CAR TROUBLE

CAR TROUBLE

A Novel

ROBERT RORKE

HARPER ● PERENNIAL

NEW YORK ● LONDON ● TORONTO ● SYDNEY ● NEW DELHI ● AUCKLAND

HARPER ⬤ PERENNIAL

HarperCollins books may be purchased for educational, business, or sales
promotional use. For information, please email the Special Markets Department at SPsales@harpercollins.com.

FIRST EDITION

Designed by Leydiana Rodriguez

Library of Congress Cataloging-in-Publication Data has been applied for.

ISBN 978-0-06-284849-9 (pbk.)

18 19 20 21 22   LSC   10 9 8 7 6 5 4 3 2 1

To my mother

I.

THE BLUE MAX

ONE

It was time to move the Blue Max. I was out front, waiting for Himself. He was probably combing his hair in the bathroom mirror and that would take forever. I sat on the cement edge of the garden, careful not to lean against the sweet alyssum on the border. I wanted to go back to bed. That's where I was, drifting off, when Mom shook me and told me he wanted me to help him. Because that's what you did at one in the morning. You got rid of the car.

After Mom left me, I thought I could close my eyes for a minute before I absolutely had to get up. I didn't doze for long, though. A memory from a summer night not so long ago woke me up for good: me pinned against the basement door, fists slamming into me, my mother and uncle pulling his arms off.

This would be the last time I helped him. In a few weeks, I would be gone.

The Blue Max was parked in the driveway, the latest in a long line of junkers Dad had picked up at police department auctions. He'd nicknamed this one, a Chevy Impala, after the German military decoration given to fighter pilots during World War I. Of all the cars he'd brought home the Blue Max was the most stylish, with blue bat wings that spread out over the trunk and red catseye taillights tucked underneath. The hubcaps had spokes like a bicycle wheel, with the Chevrolet logo imprinted in the center. I wish I'd seen the car when it was new, in 1959, the way Himself remembered it. Everything inside and outside was blue. The body and hardtop were a dusty royal color, with snazzy chrome strips running down the sides. The interior matched, down to the steering wheel, dashboard, and glove compartment. The leather seats, though, were a deep cobalt. When we went somewhere as a family, the Blue Max was wide enough to fit everyone, with our long legs and big mouths. Nobody had to sit on anybody else's lap.

We'd had the car about six months and during that time Himself had driven it into the ground, eventually falling asleep and nearly setting it on fire with a lit cigarette. That was some morning, the second time firemen had come to his aid. After the contraption cooled off, we moved it from the other side of the street into our driveway, Dad pushing the car while I steered. I didn't know where we were taking the Blue Max tonight, but I doubted we'd be pushing it. He must have something else in mind.

I had worked till eleven at the theater, and my legs were cramping up. I got to my feet, stretching, and glanced up at the sky. One or maybe two stars, very faint, were riding on the purple surface. A streetlamp across from our house buzzed. I could pick out the pungent scent of the marigolds, planted in a circle around the Japanese yew. My last garden.

Then I heard him coming, finally, his deep mumble drifting through the screens in the front porch windows. I stifled a yawn. He came down the stoop, tripping over one of the broken steps. Himself in the flesh. I stood there, hands shoved in my pockets, waiting to see what was what.

His dark pants were rumpled. The collar of his yellow polo shirt stuck up behind his neck, but his hair was freshly combed in the modified ducktail style he'd worn since high school.

"We keepin' you up?" He was fully awake, almost jaunty, ready for an adventure. The night was his favorite part of the day; after midnight he could get into anything. No doubt he'd come up with this brilliant idea while spending several hours at the Dew Drop Inn.

"Let's knock this out. Forty-five minutes. Tops."

He fished in his pocket for the car keys. I leaned against the car and looked at the house. The second floor was covered in green shingles, the first floor was done in white stucco. We'd been living here for over ten years and every year the place looked worse. There weren't enough bedrooms for all of us kids, there was only one full bathroom, and on rainy days, we had to put pots in the second-floor hallway to collect the water dripping through the holes in the roof.

The front door was still open. Mom was standing in the dark vestibule, leaning against the doorjamb. A Newport filter dangled from her left hand. "I don't see why you don't call a tow truck, Pat," she said. Queenie, our tricolor collie, poked her nose into the scene.

No way was he paying for a tow truck. He didn't go for spit, as he would say, on anything. He ignored her and climbed, headfirst, into the front seat. As long as we'd lived here, he had driven old cars. Some were even older than the Blue Max. No one used the word "vintage" then, but he defiantly preferred the nostalgic glow of an eye-shaped taillight or a sharp tail fin to anything a brand-new Buick Skylark or Dodge Charger had to offer. The cars he liked were all new when he was young, just barely out of his teens—before we came along.

He tossed junk from the front seat onto the backseat so we could sit up front. I looked up at the front bedroom windows, wondering if any of my sisters were eavesdropping from the window bench. Dad turned the key in the ignition and the car grumbled in protest, the way he did when we had to wake him up when he was conked out. The Chevy didn't want to budge. It wanted to die, whitewalls slowly deflating, fancy hubcaps collecting dust, sleek twin hood ornaments defiled by rust and passing pigeons. The nickname seemed especially ironic or sad, probably a little bit of both, since the Blue Max's fighting days were clearly over.

"I don't see why you have to do this now," Mom said, sounding more irritated than usual. The collie now sat at her feet, front paws crossed.

He stuck his head out the window. "Mother of God. Claire, would you get back in the house?"

Mom took one last drag on her cigarette and flicked it into the street. She wore a nightgown, pale green, and a cotton bathrobe, though it was hot out. I guess she thought someone might see her standing on her front stoop. "Come on," she said to the dog and went inside.

He backed the car out of the driveway, letting it roll into the street. The catseye taillights were bright as bicycle reflectors. After he straightened the car, the passenger door opened with an arthritic creak and I got in. The stench of old smoke and scorched leather still lived inside. I quickly rolled down the window.

"I know," Dad said, blue eyes looking out the windshield. "It stinks to high heaven in here."

He was six feet and powerfully built, and he shifted his weight so he could better see out the panoramic rear window. I still don't know how he managed it, backing the Chevy up for two miles. The gears were jammed, and the engine sputtered when he tried to drive normally, which is how we had ended up pushing it into the driveway. And here I was, about to take a backward journey to God-knows-where—an insane scheme, yes, but so Patrick Flynn. Pick the one thing anyone with half a brain would never attempt to do and you would find my father doing it, with a grin on his face.

I was sure he was tanked; he always was when he came home in the wee hours. But I couldn't smell it on him, at least not under the mantle of Old Spice. He steered the car carefully, and it moved, in spurts at first, and then in a more fluid motion till he was just cruising in reverse. Through the back window I could see a procession of parked cars, telephone poles, and the houses of friends I used to know—the block I'd soon be leaving behind.

"Do we really have to do this?" I asked.

"We have no choice, Nicky. The last time I got rid of a car, I got a ticket for one hundred thirty-five dollars. This time, no cops."

He wasn't much of a talker so there was never any pressure to keep a conversation going. But I wanted to know where we were dumping the Blue Max.

"So, what hellhole are you taking me to?"

"Ah," he said, "I thought you'd never ask. I have a place in mind."

I was no stranger to his secret errands, but this one was different because we were doing it together. Usually, I acted as his go-between. Sometimes with strangers, sometimes family members. Once, he made me go see this guy he knew from the phone company. Pete San Filippo. They played cards once a week. Himself was looking for work and thought Pete might know about any jobs coming up. And I was the one who had to ask. He gave me Pete's address and I walked over to his house, a few blocks away, wondering what to say when I rang the bell. Pete was a handsome, stocky man with curly black hair, who opened the screen door partway to talk to me. Whatever I said made him smile, but I felt like a complete weirdo, like some kind of beggar. Another time I had to go to Uncle Tim's house at the crack of dawn one January morning when I was suspended from school to pick up a check that would pay my tuition and readmit me. He should have taken care of it, but I was the one who took the bus to Rockaway so he could save face. You just didn't ask questions. Nobody did, not even my mother. Not only was I the eldest child, I was the only son. It was ridiculous, the things I was asked to do, but I would never think of handing them off to one of my sisters.

The trees along Snyder Avenue were heavy with late summer, the leaves at their darkest and densest green, singed at the edges from a recent heat wave, and the air was filled with the murmur of crickets. Dad swiftly turned the steering wheel and maneuvered the car into the westbound lane to see the oncoming traffic. At first, the Blue Max went one block at a time, alongside Holy Cross Cemetery, until the sheer emptiness of the street spurred him to lean on the accelerator, gliding through bands of blackness and fluorescence until we reached Schenectady Avenue. Ten blocks. Then he stopped at a red light.

I gripped the handle inside the door. "Jesus, are you trying to get us killed?"

"I'm trying to get this over with," he said, looking through the windshield. "Don't be so dramatic."

What was he going to do for wheels now? He didn't have money to buy another car, not unless he got lucky at Pete's poker game or picked up extra shifts tending bar at the Mermaid. That's where he was working. Sometimes I'd bring him a clean white shirt on a hanger when he worked a double shift; it wasn't like the regulars, blown-out lightbulbs one and all, were going to notice if his shirt wasn't fresh. Catholic schools were charging tuition now, and Mom needed every last cent to pay for that. As the sole support of the family, she was all about the money, keeping on top of the bills, the mortgage.

She was carrying him and he hated it.

I could hear the relay switches changing in the traffic-light box on the corner before the red turned to green. Dad straightened his neck and rested a minute, looking down the long black street behind us.

"So far, so good," he said; he almost always sounded hoarse. "No cops. I really appreciate you doing this."

I tried to smile. "It's okay. It won't take that long, right?"

"You in a rush or something?"

"No. I just want to know, that's all. I have a matinee tomorrow." I'd spend more time than usual ushering the Massapequa ladies to their seats.

"We'll be done when we're done."

It was hot out, one of those Augusts that make you wish it were October. Dad resumed his reverse position and backed the car onto Schenectady Avenue. The graveyard came into view again, the headlights revealing the polished granite surface of the tombstones. Their silence seemed to guarantee our success.

"We are going to the Brooklyn Terminal Market," he said suddenly.

In that case, we weren't that far away. The streetlights cast faint beams on a deserted, concrete playground on Tilden Avenue. There were silver baby swings and a torn, twisted chain-link fence, benches without seats, graffiti scrawled on the concrete wall in the handball court. I knew he was worried about a cop car pulling him over. But neither of us was thinking about fire engines. We were coming up to the intersection at Utica Avenue when I heard a siren, at first distant, then louder, more urgent and shrill. I looked out my window to see if anything was coming from the southbound lane. Then Dad said, "Holy shit." A nasal horn sounded and a fire engine came barreling out of the darkness from the north. He hit the brakes hard. The Chevy swerved and he bumped his head on the steering wheel. I steeled myself against the seat, pushing my feet on the floor. We were going to get killed. That's how the night would end—cops ringing our doorbell.

"Are you okay? Didn't you see that coming?"

He released the brake and looked out the windshield. The car was aslant in the middle of Utica Avenue. He got out of the car and looked down the street. I got out too. No sign of the phantom fire engine. I knew we hadn't dreamt it, but it was almost like we had. He slapped his meaty hands on the roof of the Chevy and stretched his bulky legs, head bowed.

We just couldn't leave the car here; we'd have to push it back to Holy Cross. That would be the easiest thing; it wouldn't take long, fifteen minutes maybe. I knew too well about his superhuman strength. He once carried a broken washing machine out of our basement and up the cellar steps and into the backyard, wrapping his massive arms around the gleaming white contraption and picking it up, tilting it against his chest, and finding his way out of the cellar. When he'd put the thing down, scraping the cement, his face was boiling red but he wasn't even breathing heavily.

Why had I let my mother talk me into going on this joyride? "So what are we going to do now?"

He said nothing; he just stared down the length of Utica Avenue as if the answer were written on the asphalt's double yellow stripe. The longer we waited there, the more likely a cop car would eventually find us. I suggested pushing the Blue Max back toward the cemetery, but then he said, "Gotta keep going. We're almost there."

That wasn't really true. And then he had another brilliant idea—that I should take the wheel.

"Me?" My voice went up half an octave. "I can't drive in reverse."

He was getting in the passenger seat. "Piece of cake. I'll show you."

I wiped the palm of my hand on my dirty denim shorts and slid in next to him. My wristwatch said one thirty in the morning. I hoped Mom wasn't still up. I adjusted the rearview mirror. "And if we get stopped by the cops, I'll be the one who gets a ticket."

He winked. "You have more money than me. You can pay it."

That much was true, but I needed all of it to live on when I went to college.

"Come on, Nicky," he said. "My neck is killing me, and I don't see too good at night. Fifteen more minutes, you'll see. And then I'll never ask you for another favor."

Famous last words, but his pleading took me by surprise. And then it dawned on me that he didn't need me for the company; he had always planned for me to do part of the driving. Was I a moron or what?

"All right. Let's just get out of here."

As I turned on the ignition and backed the Chevy down the street, the Blue Max swerved and lurched.

"Easy on the gas. Keep the wheel straight," he said. Even with half a bag on, Himself was a much better driver than I would ever be.

I stared out the back window, determined to make the car behave. The engine muttered all the way. At Kings Highway, an ambulance idled past the eight lanes while we stopped at a red light. When it changed, I asked Himself to guide me. He walked into the middle of the street, about fifty feet behind the Chevy, and beckoned the car to him like a reluctant pet. My high school, St. Michael the Archangel, was a five-minute walk from here. This was one story about Himself I could tell in public. But there was no one to tell it to. The friends I had made in high school had receded—some were ghosts—and I was only looking to tell new stories when I got to Carnegie Mellon.

When I made it to the other side, I looked back and grinned. Himself leaned on the windshield and smiled. "See? Driving backwards, there's nothing to it. Want me to take over?"

"Maybe you remember that McDonald's near St. Mike's. It's open all night. Someone might see us. We can go around."

He was in my head now and that was never a good thing. The longer I sat in the driver's seat, the more I began to think like him. Like a sneak. I did know one way to get where we were going that would attract the least attention. In two lurching maneuvers, I backed onto East Fifty-Seventh Street, where Tilden High School took up one side of the block. We called the school Killden, after race riots there made headlines.

I was getting better with the steering wheel, straightening out the Chevy while I looked out the back window. The Blue Max slipped across the dark intersection at Clarendon Road. St. Mike's was the long, tidy, rectangular building on the right side of the street. We were almost done and I was pleased that I had found the best way to get there. I half-expected the principal, Brother Theodore, to sidle up to the front window and ask in his merry brogue, "Fellas, that's quite an automobile you have there, but have you noticed that you are driving in reverse?"

Looking out at the rose granite façade and the steps that led to the front doors, Dad said, "Jesus, I forgot this place was in the middle of nowhere."

I pressed on the accelerator. The forlorn playground across the street floated by. "Is that why you only came inside the building like once? Because it was out of the way?"

He laughed. "When was that?"

"You came looking for me one day, all worked up over nothing." In my sophomore year, when I played Conrad Birdie in a gold lamé jumpsuit.

"Vaguely."

"You threatened my English teacher." The director of the school play.

"I've threatened a lot of people—even hit a few—but never a teacher. Shame on me."

He seldom felt ashamed of any of the stunts he pulled, but I couldn't argue with him when we were going backward. Besides, I had another left turn coming up. The grim sign Collisionville, blue lettering on dented white metal, appeared as I neared the edge of the school property. Stacks of stripped cars, chassis exposed like entrails, teetered high above the sidewalk on container boxes. Old hubcaps and bald, greasy tires were strewn about. I heard one of the hubcaps crush and crackle under our wheels as I ran over it. Unseen guard dogs yowled into the night.

We were almost there. Ditmas Avenue, little more than an alley between St. Mike's and the wrecking joint, would take us past the Wyckoff House and to the market. Then we got a flat. A loud flat. It sounded like a gunshot. I'd never be able to get Himself out of his predicament now.

"What did you do?" he asked, turning to me, annoyed.

"I think I hit something."

"What'd you do that for?"

I stopped the car. "I don't know why you're busting my balls when you're the one who got me up to help you do this. Do you want me to help you or not? Because I can go home right now."

Two years ago, he would have smacked me across the face for that kind of back talk, but he merely got out of the Chevy, slamming the door. I got out too and looked at the rear wheel on the driver's side. It wasn't like we could see much. There was one streetlight, half a block away. I couldn't see what caused the flat, but it didn't matter. The situation was completely hopeless.

Dad was still crouching, looking at the tire. "Guess you don't want to leave this by your school. What will the good Brothers say?"

"It's not my school anymore," I said, rubbing my eyes and looking down at the asphalt. "So now what?"

We were going to have to push the car after all. He lowered his weight against the front of the car and shoved. I copied his stance and stretched my hamstrings and whatever muscles I had back there to the max. I used as much force as I could, but I didn't have it in me. Finally, the Chevy lurched. I didn't even look up, just gripped the headlight as we forged ahead. Soon, we reached the end of the alley. Across Ralph Avenue there was a UPS warehouse and a sagging concrete train trestle that supported a discontinued freight railroad track. We pushed the car across the empty street, and then it rolled down another short alley, the deflated tire flapping against the asphalt. The car came to a stop.

"Man, I am so sick of this," I said. "Can't we just leave it here and go?"

"Pipe down, mister. Ten minutes, I promise."

I wouldn't look at him. "Mom was right. You should've called a tow truck. We could have paid for it."

"I don't need your mother's money, young man."

Yes, you do. I was making him angry. He wouldn't look at me. I wiped my hands on my sweaty shorts. He put his hands back on the car hood and waited for me to join him. I could almost hear him count to ten. A couple of good shoves, and we were able to ease the Chevy under the train trestle. I thought I was being sucked into some sooty tunnel, but the market appeared on the left, an open-air collection of wholesale and retail vendors locked up behind a high chain-link fence crowned with hoops of razor wire. A tall spotlight inside the market shone on the vendors' signs: M&M Smoked Fish, Mr. Pickle. Raindrops spattered on my neck. Great. Now we would get good and soaked.

Dad straightened all the way back up and walked over to the fence. He pointed to an eighteen-wheeler parked next to the loading dock of Mr. Pickle and said, "Wonder how I can get a job like that. Out on the open road. Like I did in Florida."

Another venture that didn't work out. I said nothing.

"I know I can drive, even in reverse." He laughed heartily. "Any job would do, Nicky. Any job."

Sometimes I felt sorry for him. "I know, Dad. I know."

I could picture him trying to scale the fence, ripping his pants on the razor wire, just for the chance to hide in the back of one of the trucks and wake up someplace else—while Mom waited on the couch for the click of the front door that wouldn't come.

But now it was my turn to leave. In one of his sober moments, he once told me, "You have to have some kind of drive. Me, I never had one." Before I even knew what he was really telling me. I didn't know how things would go without me in the house, whether it would be easier or harder for my sisters, or if they would just bide their time and get out.

"Let's do what we need to do and get out of here," I said.

There was always plenty of sky in Brooklyn and that night, I stood under an upside-down bowl of clouds. The sky was the color of a trash-can lid. A brick building across from the market housed the city's garbage trucks. The rain stirred up a rank residue from the day's collections in those trucks that were parked outside.

"It's enough to gag a maggot," Dad said, nodding at them.

I laughed, despite myself. It was one of his better lines. "Where're you going to put the car?" I thought: *And then what? We look for a taxi?*

"I think over there." He indicated a spot where the security fence met the train trestle. It was bursting with waist-high weeds and a thicket of Queen Anne's lace. I wondered if this was the spot where he junked all the cars over the years—the Green Hornet, the Black Beauty, and the other glamour tanks that rumbled into our lives for a short time and then vanished.

We pushed the Blue Max into its final resting place.

He handed me a long black flashlight from the glove compartment and got his toolbox from the trunk. The driver's-side door was still open; he told me to aim the beam on the lower left-hand corner of the blue dashboard, in front of the steering wheel. "First I'm taking off the VIN tags," he said, peering at the dashboard. His voice was muffled as his right hand poked around with the screwdriver. "That's short for Vehicle Identification Number. You have to destroy them or they'll trace the car to you. I'm looking for two rivets here. Mother of God." He paused, then his blue eyes suddenly lit up. "Got 'em."

The light shone on a scar that ran below his cheekbone to his chin, and I tried to remember how long ago he had been stabbed in the face while breaking up a fight at Harkins, this bucket of blood in Park Slope. I stepped away from the door, sticking the flashlight between the door and the dashboard while he worked with the screwdriver and a pair of pliers. Next, we took the plates. Crouching, he removed the front license plate while I shone the beam on the screws. Empire State. Orange and blue.

"I talked to your uncle about borrowing his car to drive you to Pittsburgh," he said, removing the rear plate. "And he thinks it should be okay. Who knows? Maybe he'll come."

I could smell the VO5 he used to slick down his hair. I planned to borrow a friend's van, but if Himself wanted to drive me, there was no way I was getting out of it. "Sure. That would be great. I don't have that much stuff."

He rose, the plate in his left hand, screwdriver and pliers in his right, and winked at me. "Everybody says that, until they pack up a car."

I thought we were done, but he wanted another minute with the Blue Max. He ran his hand along the back of the car, from the right wing tip down to the center of the trunk and up again to the left tip. He reached below and caressed the taillight's ruby-colored bulbs, as if he were copping a feel. It was still more than a car to him. Before he'd picked up the Impala for sixty bucks at the Sixty-Ninth Precinct, it was designed like other cars from his era—to take flight; to make drivers in lesser cars gaze longingly at its sleek form, with the trunk forming a brow over the recessed taillights that watched the street behind you like a second pair of eyes. It was sad—an insult, really—to leave it behind like this.

It was drizzling, the rain stirring up pungent odors from the thickets of weeds everywhere. Dad pocketed the keys and the VIN tags, tossed the flashlight into the yellow tool kit, and picked it up. I carried the license plates. And that was it. The Blue Max could now be picked over by junkmen and junkies, scrap metal vendors and hobos looking for a place to sleep.

We walked under the crumbling trestle. A couple of rats brazenly scampered past; they were as fat as the ones on the subway tracks. The rain fell heavily now, ruining Dad's coiffure and matting his thinning hair and dampening my brown curls. Out there in the tungsten-colored streetscape, he looked older and diminished in some way after driving in reverse.

"How do we get out of here?"

The raindrops rolled down his neck, soaking through the collar of his yellow polo shirt. My T-shirt was pretty wet too, but I didn't mind the rain. At least it was washing off the smell of the Blue Max.

"Well, I guess we have to walk," he said.

I checked my watch; it was two thirty. The Church Avenue bus wasn't running. "Okay. I don't want to go past the cemetery again."

We headed down Ralph Avenue. Two hours had passed since my mother had nudged me awake to join in the fun and the night wasn't over yet.

"That was some forty-five minutes," I said.

"Yeah, well, I don't wear a watch."

I laughed. He always had a comeback.

On the next block, we passed a bar, the Midnight Pearl Lounge. Himself stopped outside the humble building, black stucco with a pink neon sign of tilted martini glasses over the entrance. A cop car shot past us, heading toward Church. It was a good thing we hadn't been seen coming out of the alley.

"A man might be thirsty after tonight's endeavors," he said.

My real job wasn't to help him junk the car or avoid getting a ticket, but one I had performed since I was a kid: making sure he made it home. I was about to flunk. But I gave it one more try. "Mom's waiting up for us. I think we better get going."

He was scoping out the joint through the darkened window. The shank of the evening had long passed, but he flashed an Irishman's smile at me, game for anything as long as the devil found out about it before the Lord. "Come on, Nicky, don't be a deadbeat. You helped me out of a jam."

"All I did was hold the flashlight."

He was staring me down, the blazing blue eyes twisting my arm. "You can have a drink with your old man before you leave your mother and go off to parts unknown."

He handed me the tool kit. The door, warped oak with three recessed panels, creaked as he opened it. I guess I was having a nightcap.

II.

THE GREEN HORNET

TWO

My father never said anything about buying a car, but one Saturday afternoon he drove down our block with the Green Hornet. It was the middle of May; I was ready to graduate from grammar school. I was crouching in the garden, making a pile of the crabgrass I'd pulled from around the spring flowers, purple and white tulips and hyacinths in pink and Wedgwood blue.

Dee Dee ran up the stoop and yelled through the window screen in the front porch, "Daddy's here! And he's got a car!" Her face was flushed, her brown curls wild. She held a jump rope in her right hand. "Nicky, did you hear me?"

"I heard you." I stood up behind the Japanese yew. Dad was in the street with his new car, looking under the hood. Dee Dee was down on the sidewalk, standing next to the car. "Is that your car, Daddy?" she asked. He mumbled a reply. I threw the clumps of crabgrass into a garbage pail in the driveway and wiped my hands. I had spent an hour cutting old cane off the rosebushes, the kind with the big, stabbing thorns, and planting them around the tulips and hyacinths. I was ready to see how fast our neighbors tried to pick them now that they had protection.

It was our first car, but my first thought about it was: *It's not even new.* My second thought was: *How old is it?* In fact, the Green

Hornet was a 1956 Ford Fairlane. In its day, it must have been something, a two-tone flourish of greens. Nobody made cars in those colors anymore—sea green from the hood to the trunk and pine green for the hardtop and the sides. Even better, the greens were bisected by an ornate chrome wave that rolled across the sides of the car, moving from the recessed headlights and cresting to a bold, sharp point on the front door and tapering near the tail-lights. If someone had taken the time to shine it up and reattach the front fender, dangling from the grille like loose bridgework, the Green Hornet would have been the envy of every family on our block. Right now, it had the air of abandonment about it, like something from an old movie.

Maureen, my eldest sister, came to the front door. She stood in the vestibule, skinny and tall, straight brown hair pulled back in a ponytail, a paperback in her left hand. She was fourteen months younger than me. "Did someone say we have a car?" She looked suspicious but then saw the Green Hornet. Then she went back inside, probably to get Mom. Soon, Patty, who came after Maureen in the birth order, rode up on the sidewalk next to me on her blue Schwinn, a sheen of sweat on her lightly freckled face.

"What do you think?" she asked.

Dad still had his head under the hood, fiddling with the insides.

"Let's see if it actually runs."

The car was some kind of make-up present. I couldn't wait for Mom's reaction.

Mary Ellen came along next, trailing her hand along our neighbor's fence, from one black wrought-iron bar to the next. She was the baby of the family.

Maureen came out of the house with Mom. She was wearing a yellow apron, the one with rickrack trim and a safety pin at the waistband, over a blue checked dress. Her face was flushed with surprise.

"Jesus, Pat, where the hell did you get this?" She didn't exactly sound pleased. Like I said: make-up present.

"Sixty-Ninth Precinct. Fifty bucks."

"What's he talking about?" Patty whispered.

I shrugged. I would ask Mom later. Dad was chuckling as she walked up to the car and peered inside the window. The set was falling out of her chestnut hair, her curls drooping at the nape of her neck. "Did you have to get this color?"

He looked up from the car's guts, a smirk on his face. "It only came in one color, Claire." He was still thin, in his gray work pants and button-down gray shirt, always with the five o'clock shadow and the sleeves rolled up halfway, black hair bristling on his forearms. He said, with a flourish, "I'm going to call it the Green Hornet."

She took a closer look at the Ford. "I hope you're going to wash these windows."

"I'll have one of the kids do it tomorrow. Maybe Nicky will volunteer." Dad turned to me and smiled.

"Why do I have to do it?"

"Because I said so. Your sisters can help."

Great. He brings home a jalopy, and we have to clean it.

We didn't have the dog then, so it was just the five of us out there on the sidewalk, standing around nervously, wondering if Mom was going to make Himself take the car back. Then Mary Ellen went over and ran her hand along the tarnished chrome wave on the side of the car, grinning. That week, she had impulsively cut her bangs off and her light brown hair stuck up like the bristles of a typewriter eraser. She looked like a goon but was too young to know it.

"At least somebody likes the car," Dad said, scooping her up with one arm and carrying her to the front door. He opened it with a flourish. "Come on, short pants, let's go for a ride. Anybody else wanna come?"

Mom shoved her hands into the pockets of her apron. "Now? Pat, I'm in the middle of making supper."

Nobody was hungry now that we had a car. All Dad had to do was drive up with a weird old car and the very air changed. Suddenly a lazy afternoon turned into an exciting Saturday night, humming with possibilities. Patty rode her bike into the yard and stashed it in the garage. I finished with the garden and went into the kitchen to wash my hands. The table was already set, white plates on a plastic, flowered tablecloth. Frozen green beans were defrosting in a pot of water on the stove. The cast-iron frying pan was out on the adjacent burner. Mom was wrapping up a platter of seasoned chop meat and putting it back in the refrigerator. The paperback lay open on the dishwasher, its spine bent in the middle. *Lisa Bright and Dark*. Maureen's book. She was rereading it, morose even at twelve.

I dried my hands with a towel and looked at Mom for some sign of how she thought this joyride was going to go, because you couldn't tell with Dad—his moods changed so quickly—but I couldn't read her face. All she said, pot cover in her hand, was "You go ahead. I'll lock up." The yellow apron was already hanging on the kitchen closet doorknob.

My sisters squeezed into the backseat of the Green Hornet. Maureen climbed in first, tucking her ponytail under her chin, as if it was going to get in the way. Mary Ellen and Dee Dee followed. There was just enough room for Patty, who got in on the opposite side. She sat next to the window.

Although the Ford looked cumbersome, weighed down by its faded glamour, Dad made it move once he fired up the engine. He tore out of our block, driving it like a getaway car. The one thing everyone remembers about Himself was the way he drove, like he was on the lam. He hung on the steering wheel, tailgating drivers, jockeying for position, slicing across the lanes on Linden Boulevard like a speed skater going for Olympic gold.

I was sitting up front with Mom. I rolled down the window and rested my arm on the creamy green door. The girls were all smiling in the backseat, hair touching one another's shoulders. The car was pretty dingy inside, with frayed pine-green leather seats and a stale smell of rust and cigarettes, but we didn't care. We were going somewhere, and we never went anywhere, because we didn't have what everybody else had: a car! Now, there'd be trips to the beach, trips out of the city. If Dad let us, we could stick decals of the places we visited to the back window, the way the Martinucci family did with their Dodge station wagon: Howe Caverns, Hershey's Chocolate Factory.

Riding in the front seat of that car was like being on a roller coaster. First we passed the world we knew: the schoolyard at St. Maria Goretti and the white brick rectory where Mom sent me to buy mass cards for dead relatives. Everything dramatically changed, and for the worse, as we drove east. In two minutes, we were passing the slums of East New York. I stared at the grim, collapsing houses, with broken stoops and peeling porches— Brooklyn's rotted edge.

Mom put her hand, with its thin blue veins, on the dashboard. "Pat, do you think you could slow down?" she asked as the needle in the speedometer edged past fifty, sixty, seventy.

"What for?" he shot back, smiling. "I've been waiting to drive like this for years, Mrs. Flynn." He looked in the rearview mirror. "Anybody back there want me to slow down?"

"No, Daddy," said Mary Ellen.

"That's my girl."

I gripped the door handle as we barreled ahead, my feet firm against the floor, my eye on the silver hood ornament at the tip of the creamy, sea-green hood. It was bird-shaped, sleek, and savage. I didn't use the seat belt. Back then, if you strapped yourself in, it was considered an insult to the driver. We were a captive audience no doubt, but I thought I could get him to slow down if I got him to talk.

"How'd you come up with the nickname the Green Hornet?"

He passed a Mister Softee truck in the left lane. "I used to listen to a program on the radio"—he went a little Irish here, pronouncing *radio* with an exaggerated brogue, as if he had just stepped off the boat—"called *The Green Hornet* when I was a young lad. Me and your uncle George, in the living room on a Tuesday night, but only after we'd finished our homework. Of course."

The blarney was piled pretty high. "Maybe your mother listened too. Remember the music, Claire? 'The Flight of the Bumblebee.'"

"Yes," Mom said brightly. She was beginning to come around, forget about the dinner she wouldn't have to cook tonight. "I remember."

I had no idea what he was talking about.

"Does the radio work?" Maureen asked.

"I don't know. Let's try it. Which station, my dear?"

The speedometer dipped as Himself fiddled with the dials. We mainly heard a lot of static, but then something came through: WABC. Dad didn't hate rock 'n' roll as much as he hated "jigaboo music," as he called it, and luckily, we tuned in, in the middle of the Beatles singing "Hey Jude." He could deal with the Beatles. Everybody had to then. Half the song was choruses and soon my sisters were singing along. The slums receded as the octopus of highways and their grassy embankments—green like our new/old car—took over. An oldie by Martha and the

Vandellas followed the Beatles, and Dad switched stations to the Mets game. The score was 3–3 at the bottom of the sixth.

I looked at the highway signs—the Van Wyck, the Grand Central—and thought now that Himself had the Green Hornet, he could take a detour on any one of them the next time he didn't want to come home.

Soon we were cruising past Flushing Meadows Park and the Unisphere, a giant steel globe, a memento of the 1964 World's Fair, it rested like a giant Christmas ornament on the grass. Dad and Mom reminisced about the day they took us there, a summer day none of us could remember, except Patty, who liked the Clairol exhibit because it had a booth that showed what your hair would look like in different colors. The Green Hornet slowed down as cars were boxing Himself in on all sides now. The wind stopped whipping my face and I pushed my hair, which was all over the place, behind my ears. The air, even though it was kind of metallic, felt great and I knew I would love driving myself one day. Maybe I'd break the speed limit too.

Dad said nothing about the traffic but I could see him looking to wedge his way into a line headed for the eastbound exit. Vermilion and black clouds streaked across a sapphire sky as we headed back on the BQE. The Midtown Manhattan skyline rose above the flat tableau, boxy and dazzling.

Dad didn't talk much about the city across the river; that was public domain. Brooklyn was his.

"Now this here is the Kosciuszko Bridge," he announced as we crossed a half-moon-shaped green span overlooking a narrow waterway. He drove with his right forearm on the steering wheel and his left out the window. "It separates Queens from Brooklyn. That down there is the Newtown Creek. Don't fall in."

He knew everything there was to know about Brooklyn. When he was a boy, he had delivered papers for the *Brooklyn*

Eagle; he had worked all over the borough for the telephone company, installing phones, climbing up wooden poles, and entering some ugly apartments overrun with roaches and worse. His version of the borough's shocking, sad decline was a little hard to take, especially when he droned on about it. And he always knew whom to blame—the blacks, the spics, the usual suspects. There was no way for me to contradict him because that was his world; mine was just taking shape.

We were getting closer to home, passing a Russian Orthodox church topped with an exotic green onion dome. Then the Brooklyn Bridge flashed by. He swept past the white-fortress factory buildings of the Bush Terminal and the ocean liners trudging up Lower New York Bay. The Verrazano-Narrows Bridge hovered over them, majestic in its sleek lines and elongated arc.

"Longest suspension bridge in the world," Dad said with pride, as if he had helped build it.

We weren't used to him showing us a good time or talking so much. Especially since he hadn't come home after work on Wednesday. And he hadn't been there when we'd gotten up the next morning and got ready for school. While Mom had made bologna-and-cheese or peanut-butter-and-jelly sandwiches for our lunch, the phone rang. Before any of us could jump up from the kitchen table, she'd put the knife down and said, "I'll get it."

She took the call upstairs in her bedroom, and we'd all stared at one another around the table, awkwardly chewing our Cheerios and buttered English muffins. We had to eat and get going, run off to our separate schools. When Mom came downstairs, she said nothing. She'd just finished making lunch and hustled us out the door. Then, I suspected, she had cleaned up the kitchen and sat and waited for Himself to come home. Dee Dee and Mary Ellen were the first kids home from school that day. I passed them playing double Dutch when I walked down the street. I went upstairs to change into jeans and saw the black door of the master bedroom shut, impregnable as Fort Knox. He was in there, sleeping it off. Nobody wanted to guess why he hadn't made it home—he'd called, so he wasn't dead—but his absence, even for one night, was hard to fathom. When was he not there? He had his chair, a recliner upholstered in earth tones, in the living room. He had his cup—clear glass—for coffee in the morning. Both remained empty and untouched that day.

It was his first step away from us.

The Green Hornet rounded the curve on the Belt Parkway that would take us to Coney Island. The Wonder Wheel lit up the sky with pink and green neon. The dark tower of the Parachute Jump stood off to the right, a rusted sentinel.

Mom had taken her hand off the dashboard and said, "Pat, don't you think it's time we got something to eat?" We were way off schedule.

The cars in our lane were slowing down, and we soon saw why. A motorcycle had gone down in the middle of the westbound traffic; there was a kid, wearing jeans and boots, black-helmeted, facedown on the asphalt. Dad drove onto the shoulder and got out.

"Stay in the car," he told us.

My sisters crowded around the back window to watch. I couldn't see well enough over my mother's shoulder, so I stepped out of the car and leaned against the side, warmed by the engine. The curve of Gravesend Bay was out my window and a light breeze came off the water, tickling my neck.

"Nicky, your father said to stay in the car." Mom bit off the words.

"I want to see. Just for a minute."

He waded out into the traffic, straight-backed and fearless. The cars made way for him as the drivers saw where he was going.

He stepped over the lane divider and walked into the oncoming traffic in the eastbound lane. Big cars shot by, honking. Oldsmobiles. Buicks with heavy chrome fenders, not the plastic crap they use today. They must have been going sixty, seventy miles an hour, engines droning like insects. I don't know how he didn't get hit, but somehow he didn't. He kept his hands up and strode to the spot where the motorcycle rider lay sprawled on the asphalt. Hit and run. Dad bent over and scooped the kid off the ground and put him over his shoulder, like he weighed nothing. A siren cried in the distance and we watched the traffic finally slow down as a white ambulance edged across the lanes to where Dad stood holding the injured boy. When the paramedics wheeled a stretcher out of the back of the ambulance to meet him, Dad turned and came back the same way, with a hero's slow stride. This time, the traffic stopped for him.

I got back into the car. My mother wiped a tear from her eye.

My sisters sat openmouthed until he opened the car door again.

"Goddammit, Pat, you could've been killed," Mom said.

Dad shrugged it off and started the engine. "Yeah, well. Better luck next time."

Another driver would have stayed on the road until a rest area with a pay phone presented itself. Another driver would have passed the accident by in a big hurry. But Dad operated purely on instinct, which didn't always work in his favor. Tonight it did. He had seen the kid before we had, and then he was out of the car. The other drivers should have honked their horns in tribute but were too dead set on getting where they were going.

My sisters were grinning in the backseat. I knew they were going to brag about him at school to their girlfriends.

By the time we made it to Brennan and Carr, a Sheepshead Bay restaurant famous for hot roast beef sandwiches, we had forgotten about the night Himself hadn't come home and what that might mean for the future. We didn't usually eat roast beef, or even pot roast, until Sunday, so this was a treat. As the waitress, a girl with straight blond hair and a nameplate necklace that spelled DENISE, passed out menus, my sisters asked Dad for the gory details of the accident: was the guy dead, what did the guy look like, was he cute.

"I didn't have time to look. The guy was pretty banged up."

"Your father was too busy saving his life to see if he was cute, Maureen," Mom said. She was in a better mood than when we left the house, but she was still studying Dad's expression while he perused the menu.

"I hope you can cover this," she said.

"Not to worry." He flashed some bills in his wallet. "We're covered."

"I hope there's enough in there for the mortgage," Mom whispered across the table.

Dad raised his eyebrows as if scandalized. I knew he would file that remark away. "There's enough for everyone, and the bank, Mrs. Flynn," he said, opening the menu in front of his face.

Poker, I thought. *So that's how he paid for the car.* Plus, he saved a kid's life. He was having a good night on our first drive in the Green Hornet. Most amazing of all, he didn't so much as order a beer.

THREE

We took many trips in the Green Hornet that summer. We drove up to Palisades Amusement Park. We went to visit Mom's sister in Staten Island, and to Rockaway for barbecues at Uncle Tim's house. He lived one block from the beach. Dad tried to teach my sisters to swim. The waves were loud and sandy with a vicious undertow that sucked Mary Ellen into the surf. We got fried—the sunburns made us squirm in bed at night and led to a contest to see who could pull the biggest pieces of skin off when we started peeling.

We'd cleaned up the Ford, inside and out, until we could see out the windows. I Brilloed the chrome wave that crested on the side of the car and used some kind of stinky polish that restored a little bit of the sheen to the green-on-green body. I'd found some holes on one side of the car that I figured were made by bullets. So the Green Hornet was a real getaway car. A stick of air freshener now adorned the rearview mirror, but that old ashtray smell lingered.

While Dad was getting to know the features of his brand-new baby, like the built-in tissue box next to the glove compartment, he accidentally found a record player hidden beneath a drop-down door under the dashboard. You opened it by pushing a button. The turntable was only big enough to play 45s, but I had four boxes of them in my bedroom closet, including hits by the Supremes in their original, glossy Motown jackets, and once he found the button that switched the power from the radio to the record player, I was ready to be the Death Seat DJ. If there wasn't a Mets game on, we could play a few oldies while we were on the road. The sound crackled in the speakers and sometimes the Green Hornet would hit a bump and the record would skip right over Martha Reeves's growling "Yeah-yeah, yeah-yeah"s at the end of "Heat Wave," but otherwise I loved it. Now I saw why he didn't covet the Buick Skylarks and other new cars parked on our street. None of those vehicles were like the Green Hornet, with its colors like the surface and the depth of the ocean and where you could play your own tunes.

One of our strangest journeys came just after we all went back to school. Dad's older brother was moving to Germany and my grandparents were throwing a goodbye bash, not at the house, where all the holidays were usually celebrated, but at a rented hall in Greenpoint.

It would be a night to remember.

When Himself appeared in front of his family, everything had to be perfect, like he was going to the Oscars. After he showered, dressed, and splashed himself with Old Spice, he squeezed some VO5 into his palms and massaged it into his hair, which was straight, the kind of brown that is almost black, and cut short, with a brush effect at the back. He then took a black pocket comb and drew it over the front of his hair and shaped it into the ducktail style, with a cannoli-shaped curl in front.

I shined his shoes in the kitchen. He kept his supplies in a brown paper bag so old it had become soft and crinkly, like a piece of chamois. Inside, there were tins of Kiwi black shoe polish, the rags I used to rub it into Dad's old shoes—Thom McAn slip-ons—and the wooden brush I used to put some luster into the cracked leather. I worked on the shoes for ten minutes and brought them upstairs. The bathroom was still steamy from the shower and smoky from the lit cigarette balanced on the tile ledge under the mirror.

How could one person spend so much time in front of the mirror? Even if I had a pimple I was trying to beat into submission, I would give it a quick scrub and reach for the Clearasil.

I wondered if I would grow up to be as vain as my old man.

I handed him his shoes while he inspected his freshly shaved face. "Nice job," he said, taking a drag from the Lucky Strike. He wore navy trousers and a white shirt, open at the neck. The aroma of the Old Spice pinched my nose.

He nodded at my chest. "Is that the shirt you're wearing?"

My hand immediately flew to the buttons on my shirt, as if a pigeon had just pooped on me. The shirt was short-sleeved and purple, with a pattern of small black and white tulips printed on the fabric. I had spotted it two weeks ago at Benhil on Flatbush Avenue and loved it. I waited until the shirt went on sale and begged Mom to buy it for me, for the party.

Leave it for Himself to find something wrong with it. "It looks like an LSD trip," he said.

I came downstairs and sat on the living room couch with my sisters. Mom came in from the kitchen, a lit Newport in her left hand, and stood on the staircase landing, two steps up and next to a red-leather telephone bench. "Anytime you're ready, Mr. Flynn."

She was wearing an outfit that was very different for her—a white dress with giant, diaphanous red and black flowers that looked like nasturtiums, cinched by a thick black belt. She was even wearing makeup—green eye shadow and red lipstick—so we knew this party was a big deal. The last time she had dolled herself up was at my aunt's wedding in July. With five of us to take care of, there wasn't much time to get dolled up, but she also didn't have the inclination. She let Himself hog the mirror.

He finally came downstairs, whistling as the steps creaked beneath him, wafting Old Spice. "Let's not keep everybody waiting," he said.

"Right, Daddy," Maureen said. She stood and smoothed the front of her dress, pale pink eyelet with a lace collar; she'd sewn it herself from a McCall's pattern. She flicked her long brown hair behind her ears and led my other sisters out the front door.

We all piled into the Green Hornet, party clothes swishing as the girls and Mom, who sat in the backseat now with one child on her lap, found places. It was a hot evening in late September. I sat in the Death Seat, prim and neatly pressed in black chinos and my acid-trip shirt. The engine grumbled and the muffler coughed as the car warmed up. The Ford probably had two hundred thousand miles on it and the chassis was groaning for automotive euthanasia. I had a five-dollar bet with Maureen that the Green Hornet wouldn't make it to the end of the year.

Our destination was a Catholic War Veterans hall in Greenpoint. By then, we were accustomed to Himself's daredevil driving and knew we were going to get anywhere we were going fast. He took his predictable path through urban squalor, corner boys staring at our car like it was from another planet when we stopped for a light in Bed-Stuy, and we made it to Greenpoint in half an hour. This was an old, old part of Brooklyn with narrow streets. Brick buildings leaned against one another for support. Taverns with neon shamrocks in the window bumped up against butcher shops with neon signs written in Polish.

Dad let us out in front of a one-story building on Java Street while he parked. Nearly everyone in the family was already at the party, plus a lot of people I didn't recognize. Priests. Friends of my aunt and uncles, I guessed. But no one my age, and no girls. I was at a weird place socially. I was finished with grade school and hadn't seen much of my classmates this summer. I wasn't really friendly with the few guys from my class who were also going to the same high school as me. St. Mike's. All boys.

Grandma and Grandpa stood near the entrance, shaking hands and patting guests on the back. I was always happy to see Grandma. Dad inherited his eyes, that flash-cube blue, from her. She was a small woman, with thin arms and hands that quivered slightly; tonight, she was decked out in a lilac pantsuit with her gray hair styled in a gentle bouffant. Grandpa was robust, with a deep, clear voice, a strong handshake, and a ring of snowy white hair around his scalp. He was the first person to notice my shirt. I was thrilled.

"What have we here?" he asked, staring at the busy pattern. He wore a blue blazer with gold buttons and beige trousers. "I guess flower power has come to Church Avenue. Marion, did you see this?"

I laughed out loud. Flower power: he must have heard that phrase on TV.

Grandma was inspecting the workmanship on Maureen's dress. In one hand, she clutched a leather cigarette case that snapped shut. "Oh, for heaven's sake," she said. "I think you're turning into a hippie, Nicky."

I laughed. How I wished I were old enough to make that happen!

Uncle George came up next, telling me how tall I was, nearly the same height as Himself. He had some kind of top-secret government job that took him to many different places. "Hey, Nicky, how was your summer?"

"Good. We went to Palisades Park. And Robert Moses on Long Island. My father got a car. Have you seen it?"

"I heard it's very green."

"And it has a record player under the dashboard." He seemed impressed. "My dad says you're going to Germany to hunt down Communists."

He laughed, revealing a set of smoker's teeth. "Your father has a vivid imagination."

While most of the Flynns had stayed put in Brooklyn, my uncle had already lived in North Carolina and California. I had only seen him a handful of times, and now he was leaving the country. He looked like Dad—same long face and huge ears— but he had brown eyes and reddish hair. I stared at the tufts of hair growing out of his ears, wondering how he didn't see that.

Mom came over and kissed him on the cheek.

"Claire, you're looking well," he said. "I was hoping to get a little time with you and Pat later on." Mom wrinkled her brow. Then he turned to Dee Dee and Mary Ellen. "Hey, remember me?" Mary Ellen nodded, but I'm sure she was too young to remember him. "I'm your old man's older brother."

The room was decorated simply, with blue and white crepe paper and white and yellow balloons. Uncle Jimmy mixed drinks at a makeshift bar, a long folding table covered with a green paper tablecloth. He was Grandpa's youngest brother—the last of eleven kids—and not that much older than Himself. He made sure that everyone had their first round. How the Flynns could put it away! Whisky sours, Seven and Sevens, Tom Collinses, manhattans—they knocked them back the way my sisters and I drank Hires root beer.

Himself was mostly a vodka man. He mixed it with grape-fruit juice or tonic water, and as soon as he came in from parking the car, Uncle Jimmy handed him his cocktail, already poured. Now that was service. Uncle Tim, Dad's youngest of three brothers, was standing there too, with Aunt Julie. They were already red-cheeked, eyes bright and watery as they laughed. The guest of honor, though, was nursing nothing more dangerous than a 7-Up. Dad passed me a Shirley Temple to give to Mom and went back to the bar to get our sodas. She was the sober stopwatch at Flynn events, keeping one eye on us, the other on Himself.

Uncle George's wife, Aunt Linda, came over to say hi. "I can't believe you're moving so far away," Mom said. "Do you speak German?"

"*Gestapo* is about the only word I know," she said. Like Mom, she was tall and skinny, but she had short blond hair and soulful dark brown eyes. They exchanged small talk about finding schools for their two daughters.

Mom checked her watch and decided it was time we ate. Dinner was served buffet style in aluminum trays heated by Sterno canisters. There were chicken cutlets with brown gravy, chicken parmigiana, a carved roast beef, boiled potatoes, and lasagna. Maureen helped Mom spoon the food onto Chinet paper plates, standing slightly away from the serving trays so no sauces or gravies splashed on her pink creation.

We ate at one of the round tables that filled the wood-paneled room. The tables were covered in real white tablecloths and decorated with more balloons and crepe paper.

"Looks like Aunt Julie's pregnant again," I said to Patty as we sat. Aunt Julie was festooned in a go-go maternity dress of some fluffy yellow material. Her legs were very tanned from spending the summer at the beach.

Patty smiled and took a plate of chicken parmigiana from Maureen. She was the only sister wearing pants tonight, navy bell-bottoms with a white muslin blouse. "Uncle Tim's trying to beat Daddy in the grandchildren sweepstakes."

The room was full of stories and I was old enough to know a few. Uncle Jimmy had been exiled from the family for a long time—he was divorced!—until Grandma finally gave absolution. Uncle George had been in some bar getting plastered the night Aunt Linda went into labor with their first kid and Grandpa drove around Brooklyn, hunting him down. When he found him, he beat the shit out of him right there on the sidewalk.

I was sure Himself hadn't done anything that bad, but I was afraid to ask Mom.

Mom and Maureen handed out the rest of the dinners. I chose the chicken cutlet–boiled potato–brown gravy combo. I loved Italian food, but the tomato sauce made me break out big-time.

"Is there anybody for us to go play with?" Dee Dee asked.

"After you finish eating, you can play with your cousins. They're over at Aunt Julie's table," Mom said.

Mom didn't eat much, half a chicken cutlet and some vegetables. She was glancing around the hall, looking for Himself. We were seated at the opposite side of the room from the bar, but without even turning my head, I could tell her where he was. She lit a cigarette and helped Mary Ellen cut her lasagna. I knew she would steer him away from Uncle Jimmy and make him eat something.

He hadn't always gone right for the bar every time his family got together. This was a new thing. Or maybe I was old enough to notice. When I was a little kid, not even five, we were still living in a basement apartment off Flatlands Avenue. I remember standing in the kitchen with my mother early on a Sunday when he bounded through the door wearing a football uniform, carrying a helmet, a big grin on his face. He seemed happy but I was afraid of him, for some reason. Something was off about him. You didn't play football in the early morning, so what was he doing? And why was he coming home at that hour? Little things like that. And so I fell into the habit of watching my mother watch him and constructing my own story.

Mom stubbed out her cigarette in one of the tin ashtrays on the table and got up. "Make sure Mary Ellen eats her vegetables," she said, heading to the bar.

Patty and Maureen were working their way through the chicken parm and the lasagna. Everybody's soda cups were empty. "Who needs a refill?" I asked.

"I don't want 7-Up this time," Dee Dee insisted.

"I'll surprise you." Family-sized soda bottles were lined up at the far end of the bar table. I planned to sneak in, get the drinks, eluding the tipsy Flynn fraternity, but I was waylaid by two of my aunts.

"Oh, Nicky, you're getting so tall. You look just like your father." Aunt Mary, Grandpa's sister and technically my great-aunt, was sitting at a table with Dad's sister, Aunt Regina. Newly married, Aunt Regina was showing off her wedding album. Aunt Mary was oohing and aahing over the photos. The wedding had taken place on a hot Saturday morning. We—me and my sisters—were not invited, and were packed off to Uncle Tim's house to spend the day at the beach.

Thick, cream-colored mats, trimmed in gold, framed the black-and-white photos. Each eight-by-ten was protected by a sheet of plastic attached to the mat. Aunt Regina turned the pages and gave a running commentary. She was only about ten years older than I was, and had a slight case of lockjaw, speaking as if she'd grown up someplace fancier than Brooklyn. It was hard to imagine her and Dad, with his mumbling half sentences, as part of the same family. She turned next to a photo of her dancing with Grandpa, the first dance at the reception. "They tried to get us to dance to 'Sunrise, Sunset,' but my father wouldn't hear of it. We went with Cole Porter instead," she said primly. And then there was the group picture on the steps of Our Lady Help of Christians, Regina in the center in her sleeveless wedding gown and weird veil, attached to her Dutch-boy haircut by some kind of satin halo. She was smiling with her lips stretched tight, her crooked front tooth barely perceptible if you didn't know it was there, and her arm linked with her husband, a handsome throwback in a morning coat, his hair cut extra short at a time when even kids' dads were growing their hair long.

Aunt Mary pointed to a woman standing two steps above the bride, brown hair teased high and wearing mod earrings— little spheres dangling at the end of a chain. "Your mother is a beauty," she said to me. I smiled. She really was—when she had the time to do it up.

Aunt Mary said to Regina, "But where's Pat?"

Himself was standing on the other side of the church steps from Mom, eyelids drooping. He barely managed a smile. Half in the bag.

Regina pointed to my father. "There he is. All my brothers are with their wives except Pat. Oh, for heaven's sake. I didn't even notice that until now."

She gave an irritated laugh, the crooked tooth sticking out like a wagging finger. I saw her studying the photo while Aunt Mary drained her cocktail and waved to somebody at a nearby table, maybe eager to get up and say hello.

Regina locked eyes with me. She had large brown eyes like Uncle George. "Your father could have shaved."

"What?" I said, blushing violently and touching my cheek, as if I was the one with the stubble. She turned back to the album, and I looked down at the photograph, at Dad's face, the five o'clock shadow.

Well, of course he hadn't shaved. He wasn't even *home* when my mother was getting ready, ironing her dress in the kitchen, black wire curlers still in her hair. She had packed our bathing suits into a small blue Pan Am bag so we could go swimming at Uncle Tim's house. One of my distant cousins was supposed to pick us up at my grandparents' house and take us to Rockaway. When her dress was ironed, she went upstairs to the master bedroom and opened the jewelry case on the maple dresser. She'd chosen the earrings—little aqua balls at the end of a three-inch chain—I'd bought for her one Christmas at Discount City.

"Where the hell is your father?" She was taking the rollers out of her hair and dropping them on the white bedspread.

As if on cue, we heard his weary voice come from the bottom of the stairs.

"Hello, the house . . ."

He trudged up the stairs, leaning his weight on each step. "Ah, yes. Mrs. Flynn. Don't you look lovely?"

"Don't *lovely* me. Get in the shower. It's your frigging sister's wedding, not mine."

When Mom and Himself got into it, we got out of the way. And if she was right, he never gave her any lip. That day, he didn't even complain when he was getting dressed and discovered he was out of razor blades.

"Send one of the kids to the drugstore and get me a pack of Gillettes."

"We don't have time. You'll have to shave before we go to the reception."

End of discussion.

I hated Aunt Regina for trying to embarrass me, but if I made a smart remark and it got back to Himself, he would clean my clock. So I glowered at her until she looked away, turning the page in the album so Aunt Mary could admire the next photo. If I had been carrying one of those refills I was supposed to be getting, I would have pretended to trip and spill soda on her precious pictures.

"I'm going to get some drinks for my sisters," I said.

Aunt Mary squeezed my hand. She looked like Grandpa but with a lot more hair. "Please tell your mother to come over and say hello."

Over at the bar, Uncle Jimmy was still pouring, for a couple of priests and my grandmother, who was arguing with Jimmy about the sacraments.

"You haven't been to mass in seventy-five years," she said, looped to the skies. "What would you know about Holy Communion?"

Before he could hit the ball back, I asked for three sodas. "Have you seen my father?"

Uncle Jimmy nodded to the tables in the back of the room. He wore this gray Howard Cosell toupee that was a little too small for his head. "Over there with Georgie. Bit of man talk, looks like."

They were deep in conversation. Dad was holding his head up defensively, taking in what Uncle George had to say. Mom was sitting on Dad's right, fist pressed against her mouth.

It didn't seem like the right time to go over and say hello.

Like all Flynn parties, this one ended with Aunt Regina at the piano. She played songs from my grandparents' generation, "Heart and Soul," "Alexander's Ragtime Band." They weren't for me, but as I watched Grandma lean on the upright—which sounded the occasional sour note—singing, the chain on her eyeglasses grazing her shoulder as she tilted her head, cigarette case resting on top of the piano, I saw that they comforted her: her eldest son was going away and she was surrounded by her family and friends, people with hair in several shades of gray, some with a blue rinse.

Uncle Tim wheeled out a fancy sheet cake from behind a set of double doors. It was iced with buttercream frosting and inscribed with the cheerful send-off, in red lettering: Auf Wiedersehen, Georgie! My uncle cut the cake and posed for a Polaroid, which was passed around the room so everyone could remember the last time they would see him this year or, for the older folks, maybe forever.

We left right after the cake and coffee, ushered out the door on a parade of hugs and kisses, and waited for Dad to pick us up. Mom was smoking a cigarette, with her free arm around Mary Ellen's shoulder. The nights were cooling off, with the briny smell of the East River in the air.

Uncle George came rushing out on the sidewalk. He was holding a paper bag. "Hey, Nicky. I meant to give this to your father. He ran out before I could catch him. Would you mind giving this to him for me?"

He had an anxious look in his eyes, which he tried to hide from me with a broad smile.

"Sure," I said.

The Green Hornet came rumbling into view, and Uncle George waved good night to us. I sat in the Death Seat. Mary Ellen fell asleep on Mom's lap. My other sisters talked about how much fun they'd had playing hide-and-seek in the Catholic War Veterans building.

I showed Dad the package. "Uncle George asked me to give this to you."

He glanced at my lap. "Is that a fact?" he asked, annoyed. He was reasonably soused, eyes just turning bloodshot. He reached over and flipped open the glove compartment. "Do me a favor. Put that away."

I squeezed the package—solid and square—in, above a stack of maps. I closed the compartment and wondered what it was he didn't want me to see.

We left Java Street and proceeded to get lost. We could not get out of Greenpoint. Dad turned left when he should have turned right and right when he should have turned left. We passed the marquee of the Loew's Meserole, where *Rosemary's Baby* was playing, a bunch of times. At first, Dad said nothing, but as his exasperation increased so did his sense of righteous indignation. "You rat bastard, you've got to be kidding me," he said to himself.

Franklin Street was bumpy and pitted. We passed playgrounds with teenagers lounging on benches, cigarettes glowing in the dark, and warehouses hulking with sinister intent. All we needed was one good pothole and we'd be stuck here all night. "Are we going in the right direction?" I asked.

"I'm trying to get to McGuinness Boulevard."

Wherever that was. Soon we were going under a bridge ramp, and things looked very wrong. He turned left and hit the brakes; we all felt the bump as the car went up on the sidewalk. We stopped short.

I shot up in my seat. "Watch out!"

My sisters screamed. Himself pounded the dashboard and I jumped. "Everybody pipe down!" he shouted.

The Green Hornet's headlights shone on a chain-link fence; on the other side of the steel diamonds lapped the brackish black water of the East River.

"Daddy!" Maureen said. "Are you trying to get us killed?"

"For crying out loud, we are not going into the drink."

It was one of the first times I thought: *Just get out of the car.* But of course I didn't. I could picture the Green Hornet sinking like a stone, with us inside, my worn-out 45 of "Heat Wave" floating to the top.

Dad hung his head and belched expansively, a bass note that perfectly captured the end of the evening. Then he slurred, "Excuse me." His carefully sculpted front curl grazed his forehead and the scent of Old Spice had become mixed with something smoky and chemical, a sour odor, coming from his body. All that time in front of the mirror, undone.

I opened the glove compartment. "Let me see one of these maps." The package from my uncle fell on the floor, along with some maps. I picked up one. New Jersey. Then another. Upstate New York. I reached for the package. The brown paper was torn at the top. There was a book inside, with a blue dust jacket. While I stuffed the maps and the package back in the glove compartment, Dad pushed on the lever on the side of the steering wheel and backed up the car.

Very quietly Mom suggested he go back to the party and ask for directions. "I'm sure there's still someone there."

Dad looked daggers at her in the rearview mirror. "I'll get us out of here. I know Brooklyn like the back of my hand," he said.

I wished I'd gone to the bathroom before I left the party.

He made a sharp left on Manhattan Avenue. It wasn't as if Mom could have taken over—she didn't have a license. Not that he would have turned over the wheel to her. He floored the accelerator and the street names flew by: Clay, Dupont, Eagle, Green, Huron, and Java. Out the window the red letters that spelled MIA FARROW on the marquee of the Loew's Meserole caught my eye and my mind flashed on the scene where she is led naked to meet Satan in Minnie and Roman's apartment and how shocked I was by the sight of her pale flesh.

The Green Hornet swerved to the right and onto a ramp

that should have taken us to the BQE. But the road kept rising, higher and higher, above aluminum-sided homes, and then it curved, away from the streets. I saw a strand of white lights, the skyline of Manhattan, and the tarnished towers of the Williamsburg Bridge.

We were crossing the East River.

Dad's mouth hung open. He said, "I must be Mickey the Dunce."

"You said it, not me," Mom said.

I thought, *Maybe we'll go back over the Brooklyn Bridge.* He would know how to get home from there. But no. That would have been too rational. He made a U-turn on Delancey Street and went back over the Williamsburg.

"Jesus, Pat, where are we going now?" Mom said, her voice sharp. "We're going to get lost again."

"Daddy—" I said.

On our left, a train rumbled up out of the guts of the subway system and onto the bridge, oxblood-red cars scarred with graffiti. The train rode sidesaddle with us on an elevated track in the middle of the bridge. On the Brooklyn waterfront, I saw the yellow neon letters of the Domino Sugar factory. I looked back at my sisters' bewildered expressions. The shouting between Mom and Dad had wakened Mary Ellen, and she moved off Mom's lap onto the seat, rubbing her eyes. "When are we going to be in our house, Mom?" she asked.

"I was just about to ask your father the same question."

He tuned everybody out. He stared out the windshield, hugging the steering wheel. The needle on the speedometer fell back to forty-five, forty mph. We came off the bridge into a large plaza where buses from points all over Brooklyn ended their routes. They were lined up, ten across, lights on, cabins empty.

The car stopped. "I have to find Flushing Avenue," he said. "That's what I have to do."

I really had to pee. Thinking that if I told him I needed to go to the bathroom, we would get home faster, I told him I had to go.

"You're going to have to hold it, mister. Till I can get out of here."

Storefront signage in Hebrew sluggishly passed by as he searched for the right street. "What else did your uncle say?" he asked suddenly.

"Say about what?" I was distracted. I was thinking how long I would have to wait until I could get out of this car and take a leak.

"About anything. The sun, the moon. Your LSD shirt."

"He didn't ask me about my shirt."

He reached over and slapped my face.

"Pat—"

Mom's warning voice. I shot up in my seat, the tears pricking. "What was that for?"

"Don't be facetious, young man. I am asking you a question. Did he say anything to you when he gave you the package?"

"What package?" Mom asked.

Himself didn't answer and I couldn't think straight. He had a heavy paw and I felt its sting on my cheek. I turned my face to the window. "He didn't want you to leave without it."

He said nothing. We drove along a dark brick wall that I thought was a prison. It was the Brooklyn Navy Yard. He pulled over on a nearby street.

"Now where're we going?" Mom asked, exasperated.

He ignored her. "Okay, Mr. Flower Power, get out and take your piss."

I looked out the window, my face still warm, at a series of desolate loading docks. "I am not peeing in the street like somebody's dog."

He wouldn't look at me. "You're the one who said you have to go."

Why was he pulling this stunt in front of my mother and sisters? I wiped my face and looked back at Mom for some intercession. Let her play referee. "Knock it off, Pat, and get us out of here. These kids need to go to bed."

He eyeballed her in the rearview mirror. "You sure? Once I start this car again, I am not stopping until we are home."

It was another fifteen minutes before we turned the corner onto our block. I was the first one out of the car, before Himself backed it into the driveway. I made it up the stoop and into the darkened house, Mom's set of keys in my hand. With all the windows shut, the house was hot and stale-smelling inside. I slammed the bathroom door. One of the loose tiles in the wall behind me fell to the floor as I fumbled with my fly. After I flushed the toilet, I washed my face.

I picked up the two pieces of glazed white ceramic tile and added them to the pile of broken tiles on the floor next to the radiator. There were ten now.

Himself was standing in the hallway when I opened the door, shirttail out of his pants, sweaty face creased by a smirk. The last person I wanted to see tonight. The driving, the panic on the bridge, seemed to have sobered him up, but I still didn't want to get too close.

"C'mon, Nicky. You think you're the only person who has to take a piss?"

He was half-smiling at me, as if he hadn't just hit me half an hour ago. I had to pass him, uneasily, in the hallway. He closed the bathroom door behind him and turned on the faucets at the sink, which he did sometimes when he didn't want everyone to hear he was going to the bathroom. I looked over my shoulder into Mom and Dad's room. The beam of light from the lamp on the end table fell onto the white bedspread where the brown paper package lay, tantalizing as a diamond. I poked my head in the doorway. I had to know why Himself had rushed it upstairs. He never cared where he left anything: dirty underwear, dirty dishes, kicked-off shoes.

The faucets were still running in the bathroom. I had a minute, maybe less, to see what the mystery was all about. I walked to the edge of the bed and picked up the package. It was a book all right, a hardcover. *Well, so what?* I pulled it out. The dust jacket was blue and the first word on the cover was *Alcoholics*, written in large letters. The word made me shiver and my face went hot with shame. This was bad. Not just for Himself, but for Mom and the five of us kids. I couldn't explain why. I just knew it.

I slid the rest of the book out. The second word on the cover, stacked underneath *Alcoholics*, was *Anonymous*. *Alcoholics Anonymous*. AA. Now I didn't just suspect; I *knew*. Uncle George had given this to Dad so he knew too. And Aunt Regina. *Your father could have shaved.* The entire family knew and they'd elected George to make an appeal. Or maybe Mom had called him. That's what they had been talking about back at the party, just Uncle George, Mom, and Himself—it must have made him furious. And he took it out on me.

I heard the toilet flush and slid the book inside the paper bag, dropped it on the bed. Back in my room behind the closed door, I turned on the fan and changed out of my flower power shirt, tossing it on the bed. And that's where I sat, listening, while I slipped a T-shirt over my head. The book wasn't in the exact same place where I'd picked it up, but I hoped Himself wouldn't notice.

At last, I heard his customary trudge down the stairs. I went barefoot into the bathroom to brush my teeth. The light was still on in my parents' bedroom, but the brown paper package was gone.

III.

THE BLACK BEAUTY

FOUR

I took my first driving lesson in the Black Beauty—Himself's idea. We were on the way back from a nursery in the Brooklyn Terminal Market when he made an unexpected left turn on Schenectady Avenue into Holy Cross Cemetery.

I had to ask: "Are we taking a shortcut?"

He stopped the car in the middle of the road and cocked his head at me. "Let's see how you do in the driver's seat."

I put my hands on the dashboard. "What? You're kidding, right?"

"I kid you not." He was already getting out of the car and walking around the solid black hood of the Pontiac—his latest newish old car—to the passenger side. I pulled up the button, and he opened the door. "Slide over."

I had to move the seat up. He helped me adjust the rearview mirror. This was a crazy, crazy idea. The steering wheel, worn smooth from the many hands that had turned it, felt peculiar under my fingers, and the dashboard, with its fuel gauge, speedometer, and other, mysterious dials, looked strange now that I was behind the wheel.

The Black Beauty was a sporty, two-door tank with the improbable French name Pontiac Parisienne. The pride of Detroit, circa 1958. It had appeared in our driveway early in 1969, not long after the loud, wheezing death of the Green Hornet, when the floor of that car was rotting out and anybody in the backseat could see the asphalt beneath their feet as we drove along. Naturally, the Black Beauty came courtesy of one of those police department auctions that Dad preferred to a used-car lot or actual new-car showroom.

We had Holy Cross to ourselves. It was May, my favorite time of year, and the cemetery couldn't have been more beautiful. Through the windshield, the new green leaves had a bluish tint. The trees were massive, staggering—sweet gums, scarlet oaks, silver lindens, and black maples. Dad had picked a good day for this impromptu lesson—Saturday. There were no burials, no chance of running smack into a hearse or upsetting a funeral cortege.

The engine was humming. "Anytime you're ready," he said, reaching in his shirt pocket for a Lucky Strike. I pressed down on the accelerator and the Pontiac lurched. I took my foot off, like I had touched a hot pot. Dad clapped his hand on the steering wheel. "Easy," he said, laughing. It was good to hear him laugh. I hoped his mood would last.

"It figures you would have a heavy foot like your old man."

I took a deep breath and pressed down lightly on the gas pedal. We were moving. The car was moving—past the beds of new crocuses and daffodils blooming in front of the polished tombstones. I wouldn't be allowed to touch a steering wheel at St. Mike's until I was a junior, and that would be with Mr. Monroe, the bovine driver's ed teacher, and a car full of pimply upperclassmen. Getting behind the wheel with Himself, without a learner's permit, that was a gas. And no one knew, except the majestic melancholy stone angels watching over the dead, and the blinking pigeons perched on their heads.

The car moved like a turtle, ten, fifteen, twenty-five miles per hour.

"How does it feel?"

"Really weird." The roads in Holy Cross were old and narrow and the Black Beauty's hood eclipsed the asphalt. As the big car moved beneath me, I couldn't imagine what it would be like to steer this thing in traffic. Did all other cars get out of its way?

"Looking down this hood is like staring into an abyss," I said.

"You have to leave yourself extra room when you park," Dad said.

A green flatbed truck with a couple of gravediggers in back crossed in front of us, but not so close that I had to brake. Dad told me to make a left turn, away from the Albany Avenue gate, and I did, but it was very wide and the Pontiac came up on the sidewalk. I kept waiting to get yelled at, but Dad did not make a peep. He smoked his cigarette, right arm dangling out the window. I went up and down on the sidewalk, and the trees and road came at us in a leisurely fashion, as if I were watching someone drive in an old movie. What a change from the Green Hornet's Death Seat. I didn't have to grip the door handle. Here in the driver's seat, white leather with black contrast stitching, I was surprisingly calm.

We passed the statue of St. Patrick holding a stone shamrock and on the right, a massive white stone building called the Cloister, which had two floors of graves stacked behind white marble walls. If Dad was surprised at how well I knew the turns in the road, he didn't let on. You don't grow up down the block from a cemetery without exploring it, and I had first come to Holy Cross with my friends from St. Maria's during my gothic period, when we were all watching *Dark Shadows* after school. We'd pre-

tend that we were the characters in the show—vampires, were-
wolves, witches, and their unfortunate mortal companions. We'd
go to Holy Cross on a stark Sunday winter afternoon, bundled
up, crunching on the frozen grass and then hide behind the
tombstones, shrieking the names of the characters—Barnabas!
Angelique!—until the groundskeepers chased us out. Now I just
slipped inside through a break in the fence on Cortelyou Road
and wandered through the field of graves until I saw the back of
St. Patrick's mitre.

"Once you get your license, we can get you a cheap car, and
you can see the USA in your Chevrolet!" Dad said, keeping his
eye on the road. We were back at the Schenectady Avenue gate.
I wasn't sure how much longer he'd let me drive. We had a trunk
full of gardening supplies—bags of peat moss, a flat of portulacas
and phlox, and two rosebushes I picked out myself. Mom was
waiting for us to bring them home. No doubt we should have
been there by now.

"Let's go around again," he said. "You're handling the wheel
well."

"I'm not going very fast."

"You don't want to speed in the cemetery. The residents don't
like it."

I smiled. "Where did you learn to drive?"

"My old man, your grandfather, used to take me and your
uncle George out to Breezy Point and we'd practice out there, by
the bungalows, and then in the parking lot at Riis Park. We used
to chase after the pigeons with the car."

I smiled, thinking of Himself and Uncle George as teenagers—
shorter, skinnier, with their Flynn ears sticking out like open car
doors—taking turns behind the wheel in the windy parking lot at
the beach.

"What kind of car?"

"A '48 Packard. He eventually gave it to your uncle and bought an Oldsmobile."

I was getting used to the size of the Black Beauty. The massive hood that stretched far out like a dusty black carpet. We were back at the road that led you out of the cemetery and I was sure the lesson was over.

"Let's go over by Brooklyn Avenue."

That was the other side of Holy Cross, the one closer to our house. It had its own, grand entrance. I crossed the road, passing pristine limestone mausoleums with the names Sweeney and Anzalone engraved over slender doors. They were fancier than any home on our block, with its strip of semiattached A-frame houses in brick or stucco, and must have cost a fortune. Sweeney's house looked like a Greek temple with Doric columns and Anzalone's was like a miniature church with stained-glass windows, statues of saints stationed out front, and oxidized doors with windows, as if you might look inside and find parishioners attending mass. All this decoration for people who would never see it. But I appreciated the attempt to create some lasting memory, however extravagant. I felt like I was transported to another country, where imagination gave weight to sorrow and produced these mansions of the dead.

On my right, a large field of tombstones ran all the way to the Snyder Avenue cemetery fence. Somewhere in there the Flynns were buried, dating back to my great-grandparents. Mom's real mother was buried on the other side of Holy Cross, next to the Cortelyou Road fence. I knew that modest tombstone by heart.

The road curved, and I saw a man and a woman getting out of a parked car. They were dressed in blue windbreakers. The woman was carrying a potted lily, the white trumpet flower

standing out sharply against the green afternoon. The man carried a small red canvas duffel bag. They disappeared among the
angel-topped tombstones.

It was time to go home, switch places behind the wheel. People were starting to pay their respects on a Saturday afternoon,
and we didn't need to practice my driving, but Dad said, "Pull up
next to that Buick. Let's see how you do with parking."

The Buick, a Skylark, was parked next to a large limestone
mausoleum with the name Cutrone engraved above the entrance.

"I don't know if I'm ready to do that."

"You'll never get your license if you can't parallel park. Give
it a shot."

It was useless to argue. And everything so far had gone so
well so I didn't. I hadn't crashed into any bushes or graves—or
even knocked over a garbage can. If I didn't at least try this
tricky maneuver, his good mood might change for the rest of
the day, possibly the weekend.

He helped me position the Pontiac next to the Buick, put
the car into reverse, and back it up slowly until the cars were
aligned. Then he had me turn the steering wheel all the way to
the right as I backed up the car some more. He looked out the
passenger's side to check the clearance. The Pontiac sat at a funny
angle to the Buick. The Black Beauty was longer than the Green
Hornet, with a once gleaming black body, a white hardtop, and
sleek white side panels that extended from the taillights to the
front tires. A pointed white strip trimmed in chrome bisected
the black, again, from the front door to the headlights so that
the sides of the car gleamed like white daggers. In a street fight
between the two cars, the Black Beauty, named after the car
driven by Kato, sidekick to the Green Hornet in the radio serial,
would easily take the Buick.

After I turned the wheel as far as it would go, I braked. My palms were moist. I hoped that the man and woman still had a couple of Hail Marys or Our Fathers to say because I didn't want them to see a kid without a learner's permit trying to park this big old car.

Himself was ready for the next step. "Okay. Now crank it all the way to the left."

The only thing I had cranked up to that point was the volume on the stereo in the front porch, but whatever I did to the steering wheel, it worked. The Black Beauty smoothly rolled into place behind the Buick.

Dad was grinning. "Damn if you didn't get it on the first try."

He was delighted, nodding, the corners of his mouth turned down. This was awe; this was respect. This really meant something, but what I didn't know yet. No matter. I would always remember this moment as one of the times Himself and I approached something like harmony.

We switched places with the engine still running. The couple appeared from behind the Cutrone tomb and got back in the Buick.

I decided I was going to have a Ring Ding after lunch, the hell with the pimple patrol. I had just parked a '58 Pontiac Parisienne and the austere angels at Holy Cross Cemetery were my witnesses. I sat back in the Death Seat and looked out the window at the sky. A light scudding of cirrus clouds across the blue heavens promised a good afternoon of planting. We could probably get the rosebushes—one yellow, the other coral-colored—in the ground and watered in an hour. Then I could take off on my bike, down Ocean Parkway to Brighton Beach, until it got dark. I'd do my homework—algebra equations and Act III of *Julius Caesar*—tomorrow.

I felt and heard the bump at the front end of the car. We were hit or had hit something. I looked over at Himself. "You mutt," he said under his breath, already getting out of the car. I looked out the windshield. The back fender of the Buick was sort of tucked under the hood of the Black Beauty. The driver got out of his car slowly. He was older than Himself, with a thick head of silvering, wavy dark hair and a deeply lined forehead; frowning, he walked past him to look at his fender and taillights.

In the few minutes it took me to check the weather, something clumsy and stupid had happened. Through the tinted windshield, Dad's eyes looked bluer than usual. I heard him say "I didn't hit you, pal. You must have backed into me."

He was lying. I hoped he wasn't going to slug the guy.

The Black Beauty came with a thin green sun visor you could pull down like a shade to keep the sun off the front seat while the car was parked. I didn't want to watch Himself do what he was doing and I checked at the top of the windshield to see if I could pull down the visor. I'd only seen him use it once, this summer in the parking lot at Manhattan Beach. I began to pull it down when I saw the driver's wife come around the front of the car, to hand her husband some folded papers—insurance? registration? Then Dad reached inside his jacket and pulled out his wallet. Bills—I couldn't count how many—were passed from one driver to another. And then he walked away, while the couple from the Buick wrote something down, perhaps the Black Beauty's license plate number.

He opened the door with such force I half-expected it to come off. The sunshade snapped back into position. I slid over to the passenger seat. "What happened?"

He slammed the door behind him and turned on the ignition. "Nothin'. Dumb guinea has a dented fender." He shifted the car into reverse. "He wanted to see my insurance. In a pig's eye."

No way did he have insurance for a crate like this. "Why did you give him money if you didn't do anything wrong?"

He shot me a look. "That's a case where you give the guy fifty bucks to make it go away. No information exchanged."

Why wouldn't he admit he'd done something wrong? I sat back, determined to hold my tongue. He hadn't touched me since that night we got lost in the Green Hornet—I wondered if he even remembered smacking me and had given up expecting an apology—and now would be the wrong time to set him off, even if he was sober.

He backed up the car and we tore out of Holy Cross, ahead of the Buick, shooting down the main road toward the Tilden Avenue gate. We passed under the double archway, made of charcoal-colored boulders with a green-tile roof and a gold cross on top. The first building we came upon was the King Kullen supermarket, a box in pedestrian white brick. Giant white sale signs for Tropicana orange juice, Tab, and veal cutlets papered the windows, a humdrum reminder of the lives we lived outside the kingdom of the dead.

Home was two minutes away, already too long for me. We'd started out having the kind of day we never had and then in a flash, it was gone, with Himself's temper and his petty, unpredictable—I didn't know what to call it because I didn't understand him—taking over.

The Black Beauty turned right at the Sunoco station on Snyder Avenue and made the first left. When I saw Grandpa's stately Chrysler, done in a frosted champagne color, with the brand name New Yorker written in chrome script above the front tire, I smiled. It was always good to come home to company because Himself would have to be on his best behavior.

"Not a word about this to your mother," he said as we pulled into the driveway.

Everything with him was a big secret and I agreed not to say anything.

He strode to the garden, bearing the bags of peat moss in his arms as if they weighed no more than a breakfast tray. I carried the rosebushes, one in each hand, leaving the trunk open for the second trip.

Mom was in the garden with Grandpa. Her father, who had the opposite temperament of Grandpa Flynn. "What took you two so long?" She wore a yellow kerchief tied behind her ears, her car coat, and green-stained canvas gardening gloves. In her left hand, she held a dirty trowel.

"We took a detour." Dad set down the bags on the dirt and shook Grandpa's hand. "Don, let me introduce you to the next Mario Andretti." And then he raved about my vehicular prowess. His mood had changed again.

"Claire, we've got to get you behind the wheel next," he said, walking back to the car to get the rest of the supplies.

Mom retied her kerchief. "Driving lessons with you? You must have rocks in your head."

The garden was deep and rectangular, and separated from our neighbor's by a waist-high cyclone fence. We had more flowers than the Provenzanos, though: a red climbing rosebush, a willowy Japanese maple tree, and a peony whose buds were just beginning to turn white on one side. Wild ivy crawled across the stone garage wall. The mimosa tree and the new rosebushes were going in the back of the garden.

"What possessed your father to take you driving?"

"Something about the cemetery," I said, shrugging. I picked up a shovel leaning against the fence, and with my foot on the blade, drove it into the earth. The ground was dry and brown with an orange cast. I picked out the pebbles and small rocks and tossed them aside.

"He's lucky a cop didn't see him," Grandpa said.

"Nobody saw us. We did it in Holy Cross."

Grandpa giggled. He was tall and stooped, and wore an old blue shirt over gray pants. A blue cap shielded his head, completely bald now, from the wind. He worked in a grocery store way down Church Avenue, Esposito and Sons. Mom would send me down there on the bus to pick up baskets of oranges and grapefruit, and I would wait to be called into the back of the narrow store, wedging past the women shoppers who were picking up pieces of fruit and inspecting them. In the back room, there were boxes of unpacked produce stacked on a dark wood-plank floor. And that's when Grandpa would give me the package. There were always customers asking for him so I would say a quick goodbye and get back on the bus, the fragrance of peaches in summer or apples in the fall still fresh in my nostrils.

Grandpa had driven in all the way from his house on Long Island, a sylvan retreat that we had visited a few times when we were very young. Coming from the kingdom of concrete, we called it "the country" because the place smelled like newly mown grass, with split-rail fences along the property. Out back, there was a tree house and a vegetable garden. In the evenings, Grandma and Grandpa watched Lawrence Welk. Oh my god, it was beyond boring. I would sit there with Maureen—we must have been ten and nine years old—listening to the King Family sing and staring at the dancing couples in their old-fashioned evening attire and not say a word. We were guests and if we had complained, my step-grandmother, a stern Lutheran who had some kind of secretarial job on Wall Street, would have reported back to my mother.

Dad dropped off the flat of portulacas and disappeared inside the house. It felt so good to be out of the Black Beauty and that crazy scene in the cemetery. I loosened the rosebushes from their containers by gently pressing the trowel between the dirt and the green plastic pot. The yellow bush was called Amarillo and the coral Jump for Joy. A white plastic tag attached to a branch on each bush included a miniature photo of what the flowers would eventually look like when they bloomed. After I'd dug the holes, about eight inches deep, Mom shook in some of the peat moss and tossed in a handful of bonemeal. Then she loosened and lowered the bushes into the ground, her hands protected by the gloves. She usually tended the back garden by herself. I had become involved last year when she needed me to cut down a dead peach tree. I used Dad's Sears and Roebuck saw, and the resulting flood of light on the bushes underneath the tree, a bright blue hydrangea and a pink azalea, had really helped them flourish.

I filled in the holes and patted down the dirt with the shovel.

"Good job, Nicky," Grandpa said. I didn't ever remember doing anything like this, something so ordinary, with Grandpa Flynn. We only saw him at events—holidays, parties, summer barbecues. He never visited us without my grandmother as his ally. I always got the impression he thought children should be seen and not heard so this visit from Mom's dad seemed special.

Then I heard Himself coming down the back porch steps. He was dragging over the green garden hose. The color of the hose reminded me of the visor on the windshield screen I almost pulled down in the car before he paid off the guy in the Buick.

"Nicky, go in the house and make yourself a sandwich," he said, aiming the nozzle at the Amarillo rosebush. "I'll pick up from here."

"Okay." I leaned the shovel against the fence and rubbed my hands together. I was starving. And there was a Ring Ding waiting for me in the bread box under the kitchen clock. I was happy to leave him there with Mom and Grandpa, two gentle souls who would never know about the guy whose car we hit in the cemetery. Before I went into the house, I saw the Black Beauty parked in the driveway, back end facing me, and went down the alley to take a closer look. I felt the curve of the Continental kit, half-black, half-white, like the car itself, and smiled. I drove this car today and couldn't wait to tell my sisters. The sooner I knew how to drive for real, the sooner I could see the USA in my Chevrolet. Like he said.

FIVE

B rian Ventresca was the only teacher at St. Michael the Archangel who allowed students to call him by his first name. What was even stranger, he asked us to.

The first day I walked into his English class, I thought he was a substitute. He looked so out of place standing under the black crucifix planted above the blackboard that if he were any younger, he could have passed for a senior. He even dressed like us. His idea of work clothes was corduroy pants and a tweed jacket with elbow patches. The tie and shirt didn't match the jacket and the shoes were Hush Puppies. He was skyscraper-tall—well over six feet—and rangy, with long arms and longish, grown-out brown hair that was bleached a tawny color on the ends. His hands were the size of catcher's mitts, made for playing nine innings in a Brooklyn sandlot, not holding open a dog-eared copy of Stephen Crane's stories in front of thirty-five boys on the roller coaster of puberty. But here he was, St. Mike's first hippie, telling us, with an earnestness that completely beguiled me, that he wanted to "read some good books together."

I was a sophomore now, and going to school was like attending some apostolic police academy. One year in, I still wasn't used to going to an all-boys school and St. Mike's "us vs. them" dynamic didn't help. We, the students, the long-haired, corduroy-clad assembly, were "us"; the teachers, a smattering of married, bland laymen and a phalanx of Franciscan Brothers, imperious in their black soutanes, were "them." As the only teacher with a first name, Brian was somewhere in between "us" and "them."

When the Brothers were teaching, they paced back and forth in front of the blackboard, black rosaries swinging from their waists like pendulums, so Brian's calculated casualness quickly put us at ease. I did well at St. Mike's, but I didn't love it. I may not have been the most sophisticated kid in the world, but the guys here were way too Bensonhurst for me, Vinnie Barbarino to the tenth power. Suddenly I felt I had lucked out. The coolest guy in the joint was my teacher.

How he found his way to St. Mike's, I had no idea. I was there because if I'd gone to Erasmus, the public high school for kids from my neighborhood, I'd most likely end up getting jumped or knifed. St. Mike's had opened ten years ago, the last hurrah of the diocesan school system, a four-story box built in dun-colored brick on the edge of East Flatbush, but no one would have argued with you if you'd said the school was in Canarsie. The students came from far-flung parishes I'd never heard of: Saints Simon and Jude, St. Rose of Lima, Our Lady of Grace, Our Lady of Refuge, Our Lady of Perpetual Help, Resurrection, Most Precious Blood.

The school was bordered by a playground, a brand-new McDonald's, an auto body shop called Collisionville that spit out hubcaps and greasy tires onto the sidewalk, and a desperate tarpaper shack that was actually a bona fide landmark—the Pieter Claesen Wyckoff House—whose sinking foundations dated back to 1650, when this asphalt jungle was still farmland. Classrooms at St. Mike's were situated on the first three floors and in the basement. The Brothers lived in quarters on the fourth floor so I imagined them always listening in on us. They must have hired Brian because he had been in the seminary. I didn't know that until I'd been in his car a few times, but that didn't happen right away.

An almost priest. A prodigal hippie. No one could resist his natural charisma.

He wanted every class to be different. One time he played a record of Vincent Price reading "The Tell-Tale Heart" by Edgar Allan Poe, complete with chilling sound effects. When we read some scenes from *Romeo and Juliet*, Brian also screened *West Side Story* in Kingsmen Hall, the small auditorium in the school basement. Instead of making us suffer through *A Farewell to Arms*, Brian took a class vote, and we picked *Slaughterhouse-Five*, a new book I took out of the library. I suspected the Vonnegut novel was his choice all along, but he made us think it was ours. An antiwar novel while Vietnam was still raging—I don't know how he got away with it.

Somehow St. Mike's remained sheltered from political or social schisms, as if the archangel's protection were truly in evidence. Both the Kennedy assassination and the escalation of the Vietnam War occurred during its decade of operation, but that all happened at a remove on television. Students were much more likely to join the track team than march on Washington.

One day Brian asked us to rearrange our desks around the perimeter of the classroom, so we dragged the nicked, heavy desks across the floor, exchanging sly glances through the strands of hair that hung in our faces. I was worried he'd decided to turn the class into some kind of encounter group, where I would have to share my feelings with guys I barely knew and suspected I wouldn't like. But all he wanted to do was start our discussion of *Twelfth Night*.

"We're going to try something different," Brian said, as if we didn't already know that. "We're going to do the play. Here in class."

You could hear the pages of Folger Library paperbacks turning. Even I thought Brian was expecting too much. Shakespeare wasn't written for the marble-mouthed cadences of me and my fellow Brooklynites.

Brian anticipated that reaction. "You don't have to look so petrified," he said, standing in the center of the circle, his smile not exactly persuasive. "This is an experiment. We're just going to listen to the language and talk about the play. If you see how Shakespeare made poetry conversational, maybe you won't be afraid to read more of it. But first I need some volunteers."

He looked at us a minute longer, his tapered brown-black eyebrows raised in amusement. "Okay, time's up. Thanks for that enthusiastic response. Now I get to play director. Don't worry about changing your voice for the women's parts."

For those of us who didn't know there were women's parts in the play, there was some nervous darting of the eyes. "Women's parts?" asked Larry Cahill, who sat next to me in the circle. He was a tall, stocky kid with thick blond hair and olive skin. He wore black-framed glasses, like Clark Kent. "Now you're talking. If you can get me some women's parts, I'll definitely read Shakespeare. I might even compose a sonnet."

Everybody laughed. Larry had never been in any of my classes, but I knew who he was from all the practical jokes he played. He once took the microphone used for announcements in the cafeteria and, in the middle of fourth-period lunch, intoned, "This is God. And I am tired of eating the meat loaf in that kitchen."

Brian was ready to begin. "Okay, Nicky, why don't you read

Duke Orsino and, Dominic, you can do Valentine and, Larry, you do Curio. Act one, scene one. Whenever you're ready."

I licked my lips and looked at the compressed stanzas on the page. It was just an experiment, so what could go wrong? I began at the beginning and deadpanned the opening, "If music be the food of love, play on."

The guys in this class would interpret the slightest enunciation as proof of queer-bait behavior.

I looked up, thinking how funny my voice sounded when I spoke aloud. I didn't get very far before Brian interrupted me. "Nicky, the duke is hopelessly infatuated with Olivia, and he's a little on the dramatic side to begin with, so I'd like you to put some oomph into it."

Whatever that meant. I nodded, flushing. The sun, coming in through the windows, beat on the back of my neck. I read the passage again, this time with more of a flourish, even though I felt the rhythm of the verse fracture in my mouth. Larry said his two lines with bold emphasis, like an extra who wants to be a star. His friends gave him a round of applause. Dominic Fiore, sophomore class president and member of the speech and debate team and honor society, read Valentine in a loud and clear voice, as if drily making an announcement over the school's public address system.

Brian skipped ahead to the scenes of the play that were written in prose, casting Bensonhurst wiseasses Vinnie Sorrentino and Tony Stavola to read Olivia and Viola.

"For those of you who haven't read the play," Brian said, "Viola is disguised as a man here."

Vinnie and Tony were the kind of guys who liked to "surprise" the rest of us from time to time by jumping on mayonnaise or ketchup packets stolen from the cafeteria as we walked up the stairwells. They had beauty parlor hairdos, with bangs, terraces, layers, ridges, and wings, all blow-dried to perfection. I didn't know if Brian picked them to read the women's parts because they had the right hair, but the result was pure comedy. They hammed it up in their thick accents. Everyone cracked up and the boys blushed. When the reading was over, Brian applauded. "Well, I can see we have a real bunch of budding thespians here," he said. "Let's have a round of applause for today's cast."

"Hail, Caesar," said Vinnie from the back of the classroom.

Brian nodded. "Wrong play, but thanks anyway. You know, if any of you want to try out for a play I'll be directing at school after the holidays, let me know. I'm gonna need lots of guys and girls. There'll be an open invitation sent to the girls' high schools, but you can spread the word now."

"What's the play?" Dominic asked.

"*Bye Bye Birdie*. It should be fun. You did a good job today, Dominic."

The bell rang. Brian reminded us to put the desks back into rows before we left. Everyone pushed their chairs across the floor, making a huge groaning sound, and left them in a series of jagged lines. I helped Brian straighten out the rows and walked down the hall with him, on the way to geometry class. I had to speed-walk to keep up with him. "You mean you're doing the *Bye Bye Birdie* with Ann-Margret and Bobby Rydell? They're always showing that on *The 4:30 Movie*."

"Yeah? Well, next time it's on, take a look and see if there's a part you'd like to play," he said.

We passed the bursar's office and the school's main entrance, with its statue of St. Michael, complete with wings and halo, guarding the entrance to the gym.

"I really wanted to do *Hair*, but there was some kind of roy-alty problem," Brian said.

Like that was gonna happen. *Hair* was the play where all the actors were naked on stage. Maybe Brian *was* crazy. "So you think you might want to try out?" Brian asked.

"I don't know," I said, suddenly not wanting to disappoint him. "I've never done anything like that. Let me think about it."

"Fair enough. You read well today."

We stood at the entrance to the faculty lounge. "I've got to check on my messages," Brian said. "I'll see you in class tomorrow."

The rest of my classes sagged in comparison, and at three thirty, I was itching to get out of there. I always left school by the back entrance, where the track team circled a small green track. I didn't belong to any of the clubs or teams at St. Mike's. I was present, but not engaged. As I walked the four long blocks to the bus stop, I thought maybe that should change. Maybe Brian's notice to the girls' high schools would attract some who were right for me.

● ● ●

Every time I got off the bus, turned the corner at Church Avenue, and saw our house, I winced. It had been a while since it was painted, outside or inside, but outside was what I noticed. How could Himself not see it and do something about it? The stucco was the color of old loose leaf and the cinder blocks around the basement windows were definitely peeling, showing two older coats of paint beneath. The garden still had a few roses left on the bushes, and the last of the marigolds braved the autumn weather. And you would have thought Himself would get around to fixing the front stoop by now after tripping on his way up or down the steps. A couple were cracked, and one of the flowerpots had fallen into the garden after being loose for years. I had carried it into the garage thinking one day it might get reattached, but it was still there, next to the tires that once rolled underneath the Green Hornet.

I also wondered when he would get around to painting the front door. The paint, green on the trim and white on the recessed panels, had peeled so much that the bare wood was showing on the panels. I had volunteered to fix it, with a box of wood putty I had found in the garage, but Dad said no, so I hadn't mentioned it again.

Mom had to see what the rest of us saw but something held her back from saying anything about it.

I made it home in time for *Dark Shadows*. I didn't watch it as much as I used to when it was all the rage, but one look at the screen and I knew the show was doing a complete rip-off of *Rebecca*, with the actress who usually played Dr. Julia Hoffman, one of the strangest-looking people I'd ever seen, with a flat face and blinking turtle eyes, dressed in a black maid's uniform and doing a character modeled exactly on Mrs. Danvers—but not nearly as good, of course. Not even close. She was talking to a woman's portrait, head tilted back on her neck, her mouth stretched in whispering agony.

I dropped my school books on the dining room table and sat next to Maureen on the living room couch.

"What'd I miss?"

Maureen was a freshman at St. Edmund's and she was still wearing her school uniform, a blue-and-gray plaid skirt and a long-sleeved white blouse with a Peter Pan collar. "Not much. This old bat's talking to herself again. And Barnabas just came out of his coffin."

"What else is new? Where's Mom?"

Maureen pointed to the kitchen and the open door to the basement. "Laundry."

We could watch a little bit of television before supper; then, no more TV until homework was done. If there was something good on *The 4:30 Movie*, we could watch the whole thing while Mom got everything ready in the kitchen. She was always doing something, loading the washing machine or hanging the wash out or cooking. She was the most efficient person I ever knew. She made my sisters' clothes, the same outfit in different sizes from Simplicity patterns, sitting at the kitchen table with the plastic tablecloth bunched up under the Singer, basting pins between her lips and pieces of fabric, bobbins, and strips of rickrack everywhere. She unclogged sinks, checked on homework, and only sat down once or twice a day to watch her "stories," the afternoon soaps, tales of temptation, betrayal, and regret, and love withheld. Later, when she unexpectedly went back to work and I was in charge of the housework on Saturdays, I gave myself and the sisters all the chores Mom used to do and wondered how she kept on top of it all.

After *Dark Shadows*, I did my homework, geometry and history, before dinner. We ate chicken à la king, which came in plastic pouches that Mom boiled on the stove and served on toast. She would broil a steak for Himself, frying sliced white canned potatoes and onions in a cast-iron pan. Sometimes he came home right after work and ate with my mother in the living room. They put their dinner plates on snack tables and watched television while we carried on in the kitchen. If he went out for drinks with his work buddies, Mom ate with us. That seemed to be what was happening tonight. She sat at the head of the table, I knew, in case the phone rang and it was Himself saying he was on his way home. Then she would stop what she was doing and start his dinner. The steak, thick and red with a few streaks of fat, was waiting on a platter next to the cast-iron skillet.

The phone did ring, a pleasantly jarring jingle, and Mom answered in the middle of one of Maureen's stories about her old teacher, Sister Rose Carmel, and the fact that she was be-coming stone-deaf. I could tell from my mother's surprised tone, her voice light and airy, that the caller was not Himself.

We all stopped eating to eavesdrop.

Mom was chuckling. "Well, I'll have Pat call you when he gets in. Yes. Any minute now."

"Who was it?" Patty asked when Mom sat down at the table again, her expression slightly pensive.

She ate a forkful of chicken. "That was your grandfather. It seems that they have bought a place in Florida."

"Wow."

Mom sipped her ginger ale. "First your uncle, now your grandparents. Soon, you guys will be the only Flynns left in Brooklyn." In little ways like this, she did not include herself as a member of the extended family.

"Stranded," said Maureen.

"Why can't we move to Florida?" Mary Ellen asked at her end of the table.

Mom pushed her plate away. She ate like a bird. She took off her glasses and wiped a smudged lens with the hem of her blouse. "Why do you want to go to Florida?"

"Disneyland," Dee Dee said.

"That's in California," Maureen said. "Can you pass the milk?"

I handed her the carton of Borden's.

"I wish your father would come home, so he can get all the details. Your grandfather said he wants to be down there by the end of the year."

We didn't learn any more specifics that night because Him-self never came home. The phone didn't ring, and we didn't hear the distant rumble of the Black Beauty as he backed it into the driveway. When the uncooked steak still lay on the platter next to the frying pan after we did the dishes, Maureen asked Mom what to do with it.

"Stick it in the refrigerator until Himself comes home," she said from the living room.

That's what she called Dad when she was annoyed with him or he was being unusually stubborn and I guess that's where I picked it up. The shot of sarcasm made it more than a nickname and less than an insult. And I'm not sure if he ever knew we called him that.

SIX

One Sunday morning a few weeks later, we came down to breakfast and found Himself slumped on the kitchen floor, back against the white enameled oven door. Mom leaned against the sink, sipping a cup of coffee in her pink flannel nightgown, and looked down at him, as if trying to figure out how she was going to lift him—or if she was just going to leave him there.

He was conked out. If you screamed in his ear, he wouldn't have heard you. We'd found him passed out before, usually at the kitchen table, but never on the floor. Did he fall off the kitchen chair? He looked like the guys you saw on the Bowery. How do you come home like that, so drunk you just collapse? I didn't want to see him like that and almost went back to my room until Mom hustled him upstairs.

I waited with my sisters in the dining room for the okay to walk in. Mom put the coffee cup down and waved us over. I went first.

Mom lit a cigarette on the gas burner and took a long drag on it. "She's all yours," she said, pointing.

As shocked as we were to see Himself in such bad shape, the bigger surprise was the dog. She was reclining next to his bent left leg, a tricolor collie blinking at us in the most bewildered way, as if she were waiting for us to tell her what she was doing here, in our kitchen. She was really very striking, even beautiful. Her coat was mainly black. Her forelegs were brown, her paws and chest white. Her snout was longer and narrower than most collies, with a thin stripe of white in the brown. It gave her a slightly aristocratic air. In this house she was going to need it.

Like me, my sisters were half-asleep. Ringlets of damp hair stuck to their necks and temples.

Maureen immediately knelt to pet the dog. "Look at you," she said into the dog's confused, melancholy face. She looked up at Mom. "Where'd she come from?"

"Your father brought her home from a bar. Where else? Who wants coffee?"

The aroma of a freshly perked pot filled the kitchen. I raised my hand. "I do."

Maureen glanced at Dad. "He's really smelly, Mom."

I didn't plan to get that close. A thread of drool hung from his lip, a pack of Pall Malls crushed in his shirt pocket. I checked the clock over the kitchen window. Eight A.M.

Maureen gently unbent his leg to free the animal. Now Dad was sitting with his legs spread out in front of him, blocking the way to the sink. Standing on his other side, Mom poured coffee into cups that she took from the drainboard and passed them over Dad's head to Dee Dee, who put them on the table.

"Let's get her some water," Maureen said. Mom filled a Tupperware cereal bowl and passed it to Maureen. The collie lapped up half of it and then reclined on the floor next to Himself, crossing her front paws. Master and pet, in repose.

"Ooh, she's such a lady," I said. "Definitely not the saloon sort. What did he say when he brought her in?"

"What was there to say?" Mom said, flustered. "He opened

the door and said, 'I got something here for the kids.' I looked
out at the front porch and there she was."

Having the dog there made it possible to overlook Himself,
as if he were a sofa too cumbersome to move.

"Well, she's pretty and that's nice," Patty said. "What's her
name?"

"I don't know if she has one," Mom said, wiping her glasses
on a hand towel. "I think that's up to you kids."

We all looked at her.

"Well, we could name her after the bar where he found her,"
I said.

Maureen shot me a rueful look. "Like what? Dew Drop."

"We are not naming her Dew Drop," said Patty. "Don't be
such an ass."

"No, I think we'll name her Queenie," Maureen said.

She was always so pushy. "Hey, who says you get to decide?"
I asked.

Mom took a ratty leather harness off the closet doorknob
and handed it to Maureen. "Before you worry about giving her
a name, why don't you get dressed and take her out for a walk?
Your father swore she was house-trained."

We threw our clothes on and walked the dog together, the
five of us. Me, Maureen, Patty, and our two youngest sisters,
Dee Dee and Mary Ellen. I found my sneakers under the couch
in the living room and helped Maureen put the harness on the
dog. I felt the hairless skin under her coat. Himself was grum-
bling on the kitchen floor.

"Go on now, while I get him up to bed," Mom said.

Except for other dog walkers, our block was empty. It was
a cloudy day with a raw, wet breeze. The Black Beauty struck a
lopsided pose in the driveway, its luxurious back end nudging the

orange berries on our neighbor Mrs. Garrett's firethorn bush, its grille breathing on the alyssum plants around the border of our garden. Maureen held the leash and guided the collie into the street. The dog trotted along and Maureen kept her eyes peeled toward Snyder Avenue for oncoming cars. It was uncanny how she just seemed to know which way the animal was going to move. She pulled the leash to her, stopping the dog when a car approached or even if another animal appeared in her path. You would have thought she had been doing this for years. When I tried, I held the leash too loosely, and the dog almost walked into a passing Dodge.

We took the collie down to the dirt path along Holy Cross Cemetery. Gina Martinucci was already there, walking her dog, a camel-colored mutt named Muffin. She was wearing a bright green raincoat, her wavy brown hair cascading to her shoulders. Not one pimple on her face. I'd known her for as long as we lived on the block, but she'd never looked so pretty. Next to her, I felt grubby in my blue corduroy pants and sweatshirt. And I wished I'd combed my mop of hair.

Gina was obviously ready for church. She sang and played lead acoustic guitar at the ten o'clock folk mass at St. Maria Goretti (I hadn't been to church since starting high school; maybe I needed to go back). There were almost as many girls in the Martinucci house as there were in mine, and one son, also the eldest child. The big difference was that her whole family was involved in the church: her mother sang in the choir, her father was in the Holy Name Society. Rumor had it that the Martinuccis said the rosary together—something we would not do in a million years.

"My god, is that your dog?" Gina said. "She's beautiful. When did you get her?"

"This morning," I said. My sweatshirt wasn't warm enough for the crisp air.

Gina gave me a strange look. "This morning? You're kidding me. Wow."

"It was a surprise."

She bent down to pet our new pet. "How old is she?"

I shrugged. "We don't really know." I sounded like a first-class doofus.

"What?" Gina said. "Well, she's not a puppy. Where'd you get her?"

This encounter was getting more awkward every minute. I glanced at the flower arrangements on the graves through the cemetery's wrought-iron fence. Piles of unraked red, yellow, and brown leaves colored the dying grass.

"Our father brought her home," Patty said finally.

Gina looked confused. "Really? I mean, was she a stray?"

"The dog belonged to a friend of my father's who couldn't take care of her anymore," said Maureen, standing next to me.

Gina was beginning to catch on, her knit brow registering the weirdness of this morning. "Oh, that's too bad. So I guess you didn't get to name her. It's more fun when they don't have a name."

"You're right," Maureen said. "We were told her name was Queenie."

I wanted to step on her feet. It was such a frigging stupid name.

"Queenie," Gina said, trying it out. "Well, I guess there are enough Princesses around."

"And they're all German shepherds," I said.

Muffin and Queenie were sniffing each other out, the collie ever so standoffish. Maureen didn't even grip the leash. Gina ran her fingers through the collie's thick coat. "She must be shedding everywhere. I know I'm constantly picking up hair."

"Yeah, it's a real drag," Maureen said, rolling her eyes at me.

She thought Gina was stuck up and started to lead the dog away. "Come on, Queenie."

"Her coat's a little dull," Gina told me when my sisters were out of earshot. "You should give her a raw egg. Makes it shiny."

I caught up with my sisters after Gina left. "Why did you tell her we got the dog from Daddy's friend, of all things?"

"Why do you have to broadcast our business all over the place?" Maureen said, letting the dog drag her ahead as she sniffed the ground.

"What did I say? We have a dog. We don't know how old she is, and we don't know where she came from—except some bar. Which I didn't say."

Maureen remained stone-faced. "You didn't have to tell Gina Martinucci anything. She thinks who she is."

Finally, the dog squatted and peed.

Even though they met under the most unlikely circumstances, Queenie seemed to like Himself most of all. Whenever he sat in his chair, the rust-colored recliner, the dog ran over to him and leapt into his lap, offering her neck for a good rubbing. He always obliged and the dog moaned appreciatively.

"Daddy, why doesn't she ever bark?" Dee Dee asked. That was Queenie's thing: to almost bark, moaning when she became excited but never really opening her mouth to let the full sound out. "It's like she wants to but doesn't know how."

"I don't really know," he said with a yawn. "I think she may have been beaten when she did bark."

"Poor Queenie," Dee Dee said.

There was no question that the arrival of the collie was a blessing in our lives. We could all take care of her. Dad set up a schedule for the care of the dog. Queenie was walked five times a day; I had the late shift. Soon we wanted her outside with us all the time. If there was no one else for Dee Dee and Mary Ellen to play with on the block, they could run her up and down the sidewalk between our house and Snyder Avenue or try in vain to teach her tricks, like how to catch a ball. And Queenie was always good company, whether you wanted to hang out on the stoop or walk two miles around the perimeter of Holy Cross.

There were only a few things Queenie hated: baths, firecrackers, and bars. I discovered that one night when Dad called home, asking Mom for money so he could stay out and drink. Mom was using her lowest possible voice as she talked to him on the phone; I knew she didn't want to give him five cents. Then she hung up, called me over, and asked me to give her the pocketbook on the dining room table. She took a ten-dollar bill from her change purse and handed it to me. "Take this to your father," she said evenly.

"When?"

"Now."

I had finished my French and geometry homework and was getting ready to watch *The Avengers*. Never missed an episode. Diana Rigg in a leather jumpsuit doing karate on the bad guys, then changing into something sleek at the end for a martini with Mr. Steed. I could walk from one end of Brooklyn to the other and not find any girl as cool or witty or elegant. I imagined her picking me up after school in her blue Lotus Elan convertible, long brown hair blowing in the breeze as we headed off to some adventure. She would call me Nick, not Nicky, and I'd feel about ten years older.

The only place I was going now was the Dew Drop and Mom knew from my expression I didn't want to go. "He says to take the dog with you."

Queenie, napping in front of the television, coarse wisps of hair rising off her coat, didn't look like she wanted to go anywhere. "Why do I have to bring her?"

Mom bit off her words. "It will take ten minutes. Do me a favor and take the dog."

Maybe I'd make it back in time for the second half hour of the show. Emma Peel would be kicking the villain of the week in the teeth by then and the show would really get good. Maureen could tell me what I'd missed.

I walked up Church Avenue, heading toward Nostrand. Our neighborhood was more black than white now. The streetscape I used to know was changed forever. Roti shops had replaced grocery stores. Guy's Hair Salon, with its sun-bleached pictures of women with blond beehives and champagne bouffants taped to the windows, was now called De Hair Wizzards and advertised weaves, wigs, and Afros. Himself wanted me to bring the dog for protection in case I ran into any trouble, but I didn't think I'd have any problems. Now that it was colder, the corner boys who usually lingered in front of the bodega on New York Avenue drinking Colt 45s were gone. The few guys I passed sidestepped me as if they were afraid of the dog. Little did they know that she hardly ever barked when she first came to live with us, so it was hard to imagine her biting anyone.

The Dew Drop was on the corner of Church and Fairview Place, six blocks from home. Queenie trotted along at my side, her coat shiny under a dark blue sky (I'd taken Gina's advice and mixed a raw egg into her Alpo). I wore a red-and-black plaid jacket that used to belong to my uncle George; it was a little long in the sleeves but had a great scratchy feel I always associated with old-time wool. I wondered if he had contacted my father since he moved to Germany. I was sure Himself had never cracked open that book on Alcoholics Anonymous. I needed no further proof than the morning he brought home the dog and was unconscious on the kitchen floor.

Something strange happened as we approached the bar.

Queenie pulled at the leash. I looked down at her and said, "What's wrong?" I took another step and she dragged her hind legs on the sidewalk, claws on her forelegs scraping the concrete. I stopped. She gave me a frightened look. She knew more about this place than I did. I didn't know what to do, so I bent down and petted her.

I glanced at the bar. Cardboard shamrocks were taped to the window, decorations someone forgot to take down; it was already October. Or maybe every day was St. Patrick's Day at the Dew Drop.

We went back to the corner and crossed the street. I walked the collie down to the corner of Martense Street and crossed back over. "Come on. It won't take long," I said, as if she could understand me. When we were near the Dew Drop's side exit, she allowed me to tie the leash to a No Parking sign and I stayed with her a minute.

I was hoping I could make this quick, give the old man his ten bucks, and scram. I entered the bar through the side door, not knowing what to expect on the other side. First surprise: it was a mixed crowd. I couldn't even imagine Himself drinking with black guys, especially the ones here with Afros, when he was always making jokes about blacks, but I guess in the smoky confines of the Dew Drop, racial tensions were set aside as long as everyone could watch a replay of that afternoon's Mets game against the Orioles. They'd finally made it to the World Series, giving hope to underdogs everywhere.

I was the only minor in the joint, sure I stuck out like a sore thumb. Standing on tiptoe, I saw Dad sitting on a red stool at the bar, looking at a near-empty glass. Probably thinking about this ten-dollar bill every time he saw the foam slide down the inside of the glass. He was talking to some middle-aged white guy with a sunburn where his hairline was receding. A cigar stuck out of his mouth. The TV set was poised above the far right end of the bar. They were complaining about Ed Kranepool, the first baseman Dad always called lard-ass.

I took the bill out of my pocket and placed it on the bar in front of him. I leaned in. "Mom said this was for you."

He stopped laughing and shot me a look. "Hey, who's this?" the man sitting next to him asked, and I reached out to shake another hand of someone I didn't really want to meet.

"You haven't met my son, the scholar?" Dad said, poking the shoulder of the guy next to him. "Nicky, can I buy you a drink?"

Mom didn't say I was going to have to stay. "Uh, maybe a quick one. I'll take a ginger ale. I have the dog outside."

He called the bartender over. One of the Mets scored a home run on the color TV screen, and he shouted to everyone, in the booming voice we came to fear, "One to nothing, top of the eighth. We are home free." I smiled and shook my head; when he was wound up like that, Dad was hard to resist. "Hey, Charlie, give me another beer. And a soda for my son."

Charlie was an older white man with liver-colored lips and thinning brown hair slicked back with some tonic with a medicinal odor like Vitalis; his nicotined teeth flashed garishly from the right corner of his mouth when he spoke. I bet Dad had known him for years, from one place to another. Charlie slapped another foamy beer on the bar.

So this was Himself's inner sanctum. A private world of men playing the away game from their families. Some customers were older than Dad, guys with thick-lensed eyeglasses, pudding skin, and chin lines lost to jowls, but many looked like they were about the same age, early to mid-thirties, still slim and well built. All eyes were on the television screen and the all-important game. I sipped my soda, trying to seem natural though the smoky air was bothering my eyes; it was hard not to rub them.

Compared with some of the joints I would later retrieve Himself from, this place wasn't terrible. The décor was standard: a jukebox, a pool table, dartboard, neon signs advertising Rheingold and Pabst Blue Ribbon. Two photos over the walnut case that housed the bottles of liquor and liqueurs caught my eye; they seemed so out of place. One was John F. Kennedy, in a fake gold frame, the kind we used for our school graduation pictures, lined up on the fireplace in the living room. The other was Martin Luther King Jr. The owner of this place wasn't stupid; he wanted to keep his changing clientele happy.

Dad was telling the guy sitting at the next stool—his name was Molloy, Joe Molloy—what a fantastic student I was—"This kid got one hundred in Latin, I kid you not"—and I remembered how angry I was when he signed me up for the class, mailing in my freshman elective card, without telling me. Told me Latin was the root of all languages. Like he knew.

"I'm lucky I can speak English," Molloy said.

The ginger ale tasted kind of flat. I drank it anyway and gestured to the dog when I finished. The side exit from the bar was open, and he glanced at Queenie resting on the sidewalk.

"She's some watchdog," he said with a wink. "Best game of poker I ever won."

"What?"

"I was playing cards here with Tommy Sullivan and Phil Cooney and Joe was flat broke. So he put his dog up as ante. You see, he's the owner and she was kind of like the bar dog."

The bar dog. I wished he had the sense that she did about coming here. "And you won the game and the dog." I couldn't even smile.

Dad gave a hearty laugh. "That's the way it goes sometimes."

I wondered how long Queenie had lived here. We didn't even know how old she was. My eyes stung from the smoke and I rubbed them. I looked at the guys sitting on the stools and wondered how many of them would go home now. Most, probably. So why couldn't he do that?

Standing up, I glanced at the singles on the bar, the change from our drinks. I was feeling nervy. "So I guess you'll be home when the game's over?"

He did a double take, as if I'd cuffed him on the ear. "What did you say, Mr. Flynn?"

I forgot about catching the last of Emma Peel. "C'mon. I want to take another driving lesson tomorrow. We haven't gone out in a while." We'd done Holy Cross and the Brooklyn Terminal Market, which had no yellow lines, just huge spaces between the vendors. "I don't want to get rusty."

"Yeah, well. We'll see what we can do about that."

As saves go, I was proud of myself, although my knees were shaking. An appointment with a car he could make. Spending the night with his wife and family, he was on the fence.

Queenie looked fairly miserable out on the sidewalk, panting in the dark, but I wanted to see if I could get Himself to come home. It was the top of the ninth, the score unchanged. I ordered another ginger ale, chipping away at what was left of that ten-dollar bill. Tom Seaver, the cute Met my two eldest sisters had a crush on, was pitching so that was a good sign. He could knock out the other team and when he did, the guys in the bar cheered as if they were out at Shea Stadium. Then they started to leave, settling up, shaking hands with the bartender, and going on their way.

I stood and nudged my old man. "Come say hi to the dog."

I went outside. Queenie jumped on me when I untied the

leash, thinking we were finally getting out of there. When she settled down, I petted her under the collar, rubbing the white hair under her neck, which she loved. Then Himself joined us on the sidewalk and she got excited all over again. She was ready to go. I wondered if he was too.

"Want to walk us home?"

He stopped petting Queenie and looked up at me. "Why? You afraid of the dark?"

"Game's over, Dad. Your team won."

He stood, looking down at the sidewalk with his hands in his pockets, as if giving serious thought to my proposal. "You go on home, Nicky," he said. "I've got to talk to Molloy about something."

When he raised his head, his eyes were full of regret; he knew what I was up to and he was still prepared to let me down. I wondered how much of that ten-dollar bill was left—enough for one more drink? Maybe he had to talk Molloy into giving him a free one. A buyback, they called it. Except that my mother was doing the buying here. He was doing the spending.

He left me on the sidewalk. I was a fool to think I'd persuade him to come home. Voices came from the TV set inside the bar, sportscasters falling all over themselves about tonight's game. I stood there like a jerk, looking at the mannequins in the window of Bob and Betty, the children's clothing store across the street. A stock boy from the Big Apple dragged tied-up cardboard boxes to the curb for garbage pickup tomorrow morning.

I had him, then I lost him, like an image that slips out of focus in the lens of a camera. All the elements were there to give me a clear picture of what I could expect the next time I was sent to get him. And the time after that. The corner bar, the sound of my own footsteps as I walked up the street, the kid taking out the trash as I would do when I had my own afterschool job,

scooping thirty-one flavors at Baskin-Robbins. A lingering sense
of futility, and the lonely certainty that these missions would end
only when I grew up and moved away.

I took the dog and headed back down Church Avenue. She
pulled at the leash with the same force she showed when clawing
the sidewalk. Home, that's what she wanted. Me too. Neither of
us belonged here.

SEVEN

After Grandma and Grandpa Flynn sold their house, we inherited their dining room furniture. But first we had to go get it. On a cold Saturday morning in November, I waited at the kitchen table for Himself to get ready. Mom was doing her usual five things at once. She placed two cake pans to cool on top of the stove; later, she would ice them for Dee Dee's birthday. My little sister was nine years old.

The house Grandma and Grandpa were moving to was too small for all the furniture they had, Mom said. Grandma was giving everything away that wouldn't fit in the new place, a mobile home.

I had already eaten a bowl of cereal but picked up a red delicious apple out of a bowl on the table. "What do people do in Florida?"

Mom walked to the open basement door, a basket of dirty clothes under her arm. "Your grandfather's going to play golf every day. I don't know what your grandmother's going to do. This whole thing is his idea."

I smiled and bit into the apple. It was a little dry, but I would finish it just the same. We already cleared a space in the dining room for the new table; the old one leaned against the china closet. Before Mom and I put the table aside, I folded the ivory lace tablecloth that adorned it and put it away in a drawer in the buffet. While smoothing the fabric, I found a yellowed newspaper clipping, an obituary notice for my mother's mother. She'd died when Mom was still a teenager. "Jurgensen, Catherine" was the name in boldface. The newsprint was so faded I could barely make out the lowercase letters, except to find the name of the county in Ireland, Mayo, where she had been born Catherine Staunton. She'd saved it all these years, but I wondered why the notice wasn't in some kind of scrapbook.

The weekends were turning colder now, and none of us was in any hurry to go outside. Mary Ellen and the birthday girl were still in their pjs, watching cartoons in the living room. The collie napped on the rug. Patty was upstairs with the vacuum and Maureen was waiting for Himself to get out of the bathroom, so she could get in there and scrub it. I was excused from housework today because I was assigned the manly task of getting the table.

Mom returned from the basement with a yellow basket piled high with folded clothes and looked at the empty spot in the dining room. "Well, I guess I can't put these on the table." She pulled out a kitchen chair and plopped the basket there.

"Why does he have to get so dolled up just to go get a table?" I asked.

She was back at the stove again, running a knife around the edge of the silver cake pan. "So his mother will think he looks like that all the time." She turned the cake pan upside down and tapped the bottom. The spongy yellow layer fell into the palm of her hand; it was perfect. She removed the second layer and placed it on top of the first. Mom baked birthday cakes for all of us and they were all iced and presented on a bone china cake stand that once belonged to her mother.

"What kind of icing?"

She moved the cake stand to the middle of the kitchen table, where the dog couldn't paw it. "Vanilla, but she wants me to make it green. It's her favorite color. This week."

She picked up the basket of clean laundry and headed to the staircase. I could smell Himself coming into the kitchen, the Old Spice drumroll. Every hair was in place, expertly combed and slicked back with VO5. He was wearing black pants and a blue-and-white flannel shirt.

"Let's shake a leg, Mr. Flynn," he said, heading out the kitchen door. We went through the back porch into the yard. There were leaves plastered to the sidewalk from last night's rainstorm, and the sky was gray and sudsy, as if it wanted to squeeze out a little more water. The last of the roses clung to the bushes with a stubborn, battered look, and the Japanese maple had turned a burnished tangerine. He rolled up the garage door and disappeared among the bikes, the old tires, and the garden tools. The Black Beauty, parked in the driveway, had been around longer than the Green Hornet, but signs of its demise were already visible: one of the hubcaps was missing and the muffler's rumbling could be heard a block away.

He came down the alley carrying heavy yellow ropes, which I guessed we would use to tie something in the trunk, maybe the chairs. He threw them in the backseat and backed the car out of the driveway. I got in once he cleared the curb. The car smelled better than usual: no cigarette stink or sour alcohol smell. He had been home every night this week—we kept count now—and his mood seemed steady. When we had driven far enough away from the house, over by the quiet streets near Brooklyn College, he pulled over by one of the campus bookstores and told me to get behind the wheel.

It was the first time I drove in traffic. I was ready but nervous. Although these illicit driving lessons didn't come regularly, I never forgot what I learned. By the time I was old enough to take driver's ed, I would be teaching everyone else how to do this. I made a left on Campus Road and then another left on Bedford Avenue, the longest street in Brooklyn. The street rose as we passed over an old freight rail line, and I pressed on the gas pedal.

In the rearview mirror, I saw a bus sneaking up behind me. The red light at the upcoming intersection was flashing, and Dad told me to step on it. "Lights on Bedford are three minutes long," he said.

He had to be exaggerating, but I did as I was told and sailed through the intersection. "I'm doing forty-five," I said, tapping my fingers on the steering wheel.

"Watch out," Dad said.

Bedford Avenue was lined with mighty old trees. The cloud cover made the colors of the leaves pop. The yellows of the silver lindens and the black maples were really sharp, and occasionally a leaf from one of these trees would float down and rest on the hood of the Black Beauty. Homes were set back from the sidewalk with stone porches that led to side entrances and allowed for wide picture windows on the first floor. Dad pointed to a one-story house done in chunks of rosy beige stone with a grand, curved picture window, and a double-door entrance painted white. "Gil Hodges lives there."

Gil Hodges. Savior of the New York Mets. The manager who had just won the team its first World Series. My parents worshipped him. Even better, he used to play with the Brooklyn Dodgers, the best team of all time to anyone who grew up here, when people still thought that baseball could save Brooklyn.

"When he played for the Dodgers, I used to deliver the *Brooklyn Eagle* to his house every day." His pride at having the most tangential connection to this legendary player was evident, and I smiled.

There were Hasidic couples walking down the street past the Hodges house now. "Did the house look like this?"

"The house has undergone some renovations now that he's making the big money," Dad said with a chuckle.

His voice was especially raspy this morning. I think his body was rebelling against his two-pack-a-day habit, and he spent part of every morning in the bathroom coughing so violently he ended up gagging like some desperate animal. Listening to that from my bedroom, I resolved never to touch a cigarette.

We were heading toward Kings Highway now, blocks past where we were supposed to be going. I wondered how much farther we were going to go before turning around. I could see the light turning red at the next corner, and I started slowing down; I knew I wouldn't make it. Then I saw a familiar face crossing in front of us: Brian Ventresca.

I honked the horn. "Hey, there's my English teacher."

Dad looked out the window. "I didn't know they were hiring hippies in the Catholic school system."

"They are. Can we pull over?"

"Sure. This I've got to see to believe."

I pulled over in front of a white-brick saltbox with blue shutters and a flaming sugar maple in the front yard.

Brian was carrying several books under one arm and was dressed even more casually than he was at school, in jeans, sneakers, and a bright-white hooded sweatshirt. His hair lifted in the breeze.

Dad got out of the car and stuck out his hand. "Pat Flynn."

Brian shook it and introduced himself. He towered over Dad—he had to be six-four—and I watched Himself raise his eyebrows as he calculated the height difference. "Nicky can't wait to get a car of his own, so I thought I'd give him a little practice." He chuckled uneasily. "That's between you and me, of course. The Brothers up at that school do not need to know."

"If they did, they'd start showing up at your house to take a spin in something this cool." Brian took in the length and width of the Black Beauty, the chrome dagger embedded in the white trim on the side of the car and the twin headlights. Then he crouched to read the lettering. "Pontiac Parisienne. Fancy."

"Nineteen fifty-eight," Dad said. "It was a very good year."

Patty was still a baby; there were only three children in the house. Was that what he meant? I nodded at the books in Brian's hand. They were thick, maybe anthologies. "You live around here?"

"On the other side of Ocean. I'm returning some books to the Brooklyn College library and thought I'd walk." He looked at Dad. "When I'm not teaching high school, I take night classes. Getting my master's."

Dad tilted back on his heels, his arms folded across his chest, to size Brian up. He'd never met any of my teachers, not even when I was with "the good sisters," as he called the nuns at St. Maria Goretti. He left all that meet-and-greet crap to Mom. "So I guess you could say you're a professional student."

Brian pushed a flying wisp of hair behind his ear. "I've got to get a college teaching job if I want to make more money. Living at home with Mom and Pop ain't cutting it anymore."

I wanted them to get along so badly it took me a minute to hear him say that he still lived at home. I knew nothing about what jobs paid, especially teaching jobs, but I was still floored. Brian had to be in his midtwenties.

"So how do you like teaching a bunch of teenage boys? Or maybe I should ask: Can they even be taught?"

Brian laughed, perhaps too loudly. "Well, there are days

when I realize no one's done any of the reading I've assigned and I have to talk for forty-five minutes. That's when I call on Nicky." He squeezed my shoulder. Himself took note.

I was actually a little behind on my reading for Brian, but I'd make up for it tomorrow. I also had a ton of French homework. I ditched the Latin as soon as I could and Himself didn't mind because he had proven to me I had a knack for languages.

Dad insisted that Brian accept a ride. So we went back the way we came. I sat in the backseat, pushing aside those old yellow ropes, so Brian could have the legroom up front. His knees were still brushing the dashboard.

Himself took the wheel and made a sharp U-turn in the middle of Bedford Avenue.

Brian sat back and looked out the enormous windshield. "This is some car, Mr. Flynn. Where'd you get it?"

"Sixty-Ninth Precinct. My own private showroom. Buy all my cars at auction. You look pretty young to be a teacher. First year?"

"Nah. I taught for two years at Christ the King in Queens, but the driving just killed me. So I switched over. How about you?"

He told Brian how long he'd worked at the phone company: twelve years. "I've climbed poles in some of the worst neighborhoods you've never been in," he said. "Just to install a phone. Last time I was in East New York, woman on the first floor answers the door to let me in. She's got a pistol in her bra. Stood in the yard while I was doing the wires. I thought she was going to shoot me."

This was one story about the phone company I hadn't heard, and it felt good to laugh. We passed Avenue K, a few blocks from the campus. The speedometer said forty-five mph. I wondered why he was slowing down, if it was for Brian's benefit. And then

he asked, "So what do you think of that peace march they are
going to have in D.C.?"

Why did he have to mention Vietnam? I shrank in my seat.
Every night he watched the news on TV and glowered at the
"agitators," as he called them, protesting on college campuses,
having "sit-ins" and other forms of civil disobedience.

Brian looked back at me with a questioning glance. "You
mean the Moratorium? I'm going to drive down with my brother
and a friend of mine who served and we're gonna check it out.
It's in two weeks."

Dad seemed shocked and said nothing. When we read *The
Red Badge of Courage*, Brian would talk about the Berrigan brothers and the draft records they destroyed. He wanted to tell us
priests protest the war too; anybody could. The blank stares of my
classmates told me they'd never given a moment's thought to the
draft. Me, I was just hoping the war would end before I turned
eighteen and had to register with the Selective Service System.

Himself didn't need to know Brian was a fan of the Berri-
gans, though. I leaned on the front seat. "In our last car, he had a
portable record player, and me and my sisters took turns playing
our old 45s."

Brian turned toward me. "Really? Where did it go?"

"Right under the dashboard. The needle bumped on the pot-
holes, but it was better than the radio."

Finally, the campus buildings came into view and Brian ex-
ited by a tall, green wrought-iron fence. He touched the white
leather on the seat once before shutting the door.

"Thanks for the ride, Mr. Flynn. Nicky, I guess I'll see you in
school on Monday. We're going to have a surprise quiz."

Himself watched Brian walk onto the campus and I got back
into the front seat. "Inside information," he said, as we retraced
our route. "He wants you on his side."

I didn't know why Brian would need someone like me on his side. I was just one of his students, in one of several classes he taught. Plenty of his students must have liked him. Still, I didn't know how to reply directly to this comment. All I could say was "He's a really good teacher." That must have sounded pretty lame.

"I bet you fifty bucks that guy's a draft dodger," he said.

I said nothing.

"Ask him what his draft status is. I bet it's CO. Conscientious objector."

"And so what if he is? No one wants to go to Vietnam and get their legs blown off."

"Georgie Olsen went. Died for our country."

He was a kid whose family lived on our street, in a tiny house next to a vacant lot on Snyder Avenue. I barely knew him, but Himself had raised a glass or five with his father. Many families on our block went to the funeral mass at St. Maria Goretti. I was even allowed to take half a day off from school. I was sure the war would end before I could be drafted. Eventually the *Daily News* would publish the draft lottery. Anybody over eighteen could check to see if their number was listed and what their chances were of actually getting shipped overseas. It was like finding out what day you were going to die.

We were cruising down Nostrand Avenue now, past a large public school. I didn't want to anger him—I knew what could happen—but I had to ask, "So does that mean we should all go over and get killed?"

"It means that when the government tells you to do something, you do it."

I didn't say another word until we got to my grandfather's house. It was a stand-alone, three-bedroom house with a decent-sized lawn that flanked the front stoop. Everyone went in through the side door, walking across the driveway and around the backyard, where the lawn practically came up to the house. Somebody—Grandpa, I bet—had swept up the leaves shaken from the trees by last night's storm into a neat pile at the edge.

Himself led the way through a dim pantry and then the kitchen, spotless with the appliances and counters grouped in a line under windows that faced the driveway. "Hello, the house."

Grandma pushed open the swinging door that connected the dining room and the kitchen. Her Breezy Point tan, deepened on weekends she and Grandpa spent at their cabana, had faded; her blue eyes didn't blaze the way they usually did. "Well, good afternoon. Your father thought you'd never get here."

"We stopped to help out an antiwar demonstrator." He gave a cynical chuckle and opened the refrigerator.

I wished I could go to the Moratorium with Brian, even though I suspected I was a little young to march on the White House. The protesters would end the draft. Then they would end the war.

Grandma held a red leather cigarette case in her right hand. "Pat, if you want something to drink, I can get it for you."

On a Saturday morning, my mother usually wore corduroy pants with an old flannel shirt, doing housework with her hair tied back with a bandanna. Grandma was always done up. She wore trousers, khaki with a crisp crease and a coral-colored blouse. She had to have a cleaning woman. She had to.

Dad was looking in the refrigerator, leaning on the door. Behind him, I spotted the bottle of prune juice my grandparents always kept on the second shelf. Dad handed me a root beer and took a Bud for himself.

"At least wait till you have your lunch before you have a beer," she said, frowning.

He flipped the can open and raised it to his lips. "I'm thirsty now."

I let them squabble and went into the dining room. The china closet was already emptied. Its contents were stacked in boxes on the parquet floor. The table was a deep maple, with a lived-in gleam—we'd have it scratched up in a month. I'd only been allowed to eat at it a few times; on most holidays, I was relegated to the kids' table, which was set up in the living room. The leaves were leaning against the china closet. I carried those outside right away and lay them on the backseat of the Black Beauty.

It was hard to imagine someone as rambunctious as Himself coming from such a pristine environment. Now I understood the fastidious attention to appearance—at least he started out with good intentions.

The open can of Bud on the kitchen counter was the first thing I saw when I came back into the house. In the dining room, Grandpa was helping Dad lift the tabletop off its legs. They pulled the table apart at the center and slid each half off its moorings. They then set these pieces against the wall under the stained-glass windows. I didn't have to do the heavy lifting now but would be expected to memorize and repeat the steps later. Grandma leaned on the banister of the staircase, taking long drags on her Tareyton. "I bought that table at A & S in, well, I won't tell you how long ago. It's held up very well. Your grandfather's in such a hurry to pack up and give everything away," she confided in me, as if he wasn't there.

"What's that?" Grandpa said, turning his snowy white head toward us. He was notoriously hard of hearing, but knew he was missing something. His eyeglasses looked thicker than ever. "There's a house full of stuff. You can't take everything with you."

She was taking all the living room furniture—a tweed sofa,

end tables, a coffee table, and two wing chairs, and the Zenith stereo—but Uncle Tim had already stocked up on his share of the inventory: the twin bed and chest of drawers in the middle bedroom.

"We're not moving until December, for Christ's sake. Did it ever occur to you that I might like to have one last holiday dinner here?"

"Nonsense. Tim's offered his place for Thanksgiving. Let somebody else do the cooking for a change."

Grandma made an exasperated face. "Well, I guess that's settled." She sat on the landing at the bottom of the staircase.

Dad nodded to me. "Nicky, why don't you take these two halves of the table and put them in the car?" He gave me a pair of canvas gloves.

I was glad to get out of there before Grandma started throwing the dinner plates.

When the table was fully loaded in the car, we took a break for lunch, eating at a booth set into the wall. Dad carried his open Bud and sat across from me. Two sips and he was ready for another. Grandma had already set the table and put out platters of cold cuts and fresh turkey and a jar of bread-and-butter pickles. Everyone made their own sandwiches. Grandma was sitting next to me, and I asked her what she was going to miss most about the house.

"Well, I thought no one would ever ask," she said, smiling. She ate the smallest sandwich of all of us, turkey on rye with lettuce and mayo. "I'm going to miss the activity. Having everyone around. But to be honest, I don't need a house this size anymore. My children are all married with children of their own. Well, almost. Regina doesn't have children yet. And besides, your grandfather wanted to move the minute he retired. So I guess we're going. I hope you'll come down to visit us in Florida. It's not that far away."

There was a melancholy twinkle in her eyes now, and she grabbed my hand. "We had your christening at this house!"

I blushed and looked at Grandpa. He was devouring some kind of three-layer sandwich, all meat. "Ah, Marion. Can't stay here. In five, ten years, you're not going to recognize this place. It'll be all black. The time to go is now."

"You're like a broken record," she said.

Himself often made the same end-of-the-world predictions and now I knew where he got it from. They weren't wrong, though. The white flight was well under way in my neighborhood. Church Avenue was filling up with faces none of us recognized. With the way Himself was going, somehow I knew we'd be the only white family left.

Grandma got up and took her plate to the sink. "Nicky, you look good. Looks like your skin cleared up."

The Clearasil that I had been smearing across my forehead every night was working, and I was glad someone noticed. "Thanks."

"Bet there are lots of pretty girls who'd be interested in meeting you."

"You'll be the first to know when that happens," I said. Himself was smiling at me.

"She was very quick to get me and your uncles married off," he said, winking.

Grandma brought over an Ebinger's chocolate layer cake, still in the green cardboard box, and four cake plates. I had stopped eating anything that might make my skin flare up—tomato sauce, anything fried—but chocolate was chocolate.

I cleared the rest of the lunch plates. When I came back to

the table, Grandpa was eating a huge piece of cake. The filling was mocha. The aroma of the chocolate icing—dark and slick on top—smelled so delicious that I immediately picked up a cake plate.

"Just a small piece. And I mean it."

Grandma cut me a slightly larger piece than I'd asked for and left the room. "Wait right here. I want to show you something." After a few minutes she came back, clutching a navy blue leather photo album, the old-fashioned kind where the pictures are layered on top of another in plastic sleeves. She opened it and flipped about half of the twenty photos on the left side and presented the book to me, pointing to a black-and-white horizontal shot with a deckled edge. I looked down at a very young woman in catseye glasses—a dead giveaway for Mom—holding a bundle in a summer-weight blanket. That bundle was me.

I was sure I'd seen this photo before, but I was struck anyway by the innocence of the image, how happy everyone was. The first grandchild.

There was a girl standing on the sidelines, blond hair clipped behind one ear with a barrette. She had a tentative expression on her face, as if she'd just wandered into this intimate moment and didn't know if she should enter the shot or back out.

I pointed at the girl. "Who's that?"

"That's your Aunt Regina. She was about ten years old."

The mention of her name got Dad's attention. "Here, let me see that."

I didn't want to think about Aunt Regina and passed the album to him.

"Here's lookin' at you, kid," he said. "Now he's old enough to mouth off to his old man."

Grandpa stopped stuffing his face. "Oh yeah?"

"He's a little outspoken."

I was blushing again. I didn't see myself that way at all.

Out of nowhere, Himself started talking about his child-hood. "When I was a kid, your uncle George sat across from me, where you're sitting, and I would throw my peas and carrots under the table and when my old man, your grandfather, used to say, 'Finish up your peas and carrots,' I would say, 'I already did.' And your uncle would be the one to get in trouble."

"Of course, I knew all along who the culprit was," Grandpa said. "Three boys, I had to have eyes in the back of my head to keep track of them."

We looked at some more pictures before we finished packing up the car. The one I remember most was a shot of Himself standing between Grandma and Grandpa in the middle of Floyd Bennett Field. Grandma was dressed in a light-colored coat with a wide lapel. Grandpa wore a dark overcoat with a sharp-looking hat, the kind with a band above the brim. Dad was grinning. He had a crew cut and was wearing what looked like a military uniform. The photo was taken the day he went into the army.

No wonder he didn't like me speaking out against the war; he'd enlisted. "How old were you?"

"A few years older than you, young man," he said. His serious tone made me think he secretly knew when I was going to be drafted.

"You were born while he was away," Grandma said.

That I knew, from Mom telling me how she stayed out in Long Island with her father during the final weeks of her pregnancy. The day I was born, Himself wasn't even there. "But there wasn't a war going on?"

He shook his head. "I did basic training and two years in Hawaii."

Not exactly Saigon. But he thought we should all go there if we were called. He was from that generation of men that never questioned what they were told to do. And I guessed he'd just found out I was not.

Grandma closed the photo album and took it away. I cleared the dessert dishes, putting them in the sudsy water in the sink where the lunch plates were soaking. Then I grabbed my coat and told everyone I'd see them outside.

With the Black Beauty packed to the rearview mirror with furniture, there was no room for me so I rode home with Grandpa, who filled the trunk and backseat of his Impala with the chairs. His car was only a few years old, a dashing silver-gray that matched his eminence and status in life. He could glide all the way to their new house in Pembroke Pines and neither he nor Grandma would feel a bump. They were leaving Brooklyn in style.

I'd never been alone with Grandpa. He had a reputation as a stern fellow; maybe it was the beady eyes, almost black, trapped behind those thick glasses, or the way he seemed to scrutinize you with a quick once-over.

He wore a blue peacoat and a tweed flat cap for our ride home. A blue rosary was wrapped around the Impala's rearview mirror—probably one of Grandma's extra sets—and the interior had a fresh, deodorized smell, as if Grandpa had just taken it to the car wash. The chairs bobbed along nicely in the backseat. I wondered if Grandpa was going to stick around long enough to get the table set up. I saw the Black Beauty in front of us, sloping down the hill to Foster Avenue, past the Vanderveer housing projects. I was sure Himself couldn't see out the rearview mirror.

Grandpa asked me about school and if anybody at St. Mike's was offering a course on public speaking.

"I don't think so, unless you count the school play. My English teacher is directing it and he wants me to try out."

"Do it," Grandpa said. "You have a voice that carries, as

they say." Now that was something my father would never have said, especially after meeting Brian. He already thought he was a draft dodger; God knows what he'd say if I told him he was directing the school play. "So your old man tells me you have a dog now. I heard her barking in the background when I called the other day."

I smiled. "Yeah. You'll see her when we get home. She's a beauty. Very ladylike. Crosses her paws when she sits on the floor."

The Black Beauty lumbered ahead of us. The trunk was bobbing up and down, like the rope was loose.

"She doesn't sound like a puppy."

"She's not. She's fully grown. Doesn't really bark though. Dad says she was abused; I think she was kind of the bar dog at the Dew Drop."

"Is that right? I don't know the Dew Drop. Is that where your dad spends his time these days?"

"He likes to watch the Mets game there."

Grandpa gave a knowing chuckle. "I bet he does."

I had no idea I was feeding the machine, the one that had recorded my father's transgressions since the beginning of time. I figured Grandpa had to know Himself better than any of us, except my mother. Ahead of us, the Black Beauty hit a bump and the trunk flew open. I could see the back end of one of the chairs.

Grandpa honked the horn and Dad pulled over past the light on Clarendon Road. We waited for a few cars to pass and pulled up next to him.

Grandpa was already out of the car, stepping around back to retie the rope on the Black Beauty. I could smell gasoline or oil dripping from the car. "For crying out loud, Pat, you almost lost the chair."

"Never," Dad said. "I'm only going about twenty. Not even Nicky goes that slow."

Grandpa gave me a surprised look over his shoulder. His hair looked like a white halo against the gray sky.

"I've had a few lessons," I said brightly. "Dad told me how you taught him how to drive in the parking lot at Riis Park. Was he my age?"

"A little older, I think. But who the hell remembers? I taught four kids how to drive. Pat, you follow me the rest of the way."

Grandpa got back in the Impala and pressed on. Holy Cross was coming up on our right. The polished tombstones were the same color as the sky. The storm had stripped so many of the trees, it looked like winter had already arrived behind its high black fence.

"So you like to drive? You're too young to have a learner's permit, though."

"Yes. I'm not sixteen yet."

"I believe I waited until your old man had his learner's permit before I took him out."

"It was his idea. He's a hard man to say no to."

Grandpa laughed. "Is that a fact? Well, I hope he's not taking you to bars too."

I looked at him. "No, nothing like that."

I had been back to the Dew Drop a few times since that first night Mom sent me there to tide Himself over with a ten-dollar bill, but I no longer had to bring the collie with me. I never stayed longer than one ginger ale because I knew Himself was looking for some company.

"You know, when your dad was coming up, many young men thought that going to bars and carousing and getting into fights was the thing to do. I broke up some of his battles and boxed his ears myself when he needed it."

I wanted to say: *So I've heard.*

"I don't suppose young men have changed since then—or maybe your old man hasn't changed much since then."

We made a right turn at the Sunoco station on Snyder Avenue. The vacant lot on our left was a scene of desolation: clumps of weeds, old supermarket carts, the concrete floor of the old icehouse that was there when we first moved in. At the next left, we would be on Medallion Street.

"I don't think you have to worry about me," I said. "People have been comparing me to my father all my life. Do I look like him? Am I going to be taller than him? Probably. I guess that's natural. As he's fond of telling me, I am his only son. But I feel like people are telling me not to be like him."

"Nobody said anything about that—"

"Then maybe I'm just hearing it that way."

I didn't say another word. Nobody had to tell me Himself's away games, these nights spent in the Dew Drop, weren't good. In fact, they were really bad, but Mom—and I—would never tell Grandpa about them.

We pulled up in front of the house. I didn't say another word and got out of the car. I helped Dad unload chairs from the trunk, taking two into the house. Queenie trotted down the stoop to check out the scene. I went back to the makeshift loading dock at the bottom of the stoop to bring in more pieces. Dad was petting the collie on the sidewalk while he talked to Grandpa. Maybe he wasn't coming in. Maybe that was better. Once he saw the crack in the kitchen ceiling, right over the stove, he'd be on my father's case to see when he was going to fix that. And not get a straight answer.

Once we had put the table back together, Mom took one of her frilly lace tablecloths, not as fancy as Grandma's but good enough for us, out of the buffet drawer and covered the table pads. "Well, it's certainly bigger than the old table," she said. She went into the kitchen and came back with Dee Dee's birthday cake, iced a light green. "I would like everyone to keep their junk off the table for at least twenty-four hours," she said to me. "Spread the word."

Himself looked at the cake and made a face. "Is it someone's birthday?"

"Yes. Bet you can't remember which one of your five children."

Dad smiled and winked at me. "Which one of my children was born in November? Not Nicky."

I was a July baby. Everyone else was fall and winter. I thought, *He actually might get this wrong.*

"Mary Ellen?"

Mom put her hand on her hip. "No, you big boob. Mary Ellen isn't until next month. It's Dee Dee's birthday. Don't you even know when your own kids were born?"

"It's all a blur, Claire. I figure that's your job."

She punched him in the arm. "You want to go fifteen rounds?" I didn't know how long they would go back and forth like this—the playful side of their battle—but I had to call Larry Cahill. We were going to the movies.

As I headed upstairs to change my shirt, I heard Himself ask Mom, "Did she ask for green icing? You've got to be kidding me."

EIGHT

It was our first Christmas at the beach. We were heading out to Rockaway in the Black Beauty, Himself at the wheel. I was sitting up front in the Death Seat with Mom in the middle. My sisters were crammed, coat-to-coat, in the backseat under a red-and-green plaid blanket; the heater was on the fritz. With my grandparents off to Florida, Uncle Tim made the invite. He had a fancy job in the city and lived in Belle Harbor, a neighborhood that seemed like Beverly Hills compared with ours, in a stand-alone house with an outdoor shower and a built-in barbecue grill. We normally went there in the summers when my sisters and I could spend the day at the beach with our little cousins, fighting a losing battle with the Atlantic undertow and getting good and sunburned while the adults got good and tanked playing cards at the picnic table in the backyard.

So far, it had been a good holiday. Christmas was still the one morning we could count on Himself to be home when we woke up. We always put the tree up in the front porch, and that's where we opened our gifts. By the time I came downstairs in my corduroy slippers and bathrobe, Queenie was playing with the torn wrapping paper left on the living room floor, and my youngest sisters, Dee Dee and Mary Ellen, were already showing off their presents—silver necklaces with enamel, heart-shaped pendants "given" by our step-grandmother, on the Jurgensen side of the family, who sent Mom a check for the five of us and let her do the shopping. The three eldest kids—me, Maureen, and Patty—received Bulova wristwatches. Mine had a silver, stretchy wristband; the little window on the face showed the date. I turned the knob on the side to change it to 25.

Himself was the last to open his presents and did so with exaggerated care, never tearing the paper that someone had taken the time to fold, crease, and tape shut. "You never know, someone might want to use it again," he said, smiling as he opened my gift, wrapped in candy cane–patterned foil.

"C'mon, Daddy, just open the present already," Maureen said, sitting next to the tree in her blue-flowered flannel nightgown.

Mom stood in the doorway to the living room, cigarette dangling in her left hand. Because she'd gotten up early to walk the dog, she was the only one of us who was dressed. Dad had turned to her and said, "Claire, when did your daughter become so bossy?"

We never knew what to get him for Christmas. He didn't have any hobbies or go in for fancy accessories like cuff links. If he wasn't wearing the heavy-duty chinos he wore to work, he stuck to three colors: light blue, navy, and gray. He liked his cars in loud colors, though, and that gave me an idea. After driving around in the Green Hornet and now the Black Beauty, I wanted to see if he was willing to borrow some of that flamboyance.

After he gingerly opened and removed the wrapping, his eyes popped and he cracked up. "Mother of God, what have we here?" He removed from the white tissue paper two pairs of socks, one canary yellow, the other bright purple.

"I thought they would go with your car," I said.

"Oh, did you, now?" He was still laughing. A thick, graying

stubble covered his cheeks and chin. I wondered if I was going to be that hairy when I was his age.

"Love the socks," Patty said. She was sitting on the radiator under the front porch windows, auburn hair in a ponytail. "You should wear them today."

He raised his eyebrow, sensing a plot: Maureen had already given him a pair of fuzzy dice, black with white polka dots to match the Pontiac's two colors. We found them in an automotive shop across the street from Sears.

"I'll let your mother decide if they go with what I'm wearing."

I was sure he wouldn't be caught dead in those socks at Christmas dinner, but I was wrong. He wore the purple Ban-Lons, with gray flannel trousers and a white dress shirt. All new. I took it as a sign his good mood would last all day.

It took a little while to get out of Brooklyn, even though Himself drove like a maniac, changing lanes on Flatbush Avenue whenever a car blocked him, hugging the steering wheel as he burned through the streets. I held the handle near the car roof; Mom held my left hand. We never looked at the speedometer.

Except for a newsstand at Kings Highway and a Chinese restaurant near Avenue P, everything was closed. The stores and automotive shops disappeared after the light at Avenue U. On one side of the road there was a golf course, then a marina; on the other, Floyd Bennett Field's shuttered hangars and abandoned runways. For an old car the Black Beauty moved pretty well, approaching the tollbooth at the Marine Parkway Bridge with a steady, heaving determination.

My sisters called it the noise bridge because of the buzzing sound the car made when it hit the road. I cracked open the window after we went through the tollbooth so I could smell the sea. The bridge rose over Jamaica Bay like a steel caterpillar, its

towers and girders battleship blue. As we crested the road, the
Atlantic came into view, a glittering plain of sapphire glass.

I turned to my sisters. "Who wants to go to the beach
with me?"

"I'm cold enough in this car, Nicky," Maureen said.

It was probably twenty-five degrees out, but I wanted ten
minutes at the beach before the family tango took over, so I
slipped away after Himself parked the car. There was no wind
and the sky was the hard bright blue of winter, so vast it was
impossible to measure. The air was still, bracing, and the only
sound was the occasional plane concluding its descent into
Kennedy. We had just had a storm, and snow lay in crisp drifts
in the gardens and by the curb. The houses were fantasy homes;
some with three stories, wraparound porches, and the occasional
turret facing the sea. Others went with a nautical theme, like one
mansion whose flagstone patio had a balustrade decorated with
seahorses.

Even though it wasn't going to be dark for a few hours, everyone's Christmas lights were on, stapled to the windows and
festooned on bushes and twirled around fences, bathing the
blocks leading to the beach in a Technicolor glow. Of course,
Himself would never allow us to have outdoor lights; it was too
gaudy, he said, and too expensive. We had to settle for decorat-
ing the front porch windows with a plastic wreath that had one
candle in the center and stencils of winter scenes made white
with a can of spray-on snow.

I wondered if he had started. The liquor would be out. It
was Christmas; everyone had drinks before dinner. It was no big
deal. But with Himself, you couldn't do that.

The beach was empty, the sand packed down, the tide out. An
Irish setter ran to fetch a stick of driftwood, its red coat shining,
and brought it back to a trio of kids farther down the shore. It

was too bad we hadn't been able to bring Queenie with us. She was probably gnawing on the doggy treats she'd gotten as part of her present. This morning, Maureen had tied a red bow around her neck and took several photographs with Mom's camera.

The sun cast a dull glow on the ocean through a skein of clouds; another weather system was approaching. I rewrapped my new green-and-blue plaid scarf around my neck and shoved my hands into the pockets of my parka. The cold was piercing. I walked over to see the seahorses—their heads were still capped with snow—and checked the time: three P.M. Time to head back.

There was another car parked in front of Uncle Tim's house, behind the Black Beauty, a white four-door compact that looked too new, too immaculate to actually belong to someone; probably a rental.

My ears were tingling by the time I let myself in through the back door. I heard a commotion upstairs, coming from the kitchen. I blew my runny nose with a handkerchief and climbed a short staircase to the main floor into a house filled with the rich aroma of well-seasoned roasting meat.

Aunt Julie said, in her throaty voice, "Did I hear someone say Georgie is here?"

I paused on the top step. *Uncle George? He flew in from Germany?* We hadn't seen, or heard, from him since he'd moved to take that military job he wasn't allowed to talk about.

Uncle George's suitcase, a large blue Samsonite contraption with brass buckles and reinforcements, stood in the center of the kitchen on the red linoleum. With its narrow entrance, the room looked like it might be small, but it opened up in unexpected ways. An L-shaped arrangement of appliances on two walls faced a large breakfast nook with built-in benches and a picture window that looked out onto the yard. That's where the Flynn kids would eat their Christmas dinner. The table was already set.

The grown-ups gathered near the stove and the sink. Uncle George draped his loden overcoat over the back of a chair and kissed Mom on the cheek and then Aunt Julie. Mom was wearing a white apron over her red wool skirt. She was mashing potatoes in a large pot with her usual gusto, eyeglasses pushed up on her forehead. She dropped in a stick of butter. Aunt Julie, in gray slacks and a navy wool cowl-neck sweater, was stirring gravy in a black roasting pan. Over at the counter, Uncle Tim sliced the prime rib with an electric knife. He may have been the youngest of the three brothers but he was the first to go gray, a thick crop that shone silver as he bent his head toward the overhead light.

Now that I saw we were probably ten minutes away from diving into this feast, I was starving.

"Tim, get Georgie a drink," Aunt Julie said, arranging the cut meat with a fork on a bone china platter. "I think this is enough for now." She was a tall, chunky woman with short straight brown hair and she was forever on some kind of diet, the kind found in women's magazines. The rules were always taped to the side of the fridge. She'd already tried the banana diet, the blender diet, and even the breakfast diet, but she always looked the same.

"I'll just have a club soda," George said.

Uncle Tim took a bottle of White Rock seltzer out of the refrigerator, an Amana upright the color of Coca-Cola. All the appliances were the same color and coordinated with the wallpaper, red with a busy print of yellow and white flowers that covered every inch of wall space. I was thinking everyone's here except Himself, when he appeared in the doorway like the neighbor in a TV sitcom. He was holding a yellow cocktail with a maraschino cherry floating on top. I could tell from the watery look in his blue eyes that it wasn't his first. "*Auf wiedersehen.* Where're Linda and the girls?"

It was a whole story, as my mother would say. One of George's kids had the flu and his wife, my aunt Linda, stayed behind. Uncle George sipped his drink. "It seems like I got on the plane a day and a half ago. But it's so good to see everyone." He chugged the contents of his glass like it was a cold beer and caught me looking at him when he put it down. "Hey, Nicky." He stuck out his hand. He had one of those Flynn grips of death like Himself.

I wondered how long he'd been in AA and how he felt when everyone was knocking them back, oblivious to his abstention.

"Nicky, do you mind taking the suitcase up to my room?" Aunt Julie said. "Before someone trips over it."

"And then you can help your sister set the table," Mom said. "And don't forget to take off your coat."

I lugged the Samsonite upstairs to the master bedroom, which took up half the floor. Aunt Julie had a game-show bedroom set, with matching night tables and a chest of drawers. I left the suitcase at the foot of the king-sized bed and went downstairs to the dining room. Maureen was choosing forks from a brown silverware chest. She was wearing her latest homemade dress, cut from a Butterick pattern and sewn on Mom's Singer at the kitchen table: dark green velvet with a high lace collar and a thin black belt.

"Mom said I should help you." I unzipped my parka and tossed it over one of the chairs.

"Damned decent of you to show up," Maureen said, in her Brooklyn battle-ax voice. She liked to imitate the gravel-voiced ladies who worked at Ann's Gift Shop, our neighborhood junk store, where the sales help wore bullet bras and sleeveless Orlon shells and talked with lit cigarettes hanging out of their mouths. "How was the beach?"

"Great. I think it's going to snow later."

"Your ears are really red. Good thing you didn't get frostbite.

Then we'd have to cut them off." She handed me a fistful of forks and knives from the green plush interior of the case. "I'll do the spoons." She pointed to the crystal goblets at each place setting. "Watch out for the Waterford. It's from the old country."

We started at opposite ends of the table, moving counter-clockwise. The dining room was papered in a dark navy with white and yellow flowers, large and heavy as peonies. We never ate in this room in the summer, and now it seemed intimidat-ingly small and formal.

I had to ask. "Did you see Uncle George? Do you think he's here to check up on you-know-who?"

"Now you're crazy."

"Do I look like I'm crazy?" Now that Grandpa wasn't around, I couldn't help think it.

Maureen was the only sister who knew about the Big Book, although I couldn't show it to her because I didn't know if it was still in the house.

"Well, he came at the right time. Daddy's on his third."

On occasions like these Maureen and I would meet and share the cocktail count. The alcoholic weather report. I was thinking maybe my aunt and uncles wouldn't be as aware of the changes in his behavior as we usually were. I kept vigil but I wasn't alone. Uncle George sat next to Himself at dinner, slyly glancing at his never empty wineglass.

He asked my father to pass the meat platter. "Hey, Pat, when I pulled up I saw this jalopy outside and I knew it had to belong to you. Where'd you find that?"

Uncle George broke into a wide grin and I laughed too.

"That's a 1958 Pontiac, pal," Dad said, right hand on the stem of his glass. "And not just any Pontiac. It's a Pontiac Pari-sienne."

Uncle George laughed, as if he was surprised that his brother could correctly pronounce a French word. "But it's 1970, Pat. What do you get, ten miles a gallon? You've got to step up, get a real car."

"I will when someone gives me a deal as good as the NYPD."

Everything was so delicious I cleaned my plate: the prime rib, the mashed potatoes, the green beans amandine, and, always, the creamed onions. Dee Dee and Mary Ellen were in the kitchen at the kids' table. My two eldest sisters and I were a captive audience while the adults at the grown-up table told stories. Uncle Tim relived his youth as a lifeguard at Breezy Point, diving for fish at Rockaway Point, way down at the western end of the island, where the bay met the Atlantic. In the middle of one of his stories, Uncle George leaned over to whisper in Himself's ear. Dad nodded slowly, meaningfully, flexing his jaw like he really wanted to clock his brother in the face.

Uncle George was staying a week. He had brought gifts from Germany, and in between courses he asked me to help get them out of the car. It sounded like he had a lot of presents but when he opened the trunk, there were just two cardboard boxes covered with a lot of masking tape. He took out the larger one, handed me the other box, and didn't shut the trunk.

"I wanted to talk to you for a minute."

Now that we were face-to-face, I saw I was taller than he was, about an inch. "Okay. What's up?"

"So, how's everything going? We haven't seen each other in a while. Your father says you're taking French. *Parlez-vous?*"

I got a 95 on my last test, my last of the semester. "*Oui, monsieur.* But I'm off for the next two weeks. I don't even want to think about school."

"How's your dad doing?"

In all matters regarding Himself, I took the fifth with outsiders. Even when I was related to them.

"I think he's doing great today."

That was one word too many. "Today. How about other days?"

My uncle didn't have Himself's laserlike blue eyes, but he could still look through you pretty good. As the eldest kid in the family and the only boy, I was expected to know and remember everything. I hated it.

The cold pinched my shoulders and the box felt heavier than when I first picked it up. I stared at the car fender. "Not every day's the same." Especially the days he didn't come home.

"He ever go to any meetings? I talked to him about it."

Oh, Jesus. I almost said: *That would mean he'd read the AA book you gave him.* I was going to get my head handed to me if I said another word. "You know, you can always ask him yourself."

He gave me a surprised smile and backed off. "Listen, I'm gonna be here a week, spend some time here, spend some with your dad. If you want to hang out, I can pick you up."

That actually sounded like fun. "But we have to talk about something else besides my father."

He stuck his free hand out for me to shake. "Deal. Let's go back inside."

He gave out the presents in the living room, next to the huge Douglas fir. Uncle George was stockier than the last time we saw him, though still fit. He handed the cousins—Timmy, Jane, and Erica—their gifts first: handpainted wooden dolls from the Berlin Christmas market.

"Say thank you," said Uncle Tim, pulling the mahogany coffee table away from the sofa so we could stretch out our legs. The children, towheads all under the age of six and born a year apart, followed orders.

The presents were mostly small and wrapped in shiny blue

paper; the few bigger ones were wrapped in Santa Claus paper. Uncle Tim got a beer stein from Oktoberfest, stoneware
with enameled scenes of German life and a hinged pewter lid.
Aunt Julie opened a box of Asbach Uralt chocolates, shaped
like bottles and filled with brandy. Aunt Julie and Mom got
Hummels.

Mom sat on the couch with us to open her gift, with Maureen and Dee Dee hovering on either side. "Oh my god," she
said, removing a figurine of a little boy, seated, and holding a
brown umbrella that covered his entire body. "Oh, George, this
is beautiful."

"Let me see, let me see," said Dee Dee, leaning on Mom's
lap, her corn-silk hair escaping from its rubber band. Mom let
her hold the Hummel, and she turned it over and over. "I want
one too," she said.

"I've got something even better for you," said Uncle George.
"Well, it's for you and your sisters, and your brother, although
it might not be cool enough for him."

I laughed, and Patty elbowed me. George crouched and
reached into the cardboard box and produced two gifts identi-
cally wrapped in gold paper. "Now I'm going to open these for
you because they're a little involved, but one is for the Rockaway,
or maybe I should say the Flynns of Queens, and the other is for
the Brooklyn Flynns."

He carried the packages to the coffee table and carefully
peeled back the paper, in almost as dramatic a fashion as Himself, who had vanished. I mouthed, "Where's Dad?" to Mom and
she shrugged.

"What is it?" Patty said when the packages were finally un-
wrapped, gold paper tossed on the floor.

"I don't know," Aunt Julie said. She was standing next to the tree, which had to be seven feet tall and smelled like it was cut down yesterday.

"It's a Christmas pyramid," he said. "It's very common in German households. We got one last year and the girls just loved it. So now, we'll all have something to share on Christmas, even though we don't live near each other."

The pyramids stood about a foot tall and were made of blond wood. Each had three tiers surrounded by dark wooden fences fitted with candleholders; a small propeller, also wooden, was fixed to the top, like the star on a Christmas tree, by way of a pole in the center. I was trying to figure out how everything worked when Uncle George took a small plastic bag out of the cardboard box and placed thin red candles on the lower two tiers and lit them with a match. The heat from the flames rose and turned the propeller blades, and with them, the tiers. It was like a carousel. Now we could see the brightly painted wooden figures within. On the bottom level, Mary, clad in a blue veil, and Joseph, in a brown cloak, stood on either side of a manger with beige straw and a golden-haired baby Jesus. In the middle, the Magi in white robes carried tiny foil-wrapped gifts to the Christ child. Finally, three blond angels holding red horns in front of their faces rang out the news on the top tier.

"Look at that!" Mom said, touching her face.

We had never seen anything like it. So simple, and yet magical. It was the gift everyone would remember. And cool enough for me.

Mom turned to Maureen. "Where is your father? Pat, come look at this."

Himself wandered in from the dining room with a red-wine refill. He staggered a bit, stepping back to adjust his footing or prevent the precious grape from spilling on the carpet. His face was flushed now, his eyes like blue headlights. He stood perilously close to the coffee table. "What have we here?"

"Presents," Mom said, biting off the word. "Your brother brought them from Germany."

"Is that a fact?"

I looked up at him. He had that tone. The switch inside him had turned the wrong way and now he was going to do something, say something we would regret. I braced myself.

He was rocking back and forth on his feet, the wine running through his veins like the cars on the Cyclone, straight downhill from the summit. I thought he might fall on one of us. "Dad, why don't you take my seat?" I stood up, making way for him to sit next to Mom on the couch but he stood there, lost in some reverie.

Uncle George glanced uncomfortably at him while the fans were spinning, the candles flickering, and the tiers turning. "What do you think, guys?" he asked my cousins, finally standing up with a perceptible creak. He rubbed his hands on his knees. "Did anyone else hear that?"

My little cousins, the Flynns of Rockaway, sat in front of the tree, rapt by the spectacle of color, motion, and light.

Aunt Julie touched Uncle George's arm. "They've totally forgotten about their new toys."

Dad took a sip of wine and stared down at the pyramids, a smart-ass grin on his face. "Do you think Hitler had one of these as a little boy?"

"Oh, shut up, you big boob," Mom said. She handed the cardboard box containing the Hummel to Patty and got off the couch. Her arm was already outstretched when she walked over to him. "Give me your glass."

Aunt Julie started for the kitchen. "I'm going to make the coffee," she said, backing away, taking her boxed Hummel with her.

Maureen followed. "I'll start the dishes."

Everyone was looking for an exit. Mom tried to grab the wineglass but Dad hugged it to his chest, where a red splotch bloomed on his new white shirt, over the left pocket. He looked down at the wet spot, teetering over the turning tiers, and stumbled into the coffee table.

"He's going to fall on them," Mary Ellen said. "Mom!"

And so the Flynn pyramid toppled over, flames licking at Aunt Julie's coffee table. "Stand up, I got a bet on you," Himself said.

The little kids screeched and Timmy cried out, "Mom, there's a fire!"

I watched the flames singe the table, backing away. Uncle Tim ran into the kitchen and came back with a newspaper, folded in half. My cousins also stood back, horrified, as the flames burned a black ring into the wood. With several swift strokes, he beat out the fire, swatting away the smoke curling up. Uncle George quickly righted the pyramid, blowing out the candles. Aunt Julie rushed back into the living room and surveyed the mess.

"For crying out loud, what the hell happened?" She glared at Himself. "Did you do this?"

"I stand accused," he said, nodding.

"We had a slight accident but it's under control," Uncle Tim said. "You never liked this table anyway."

I appreciated him trying to make light of the moment, since no one else knew what to say. One of the fences on the bottom tier of the pyramid had snapped in half.

"C'mon, Pat," George said, shaking his head. "I told you to knock it off already."

"Yes, you did," he said, smiling.

"Give me that glass before I break it over your head," Mom said, finally wresting the goblet out of his hand.

Patty leaned over and picked up the broken pyramid. She smiled unconvincingly and said, "I'm going to take this in the kitchen for a minute. Anyone want to come with me?"

Three blond heads followed her out of the room. Uncle Tim joined them, asking, "Hon, do we have any wood glue?"

Aunt Julie smoothed her hands on her long apron, transfixed by the ruined table. "Check the drawer next to the dishwasher," she said over her shoulder.

"Pat, why don't you sit down?" George said, reaching out as if to steady him.

"Stick it in your ear," Himself said, teetering.

My uncle went over and grabbed my father by the shoulder, saying something in his ear. And that's when Himself shoved him, not once, but twice, until my uncle staggered back, eyes widening before he broke his fall.

"I said, that's enough, for God's sake," he shouted. "Why do you have to be so belligerent?"

I wasn't going to intervene, not as long as I was on Himself's good side. When he was wound up, it was best to remain invisible. But I was worried about Mom, still holding the crystal goblet. I took it out of her hand and set it down on an end table.

"C'mon, Pat," she said gently. "Let me get that stain out of your shirt." She gestured toward the staircase.

Something about her delivery did the trick because he followed her. By the time she came down, we were eating dessert in the dining room. Our mortification was so extreme that no one could enjoy the chocolate éclairs, Napoleons, or apple pie. Mom took her seat, but only ate two bites of pie. She lit a cigarette, eyes boring into the embroidered red holiday tablecloth.

"Well, I think it's time we went home," she said when Mary Ellen, the slowest eater among the five of us, finished her last forkful.

Patty went upstairs to use the bathroom. When she came down, she said Himself was sprawled out on Aunt Julie and Uncle Tim's bed. I vowed not to be the one going upstairs to get him when it was time to leave.

That task was left to Uncle George. We overheard them having a loud discussion about who was going to drive us home. Technically, I could drive everyone home, but I had never driven at night. I didn't know if I could do it.

Everyone helped clear the table and load the dishwasher. The leftover prime rib was still out on the cutting board. Now that we had polished off half of it, it looked gross, a cold, greasy, red slab that made my stomach tighten. Aunt Julie flicked on the radio on the counter, and we heard the Ronettes' tinny voices singing "I Saw Mommy Kissing Santa Claus."

"A little Christmas music before everyone goes home," she said with forced merriment. I was sure she couldn't wait to see Himself on his way. Our first Christmas at the beach was bound to be our last.

Himself was in no condition to drive; that didn't stop him from getting behind the wheel. Uncle George wanted to ride with us, but Himself said there wasn't room in the car. Then Uncle Tim offered to take some passengers and follow from behind.

"Can I ride with Uncle Tim?" Dee Dee said, holding our Christmas pyramid in front of her like a chalice. She was only nine, but she was no fool.

"I think that'll be all right." Mom looked at Patty, pulling on her plaid parka. "Would you go sit with your sister?"

Dad raised his eyebrows in deep suspicion, but he was outnumbered. "Mother of God," he muttered as we went out the door.

The sky had clouded over and snow began falling in enchanted storybook fashion on the sleighs in people's gardens and the garlands coiled around mailbox poles. The sidewalk and the roof of the Black Beauty had already whitened. It was beautiful, and I wished I could have taken the bus home, watching the snow as it coated the rocks along Jamaica Bay. But I had to get into the car. Mom, Maureen, Mary Ellen in back, Himself at the wheel, and me in the Death Seat again. As I belted myself in, I felt defeated, as if I had done something wrong. It was great sitting next to Himself when he let me take the wheel, but now he felt like an albatross. I was stuck for the foreseeable future.

I stared down at the black threads of water below the Marine Parkway Bridge. The sky turned pinkish with snow. In the far distance, the Empire State Building glowed red and green at the top.

It was a long, glum drive home, the embarrassment and near-calamity of the fire casting an ash-like pall over the car. Not only did Himself spoil our holiday, he also nearly ruined my cousins'. I didn't have a chance to ask Patty if she'd had any success gluing the pyramid's broken fence back together.

The westbound lanes of the Belt were filled with cars trying to beat the storm. We had seven, eight miles to go and we went slowly on the Flatbush Avenue extension, the engine grinding. The traffic lights looked ethereal, colored gels hanging in the air, and flakes flew at the windshield as if churned out of some machine beyond the horizon. It was hypnotic, as if our house would magically appear in front of us if we just kept staring at the snow.

Not knowing the patron saint of snowstorms, I said a quick Hail Mary to cover the bases. If everybody was as scared as I was, they didn't let on. We all listened to the windshield wipers as they jerked back and forth, squeaking like a faulty metronome and never quite cleaning the glass. A few cars passed on the right, and I gripped the door handle as Himself cut out of the lane and nearly collided with an oncoming car, horn blaring, headlights fierce in the snow-light.

I couldn't be a passenger anymore. I moved over and put my left hand on the bottom of the steering wheel so we could stay on our side of the road. Himself didn't object. He knew the shape he was in.

An empty Flatbush Avenue bus rattled by in the southbound lane as we passed the Torregrossa funeral home. In general, traffic was heavier going toward Rockaway than away from it and I was grateful. The car groaned, its insides sounding like they were about to fall out. Uncle Tim eventually pulled up alongside and then in front of us. For some reason, I felt better even though I knew if we crashed, it would be into him.

Then we turned right onto Brooklyn Avenue. The car skidded and Himself hit the brakes. "Son of a mutt," he said. We all gasped as the car jolted and screeched, toppling a corner mailbox.

"Jesus, Mary, and Joseph," Mom said in an infernal whisper.

We were in the middle of Avenue J. I knew from riding my bike that a police station was just down the street.

There was a sharp rap on the window. My heart jumped. It had to be a cop—a cop who would see Himself's condition and arrest him, on Christmas. He rolled it down, and I saw Uncle Tim's worried face, his gray hair like a halo around his head as the snow blew all around him. "Everybody all right?"

"Yeah," Dad said. "This car has old tires, that's all." He raised his head and looked in the rearview mirror. "Everything copacetic back there?"

"Your rear end is in the middle of the street," Mom said, biting off the words. "If you don't get us out of here in two minutes, I'll get out and walk."

I had to do something and there was only one thing to be

done. "Daddy, let me finish," I said. I hardly called him that anymore: too needy.

He looked at me, incredulous, like the night during the World Series I tried to get him to come home from the Dew Drop. "You?"

"Yeah. Look, it's not far and you're tired. You know me, I never go above twenty miles an hour."

Dad chuckled, but Uncle Tim didn't think it was a good idea. "I should be all right if I follow you," I said.

Uncle Tim leaned in. "Pat, what do you think?"

"How about somebody asking me what I think?" Mom piped up from the backseat. "Nicky, you're not old enough. The last thing I need is you getting pulled over."

"He's the only one who's driven this car besides me," Dad said. It was as close to an admission of his condition as we were going to get.

"I drove from Brooklyn College to Kings Highway."

"When did you do that?" Mom was getting madder by the minute. "You told me you were only taking him to Holy Cross."

"We branched out," Dad said. "We went to Bedford Avenue. Hardly any traffic. The Jews don't drive on Saturdays."

"Well, then, I guess we should all kneel down and thank God for the Sabbath," she said.

"Listen, we'd better get out of here," Uncle Tim said. I nodded: we had to go while I still had the nerve to do this. Reluctantly, Dad got out of the car and came around to the passenger side. I adjusted the rearview mirror and waited for Uncle Tim's lead.

"Are you sure you're going to be all right?" Dad asked, the wine smell wafting off him in sick, sweet waves.

I nodded. "It's only like seven, eight blocks."

But they felt like the longest ones I ever drove. The wind-shield wipers were out of sync, and I only had the left headlight. I stared ahead into the snow, which was lighter now, making it easier for me to see Uncle Tim's car in the home stretch. Down the hill to Foster Avenue, where the Vanderveer Houses domi-nated the block like a prison, the road was sopping wet. A red light flared at the intersection and Dad told me to hit the brake hard because we were going to roll at the bottom. I pressed down all the way to stop the slide while I gripped the wheel.

"When's the last time you had these brakes checked?"

I looked over. His eyes were closed. "Stop busting my hump, Nicky. I let you drive, for chrissake," he said.

I was able to stop the car ten feet before the red light, but it felt like my lungs were going to go through the windshield. Un-cle Tim had cleared the intersection and was waiting for me on the other side. I waited for the light to turn green and caught my breath. The silence in the car was deadly. Mom was furious, but I had proven my point: I could drive. And I was going to bring everybody home, in one piece.

Dad leaned over to me. "Don't know if the Black Beauty's gonna make it through the winter."

"Five more blocks, that's all she has to do," I said. When the car finally died, I was going to miss her. I always thought of her as my first.

With the projects behind us, we soon came upon the graves at Holy Cross, tombstone angels graced by the snow. Two more turns and we were on our block. Up ahead, Uncle Tim honked his approval. Mary Ellen and Maureen were clapping in the backseat. I stopped in front of the house and jumped out of the car—and almost slipped in the snowy street. I reached for the car door handle to steady myself and helped Mom out and then the girls. Mom barely looked at me.

Uncle Tim had pulled up in front of Mrs. Garrett's house. Dee Dee carried the Christmas pyramid up the stoop. Maureen stood on the sidewalk, smiling, snow falling on her hair. "You did it," she said. "You never told me you could drive."

"I did too," I said. "You just didn't believe me."

I walked over to the car. The grille was dented, the right headlight gone. Himself came over to look at it. He put one hand on my shoulder. "They should give you that license now," he said.

I smiled and caught a glimpse of Mom unlocking the front door. Queenie jumped on her and barked. "Get off me," she said, going inside.

The dog bounded down the steps, their cracks sealed into perfection by the snow, and waited near the edge of the stoop.

"She needs to be walked," I said to Maureen. "I'll do it if you get the leash."

She went inside and I overheard Himself invite Uncle Tim in for a nightcap. Was he kidding? Ever the diplomat, Uncle Tim said he had to be heading back. God knows what it would be like crossing the bridge back to Rockaway in this weather.

Maureen threw the leash at me from the vestibule. It landed at my feet and I clipped it to Queenie's collar. Himself was backing the Black Beauty into the driveway. The snow was pouring out of the sky, backlit by streetlamps. Flakes fell all around us in a crystalline white curtain, a buffer between us and the house, keeping whatever was going to happen at bay as long as we stayed outside. Queenie blinked as I led her down the block to the trail along Holy Cross. She loved the snow.

The Provenzanos had turned off their Christmas lights, strung along the wrought-iron fence of their garden. Another holiday, dead and buried, but we made it home and I was glad it was because of me.

Uncle Tim honked once as he pulled away, his car's red

taillights pedestrian and tiny compared to the Black Beauty's exotic conical bulbs. There would be more occasions, some quite dire, when he would have to come to his brother's rescue again. Because Patrick Flynn, the not-so-artful dodger, was about to fall through a trapdoor and take us with him.

IV.

THE RED DEVIL

NINE

I went to the main branch of the Brooklyn Public Library one day after school to borrow the *Bye Bye Birdie* soundtrack. The new year was here and I decided to try out for a part in the school play.

I took the bus on Utica Avenue and transferred to the No. 2 IRT train. It was a two-tiered station. Outbound trains to New Lots Avenue rolled into the upper platform; the cars headed to Manhattan rocked the lower. Everybody going toward New Lots was black, high school kids like me, talking loudly in groups. I thought I went through the turnstile unnoticed, but somebody said "Look at the white boy" as I headed downstairs. A set of trains, battleship gray, parked on an unused third track caught my attention. The sides were spray-painted with crazy letters; the artist had also drawn a buxom woman in a red dress, a comic-strip blonde whose hair extended over the top of the car.

It was wild, it was funny. As the train pulled into the station, I made out the author's name: Blade, followed by some numbers I couldn't make sense of because we were leaving. I got off ten minutes later at Eastern Parkway. The weathered grandeur of the Brooklyn Museum, facing me as I walked up the steps, might persuade a visitor that this was a classy neighborhood, but I knew better; they were all bad once you crossed to the other side of

Kings County Hospital from where we lived. It was freezing, maybe twenty degrees, and I hurried in the late-afternoon winter sunshine past the tall apartment buildings that had once been fancy but now were shabby hulking things.

Grand Army was Brooklyn's biggest library, with a curved façade meant to look like an open book standing on its spine. Classical figures in tarnished gold leaf were molded onto the limestone. A decorative panel mounted above the entrance, also in gold leaf, displayed a tic-tac-toe board of literary characters. I could pick out Moby Dick, squat on a coil of rope, Tom Sawyer, barefoot and holding a stick, and Hester Prynne and her (not scarlet) letter—that book was the scourge of my freshman year.

There was only one copy of the soundtrack, up on the second floor in the tiny music room. I slipped the record out of the hard plastic sleeve and placed it on an old gray turntable at one of the carrels lined up against one wall. The headphones were stretched out, and I fiddled with the adjustable band on top but couldn't quite get them to fit my ears. What I mostly remembered from the movie, which I hadn't seen in years, was Ann-Margret dancing in a purple ruffled blouse and skintight pants, her midriff a golden tan, with all that sexy red hair falling in her face. She wasn't Diana Rigg, but, as my friend Larry often said, I wouldn't kick her out of bed.

The songs came back to me—corny, catchy, and short, over before you knew it. I definitely didn't like any of that goofy Dick Van Dyke stuff, like "Put on a Happy Face," and knew they'd probably find some upperclassman to play the Paul Lynde role. That left Birdie's songs, "Honestly Sincere" and "One Last Kiss," which was a goof and didn't require much real singing anyway. You just had to try to sort of sound like Elvis Presley because that's who Birdie was supposed to be—Elvis going into the army.

The album cover made me smirk. Everyone looked a little too adorable, coated with the kind of Hollywood veneer that was long out of style. Were the girls from the Catholic high schools really going to show up and audition to play these Midwestern throwbacks? I couldn't picture it. The Brooklyn girls I knew ranged from brash to brutal. Were they going to dress up like bobby-soxers in poodle skirts and pom-pom ponytails? The guys in the movie had DA haircuts, like Himself, so the boys who got parts would probably have to cut their hair.

The back of the album cover showed scenes from the movie. The actor who played Birdie was strutting around in gold lamé, leering at everyone, in one photo. Could I get away with a costume like that? Something inside me was dying to be outrageous, jump out of my own skin.

It was almost four thirty when I left the music room. I picked up my parka, gloves, and scarf from the adjacent chair and headed out, walking along a balcony that overlooked the library's main room, circulation desks, and wooden card catalog files. The ceilings were vast, about forty feet high, and the walls were paneled in a light brown that seemed warm even on rainy days. I looked down at the checkout desk to see how many people were standing in line. Gina Martinucci was talking to a gray-haired clerk at the information desk. She was still in her school uniform. She went to Bishop McDonnell, the high school that was one block east of the Brooklyn Museum. When I saw her glance up in my direction, I hung back, sure she didn't see me. I bet she was here to check out the Birdie soundtrack and hid in the room where they stacked the religion and history books till I could make it down the staircase.

I could borrow the soundtrack for two weeks. If I could memorize French verbs, the lyrics to these silly songs would be a cinch, but I also wanted to impress Brian and show him that his faith in me was not misplaced. He'd mentioned the auditions several times after class since that day we met on Bedford Avenue, as if he knew from one encounter with Himself that I needed something to do with my free time.

As I headed to the subway stop at Grand Army Plaza in the gathering darkness, the album safely encased in a thick brown envelope and tucked under my arm, I wondered what part Gina wanted to play. Not the lead, right?

I listened to the album again before supper in my bedroom. I hadn't yet realized how lucky I was, to have my own room, which I painted Antwerp blue and decorated with posters. Over my bed was a poster Mom gave me for Christmas. It was a pixilated black-and-white photo of the Parachute Jump and the boardwalk at Coney Island. Printed over the faded figures walking on the boards were some lines from Lawrence Ferlinghetti's poem "A Coney Island of the Mind." On the wall facing the bed I had taped a psychedelic Peter Max poster that came in the Sunday *Daily News*. With Himself consuming all the addictive substances available in a six-mile radius, it was as close as I would ever come to being psychedelic.

I was sitting on the old brownish linoleum while the LP turned on my portable blue-and-white record player. Maureen came in and plopped down on the blue bedspread. She had changed out of her school uniform into jeans, a red sweatshirt, and old fuzzy blue slippers.

"You've played this song three times. Why?"

"Sssh. I'm trying to get this word." I lifted the needle off the record in the middle of "A Lot of Livin' to Do" and turned to her. "Can you make this out?"

I placed the needle back down on the worn vinyl and Maureen bent her head to the record player. She cocked one eyebrow. "Did he just say 'This town's awfully square for a cat like me'?"

I laughed and handed her the album cover. "That's what he said, all right."

"Daddy-o, he's groovy with the lingo," she said, inspecting the photo on the back. "So what's this for?"

I was going to have to tell them sooner or later.

"I know: Bobby Rydell is coming out of mothballs to perform at the next school dance," she said, "and you just want to catch up on all his latest hits."

I lay on the floor and cackled like a fool. "Not exactly. You won't believe it."

She pointed to the girl with the long hair on the album cover. "Is this supposed to be Ann-Margret?"

I concentrated on the cracks in the ceiling as I told her, "They're doing the play at St. Michael's this spring. My English teacher wants me to try out."

I sat up again. I could tell from Maureen's face, with her lips stretched over her teeth, that she was trying not to laugh at me. Then she said, "First you can drive. Now you can sing?"

Brian had said he wasn't expecting miracles. "What can I tell you, I'm coming out of my shell. It beats hanging around here, waiting for Himself to come home stewed to the eyeballs."

She didn't say anything, but I knew she agreed with me.

"I mean, you have your friends. I need to go get some of my own."

Maureen had been hanging out more and more with Kathy Fitzgerald, this tough girl she met at St. Edmund's who lived on Linden Boulevard. She knew all these Puerto Rican boys and now my sister knew them. Guys who weren't from around here. I swear they were all named Richie, but there was also some guy named Angel and one called Boppo. Boppo: that's all Himself had to hear. It would be the end of her.

"You know, I bet I sound okay," I said. She was grinning at me, mocking me. "It's just a school play. It's not Broadway."

Then she grilled me: which part was I going to try out for? I didn't want to jinx it, in case I really did end up backstage building scenery.

"I'm not saying. We all have to audition."

"They're having auditions!" Maureen exclaimed. "Wow. Wait till Mommy hears this."

I gave her the Flynn Look of Death, a slack-jawed, stony stare reserved for behavior displaying astonishing stupidity. "Do you think you could keep your big mouth shut?"

"Well, yeah," she said, miffed. "But are you going to tell them how you did the minuet in the sixth-grade play and you couldn't keep time?"

I groaned. "No, I am not. I blame that on the costume. I hated wearing Mom's dusting powder and talcum powder in my hair. Besides, I was too jealous of Thomas Monjardo to concentrate." I leaned my head against the bed. "He spray-painted his hair silver. Why didn't I think of that?"

"Well, if you get a part in this, we'll have to make up for that," Maureen said.

I put the needle back down on the beginning of the song. "Let me listen to this one more time before supper. No talking."

• • •

The auditions were held in the gym. I had class there twice a week, with this former marine named Mr. Spanko, a scowling brute who ran everybody ragged on the outdoor track. The room was big, about forty feet wide and seventy feet deep, with a large stage that was mainly used for the annual school play. Rickety old bleachers, pizza-grease orange, flanked the walls on either side, folding up under each other for the school's basketball games. I could see the back of Brian's head at the front of the auditorium.

Larry was already holding court under one of the basketball hoops with a group of girls from Bishop McDonnell. You could tell which school a girl went to by her uniform. Bishop's girls wore a green-and-red plaid skirt with a green weskit or blazer. I recognized the white blouse with blue-and-gray plaid skirt and navy vest ensemble from Maureen's school, St. Edmund's. Catherine McAuley was the yellow blouse with maroon skirt and blazer. St. Brendan's was the white blouse with green-and-blue plaid skirt.

He waved me over to a group of folding chairs. He hadn't bothered to tuck in his shirttail, and he was speaking with his hands, his brown eyes magnified by his Clark Kent glasses.

"Nicky, allow me to introduce you to today's bevy of ingénues," he said.

I wished I had Larry's panache. Sometimes I clammed up when I walked into a group of girls. At first I thought I didn't know any of them, but then Gina stepped forward and grabbed my arm. "Nicky, what are you doing here?"

I didn't know Gina could be so theatrical. "Cahill is railroading me into doing this."

Gina turned to her friends, olive-skinned Italian girls like herself, all with dark curly hair, and said, "This guy lives across the street from me." I said hello. There was a Joanne, a Theresa, and a Rosalie. Brooklyn was crawling with Rosalies in those days. We had two on our block alone. Rosalie Provenzano next door and Rosalie Confuso down the block.

Gina had her hair tied in a ponytail. My brain clicked: she was here to try out for Kim MacAfee, the girl who sings to Birdie on *The Ed Sullivan Show* before he goes into the army. The only singing I'd seen Gina do was on the altar at St. Maria Goretti's. If she was Ann-Margret, I was Mick Jagger.

She held out the casting notice that had been distributed to the girls' high schools. "Who's Mr. Ventresca?" she asked.

"He's my English teacher. He likes people to call him by his first name."

Gina looked at the blue sheet again. "Brian?" She winked and nudged my shoulder. "First-name basis, wow. He'll probably give you a part."

"I don't know about that." I tapped my foot and looked around the room. "You know, there are like a zillion girls here."

Gina rolled her eyes and said, "And I bet they all want my part."

It was as good a time as any to ask. "You want to play Kim?"

"Of course," Gina said. "You can't show up at one of these things and not want to play the lead. Last year, I auditioned here for *Oliver!* but I didn't get it—the lead—although I did a great version of 'As Long as He Needs Me.'"

"Actually, I think Nicky here is going to be one of the stage-hands," Larry said. "The guy is completely tone-deaf."

He liked to joke around and the bantering broke up my day. He could have been a stand-up comic. "You don't have to be worried about competing with me, Larry. It's not like we're gonna be up for the same parts. I hear you're trying out for Hugo."

Corniest part in the show. At least Birdie had some attitude. "I thought I'd try out for Kim," Larry said. "Don't you just see me in a ruffled blouse and culottes?"

I took a seat next to the girl named Joanne. She wore her Maybelline in a Sophia Loren style, curling off her eyelid. "Do you sing?" she asked.

"Not in years," I said, looking at Brian going over some sheet music on stage with Mr. Steiner, one of the music teachers. "So I may really bomb out. Brian told us all to come down and try out. He said it was no big deal."

"No big deal?" Gina asked, incredulous. She was only a year older than I was but right now she made me feel much younger, like she'd been around and knew the score. I watched her sizing up the other girls, now milling around the room. Many had that fresh-scrubbed look of Kim MacAfee, the long hair, clear complexion, and cheerleader build—not what I was expecting. "There are two real female singing parts in the show, if you don't count Albert's mother, which I would never play." She turned to me and asked, "Do you *know* the show?"

Her keen sense of the competition made me more nervous. No doubt there was some guy here who was cuter than me who was going to try out for Birdie, but I hoped he didn't audition before I did. "I've seen the movie a couple of times. I took the album out of the library."

"Oh, was that you? I can't believe you beat me to it," Gina said. "I bought the album at Discount City."

Our little neighborhood department store, currently on the skids.

"Well, if you don't get to play Kim, you can always play Rosie," Joanne said. "That's my plan."

Gina shrugged. "That's why I have both parts of 'One Boy' memorized." She stopped studying her competition for a moment and looked at me. "Which part are you gonna try out for?"

"Birdie."

Gina gave me a very doubtful once-over. Then she did this insane pirouette and said, "Nicky Flynn, you are a pisser. I should've known."

A lone microphone stood on the stage next to an upright piano for the afternoon's vocal tryouts. Two flags—one for America and the gold-and-white banner of the Vatican—flanked the stage at either end. Brian looked out at the crowd. "Wow, what a turnout. Thanks for coming down when I know you'd rather be home doing your homework."

There was a smattering of mild nervous laughter.

His voice sounded deeper than ever with the microphone. "This afternoon, we're just gonna try to get a sense of what parts you might be right for, what kind of vocal range you have, that sort of thing," he said. "If you don't have the greatest voice in the world, don't worry. And there are choruses of guys and girls who appear as best friends of our principals, Kim and Hugo. There are lots of character parts, so if you can't carry a tune but you're a pretty good actor, you may have a shot. Your accompanist is Mr. Steiner of the music department."

Mr. Steiner, bald as a 60-watt bulb, sat at the piano with sheet music spread out on the stand, ready to get this show on the road.

"And that guy walking around and listening in is Mr. Testagrose, the music department's band leader," Brian said.

Mr. Testagrose took a ceremonious bow. He was a penguin with a pear-shaped face. Always had a five o'clock shadow, and these squinty black eyes. Most unfortunate, his lips were always wet, like raw liver. In my freshman year, he taught us to play the flutophone, a red-and-white, very distant plastic cousin of the recorder. He tried to connect with us by playing brassy groups like Blood, Sweat & Tears or Chicago. When you walked past the band practicing in their room in St. Mike's basement, they were usually playing "Spinning Wheel." For classroom humor, he told Mafia jokes.

Brian began calling names from the sign-up sheet. A girl from St. Brendan's went up to the stage, tall and stoop-shouldered with long, tangled dark hair that hid her face. She whispered something to Mr. Steiner, who turned to the piano and played the opening bars of "One Boy." The girl was a baritone. I smiled. She could sing, but Brian only let her sing a few bars before he thanked her for coming and called the next person to the stage: Larry Cahill.

I turned and said, "You never told me what song you were going to do."

"Prepare to be wowed," he said, running up on stage.

Larry whispered something to Steiner and broke into a note-perfect version of "Kids," dragging out that word with grating Mermanesque aplomb. I stared at the stage, little firecrackers going off in my brain. Larry had taken piano lessons and he played organ at Sunday mass in his parish church, but I didn't know he could also sing. He was ready for opening night. Larry acted out the song, gripping his skull as he exaggerated Harry MacAfee's predicament. After two stanzas, Brian stood up, laughing, and thanked him. Everybody broke into applause. I stood and whistled.

"Geez, Larry, where did that come from?" Brian asked.

"From the heart," he said and trotted back to his seat. I thought he would linger, to rake in the compliments from the girls, but he put on his coat and picked up his books.

"Gotta roll," he said, punching me on the arm. "Just remember, I'm not doing this show without you."

"No pressure," I said. I would have to be as good as Larry to get cast. I seriously doubted I could get up there and do it the way he just did, but I would have to.

The auditions went on past five o'clock, with people trying out for every part, from Albert and his eternally patient girlfriend Rosie to Albert's looney tunes mother. Some people were clearly wrong, singing off-key and having the wrong physical traits for the roles, but others were really good, as if they'd had musical training for years. I had no idea some of the guys I passed in the hallways at St. Mike's—and only knew by face—could get up there and sing. It was like they were from another, more accomplished world and it made me even more anxious; with Larry gone, there was no one around to distract me.

About a third of the people had left by the time I was called. Gina wished me good luck as I faced my first audience. I did not look at Brian. I was planning on doing "Honestly Sincere," a rock number that relied heavily on bass guitar, but I knew after two hours that Mr. Steiner couldn't make that upright sound like a guitar, so I asked him to play "A Lot of Livin' to Do." In the movie, Birdie opened the song, Kim sang the middle, and Hugo finished it up.

Mr. Steiner looked at me, owl-eyed. His face sagged, like he'd had enough of high school students for one day, but he knew the tempo right from the beginning. I'd never spoken or sung into a microphone before; the volume surprised me. I looked into the darkness and gave it my best shot, snapping my fingers like Conrad did in the movie.

> *There are chicks just ripe for some kissin'*
> *And I mean to kiss me a few!*
> *Man those chicks don't know what they're missin',*
> *I got a lot of livin' to do!*

The lyrics were just this side of lame. I hoped people wouldn't start laughing. But at least I sounded good, strong, and clear.

Brian interrupted me before I could sing the second stanza. "That's fine, Nicky." I stepped away from the microphone, mortified. I was being sent home. I checked to see if there were steps on that side of the stage so I wouldn't have to walk past Brian. I was about to leave when he said, "Where are you going?"

I stopped, unsure of where to go or what Brian wanted.

"Take the mike out of the stand and do it again," Brian said.

I squinted into the overhead light and removed the mike, making a crackling sound as I did. Brian directed me away from the mike stand, closer to the piano. Now I knew what Brian wanted: to see if I could move like Birdie. So I just pictured him as he was on screen, legs spread in a come-hither stance, shoulders loose, one finger tucked in his belt loop. I felt the weight of my body move into my hips.

I raised the mike and went through the song again, shaking my hips on the beat and snapping my fingers at the audience the way Conrad did in the movie. Wolf whistles, from the back of the gym.

When I was done, there was some scattered applause. My face flushed as I came down from the stage and saw Mr. Testagrose smiling. Brian grabbed my arm. "Good job," he said.

My armpits and forehead were damp. I smiled when I saw Gina.

"You were great," she said, eyebrows raised in surprise. "I think you definitely have a shot."

I should have thought to take the microphone out of the stand. "I think I was too slow on the uptake."

"No, don't be ridiculous," Gina said. "The director clearly likes you. He helped you. And you had fun, right? It's supposed to be fun."

I sat back and watched the next audition, for the part of Kim. Gina's eyes were riveted on the stage. I looked at my watch; it was almost six. "When do you think they're going to call you?"

"Not anytime soon, looks like. I should call my mother and tell her I'm still here."

I hadn't even told Mom I'd be staying after school. Trying to keep everything top secret, in case it fell through. I decided to leave.

Supper was on the table when I came in—spaghetti and meatballs: my favorite. Mom was eating with us in the kitchen. Himself wasn't there and we had stopped asking why.

Mom went over to the stove to make up my plate. "Well, the dead arose and appeared to many," she said. "Where have you been?"

"School," I said, dumping my books on the dining room table and draping my jacket on the back of one of the chairs.

"Since when do you stay after school?" she asked knowingly, with an amused expression.

I gave Maureen the Flynn Look of Death. "You told her."

"I had to. I couldn't take it anymore. She was about to call the police."

"Told her what?" Patty said, twirling spaghetti with her fork.

"I auditioned for the school play," I said.

Patty stopped eating. "What? Which one?"

"*Bye Bye Birdie.*"

"You mean, the one from *The 4:30 Movie?*"

I nodded and began to wolf down the pasta. Patty was the biggest fan of *The 4:30 Movie*. She never missed Gidget Week, featuring her favorite, *Gidget Goes to Rome*, or Troy Donahue Week, featuring *A Summer Place*. We all watched Bette Davis Week, featuring *What Ever Happened to Baby Jane?*, *Dead Ringer*, and *Hush . . . Hush Sweet Charlotte*, back to back. Bette Davis feeding rodents to Joan Crawford, Bette playing twins, and Olivia de Havilland pushing Agnes Moorehead down a flight of stairs. You could not beat it.

"So how'd it go?" Mom asked, smiling.

"Well, I don't know yet," I said, wiping my mouth with a napkin. "There were a lot of people there. Like even Gina Martinucci."

"Really?"

"My English teacher is directing, and I don't know if I'll get a part, but it was fun watching everybody."

"Did you have to sing?" Dee Dee said.

I nodded. "You'll never guess which part I tried out for."

"Not that loser Bobby Rydell played, I hope," Patty said.

I swallowed. "Oh, come on. Give me some credit."

Maureen brought her plate to the sink. "I know," she said. "The guy in the gold pants. Conrad Birdie."

Leave it to the seamstress in the family to remember him by his costume. "That's the guy."

"I don't remember him," Mom said.

"How could you not?" Maureen said. "He wore this gold lamé outfit, really tight. He was gorgeous. Oh, Nicky, you're kidding. If you get the part, can I make your costume?"

"Sure," I said. "But I don't know who else tried out for it."

Mom cleared the other plates. I was just about finished eating. "I just remember Maureen Stapleton and those squeaking shoes," she said. "Remember when she put her head in the oven? That's how I feel sometimes."

"How come I never saw this movie?" Mary Ellen said.

Patty stroked her arm. "That's right, you're too young to remember. We'll have to check *TV Guide* to see when it's on next."

"When is the show gonna be on?" Mom asked.

"Easter time."

"We'll have to tell everyone to come."

"I think you should wait until I know if I'm in the play. I might wind up building sets backstage."

But I didn't wind up building sets backstage. At the end of the week, Brian asked me and Larry to stay after English class and told us we were going to be in the play. Larry held out the palm of his hand and I slapped it with mine. He said, "Well done, my man."

My hand hurt. It all seemed too easy. I couldn't have been the best singer for Birdie at the auditions; I had just gone there because Larry cajoled me for a couple of weeks. And now I had what I wanted and it was too late to say no. I knew we were going to have a good time, me and Larry and whoever else wanted to hang with us, but as I cut through Holy Cross, I thought Gina was right. Brian was going to give me a part anyway, no matter which one I tried out for.

I had never been teacher's pet.

TEN

Maureen and I hit the discount fabric stores on Orchard Street the next Sunday morning in search of gold lamé. There was a small budget for costumes, Brian said; he gave us fifty dollars of it, whether it meant going to some store or buying the fabric to do it ourselves. Whatever was left over from the fabric could pay for labor, Brian said. Maureen's ears perked up at that.

We took the F train to Delancey Street. It was freezing, a blue, big-sky morning with a thin layer of clouds that stretched to Chinatown. Maureen and I had never been to the Lower East Side. It made a bad first impression. There was trash all over the steps leading up from the subway station to the sidewalk and an empty plaid sleeping bag smeared with crud. Delancey Street looked like it hadn't been swept in decades. The marquee for the theater showing Spanish films was cracked, with letters from the film titles missing. Behind us, the Williamsburg Bridge was a sour reminder of the night Himself had gotten us lost in the Green Hornet.

The icy wind didn't keep bargain hunters from mobbing Orchard Street. The street was closed to traffic and all the stores were open. The owners, Hasidic Jews, didn't work on the Sabbath.

We joined the crowd inching under displays of leather jackets, gabardine pants, jeans, and blouses, displays hung like clotheslines, extending over the sidewalk on horizontal poles, patching over the grimy tenements underneath. People were bundled in parkas, some knee length, hoods fringed with fur, cradling Styrofoam coffee cups. Salesmen with potbellies and cigars dangling from their mouths heckled us. "Dahling, I have many beautiful blouses inside the store," one guy called to Maureen. "I am villing to give you a very good price. Sir, mebbe I can interest you in a leather jacket."

I didn't see any sidewalk displays of gold lamé so when I saw a real store—Beckenstein's—across the street, we ducked inside. With its orderly aisles and shelves bearing bolts of fabric, it was the antithesis of the chaos outside, and the sales help, mostly Hasidic women, quietly assisted customers, unrolling the fabric on plain, wide counters. A Puerto Rican stock boy pushed a dolly of giant bolts of gray flannel across the aisle that bisected the store.

"We need something really gross but stretchy," Maureen said, marching past the bolts of corduroy, cotton prints, velvet, wool, voile, and polyester interlock to a barrel of glittery fabrics in metallic colors wound around long cardboard tubes. I loved watching her take over. We hadn't had fun like this in ages. The minute she finished her chores on the weekends she was out of the house; now that I was at St. Mike's, I didn't seek out her company as often as I should have.

"Look at this stuff," she said, beaming as she rubbed the selvage of a shiny gold fabric in her palm.

"What is it?" I said.

Maureen looked for a tag. "Some kind of polyester."

"We call that one liquid gold," said a voice behind us.

We turned and saw a young, milky-complexioned woman

with a honey-blond pageboy wig. She stepped up alongside Maureen. "What are you thinking of using it for?"

"A jumpsuit."

"For you, it's fabulous," the saleswoman said. Her voice was light and bouncy, and she had eager hazel eyes; maybe we'd be her first sale of the day. She took the bolt of liquid gold from Maureen with a soft, assured hand and held out the fabric for us. "As you see, it really shimmers. It's a tight mesh knit that catches the light. You can use it for a jumpsuit, sure, but it's also very sexy in a cocktail dress or full-length formal wear."

"Actually, it's for me," I said.

The saleswoman turned to me, frowning. "Oh. I don't know about a man. What man would wear this? Liberace, maybe, but he's a fruit."

Now I was really turning red. Is that what everyone was going to say once I wore the costume?

"He's in a play," Maureen said, shaking her head. She produced a Vogue/Butterick pattern for a man's jumpsuit from her shoulder bag. It wasn't exactly like the outfit Jesse Pearson wore in the movie—he wore pants and a shirt—but my sister thought she could make this pattern quickly. The cover illustration of the final product showed a man who looked like a Ken doll having a midlife crisis. He was wearing trinkets around his neck.

"It has flared legs," I said, slightly alarmed.

"We can make them straight if you want." Maureen showed the pattern to the saleswoman. "This fabric falls nicely and moves well. He has to dance."

She smiled, relieved she was finally in on the joke. "What kind of dancing are we talking about, the frug, the watusi?"

"Sort of," I said. "Just rock 'n' roll stuff."

"Sure. By the way, do you mind my asking what play it is?"

"Bye Bye Birdie."

She put a hand to her cheek; there was a sparkling rock on her finger that could have cut your jugular. "You mean the one with Ann-Margret and Bobby Rydell? Oy! I haven't seen that in years."

"That's why they're doing it," Maureen said, completely deadpan. "To bring back memories."

That was enough sarcasm for one day. I pinched her waist. "By the way, my name is Faye," said the saleswoman, placing her palm on her chest, maybe so we could really size up her diamond. "We get a lot of showbiz people in here. We had one of the producers from *Hair*. He wanted to give us free tickets to see a show where people take their clothes off. Like I could go see that with my husband. Can you imagine?"

Six and a half yards of liquid gold, one very long zipper, and thirty-six dollars later, we left Beckenstein's. We stopped at a deli and bought knishes and Dr. Brown's Cel-Ray soda with the change and got back on the train, eating our lunch out of grease-stained paper bags. When we got home, Maureen cleared off the kitchen table, got out Mom's beige, portable Singer sewing machine from the dining room, and I helped her pin and cut out the pattern pieces. The paper was so thin and crinkly, I was afraid it would rip.

Mom was making dinner. There was a roast beef cooking in the oven; the juices spat and crackled in the pan. Two pots were on the stove, one for potatoes, the other for string beans. Himself and Mom were watching football in the living room.

"This is going to be the best costume," I said.

"Anything for my brother, the star," Maureen mumbled, stray pins sticking out of her mouth like a voodoo doll. "I'm getting hunchbacked already from pinning," she said.

A pair of footsteps approached. Himself. He stepped into the kitchen, barefoot, spiky-haired, and grizzled. He was wearing gray pants and one of his threadbare flannel shirts tightly buttoned over his gut. He went into the refrigerator for a Bud—two down, four to go. He took a swig of the beer and picked up the pattern envelope.

"So this is the costume, I take it," he said solemnly.

It was the first time he had mentioned the play. Maureen and I looked at each other and nodded. I was waiting for him to say something, either about the play or Brian. *Bet you fifty bucks that guy's a draft dodger.* The doorbell rang. "Nicky," Mom called. "It's for you."

No one ever rang the bell looking for me. I went to the kitchen doorway. Gina Martinucci was standing in the vestibule in an oversized denim jacket and black corduroy pants. She had pulled her hair back in a thick, vinelike ponytail. She had never been in my house. I don't think she'd ever crossed the street to say hello. "Hi," I said, unable to conceal my surprise.

"Hi, Queenie," Gina said, crouching down to pet the collie. Queenie licked her face.

"Wow, instant love. I can dig it," Gina said.

"Come on in, Gina," Mom said, standing behind them and smiling at me. "Let me take your coat."

Gina slipped off her jacket and followed me into the kitchen. "I heard the news. It's great."

"Yeah, it's pretty good. But what about you?"

Himself was draining the last of the Bud, watching Maureen line up a piece of fabric to go under the needle. He crunched the can and threw it into the garbage pail. I cringed at the rotted kitchen ceiling, the exposed beams under the missing plaster. Gina wouldn't miss that eyesore; I hoped she wouldn't stare.

"Daddy, you remember Gina Martinucci, from across the street?"

His eyes were half-open. "I recognize the hair. How ya doing? I'm going to have a beer. You want one?"

Gina gave me a nervous look and laughed. Indoors, her bovine eyes looked larger than usual. I could see her taking a measure of Himself, as if to say, *This is your father?*

"Oh, excuse me, I thought you might be of drinking age," Himself said. I glowered at him as he went behind the kitchen table and reached into the fridge. Gina shifted her focus to Maureen and the pinned costume. "Wow, look at this fabric. This is outrageous."

"They call it liquid gold," I said.

"Liquid *what?*" Himself said, shutting the refrigerator door and standing next to the sewing machine. "And you're going to wear this? In public?"

"That's the general idea," I said.

"You've got to be kidding me. Does your mother know about this?"

"Yes." I tried to ignore him, hoping he'd go back to his stupid game, but I felt my face growing hot. Maybe that's why I didn't think I was good enough to be in the play; I knew Himself would disapprove.

"You're going to look great in this," Gina said. "I didn't know you sewed, Maureen."

"I'm still learning," Maureen deadpanned. "Are you in the play too?"

"Touchdown, Pat!" Mom called from the living room.

"Goooooo, Giants!" He sprinted out of the kitchen, right past Gina, leading with the can of Bud. He sounded like he was summoning a team of dogs to cross the Bering Strait.

Gina whipped around, touching her throat, as if she'd been smacked on the back. "Oh my god. That was like . . ."

"It's his favorite team," I explained quietly. "Would you like a cup of tea?"

She nodded and sat down at the table, next to Maureen, facing the wall. Now she definitely wouldn't be distracted by the bad ceiling. I turned on the kettle and sat on the other side of the sewing machine.

"Goddammit," Maureen said, taking her foot off the pedal and flipping up the guard. She raised the needle and reached for her handy seam ripper, removing an uneven stitch. She adjusted the tension with a small knob over the needle, hit the reverse button on the front of the machine, and started over. Gold thread gently unwound from a spool fixed to the top of the machine and the motor hummed with muffled efficiency.

"Where was I?" Gina said. "Well, I didn't get the part of Kim—some girl from St. Brendan's did—but I'll be singing one number with her."

"You're Rosie!" I said. "That's great." Gold fabric flowed across the table, brushing against the toaster. I checked the fabric for crumbs and began folding the sewn pant legs as they came through.

"You have a lot of dialogue to learn," I said. Fortunately, Birdie really didn't speak.

"I feel like I'm playing an old bag," Gina said. "But my mother said it's the mature woman's role."

"You are more grown-up than the rest of us."

"Really?" she asked, as if she didn't know it already. "At least I won't have to wear a bathing suit because my skin is like, forget it. I'm going to wear one of my mother's old Chanel suits."

Maureen took her foot off the pedal and looked up from the machine, as if seeing Gina for the first time. "Your mother has a Chanel suit?"

Gina smiled and nodded. She wore a black turtleneck that was snug against her tiny frame. Her stomach bumped slightly over the top of her jeans. "It used to fit her years ago, before she had kids, but she never got rid of it. It's red too. It should look great on stage. I think the play's going to be great. I guess we'll meet the rest of the cast at the first rehearsal."

The kettle was whistling. "We can go home from rehearsals together," I said, getting up to make the tea. We'd been neighbors for years, but maybe now we'd become friends.

Maureen was able to finish the pant legs and one sleeve before Mom kicked us out of the kitchen to set the table. Gina helped me carry the costume pieces into the dining room. I moved somebody's textbooks aside to make space on the table. Then I went back into the kitchen to get the sewing machine while Maureen folded the unsewn and pinned pattern pieces. Himself was glued to the TV screen, one empty and one open beer can on the snack table, as I walked Gina to the front door.

I got her jacket from the vestibule closet. It seemed way too big, as if she had borrowed it from her older brother, Sal. Or a boyfriend.

"Your father has *another* car?" she said as we walked down the stoop. You could only walk on the right side now; the left-hand side of the third step down had crumbled. "We liked the last one. Black and white, with that old-fashioned tire in the back. You could hear it coming around the block."

"The Black Beauty. It sort of died at Christmas."

Himself had gone a little while without any wheels, but his newest toy was parked in the driveway. A four-door Mercury, sleek and fire-engine red all over. It was shocking to have a car that was only one color after the two-tone wonders of the Green Hornet and the Black Beauty. This one was modern compared to those tanks. I asked him why he picked it and he said he liked the five-spoke chrome rims and the wide front seat. But mostly he said the car called to him. "There was a thin coat of snow on the windows and the exterior and I thought, *This car needs a driver*," he'd said. "And then I remembered your uncle busting my chops about having an old car, so I came forward a little bit, into the nineteen sixties."

I walked Gina over to the Mercury. "He hasn't let me drive it yet," I said. After that night in the snowstorm when I took over the wheel, Mom forbade me from driving Dad's cars ever again. I knew the Black Beauty was headed to the junkyard so I didn't object.

Gina eyed me over her shoulder. "You're driving already?"

"He takes me around. Ask your dad to take you to Holy Cross. That's where I started. No one's there to watch you."

I was only wearing a crewneck sweater and jeans, but it wasn't that cold. We went over to the car and looked down at the gleaming red trunk and the matching triple taillights. The car glowed in the dark.

"It's a Mercury Monterey, 1963." I pointed to the rear window, tucked under the red roof. "When you press a button on the driver's side, the window goes down and the breeze comes in, but not the sun or the rain. It's the coolest thing."

I had visions of California or Mexico, the only places I knew with cities named Monterey, but Gina was not catching my drift. "You do that you'll freeze your ass off," she said, smiling.

"In the summer everyone will want to sit in the backseat, though." If the car lasted that long. When Dad brought the Mercury home, he said the rear suspension was shot. I didn't know rear suspension from suspension bridge, but whatever the problem was, he fixed it because the Red Devil was a smooth ride. I told her the car's nickname. "Does your car have a nickname?"

"No," she said, slightly miffed, as if I was asking a silly question. "My father's an engineer." She headed back to her house. "See you at rehearsal tomorrow."

ELEVEN

My sisters and I were getting ready for school, ironing shirts and blouses, eating Corn Flakes and Lucky Charms at the kitchen table, when we heard Himself come in, giving the front door his usual extra push. We snapped to attention. It was the beginning of February.

He creaked his way from the living room into the kitchen with deliberate, heavy steps, a thief in his own house. Glancing at his bloodshot eyes and splotched face, I thought it was the end of another long night at the Dew Drop. "Good morning," he said. "And where is your mother?"

"Basement," Patty said. She was standing at the stove waiting for Maureen to finish washing her hair in the kitchen sink—Himself's decree: my sisters' long hair clogged the bathtub drain.

He went to the top of the basement staircase. "Mrs. Flynn? Are you home?"

She came up the stairs, carrying a basket full of dried clothes. She wore a powder-blue quilted bathrobe and slippers. "What?"

"We have to have a discussion—upstairs."

Mrs. Flynn—a dead giveaway that something was up. Patty and I exchanged glances. Mom put the basket on the dining room table and followed him to their bedroom. This time the door did not slam.

I had my French grammar book out on the table; there was a test in second period. Patty took Maureen's place at the sink, and Maureen wrapped a yellow towel around her wet head. "Jesus, what is it now?"

"I don't know," I said, finishing my cereal. "But I am not sticking around to find out. If you have any sense, you won't either."

I put my cereal bowl in the sink when Patty was done and grabbed my coat.

When I came home from school, there was one thing out of place: Himself was occupying the recliner in the living room, smoking a Lucky Strike and fixing a baleful, pent-up look at the television screen. The earliest he was ever home from work was dinnertime.

I met my sisters upstairs in their bedroom to talk about what was going on. With four girls sleeping in one room, space was at a premium. A set of bunk beds, flush against one wall with chests of drawers on either side, faced a window bench piled with books and folded laundry. Two twin beds stuck out into the middle of the room from the opposite wall. There was almost no floor space, but at least my sisters had a rug. I didn't have a rug.

Maureen and Dee Dee sat on the twin beds. Patty pushed aside a stack of clean hand towels on the window bench so Mary Ellen and I could sit with her.

"What's he doing down there?" Dee Dee asked.

Mary Ellen retied her ponytail. "We wanted to watch *40 Pounds of Trouble* and Daddy told us not to change the channel."

"C'mon, Nicky," Patty said. "You must know what's going on with him."

A bent venetian blind behind Mary Ellen and Dee Dee revealed the intrusive glow of a streetlamp. "I know nothing." The longer we sat there looking at one another, though, the more

I knew whatever was going on wasn't good. "Don't worry. They always show that movie on *The 4:30 Movie*."

But we didn't go back to the living room when we went downstairs. Whatever he was watching, we didn't want to watch it with him. Instead, we huddled in the kitchen. Mom was peeling potatoes into sheets of newspaper and plopped the white, skinned vegetables into a pot of water.

"Is Daddy sick?" Patty asked.

"He's not feeling so good today and he came home a little early," she said in a clipped tone that suggested she was not willing to elaborate. But he didn't go to work the next day either. He didn't even come down at breakfast. I didn't see him until I got home after rehearsal. I was taking off my coat in the vestibule and he was putting his on. He was telling Mom that he was going out "to see a guy."

It seemed like a casual enough remark, but I didn't realize this was going to be one of his catchphrases, Himself standing in the center of the living room, one sleeve of his jacket already pulled on, face splashed with Old Spice, hair slicked back. These "guys" he was meeting never had names, but the bars where he met them did. The Dew Drop, Martin and Joe's, Harkins, and, dive of dives, Shanahan's at the Junction.

● ● ●

Something was seriously wrong, and I was the first to get the official word, before the week was out. "Your father's not working for the phone company anymore," Mom said. We were in the kitchen alone together, sitting at the kitchen table and looking through seed catalogs for flowers to buy for the summer garden.

My back clenched. "What happened?"

She drummed her fingers on the table. "Somebody found him sleeping in his van and reported him."

"So?"

"Well, it seems that he was also drunk and that's when they told him not to come back," she said, her voice cracking.

"Don't cry, Ma." I took her hand. "It's not your fault."

She took off her eyeglasses and wiped her eyes. "I know that."

We're going to lose the house. The sunlight bathed the windows of the back porch and kitchen in a single swath. This was the time of day—late afternoon, when she would be seasoning meat or chopping vegetables or sitting at the table just drinking a cup of tea—when I felt closest to her, watching her take her simple pleasures without having to rush around keeping us going. Now moments like this would vanish. In fact, they were already gone.

"Why doesn't he go to AA?"

"Do you know how many times I've told him he has to stop?"

I didn't know what to say or do. My eyes welled up; I wasn't prepared to see my mother in this state, confessing her desperation. She couldn't cover for him anymore, and the disappointment and anger I'd seen cross her face had turned to hopelessness. I couldn't believe he let her down like that. As her soldier, I'd make sure he never hurt her again.

"So what are you going to do?"

She was close to tears again, and I couldn't bear it. "I don't know. But obviously I'm gonna have to do something."

We all knew this day was coming. If we saw him stumbling from the front door to the kitchen and up to the bedroom, they had definitely seen him fall down at work. But if my mother felt a sense of reckoning, she didn't show it. She addressed her next task—dinner—and got up from the table to start cooking. I paged through the seed catalogs, but the splashy displays of zinnias and dahlias and bachelor buttons could not cheer me up. Who knew if we would even be living here in the summer? We had lived in this house for ten years. I remembered the day we moved in. Every room was painted green. Mint. It was just awful.

That morning when he came into the kitchen of our basement apartment after a night of football and boozing was the beginning of the story. I didn't know yet if we were in the middle, but I was sure we weren't at the end. Chapter to chapter, we would walk on eggshells.

"Can't he get another job?"

"I don't know," Mom said from the stove, as she pulled out pots and pans from the drawer below. "I'm going to look for one. Your father's not too happy about it, but he should have thought about that when he was out every night on Church Avenue."

I held my breath. I was afraid she was going to start throwing things. But she never did. There was always the business of living and that's where my mother found her focus.

Very quickly, the axis of the house shifted. There was some kind of conference out in Rockaway at Uncle Tim's house—we were not present—and when it was over, Mom took over and Himself became a supporting character in our story. She took the New York City civil service test, scored well, and applied for a job as a school crossing guard. A New York City hiring freeze prevented any jobs from opening up. Then she applied for a job at a bank on Church Avenue, the Lincoln Savings. She was hired almost immediately. To prepare for her reentry into the working world, Mom bought a can of hair spray and some new eye shadow, and a new wardrobe of blouses, skirts, and stockings— nothing fancy—and a pair of flat black shoes.

The best part: the branch she worked at was seven blocks from home. We stopped by after school to say hello, to see Mom do her job and meet the other tellers, mostly mothers like herself who had gone back to work to supplement the family income. She worked a lot, more hours than Himself ever did, with occasional Saturdays (till one P.M.) and a late Thursday. Getting out there in the world, earning money, boosted her confidence. But she was on her feet all day. Come the weekend, she just relaxed, and we took her place in the family dynamic, doing some of the cooking and all of the housework.

I made up a chart, matching chores with our names, so we alternated doing laundry with vacuuming or washing the kitchen floor. And I learned where everything went in the house: all the respective drawers for the clothes we wore, the utensils we ate with, and the plates we ate on. One day, I carried folded clothes into the master bedroom and went to Himself's dresser to put them away. The T-shirts and socks went in the middle drawer, the sweatshirts in the bottom. As I arranged the sweatshirts in the pile that was already there, I noticed something blue beneath the last white sweatshirt in the drawer. I pushed the ribbed cotton shirt aside and saw a book. For a minute I didn't recognize it. Then I turned it over. The title hit me between the eyes: *Alcoholics Anonymous.* So this was where he had stashed the Big Book. Everybody was in the house, doing their own chores, and Himself was in the living room reading the *Daily News* and watching some John Wayne western on TV. So I didn't go through the book. But it looked like, from touching the smooth cut of the pages on the side, he had never read it.

When Mom worked Saturdays, she checked in midmorning to see how everything was going; she ran the house so efficiently from the bank that not even Himself's dissipation could shut down the domestic machine. If he was sleeping at the kitchen table, his head plopped down next to a plate of last night's mashed potatoes and gravy, we worked around him, saving the washing of the kitchen floor until he came to and crawled upstairs. We learned from Mom how to do this. Scrubbing, polishing, ironing, we worked in silence so we would not wake him up.

On one of his excursions to "meet a guy," Himself picked up a couple of shifts tending bar at some joint called the Mermaid on Bergen Street, way down the losing end of Flatbush Avenue. Maybe it was the best he could do, but it was the worst possible place he could have ended up. Now he was surrounded by booze all the time, measuring, mixing, serving—and consuming it. Then he went to an after-hours joint on Seventh Avenue to work a poker game, for tips. As our lives sped up in the daytime world, his stalled in a netherworld, an unobserved region that made him solitary and unaccountable. He became the phantom father.

The word about Himself trickled out and the far-flung Flynns bore down on us. I couldn't tell whether they were concerned or just scandalized. The phone rang more in two weeks than it had since Christmas. When Grandpa called long distance from Florida, Himself went upstairs to take the call in the master bedroom. I could only imagine what belittling comments passed through the receiver. From then on, Grandpa would call every Sunday, looking for Himself, checking up on him. Naturally, he never answered the phone. So one of us would have to stall, listening to Grandpa brag about the perfect weather in Pembroke Pines until it was time to hand the receiver over to Mom, who would tell Grandpa that Dad was sleeping or was out doing food shopping (like that would ever happen). He could be upstairs in bed, sleeping it off, or out on the street. Mom protected him. We all did.

For instance, she never said the word "fired," and neither did we, not to one another and certainly not to Dad's face. The phrase we used was "lost his job," as if the means by which you supported yourself and your family was something that fell out of your hand, like a set of keys, or slipped off your wrist, like a watch.

There was a whole series of hushed phone conversations in the dining room when Himself wasn't there. Mom sat on the red-leather telephone bench as if she were in the confessional at St. Maria Goretti, as if these were her sins she was imparting to the absolver on the other line. One of these calls came from Aunt Regina. That was some conversation. Mom hung up, lit up a Newport, and told me, "Well, she called to offer her sympathy. And then she has to say 'Of course, we can't offer any financial support.'"

She had kicked off her shoes after coming home from work and was now wearing blue slippers on her stockinged feet. She sat in the wing chair and looked uncomprehendingly at the television screen, where an episode of *Dark Shadows* was playing. Barnabas was in the crypt again, with Willie Loomis. "Like I ever asked her for money," she said, tapping the cigarette into an ashtray on the coffee table. "I don't need her money. Frig her. I hope I'm here the next time she calls here looking for your father to come out and fix her broken toilet."

I didn't know anything about money or even what a mortgage was, or how a bank could hold a lien against someone who was late with their payments, but I knew that whatever Himself made at the Mermaid wasn't the same as having a salary. When he drove out to Rockaway early one Saturday morning in the Red Devil to see Uncle Tim, I suspected money was the reason: he needed a loan.

He was as clean as a whistle, having stayed in the night before. He wanted me to go with him. I said I had rehearsal. And then he insisted on driving me there.

It was harder to enjoy the pleasures of the Red Devil now that Himself wasn't working a regular job. Before, his fascination with old cars with a trace of glamour seemed part of his charm—it gave him some style, like his outdated way of combing his hair—but now, having an old car made it look like automobiles were just one more thing Himself wasn't paying attention to.

I looked at the garden while he backed the car out of the driveway. The mulch that I put down in October was still crusted over with old dirty snow, and we were supposed to get more today. I was bundled up in my parka, but even with the heater on, the car still felt cold. Himself never wore a big coat, just a red-and-black Woolrich jacket and a black wool hat. We hadn't been alone together in the car since he was fired. And you'd never know there was a problem to look at him. But I knew we weren't supposed to talk about it.

We headed out onto Church Avenue, past women wheeling shopping wagons piled with clothes to the corner Laundromat. The sky was full of low-lying bands of clouds like ermine collars. I cracked open the window because I thought the Old Spice aroma coming off Himself was going to make me sneeze.

He took a right on Schenectady Avenue. "How's life in the musical theater?"

I smiled. "It's great." When we first started rehearsing, I didn't know what I was doing, but I studied the kids with more experience, who knew how to project their speaking and singing voices. The belief in their eyes, when they looked at me when I strode out onto the stage—that what we were doing was real—convinced me that my scenes, though short, were somehow real too. And that blew my mind.

By now, Maureen had finished my costume, down to the eighteen-inch, evening-gown-style zipper, gold belt loops, and hemming. It hung in my closet, waiting for the dress rehearsal; I had modeled it last week in the kitchen for Mom and my sisters. It fit me like a glove. I took one look at myself in the full-length mirror in my sisters' bedroom and thought, *Who is that rock star?* And then: *I can't wear this with white tube socks.*

"I have to work on my dance moves, Brian says." We were passing Holy Cross. The cemetery, granite and white amid the bare bones of trees, lay stark and beautiful out my window.

"Does he now? Ah, yes. The famous Brian."

I straightened my back against the seat. I was waiting for the remark.

"I don't know why you want to be in this play, Nicky. That costume is just ridiculous."

It was bad enough that he had said, the night after Gina Martinucci had come over, "I hope this doesn't interfere with your schoolwork." I was carrying a 92 average and he knew it. And every time I had rehearsal, I sat on a folding chair in the back of the gym, doing my French exercises and translations and my boring geometry homework until it was time for me to go on. I read *Huckleberry Finn* on the bus rides home. And on Saturdays, I was the first one to finish my chores. Unlike Himself, I obeyed all the rules.

"It's supposed to be ridiculous," I said. "We're spoofing Elvis. That's the character."

"You look like Liberace."

Not that he'd seen me in costume, but I knew what he was implying—that doing the play would make me effeminate or something. We were cruising along Clarendon Road, a four-lane street with many brick two-family homes. "I like the play. And I'm making friends. You don't have anything to worry about."

Himself looked over at me, blue eyes clearer than usual. "This teacher of yours, he wouldn't be a little queer, would he?"

"Oh, come on. Don't be like that. What did he ever do to you?" I couldn't even look at him. He put me on the defensive and I couldn't back down. "You met him. He thought your car looked sharp or whatever he said. So what's the problem?"

"You just be careful is all I'm saying. He's taken a shine to you."

I was trying not to sound facetious, but he made it so hard to hold my tongue. "Maybe it's because I'm a good student and he likes me. Did you ever think about that?"

"Why are you talking with your hands?"

My arm was in the air. I dropped it to my side. "What?"

"You're talking with your hands. I can hear you. What I'm saying is that he's taken a shine to you and I don't like it."

Kings Highway could not come fast enough. St. Mike's was within spitting distance.

I didn't know why I was rushing to Brian's defense; I would never have put him in that category, with those other teachers at St. Mike's—some of them Brothers—who got a little too friendly, almost caressing students' backs when they had to write equations on the blackboard, or who seemed a little fey in their delivery. We joked about them. And then there was creepy Mr. Carter, the prefect of discipline, who, I swear, followed me off the subway once at the Brooklyn Museum stop and waited at the back of the station, down the dirty platform, with the look of lurk scrawled all over his face. But Brian wasn't like them, and I didn't want to think about him that way.

But what I was learning about him was a gas. He once told me he lived in a commune upstate after college, which made his parents freak out; it made me laugh. It was so out there. I felt like telling Himself that, just to see his reaction, but I kept my mouth shut. I didn't want to start my day with a smack across the face.

I asked to be let out on the corner—St. Mike's was on a one-way street—rather than go all the way around the block, but he insisted on taking me to the front entrance where a reddish marble set of stairs dressed up St. Mike's ordinary façade. So we had to go all the way around, not speaking, and I fidgeted with the zipper on my coat. I was already thinking the worst: he would make me quit the play. And if he did that, I would never forgive him.

There were parting words. "What time you get through with rehearsal?"

Now that he was home all the time, he had to know your schedule. "Three thirty, four."

"Maybe I'll see you later."

Man, I could not get rid of him. "I can take the bus home. I do it every day."

He gave me one of those looks and I got out of the car. "Let's see what happens with the snow."

Flurries drifted down to the sidewalk and melted. The Red Devil disappeared down the street, a bright splotch under the gray sky.

TWELVE

I took a seat in the back of the gym where it was dark, wrapped in my coat, trying to shake off that encounter in the car. Brian was directing a scene with Hugo and Kim. A wiry freshman named Steve Kirkland was playing the role and Mary Zaleski, an imp with long blond hair and a big colorful voice, was Kim. She had a compact, athletic body that wouldn't quit, with huge tits and shapely legs. I heard she'd been a majorette in a marching band, and last year, she had played Nellie Forbush in St. Mike's production of *South Pacific*, but I never saw it. Back then, I still hated musicals.

The band sat on folding chairs in front of the stage, at attention with their instruments while Mr. Testagrose reviewed the sheet music on his stand.

Brian was near the front of the stage, the play in his hand. "Remember Kim is acting more mature than Hugo here. She wants him to be jealous," he said. He was doing all the acting coaching while Mr. Steiner played the piano and gave the dance instruction. It turned out that Steiner had become a teacher after a brief career in summer stock. What he remembered about dance was good enough for St. Mike's.

Before I did anything on stage, I had to see my friends. I

draped my coat over one of the folding chairs and went backstage. Larry was already there, clowning around with this girl from St. Brendan's. She had the most amazing name I ever heard, Italian to the tenth power, Immaculata Rainone. I was afraid to ask her middle name. She had already used all the vowels in the language. She was playing Albert's mother. Everyone just about died when she showed up to audition in an old fur coat and her grandmother's orthopedic shoes.

"She has two pair," Immaculata explained.

She and Larry were leaning against the wall by the exit door to the schoolyard. Larry nodded at me, adjusting his Clark Kent glasses. "Hey, listen to Immaculata make her shoes squeak."

Immaculata was a tall, earthy girl with droopy brown eyes and curly brown hair that she pinned up when she came to rehearsal. "I brought my mother's plant spritzer from home, and I spray the shoes a little bit before I go on stage, and I kind of squeeze the rubber sole against the floor." She demonstrated, smiling as she made little mouse peeps with the shoes. "It works. You can hear it from the tenth row. After that, you're out of luck."

They had already done their song, "Kids," and were just hanging around. We were getting ready to rehearse my first number; it was the second time we'd done it with the band. The first time had been a disaster, and Testagrose nearly threw one of the trombone players, Sal Fortunato, out of the show when he couldn't keep time.

"Are you blowing into that trombone or sticking your dick in the other end?" he thundered.

Rehearsing with Brian was a piece of cake compared to Testagrose. He didn't make a pretense of being anybody's friend.

Suddenly, Brian poked his head backstage. "You ready, Nicky? Five minutes."

I heard the chorus humming "We love you, Conrad, oh yes

we do," and I took several deep breaths. I went over the plot in my mind. After Kim, as president of the Conrad Birdie Fan Club, presents me with the key to Sweet Apple, Ohio, I would sing "Honestly Sincere."

Brian wanted Conrad Birdie to arrive on a motorcycle, but he couldn't persuade any of his friends to lend him one, so he picked up an album of recorded sound effects that featured a track of revving motorcycles. The track lasted about three minutes; at the end of it, I stepped out on stage, in a pose I had copied from a Jim Morrison poster I had seen in the record department at Discount City: legs apart, ass up, crotch down. I had on these ultra-black racer sunglasses Brian had picked up at a drugstore. The black bass slung across my pelvis was borrowed from this guy he knew named Zodiac. He taught me the opening chords of the song and that was all I needed to know. I was ready.

The girls squealed, not in unison. They sounded like they were falling out of windows.

"Maddone," said Testagrose from the gym floor. The drummer hit the cymbals.

There were some guffaws from the band. We weren't expected to wear our costumes yet, but Mary wore a flowered dress with a scooped neckline. Her long, tapered waist made her look taller than she really was. Her hair, blond and usually worn straight, was set in a kind of retro flip. She moved to the set, a plain bandstand with three steps. A banner that said "Welcome, Conrad Birdie" in pink paint and gold glitter was strung across the rafters. The Conrad Birdie Fan Club gathered on tacked-down sheets of kelly green felt.

"As the president of the Conrad Birdie Fan Club I would like to present you with the key to Sweet Apple, Ohio," Kim said.

I stared at the rise of her breasts and said, "And sweet apples, they are too."

Larry hooted in the wings and I could see Mary's mind go blank. Then her forehead crinkled, like she was going to hit me.

"Give him the key," Brian whispered behind her. Mary followed the direction and stood on tiptoe to kiss me on the cheek. Very chaste. I strummed the opening chords of "Honestly Sincere" and removed the mike from the stand. The guitars strummed again and I started singing, mouth pressed up against the mike:

> *You've gotta be sincere*
> *You've gotta feel it here*
> *'Cause if you feel it here*
> *You're gonna be honestly sincere.*

The girls moaned between each line, the bass kicked in, and the rest of the scene went the way we had rehearsed it. The band joined in, changing the tempo. I threw the mike to my groupies and swung the guitar to my side. I jumped around the stage, calling, "Are you going to be sincere?" till I ended up back on the bandstand with the band, rocking the guitar on my pelvis in the faces of my groupies. With each thrust, columns of girls began to faint away on the padded green like falling dominoes. I felt the muscles in my ass clench and saw the panic on Carole Esterhaus's face as the guitar neck nearly collided with her nose. When the stage was littered with female bodies, I raised the guitar over my head.

The curtain closed. I stood there, panting, looking at the curves of legs, hips, and breasts below me. It was like a bobby-soxer harem. I went from having no girls in my life to being surrounded by them: a magic trick.

Then the curtain opened. Silence fell as we waited for the verdict. The penguin maestro came up on the stage toward me.

"You're Flynn, right?"

I nodded and did a quick scan of the stage for Brian. Testa-grose was grinning at me. I didn't trust it: he could smile at you one minute and curse you out the next. "Tell me something, where did they find you?"

"He's one of my students," Brian said, from somewhere behind me.

"Well, Mr. Flynn, you are one crazy motherfucker," he said. I swallowed. "Excuse me?"

Brian came around and faced Testagrose, hand over his mouth, eyebrows pressed together. It was funny to me that some-one who towered over the maestro should be so worried about his opinion. Then Testagrose stuck out his hand. I shook it.

"Now we're getting somewhere," he said. He turned to the company and said, "When the rest of you are as good as this guy, we will have ourselves a show."

Brian called for a five-minute break. After everyone dis-persed, he came over and patted me on the shoulder. "Well, at least one of us is off the hook." He smiled and said they didn't think they would get around to rehearsing "A Lot of Livin' to Do" today if I wanted to go home. But I never wanted to go home. I stayed at rehearsals as long as I could on Saturdays. While on a break, Brian and I would sit side by side on folding chairs in the gym and he'd start talking about the performing arts. "Talent's a wonderful thing, Nicky," he said, "and when people come to-gether in an environment like the theater, it's kind of utopian be-cause each person is the best they can be and they end up feeding each other ideas and giving each other creative insights. There's a lot to learn just by osmosis. You watch people do their scenes and sometimes it helps you do yours."

I could listen to him for hours, even if I didn't always know what he was talking about.

After Gina and Mary sang "One Boy," the second corniest song in the show, Larry, Immaculata, and I went to the McDonald's across the street. The restaurant hadn't been open that long; it was the only place to eat, it seemed, and now all the students, from St. Mike's and Killden, which was our nickname for Tilden High, piled in at lunchtime.

Snow dusted the sidewalk and coated the stiff black tarp covering the wreckage of the Wyckoff House. The air was brisk and wet and made my eyes pop open after looking into those footlights for so long. The smell of fryer grease hit us as soon as we walked in the door. Larry ordered a Big Mac, fries, and a chocolate milk shake for himself and a vanilla milk shake for Immaculata. I never ate more than a cheeseburger, which cost forty-nine cents, and a Tab. Two bites in and the grease from the meat seeped into my skin. I was determined to be zit-free on opening night, and I put the burger down in the yellow wrapper.

Immaculata had saved a booth that faced East Fifty-Eighth Street and the back of the school. We were a solid trio, but never more than friends. I suspected Immaculata had a crush on Larry, the way she doubled over at his jokes. I mean he was funny, but not that funny every time out.

I nodded at Larry's junk feast. "And now you're gonna go home and eat supper?"

He grinned broadly. "My brothers steal all the food. I have to eat on the sly."

I sank into the booth, thinking about the tall black kid, probably the same age as me, who had waited on us. His red uniform shirt with golden arches above the pocket, and the cardboard hat that sat on top of his Afro like a crooked crown. That's what I should be doing with my Saturdays, making some money to give to my mother—and getting some for me so I wouldn't have to ask her every time I went out somewhere.

I hadn't told anyone in the play yet about Himself getting fired. Or anyone at school. If I told one half of the story, I'd have to tell the other, and I didn't want to get into it. I wanted a different story, the one with the happy ending, and *Birdie* was it.

Immaculata smiled and patted my arm. "So, how you doin', Nicky? You're so quiet now."

I stole three French fries from Larry's mound. "I guess I'm a little tired after doing that song."

"You were great," Immaculata said. She had a milk shake moustache.

"I had three girls ask me for your phone number," Larry said. "You ready for that kind of attention, playboy?"

I laughed and shook my head. "You are so full of it. It was a three-minute song."

"Yeah, but wait till they see you in that costume," Larry said. "You'll be fighting them off."

I doubted it. The girls in the play hadn't really noticed me, much to my chagrin. They were too busy hanging on Brian's every word. He was like a rock star to them. Or maybe I should say a folk-rock star.

"My old man is not exactly thrilled I'm doing the play. He saw my sister sewing my costume and made a few choice re-marks. And he thinks Brian is—"

"Don't say it," Immaculata said. "It doesn't matter what he thinks. Just have a good time. Isn't that why we're all here?"

"She's right," Larry said. "Brian's cool. He lets me ham it up all over the place, so what's not to like?"

"But Testagrose has the last word. You don't want to get on his bad side."

"Oh, he's a fuck," Immaculata said.

Larry and I burst out laughing. "Tell us what you really think," Larry said.

"My aunt Chickie knows him, from Our Lady of Grace." She had borrowed her aunt's beaver coat for the play. "He thinks who he is."

I glanced out the window. It had started snowing again. I looked down the street and saw the Red Devil pass by, headed toward Collisionville.

Himself was back. Looking for me.

"Oh, shit." I grabbed my coat. "My old man's here. He said he was going to pick me up. I forgot."

"Wait a minute," Larry said. "We'll come with you. I've never met your father."

I thrust my arms through the sleeves of my parka and pulled up the hood. Immaculata stared at me, puzzled. "Are you sure you want to?" I asked.

I took off, shoving open the restaurant's double doors, and broke into a trot on Clarendon Road. The cold made my eyes tear. Larry was calling my name but I didn't turn around. When I rounded the corner of East Fifty-Seventh Street, I saw the Mercury parked in front of the school. I waved wildly at the windshield, thinking Himself would see me and drive up. But as I got closer, I saw that he wasn't behind the wheel. My heart pounded. I stared in panic at the entrance doors.

He was inside. I hoped he hadn't stopped for a few along the way.

I took the steps two at a time and shot through the darkened lobby. I walked into the gym and saw the empty stage and the empty folding chairs; everybody was still on break. Then I saw Brian and Himself standing off to the side over by the bleachers.

His voice was booming. "Look, pal, I know he's here. I dropped him off. Are you pulling my mickey or what?"

I couldn't hear Brian's reply, but I could tell from the way

Brian was standing, arms folded across his chest, that he wanted Himself to back off.

I hurried across the scuffed, golden floor. "Dad, I'm right behind you."

He turned around, eyebrows raised in indignation. I had to defuse.

"How was Rockaway?"

"Colder than a witch—"

He stopped. Then I saw the easy smile, the one that came after a few cocktails. Over his shoulder, I saw Brian make a face that said "Time for Dad to go."

He walked over and clamped his hand on my shoulder, squeezing it until I flinched. "The director here said you might be out in the lobby signing autographs, but I didn't see you."

I couldn't smell anything on him.

"I didn't know you were still around," Brian said. "I told your father you had gone home."

"We went to McDonald's."

Brian shook my father's hand. "Glad you two have found each other. I have to get back to rehearsal. Sorry we can't give you more of a preview."

I started walking out. "Come on, Dad. Let's go."

I waited until we were in the lobby before I turned on him. "Why were you giving him the third degree? He's my teacher, for god's sake."

The lobby statue of St. Michael the Archangel frowned upon us, life-sized with wings like javelins. "That's enough now, Nicky."

I didn't notice Larry and Immaculata waiting in the vestibule until I pushed open the double doors. She was pacing in her beaver coat. Larry walked right up to Himself and said, "Might you be the owner of the red roadster outside?"

Himself took a full measure of my stocky friend. "I might be." Then to me: "You know this guy?"

We ended up driving them home. I let Larry sit in the Death Seat so Himself could explain all the features of the Red Devil. While he hung on the steering wheel and the speedometer shot past forty, he talked about the transmission, the power steering, and the Marauder V-8 engine. He directed Larry's attention to the rear window, pressing a button on the door handle. The automatic window came down and the sharp wintry air wafted in.

"Cool," Larry said. He looked over the front seat at me and grinned. "Flynn, you've been holding out on me. When were you going to tell me your father had these dynamite wheels?"

"I'm the family secret," Himself said, taking a sharp left on Flatbush at Kings Highway. "You might say."

I rolled my eyes in the backseat. Immaculata sat across from me, relaxing into the white leather seat. "Nicky, I feel like I'm in a Troy Donahue movie." She slapped her knee and giggled. "Paging Connie Stevens."

An image of these toothpaste-white Hollywood actors drifted into my mind, and I laughed too.

"Hey, Dad, I think you can raise the window now."

Larry lived the farthest away, so he was dropped off first. Himself pulled up in front of an unattached house on Hendrickson Street, down the block from St. Thomas Aquinas and the Brook movie theater. His house definitely looked better than ours—a neat brick saltbox with a bay window and an intact stoop.

He shook Dad's hand and said, "A real pleasure."

Immaculata lived to the west, in Midwood, on a dark street where the homes were larger than those in Marine Park and set back from the sidewalk with bigger gardens. Her father was a professor at Brooklyn Law School.

We waited until she had gone through the front door before taking off again.

"Well, there's the gang," I said, after I moved up to the front seat. "So now you know what I do when I'm at rehearsal. And now you know where my friends live. Anything else?"

"Come on, Nicky. I'm not that bad."

"I don't see why you have to make everything a federal case."

"There you go again, talking with the hands."

The Red Devil rolled through the frosted streets as the sun set in orange slashes across the sky. We drove north toward home. Some of the Victorian houses still had Christmas wreaths hanging on front doors.

He started talking about the phone company, his last day. How he thought he knew the guy who was behind everything. Another lineman who worked in the same neighborhoods as he did. His elected enemy.

"I'm gonna find this son of a bitch who kicked my ass," he said with raspy urgency.

We were heading west now, crossing Ocean Parkway. The black rags of clouds hung in the red sky and the traffic, six lanes of it, was bound for the beach. Brighton, Coney. It was snowing again. The tender flakes melted on the windshield.

"Now I'm down in the dirt, and your mother, she's carrying me. This working of hers, I see it as a necessary evil." He was staring straight ahead, the blue glare boring through the windshield.

Necessary, yes. Evil, no. I tried to think of something to say. "It'll be okay."

He was still a young man then. Only thirty-five. There was still time. Plenty of time ahead to turn things around, find his way out of the hole he was crawling into.

I didn't know the neighborhood we were driving through. "Where are we going?"

"I have to see a guy. I need you to watch the car." He gave me a piece of paper. "Read that address to me."

His handwriting was like chicken scratch. But I could make out the numbers: 6225 Nineteenth Avenue.

"Who lives there?"

He rolled down the window. "My nemesis, I believe."

"What are you going to do—ring his bell and knock him out?"

"We may have a discussion."

He was going to get arrested. That was all we needed.

I leaned back against the seat, my stomach filling with dread. We were driving on Twentieth Avenue, closing in. The neighborhood was purely residential. I didn't know the ethnic makeup—Italian or Irish, Jewish or Catholic. I didn't see so much as a Blessed Virgin statue in the iced-over gardens. A man in a parka smoking a pipe was walking his dog past a public school with snow from last week's storm shoveled against a cyclone fence.

"Don't do this."

"Don't do what?"

"What you're thinking. Don't get into a fight."

"Who said anything about fighting?"

He was looking for a parking space. I sank down in the seat, unzipping my parka. I was getting overheated, sweaty. And I was frustrated; I could not get through to him. My mother was right: talking to him was like talking to a brick wall. But I was going to try to stall him, until this vengeful mood passed. His mood had already changed three times from St. Mike's to this godforsaken spot.

"You don't need any more trouble."

He found a spot next to the public school and around the corner from the address on the piece of paper. He lined up the car with one that was already parked. Looking over his shoulder, out the back window, he said, "What I need to do is find the son of a bitch who kicked my ass."

I was going to get killed for opening my mouth, but I did anyway. "If you ask me, you need to get some help."

He finished turning the steering wheel until the front wheel was straight. "I'm a broken-down alcoholic without a friend in the world, Nicky. No one's going to help me."

The last thing I was expecting was self-pity. I no longer felt like the kid in the front seat. "C'mon. Don't think that way. You can turn this around."

The car slid into place and he straightened the steering wheel. All he had to do was pull out, and this would all go away.

He opened the front door. I had one more chance.

"What does Mommy do if you get arrested? Have you thought about that?"

He didn't say anything; the last person he was thinking about was my mother. And then he cuffed me on the ear. I put up my hands and backed myself against the car door. My ear was stinging.

He was breathing in my face. "Listen, pal, I need you to watch the car while I take care of this. That's the only help I need right now. You got it?"

I nodded and he got out of the car. But he left the motor running. "I won't be long."

He walked back to the trunk and opened it. I looked out the back window but couldn't see much. He closed the trunk and began to stride down the street, carrying a flashlight in his right hand and something heavy in his left. A crowbar? A two-by-four? He disappeared around the corner.

I wanted to get the hell out of there, but if I did he'd really beat the shit out of me.

I hoped whoever he was after wasn't home. I looked at the

dashboard, missing the portable record player we'd had in the
Green Hornet, and settled for the radio. I found the oldies station. First song? No lie. "Rescue Me," Fontella Bass.

I was tempted to get out of the car and follow him but knew
that whatever I saw would ruin him in my eyes forever. And I
wasn't ready for that. So I waited, expecting to hear the sound of
breaking glass and popped car tires. Then I decided I didn't want
to know the minute things started going wrong. I raised the volume on the radio till poor old Fontella was bleating, high distress
with a backbeat. Maybe she would drown out the police sirens
when they came. Himself was turning into a criminal—and he
didn't care if I knew it.

I turned the radio off when Fontella faded out and listened
to the branches creaking on the trees. The silence was so wintry
and deep I expected to look at my watch and see it was midnight,
but it was only six thirty. Where was everybody? I didn't hear
another car or even a city bus.

The door on the driver's side suddenly jerked open and he got
in. I shot up and moved over, as if he was going to set something
down on the seat between us, like the flashlight he took with
him. But he was empty-handed.

He put his hands on the steering wheel. Snow melted in his
hair and on the shoulders of his jacket. A white handkerchief
was wrapped around his knuckles; dark spots soaked through the
cloth. He looked in the rearview mirror for a long minute, as if
someone was following him. Then he pulled out, taking the first
left. The roads were deserted, and the snow was sticking.

My stomach growled; maybe I should have finished that
cheeseburger back at McDonald's. "Are we going home now?"

"Yes. I did what I came to do."

"You shouldn't have made me sit there," I said.

"Why? Did somebody try to steal you? It was ten minutes."

More like twenty. I remembered that day in Holy Cross, when he hit the car parked by the mausoleum: *Not a word about this to your mother.* "Mom must be wondering where we are. I mean, does she even know I'm with you?"

The speedometer climbed as we headed east. "I might have said something."

I didn't believe him; it was silly to ask. He was never going to tell me the truth. All I knew was this afternoon, I was pretending I was a rock 'n' roll star in the school play. Now I was an accomplice in his getaway car.

THIRTEEN

After that adventure in the car, staying on his good side wasn't so important anymore. He was going down some scary path and I wasn't going with him. Even when I helped him—I did what I was told to do—I still got smacked. But as much as I wanted to walk away, I didn't. And as we discovered, he couldn't be left alone.

One Thursday a week or so later when I came home after school he found me in the kitchen. It was my mother's late day at the bank, none of my sisters were home yet, and I was headed down to see her to get the money for groceries. I agreed to do the cooking as long as one of my sisters lit the pilot light on the stove. I was afraid of fire and wouldn't even light a match. I feared the flame would spread from the matchstick to my fingers and soon my whole hand would turn into a red-hot burning coal. It made no sense, I knew, but I couldn't shake that feeling. I just wanted to be able to function, hold up my end of the domestic bargain.

I was on my way out the door, shopping list in my hand. He came downstairs and stood in the doorway between the kitchen and the dining room. His eyelids were falling down like broken window shades and he was wearing the same clothes he wore when he left the house the night before.

"Well, if it isn't the Anointed One," he said.

I looked up from my shopping list. "What?"

It was three thirty. Now that he was a "bartender," you never knew what time he was coming home; our encounters with him mostly took place at the crack of dawn, when he would stagger in and sometimes summon us to the kitchen. We would troop downstairs and park ourselves at the kitchen table, pasty-faced and bleary-eyed, while he delivered a lecture on how to properly wash a kitchen floor or how to defrost a steak. Or he might check our arms for needle marks. "If I ever find that any of you have been fooling around with drugs, I will have you put in jail. I kid you not. I will call the police. If I find a mark from a needle on your arms, you are dead. Do I make myself clear?"

The response to this threat was always the same. "Yes, Daddy."

The obsession with drugs took me by surprise. He just wanted to scare the hell out of everyone, now that he was spiraling down, but I still couldn't believe he would talk to my little sisters with such vehemence. Me and Maureen, we were getting used to being browbeaten and if it wore us down, I can only imagine how he intimidated Dee Dee and Mary Ellen, who were nine and seven years old. A lifetime of being afraid of your own father.

"Let me ask you a question: How's your peripheral vision?"

"I don't know, I never thought about it." I glanced at my list; I forgot to add Alpo to it. Himself was standing in the doorway, scratching his back on the doorjamb, moving back and forth against the wood. "Well, come over here and let's see how you do."

I sighed. "Do I have to do it now? I sort of have to get going."

I couldn't tell him to go to bed even though he'd been out all night; it would sound too much like a lecture and that would turn into an argument, and I would never get to the bank or the store.

"Oh, come on, give it a try. It couldn't hurt." There was no way around it. I knew he wouldn't give up unless I tried. I put down the pencil and turned around in the doorway.

He stood behind me. The fumes coming off him made me tilt my head away from him.

"Now, look out of your left eye and tell me what you see."

I saw the old enamel paint job and the side of the buffet. "Can you see the dining room table?"

"Not unless I turn my head," I said.

"Okay, now look out of your right eye and tell me what you see."

More enamel and some of the beige dining room wall. I dropped my hands and looked back at him. "Guess your peripheral vision isn't so good," he said, smirking.

"Why does it matter?"

"Because it's good to know who's coming up behind you, that's why."

Like when you went to find the guy on Nineteenth Avenue who supposedly ruined your life? I kept expecting the story of what happened that evening to surface in the newspaper, and I looked for it, scrutinizing the pages of the *Daily News*, but whatever happened slipped by, unrecorded.

He lumbered over to the refrigerator like a tugboat moving through wet cement, shifting his weight on swollen ankles at the open door. He grabbed the bottle of grapefruit juice, the antidote to the booze he'd consumed the night before, and sat at the table.

"Vodka. Drink enough of it and it swells up in the ankles, the fingers," he said. Then he asked me what I was cooking tonight.

"It's called Chicken Marengo," I said politely. I had found the recipe in *Family Circle*, one of Mom's magazines.

"You're really getting into this cooking thing." He knocked one glass back and poured himself another. "First the play, now Chicken Go Tango. I know you like it, so I figure I'll let you cook. But you sure do like to lay on those spices."

I doubted if he'd ever eaten anything I'd prepared, but I was more annoyed that he thought I was waiting for his permission to do anything. He was baiting me and I decided to let the moment pass. I checked the kitchen clock again and reached for the food stamp booklet.

It was ten after four when I got to the Lincoln Savings Bank. I loved the smell of the place, with its waxed marble floors and freshly shampooed rugs. The bank had two large rooms, one in front with desks where customers opened new accounts and a rectangular room in back where the tellers worked behind a high, wood-paneled counter. Mom came to the marble-topped ledge of the teller partition and handed me a white envelope containing fifteen dollars.

"This should cover what you can't get with the food stamps," she said. "Remember we need dog food." She paused a minute. "What's going on with Himself? Is he home yet?"

"He just got in."

"Terrific." She sighed. "Well, I hope he goes to sleep. I don't know how he does it, living on no sleep." She seemed distracted. The bank was hopping, the line of customers snaking behind burgundy velvet ropes. "God knows what time I'm getting out of here tonight."

She went back to her customers, and I went to the Big Apple. I bought chicken legs and crushed tomatoes and onions, frozen spinach, dog food, soda, and a half gallon of ice cream for dessert. I bought Himself a steak, not too thick. He could send somebody else to the store for his beer.

It was a seven-block walk home. I could see the back of the

house from the corner of Brooklyn Avenue. The missing green
shingles by the back bedroom, the exposed tarpaper beneath. I
saw smoke drifting up to the back bedroom window. At first I
thought it was the incineration from the apartment house on our
corner; but they only ran that at night. I panicked and rushed
home, cradling the groceries against my chest.

There was a fire engine parked directly in front of our house.
The Red Devil was in the driveway. "Oh, Jesus," I said.

Mrs. Garrett from next door and some of the other neighbors were standing out in front, gazing at the house, as if waiting
for a sign. They touched my shoulders, saying things to me as I
raced past them up the stoop. The front door was wide open. A
fat hose limped up the steps and into the front porch. Then I was
inside, choking on smoke.

The rooms on the first floor were full of it. My eyes stung. I
tried blinking through the haze. Two hulking firemen wearing
black slickers and tall hats stood in the living room, one hosing
down Himself's chair; the cushion glowed with burning embers
under the right arm. Himself lay in a heap on the rug, with the
coffee table pushed up against the couch.

"Daddy!" I cried, stepping closer.

He didn't move. One of the firemen spoke to me. Beads of
sweat ran down his face. "He was in the chair when we came in.
We hauled him out. Who is he?"

I nodded. "It's my father." Then I looked around; the house
was fractured, like someone had thrown it up in the air and it
had landed with a thud, dislodging the foundation. "Queenie!" I
put the groceries on the coffee table. My mind was reeling. Was
anybody else home yet? "Where's the dog?"

"Do you know what's wrong with him?" the fireman asked.

"He's drunk," I said, mortified. I could picture these men
breaking into the house and seeing Himself sleeping in the

burning chair, too crocked to know he was about to go up in flames. I took a good look at him. His pants were singed on the left leg all the way to the hip. How could he still be conked out?

I heard Queenie whimper. The dog poked her head into the dining room from the kitchen. Then she backed away.

"Looks like he fell asleep with a lit cigarette," the fireman said. He was the older of the two, with deep crow's feet around his eyes. "What's your name?"

I felt like I couldn't breathe. "Let me call my mother. She's at work."

The two firemen picked Himself up off the floor and settled him on the couch. He slumped over. The fireman with the crow's feet shook his shoulder, calling his name. Maureen and Patty came running into the living room from the stoop, coats half-unbuttoned. "Oh my god. Where's the dog?" Maureen said.

I nodded to the kitchen. Maureen went running out of the room. "Here she is," she called from inside. "She was under the kitchen table."

"What's wrong with Daddy?" Patty said.

"What do you think?" I snapped at her.

While the firemen gradually roused my father, I phoned the bank. I heard Mom's work voice, cool and controlled. "Mrs. Flynn speaking."

"You'd better come home right away. Daddy set the house on fire."

"What!"

The receiver shook in my hand. My voice was cracking. "He fell asleep in his chair with a cigarette. I came home and there are two firemen in the living room with Daddy."

She muttered something away from the receiver. Then her voice came on, hard-edged. "I'll be right there."

I hung up. My hand was shaking. I went back into the living room. The smoke was dispersing as cold air came in through the open front door. One of the firemen was fitting an oxygen mask over Dad's face. His eyes were partly open. "My mother's on her way. She'll be here in five minutes," I said.

I wasn't sure what I should do. I had reached my limit and all I wanted to do now was be with my sisters. I went into the back porch and found them in the yard, wrapped in their coats, standing around in the cold with Queenie. Their schoolbooks were stacked on the back porch steps. Maureen had brought the dog's bowl outside, filled with fresh water.

I sat down on the steps and started crying. In front of my sisters. I hated it, I couldn't stop. Maureen came over and put her arm around me. All the weird things I alone had witnessed— with the man he paid off at Holy Cross, when I couldn't get him to come home from the Dew Drop, waiting for him in the front seat of the Red Devil—crystallized in that moment. That guy lying on the living room floor, who was he? If he was my father, I didn't recognize him.

"He's gonna get us killed one of these days," I said. "You know that."

"Don't say that, Nicky," Patty said.

"Why not? It's true. You were there when he almost drove into the East River. We were lucky there was a fence. Next time, there won't be."

The light came on in Mrs. Garrett's kitchen, which faced the backyard. She pulled down the window shade to give us some privacy. My sisters made me tell them the whole story and I tried but Mom came down the alley, beige car coat not even buttoned, black pocketbook swinging on her left arm.

"What are you doing out here?"

"It's pretty bad in there," Maureen said.

Mom glared at me as she stomped up the back porch steps. "I suppose none of you checked on your father," she said.

"He's in there with the firemen," I said as she went charging into the house.

"What the hell is the dog's dish doing on the concrete? Come inside now," she said. The door connecting the porch to the kitchen smacked against the wall. My sisters filed in, Maureen carrying the dog's dish.

"C'mon, Nicky," she said, touching my arm.

"I'm not going in."

"Where're you going?"

"I don't know. I can't go in there."

I squeezed past the Mercury in the alley and gripped the car's red hood. I kicked the fender and then kicked in the left headlight. Nothing I did mattered. Our father would burn it all down.

FOURTEEN

The smell of the fire followed me. I could smell it on my shoulders, I could smell it in my hair. It was like having Himself's hands on me, pushing me down on the floor with him. I unzipped my coat halfway and walked toward Holy Cross, not sure where I was headed. If I walked around the cemetery—about two miles—my head would probably clear.

The Tilden Avenue gates were still open. I had just enough time before Holy Cross closed to walk to the chapel and maybe out the Albany Avenue exit, by the big tombs.

The chapel was a ten-minute walk from the entrance. The room was empty and dimly lit, with a modest-sized altar and a plain gold tabernacle. Some sharp fragrance—incense from morning mass—still lingered. I sat down in one of the light wood pews. The colors on the stained-glass windows—square panels of lilac and mint green—offered some cheer, but the red, blue, and yellow figures of the saints trapped there seemed tortured and remote, more intent on brandishing their wings than offering consolation. They didn't know how this story was going to end and neither did I. I wondered if Mom was going to tell someone—Uncle Tim or Grandpa or even her own father—what was going on. As the light faded from the glass, I imagined myself knocking on Uncle Tim's door. Would the story of what was happening to his brother shock him, after that drive home on Christmas? He was already lending Himself money, I was sure, and moral support. What else was there to be done? I didn't know.

An engine rumbled outside. My first thought: *It's Himself, hunting me down in the Red Devil.* I left the pew, tripping over the kneeler, and moved to the corner of the chapel, next to a stand of blood-red votive candles. A gust of cold air blew in as the chapel doors opened. Dried-up leaves skittered across the stone floor in the vestibule. I realized it couldn't have been Himself driving. He was conked out. Not even he could bounce back that quickly.

An older man with a green cap and a heavy burlap-type jacket walked down the aisle and genuflected next to one of the pews close to the altar. I pegged him for a maintenance worker. He went into the pew and knelt, bowing his head in prayer. I eased my way toward the vestibule, behind the brass stand of candles, and slipped outside. A pickup truck like those I had seen when I took my first driving lesson in the Black Beauty was parked next to the chapel.

It was nearly dark. I jogged down the street, past graves on both sides, many of them taller than I was, heading for the Tilden Avenue gates. The sky was streaked with silvery yellow light and the moon, white as a cue ball, rose over the hulking edifice of the Cloister. The only sound was the crunch my sneakers made on the occasional patch of old snow. I reached the main road in a few minutes. A bright spotlight shone down on the chunky stone archway and the adjacent yellow brick building where the cemetery kept its records, but I could see that the gates, black as night, were closed. That meant the gates at Albany Avenue were closed too. There was no point in even looking. The only way out was to climb the fence.

I headed into a labyrinth of headstones. The path between graves was not always clear, and I had to straighten myself out, keeping an eye on the houses across the street from the cemetery on Snyder Avenue. A horn honked behind me, and I turned. The truck I had seen parked outside the chapel was advancing; its headlights appeared between the graves like twin suns. I didn't feel like stopping or getting to know the driver, and I moved behind a crumbly, oval-shaped mausoleum with ridges in its cement façade. The fence, black and peeling, even in the poor light, wasn't that far away. Maybe a hundred feet.

Then he called out to me. He was out of the truck.

"Cemetery's closed, son."

He thought I was trespassing. I looked over my left shoulder but didn't see him. "I was in the chapel," I called out. "I lost track of time."

I kept moving, walking as quickly as I could. It was going to be awkward climbing the fence in my parka, and I unzipped it all the way so my hips would be free.

"Why don't you come over here?" His voice was closer and sounded ragged, as if he were out of breath from trying to catch up with me. "Come with me and I'll let you out by the gate."

I didn't like this guy. My scalp tingled: I was beginning to sweat and something bad stirred in my stomach. I looked over my right shoulder and there he was—tall, stoop-shouldered, and very pink in the face, like he'd been digging graves all day in the cold. He carried a flashlight, and I backed away from its beam, behind a tree. He stood behind a headstone that almost came up to his waist. He wore wire-rimmed glasses that made his eyes look very small. He wiped his nose with the sleeve of his jacket.

I kept moving. The fence, about seven feet high, was a few feet away. The flashlight beam bounced on the dirt, along the bottom of the graves.

"Son, there's no harm in getting locked in, but you could hurt yourself trying to get out that way."

I shouldn't have turned around, but I was having trouble shimmying up the fence. My palms slid down the black wrought-iron bars, so I wiped them on my coat. Then the coat seemed too heavy. I took it off and tossed it over the fence. That's when I looked over my shoulder. The gravedigger was leaning on the other side of the headstone now and I could see the brass teeth of his open zipper and the white cotton of his briefs.

"Get away from me," I shouted.

"You don't want to be climbing up there, son. I could pull you down in a minute."

When I thought of him touching me, I found my way out. Two back-to-back tombstones, one a little shorter than the other, stood close to the fence. I climbed on top and put one foot on a slanted black rod that branched out from the fence. I leaned over and grabbed the top of the fence and hauled myself up, lodging my left foot on top in the thin space between spikes. When I had both feet on top of the fence, I jumped, landing on the dirt path where I walked Queenie. I broke my fall with my hands.

I stood up and wiped the dirt and pebbles from my hands. Inside the cemetery fence the cold granite graves stared back at me. The perv was gone. I gathered up my coat and took off down my block. The fire engine was gone. When I squeezed past the Mercury in the driveway, I saw that someone had carried the charred recliner out through the back porch door and left it on the cement, next to the garbage pails. That couldn't have been easy; the chair was heavy and cumbersome. I wondered if Himself did it or whether that job fell to the cleanup crew of my mother and Maureen. I felt a twinge of guilt: I should have done it.

The light from Mrs. Garrett's kitchen—she had raised the

shade—shone on the burned fabric. An old kitchen towel masked the crater of fried stuffing, like singed cotton candy, where the cushion once provided a seat.

I heard a screen door squeak and snap shut and soon Mrs. Garrett was inching down her back steps, on the pretext of throwing out her garbage. She dropped a brown paper bag in the can next to the stoop and came over to me.

"I called the fire department. Your daddy could have died." She was originally from Virginia and still had traces of her Southern accent.

"I know," I said. "You probably saved his life." Then I burst into tears again.

Mrs. Garrett was somewhere in her seventies. She had worked as a nurse at Kings County for forty-five years and bought this house after she retired. Her husband had died last year while pruning a tree in the backyard. She knocked on our back door and asked for Mr. Flynn. "I found John in the yard," she said, her voice shaking. We weren't allowed back there—the Garretts' yard extended behind our garage and garden, and actually was a remnant of an old Indian road that led all the way to Canarsie—while Himself carried the body into the house and waited with Mrs. Garrett for the coroner.

Now she lived alone in the big house, which was not semi-attached like ours, but freestanding, with four bedrooms and a dining room with mahogany beams in the ceiling.

She took my hand; her skin was dry as paper. In this light, the silver of her eyeglass frames was sharply etched. "You came down the block in such a fright, but everyone's all right now. Nobody got hurt."

"I guess so," I said, wiping my eyes on my sleeves. "But it's been one thing after another, all day."

I heard another door open, on my side of the yard. There were footsteps on the back porch, then Mom's solemn voice. "Are you ready to come in and have your supper?"

She did not say hello or anything to Mrs. Garrett, but waited for me to end my conversation and walk up the steps. I couldn't tell if she was angry or just impatient. Had I been gone that long?

"You take care, then," Mrs. Garrett whispered.

FIFTEEN

The rearrangement of furniture made it easy to pretend he hadn't almost set himself—and the house—on fire. Mom moved the wing chair over to the spot where the recliner stood and I carried the rocking chair from the front porch into the living room. She didn't talk about what happened. And we never, ever mentioned the fire to Himself. The only trace was the ointments Mom had purchased to help his skin heal and in his walk: slow, creaky, every step a reminder that he was a lucky devil.

A week or so later, he needed our salvation again.

Mom woke me up in the middle of the night. I turned over in bed and saw the black frames of her eyeglasses.

"I need you," she said in a low whisper. "Your father's been hurt."

I didn't even know he was home. Usually, I heard the front door open, and then the groaning staircase as he dragged himself upstairs.

"What's going on?"

I followed her into the bathroom, the overhead light catching on her pink plastic curlers and the collar of her blue flannel bathrobe. Himself was lying on the floor between the pedestal sink and the radiator; the tub was behind his head.

I thought he was having a heart attack. I gasped and Mom turned to me and said, "Don't wake up the whole house."

He was bleeding from a cut on the bridge of his nose. Blood ran down the side of his face onto the tile floor. He stared at the ceiling, mesmerized, as if the Almighty had him under a microscope. He didn't seem to know we were there.

"What happened to him?"

"There was a fight at the bar. He tried to break it up."

"He needs stitches," I whispered.

She handed me some tissues to mop up the blood. "I already told him that."

I crouched down. "Dad, are you all right?"

His breathing was ragged. "Son of a mutt clocked me good."

"Hold his shoulders down," Mom said. She took a handful of cotton swabs, poured some boric acid on them, and knelt down next to the sink. It was a tight squeeze, the three of us there on the tile floor. My back was flush with the cool marble of the tub. Himself instructed her how to clean the cut. She pressed the swabs down on his nose and cleared out the dirt and blood. He hissed and kicked as I held him down. It looked to me like he'd been cut, not hit with a fist, but now wasn't the time to ask.

And then he did something I'll never forget. He pressed the torn flesh together and turned purple from the pain. I winced, but he groaned, like a wounded animal. "Mother of God."

"Now, put this on." Mom handed me a peeled Band-Aid to put on his cut. Her focus was impressive, like she'd done this kind of patchwork before. Me, I was a little dizzy.

A voice whispered in the hallway. "What's wrong?"

Maureen, in her yellow flannel nightgown and socks, stood in the hallway. She pushed loose strands of hair out of her face.

"Go back to bed, please," Mom said, without looking back.

I looked at Maureen and shook my head. She crept away.

Mom screwed the top of the bottle back on and put it back in the medicine chest. The circles under her eyes looked deeper than ever in the harsh light. In a few hours, she and I would be getting up again for our lives in the daylight world. "Pat, you're gonna be the death of me yet."

"Yeah, well. Don't get your hopes up," he said. "Help me up, Nicky."

I hooked my left arm under his arm and gripped his shoulder. I placed my right hand around his shoulder. He weighed a ton, and I had to plant my foot against the tub to get enough traction. Once he was able to put his hand on the sink, he stood up and I was able to get out from behind him. He checked his face in the mirror and approved of the emergency wound cleaning. Ever the pretty boy. "Scar won't be too bad."

"You can go back to bed now," Mom said, nodding toward the door.

Like I would ever fall asleep now. I had to say something before I left. I put my arm around his shoulder, looked in the mirror, and said, "Dad, I think you need another line of work."

"You might be right about that," he said, almost laughing.

As I left the bathroom, I looked back at them, and saw the way Mom tenderly finished cleaning his face with a washcloth. No matter what shape he came home in, she would fix him up. And now I was her accomplice too, the good soldier being trained to mend Himself and send him back out into the world for another day on the battlefield.

SIXTEEN

The night he spent on the bathroom floor while his split face was repaired seemed to give Himself pause. He stopped: drinking, carousing, closing out the night. He came home after locking up at the Mermaid, ate something, and went to bed. Maybe he had been scared straight.

"Maybe this time he'll stop," said Dee Dee one afternoon in the girls' bedroom. We were discussing the alcoholic weather report. Forecast: partly sunny.

The other three sisters were looking at me for my verdict.

"It's hard to say," I said. Their expectant faces told me I wasn't telling them what they wanted to hear. And I remember how I thought there wasn't much more I could take, but from day to day you never knew how much more you might be asked to process. I mean, if Tuesday was good, Wednesday would be bad. Before you digested that he had set the house on fire, he would wind up on the bathroom floor, his face gushing blood. The close calls were growing more frequent and they set me on edge. That day talking to my sisters in the front bedroom, I was feeling pretty numb from having absorbed one shock after another. If it wasn't for the play, I don't know if I would have made it. That land of make-believe was the only reality I could take.

While we waited to see whether sobriety was a commitment

or just a hiatus, we had to get used to him being around more often. He was intent on playing the patriarch. He told us to turn down the kitchen radio, which we blasted when we did the dishes after supper. And watched us as we went to the telephone bench to talk to our friends. We were no longer getting free service and he began to ration how much time we could spend on the phone, especially when Maureen was using it. He also hadn't been home when she started going out at night with her friends, wearing makeup and perfume and a vintage black velveteen coat that had once belonged to my mother. But he didn't like it.

One night she was heading out, and the closest she got to the front door was the wing chair in the living room. He glanced away from the television screen. "What do you have on your face, young lady?"

Maureen looked over at Mom, stretched out on the couch, wrapped under a multicolored afghan—crocheted by Grandma Flynn—with an ashtray balanced on her lap.

"Don't look at your mother. I'm the one who's talking to you."

I was sitting in the rocking chair between Himself and Mom, reading my European history textbook. Queenie sat at Dad's feet.

Before Maureen could even say the word "eyeliner," Himself ordered her to go upstairs and wash her face. "You're not walking down Church Avenue looking like that," he said.

Maureen wasn't wearing that much makeup, but she did a quick save, turning around and stomping upstairs to the bathroom. When she was done, she left the house by the back door. If he was going to be like this with her, my other sisters were in for a hell of a time. We were all growing up, bodies changing and maturing, involved in athletics and theatrics, but it was clear Himself wasn't going to keep up with us.

Maureen needed another place to hang out besides Church

Avenue, and I invited her to come with me to dress rehearsal. We left early on a Saturday morning, the only white people on the Church Avenue bus. The passengers were doing their errands, carrying bags of groceries and dry cleaning. We sat side by side toward the back, the garment bag holding my costume folded on my lap. When the bus stopped at Utica Avenue, I looked out the window and saw construction workers putting a new plate-glass window in the frame of an empty corner store.

"So tell me about the play. Who am I going to meet?"

"Well, there's Larry, he's a total crack-up. He has these Clark Kent glasses and he kind of talks like a radio announcer." I tried, lamely, to imitate him, calling me "sport" and his other nick-names. "He's in my English class. He has the Paul Lynde part and he's just as loud."

Maureen laughed.

"So I hang out with him backstage. He knows everyone in my school and seems to know all the girls from the high schools. He knew them at the audition."

"All the girls in the play are from Catholic high schools?"

I nodded. We had to get off at the next stop. "The star of the show is from St. Brendan's. This other girl, her name is Immaculata."

"Jesus. You're kidding?"

I walked to the rear door exit. "No. That's really her name."

"We have Scholastica Del Vecchio at St. Edmund's." She made the sign of the cross. "Very pious. The nuns love her."

I opened the back door and we stepped out into the windy morning on Kings Highway. "Oh, Immaculata's nothing like that. Between her and Larry, I'm laughing all day long."

The blocks leading up to St. Mike's were always so quiet I sometimes wondered if the houses were empty. "They're very, very dramatic. They all think they're going to go on to Broadway."

I told her about the day a bunch of us went to the movies after rehearsal and Mary Zaleski told me she was going to go to this school Juilliard. We were at Kings Plaza, the new mall, sniffing the candles in the Plum Tree afterward and she spoke with such conviction I forgot about her three-octave range (we all knew she could sing high, but Immaculata gave me the exact number) and her gymnast's figure, those balloons in her shirt swelling against the pink corduroy, protected by the good-girl crucifix. She took ballet and voice lessons. She could play piano. All of the guys in the show were trying to get with her, but she only had eyes for Brian. It made me think she was a little ridiculous, even though she was obviously a hot girl. Especially when she started asking me where Brian lived. And did he have a girlfriend? Was it true that he was in the seminary?

"What's his astrological sign? I'm a Leo," she said, tossing her blond mane behind her shoulder. "We might be compatible."

I answered some of her questions and that's where I made my mistake. I became more invisible in her eyes.

Maureen and I crossed Tilden Avenue and passed the high school. I heard a coach blowing a whistle behind the brick wall circling the football field, and the thud of bodies hitting the ground.

She told me the phone company was about to shut off our service. "I heard Mommy telling Daddy that they got the warning notice. First they shut off the outgoing calls. Then they give you a week to pay the bill or they shut off the incoming calls, and then you have to pay a huge security deposit for them to turn it back on."

"Great," I said. "Maybe Daddy wants it that way. Then he can't bellyache about how much we hog the phone. And Grandpa won't be able to check up on him on Sunday mornings."

It would be just us against him in the house, no outside interference; a grim prospect. "I don't even know where the nearest pay phone is."

"It's in the gas station on Snyder Avenue," she said.

Who was she calling from down there? We were at the school, and I took the front steps two at a time. "Once we go inside, we don't talk about home."

Rehearsal was already under way when we entered the gym. I showed Maureen to a seat in the back and pointed to Gina on the stage, gamely singing the show's first song, "An English Teacher."

"It'll only take me five minutes to change," I said, heading into the locker room. My locker was in the back. To get there, I had to pass Larry prancing around in a V-neck T-shirt and boxer shorts decorated with little red diamonds. His pale, fleshy legs were exposed, his dainty feet sheathed in black Ban-Lon socks.

"What's up, there?" Larry said. "Look out, he's got the big costume."

"Prepare to eat your heart out." I undid the combination lock and hung the garment bag inside. The jumpsuit felt great against my naked chest, the fabric shimmering yellow-gold from my shoulders to my ankles. I laughed; Maureen and I had really pulled it off. I couldn't wait to walk out on stage. Now I would really look like Birdie. I had cut my hair last week, short on the sides, with plenty of stuff to play with on top; Brian said he would probably add gel or hair spray at the end. I tied my black shoes and locked up. When I walked out, I saw Larry had gotten dressed. He was talking to Vinnie Sorrentino and Al Doyle, who were in the chorus, playing Hugo's friends.

"Wow," Larry said, touching the sleeve. He was wearing baggy gray pants with red suspenders over a white shirt, and a blue-and-beige plaid jacket. "Your sister made this? Spiffy."

"Let me ask Nicky a question," Vinnie said. "Who would

you rather do, Gina or Mary? I know which one I'd like to fuck, but what about you?"

He was compact and muscled with nosy, bulbous eyes. He was wearing crisp chinos and a V-necked white cable-knit sweater with navy and maroon trim around the cuffs. He looked like a Sicilian Doublemint twin. When I didn't answer, he turned to Al. "I bet he doesn't want either one."

I rolled my eyes. "Don't be an asshole, okay? And lower your voice. My sister's waiting right outside."

I kept walking and Larry caught up with me.

"Hey, Sorrentino, go beat your meat with the chorus," he said over his shoulder.

I walked over to where Maureen was sitting. "How does it look?"

She stood back and then forward, adjusting my collar. "I should take down the hem on the legs."

"You'll have to do it tonight. Our first show is tomorrow afternoon."

The scenery had changed for Kim MacAfee's bedroom. Brian was talking to Testagrose, all turned out in a snug tuxedo. He really looked like a penguin now. I called Brian over.

"You didn't tell me he was gorgeous," Maureen whispered.

"This is my sister," I said to Brian. "And this is the costume she made."

"Holy moly," Brian said. He wore a fisherman sweater and jeans. And he looked like he'd had a haircut, the brown locks brushing the collar of his sweater.

He broke into a broad grin. "You did a fantastic job. I never expected anything like this. This costume will really let your brother strut his stuff, which he has no trouble doing," he said, walking to the stage. "You guys can hang out backstage if you want. I have to get back to work."

Maureen grabbed my arm as Larry and I walked up the short staircase to the backstage area. Immaculata was already there, signature coat draped on her lap.

"My nerves! Look at this," she whispered, standing up and touching my sleeve. She wore a baggy print dress with a sprung seat and a waistline that hovered in the vicinity of her backside. "Your sister made this? She's so talented. Where did you get the fabric?"

I slung the bass guitar over my shoulder. "Orchard Street. They call it liquid gold."

"Liquid gold," she repeated emphatically, with a demented smile. "I'm standing here in my grandmother's orthopedic shoes next to a man wearing liquid gold." She nodded at my hips and squawked. "Well, baby, you can pour it all over me."

It was my turn to blush. Then Larry pinched my ass. I turned on him.

He shrugged. "Sorry there, sport. I guess I forgot you were a boy for a minute."

I pushed him away. "Hands off the merchandise."

Immaculata reached out for Maureen. "Hello, allow me to introduce myself. I'm Immaculata Rainone. I was born on the feast of the Immaculate Conception. My mother was very literal."

Maureen cracked up and asked her who she was playing.

"I'm the Maureen Stapleton of the piece. I know what you're thinking: a little young for the part. Pull up a chair and I'll give you the dish."

Maureen smiled and sat in an empty folding chair. She was pretty, I could see that, even though she was my sister, with a long, lithe figure and hair spilling over her shoulders onto a purple turtleneck. She was laughing at everything Immaculata said. I should have brought her here a long time ago.

I could hear Mary sing "How Lovely to Be a Woman" through the heavy beige curtain. Her voice was clear and bell-like; she should be in a high school like Performing Arts rather than St. Brendan's. After she hit the high note at the end of the song, the crew would be changing sets for "The Telephone Hour," my second favorite number, and I parted the curtain. There were only six guys, but they got the job done, carrying out this odd rectangular version of a jungle gym, connecting wooden boxes painted black that were big enough for people to move around in as they sang. Red, black, and white Princess and wall telephones were nailed to the inside of the boxes. From the other side of the stage, the actors—all chorus members—came out and installed themselves inside the set.

The band gave a cue and the first girl jumped out of her box, red telephone receiver in her hand. I waved Maureen over and held the curtain open so she could see the whole thing.

"Hi, Margie. Hi, Alice. . . . What's the word? Humming-bird? Have you heard about Hugo and Kim?"

The number came off without a hitch. Brian jumped up on stage, to give notes to the chorus.

"So what do you think?" I asked Maureen.

"It's not Al Green, but I can live with it," she said.

"Don't be a snob. Remember: you made the costume."

Gina came backstage after her scenes with Vincent LoPresti, the kid who was playing Albert, Rosie's fiancé. Gina's mother's red Chanel suit fit her like a dream. We hadn't seen much of her since rehearsals started; she was always hanging around with this drummer from the band. Lenny Plonski. He was a senior.

"Nice circle pin," Maureen said. "Was that your mother's too?"

Gina nodded. She pointed to her hair. "Tell me the truth."

Her hair was set in a chestnut-brown bouffant. So long, Judy Collins; hello, Rosary Society.

"I look like Sadie Scotto at her daughter's First Communion," she said, distressed. That was Gina's mother's best friend. "It's okay," Maureen said. "It's only for a few more weeks. You'll survive."

Gina had some downtime so she sat with us while Larry did his scene with the MacAfee family, with Kim monopolizing the telephone as she talked about Conrad Birdie with her girlfriends. The girl playing Kim's mother went blank on one of her lines and Larry saved her, ad-libbing, "As your mother says" and helping everything move along. He always knew what to do on stage, where to stand, how to make the set where the MacAfees lived feel like it was his own. I loved watching him from the wings.

Brian called for a fifteen-minute break. He huddled with Testagrose and the band. The guys and girls in the chorus cleared the stage, dispersing throughout the auditorium in a few minutes. Vinnie came backstage looking for Gina, practically pleading with her to make a McDonald's run. When Larry overheard that, he wanted a milk shake too. Immaculata was staying put.

"If I drink any more milk shakes, I won't need padding for my costume," she said.

"Don't you want to take a walk at least?" I asked. "I need some fresh air."

Immaculata shook her head. "No. This neighborhood has nothing to recommend it."

Sometimes Immaculata said things I swear she heard in an old movie. But she wasn't wrong about the neighborhood. Maureen decided to stay with her and I ducked out the back door onto East Fifty-Eighth Street. Guard dogs yowled behind the fence at Collisionville and the tarpaper roof of the Wyckoff House looked a little more sunken than the last time I passed it. The cold air was biting, but I didn't mind it after the stale smell of the gym.

McDonald's was jammed with the Tilden football team. Big guys, mostly black, in parkas, some still in uniform, white jerseys with their names and numbers in red lettering, had taken all the booths and many more were still in line. We would look like fools standing behind them. Vinnie was ahead of us in line with Gina. Her hand kept going to the circumference of her chestnut sphere, as if she was checking for dents.

I tugged on the sleeve of Larry's sports jacket. "The line looks kind of long for a fifteen-minute break."

"I see your point. What do you think the chances are that we could get Sorrentino to order for us?" Larry whispered.

Between me and Vinnie, there were three football players holding their helmets, shoulder pads rising from their bodies like rocks. "Slim."

The odor of fryer grease grew stronger as we moved closer to the counter. I could feel my forehead turning slick, as if five lurking pimples had received permission to sprout. Larry never needed to put Clearasil on his face. I once asked him why. He said, "All of my pimples are on my backside."

Some of the guys in the line on my left were laughing. Then I heard one of them say, "Looks like James Brown's gonna order a Big Mac."

I blushed and looked straight ahead. James Brown was a big step up from being compared to Liberace, so I guessed I was safe. Even so, something—maybe the risen hairs on my neck—told me we were attracting too much attention. I turned to Larry. "Hey, this line is dragging. What if I meet you back at school? I'm not that hungry anyway."

"Oh, come on," Larry said. "It's only a few more people."

Vinnie and Gina inched back toward us, carrying soda cups and two yellow-and-white bags. There wasn't a head that didn't turn to take in the full effect of Gina in her bouffant and Chanel suit. Vinnie saw them all and leaned over until his chin brushed Larry's shoulder. "Fucking mulignan taking over the joint."

I didn't know what that word meant, but Larry did and he raised his eyebrows. "Hey, dickhead, you're not on Eighteenth Avenue. Cool it."

Vinnie shrugged. He lived in Bensonhurst or Bath Beach, one of those all-white outposts I had never been to. The football player in front of me, six-two with shoulders as broad as the Shasta Dam, apparently didn't hear him. He just cocked his head and smiled at Gina. "What's goin' on?"

Gina looked straight ahead, her bouffant a compass. "Nothin's goin' on, that's what," Vinnie said, all snotty-faced.

"Vinnie!" Gina rolled her eyes. Whatever traction Vinnie thought he was getting with Gina was slipping. "We're doing a play over at St. Mike's," she said. "It's dress rehearsal. That's why we all look so ridiculous."

The football player laughed. He must have been around our age but he looked like he was in college, handsome with soft lips and deep-set eyes that squinted when he smiled. "My name's Lamont," he said. "Maybe I'll check you later."

Gina blinked and blushed at the same time, unprepared for such admiration, and Vinnie watched the football player saunter over to his buddies. "Maybe in your dreams," he said under his breath. He took Gina's elbow. "Don't talk to him. C'mon." He nodded to a corner booth. "Let's sit for five minutes."

Gina was looking toward the door. "Shouldn't we go back?"

"Why would you have to go? You're not in the next number."

"But you are."

Vinnie's brown eyes were begging. "Just sit with me while I have my milk shake. I drink fast."

He was determined to grab any time with her. But I thought she should have left. Then he would have followed her and consumed his milk shake on the walk back to the school. Instead, Gina trailed after him to a booth that had emptied out when four football players took their gear and left.

Larry and I were next at the counter. I only had money for snacks for me and Maureen. I ordered two cherry pies, one 7-Up, and one coffee. The girl waiting on us had long pink fingernails and a name tag pinned to her uniform: Rolonda. I counted out the change on the black Formica counter. Rolonda took one look at my getup and asked, "You goin' to a costume party?"

"Yeah," Larry said, stepping up. "It's a costume party called *Bye Bye Birdie*. We're doing it at the school across the street. Tomorrow afternoon and next weekend. Maybe you'd like to come. We'll sing and dance for you."

She flashed a neon smile and took Larry's usual gargantuan order. "Well, maybe next weekend."

"Yes. But it's at night. You can come after work."

Rolonda lowered her head as she handed Larry his change. "I'll keep it in mind. Your fries will be ready in a minute." She called the next customer and Larry had to step aside.

I opened the cherry pie box. The pie looked more like a turnover—a small turnover—and smelled achingly sweet. "You make friends wherever you go."

"I've never seen her here and I'm a preferred customer. Killer smile."

I half-listened to what Larry said, watching the horde of kids scarfing down cheeseburgers and milk shakes, helmets on the floor. I shut the box and put the pie back in the bag. It was really time to get back to rehearsal. "A Lot of Livin' to Do" was about ten minutes long, with three singers and lots of dancing with the chorus. It was a workout, and Testagrose and Brian were not yet satisfied with the way the parts fit together.

Rolonda put Larry's large fries in the bag and gave him one

last smile. The line behind us now stretched to the door. As we headed out, I glanced between the waiting people and saw Vinnie standing over the football player who had chatted up Gina. They were arguing. I heard Vinnie say the one word he shouldn't have said. He was going to get his ass kicked and I hustled Larry to the exit.

"You don't want to be talking like that to me," Lamont said. "Go back and sit down with your pretty friend."

"Why don't you go back to the fucking jungle?"

"You're already in the jungle," said a guy in Lamont's booth. He was dipping French fries in ketchup and laughing. "Or ain't you noticed?"

I could hear my heartbeat knocking in my ears. Something terrible was about to happen and I wanted us all to get out of here. "C'mon, Larry, let's go," I said, stepping in front of him. Gina stood up, smoothing her skirt. "Vinnie, let's go back. We're late already."

Larry went over and tapped Vinnie on the shoulder, but he didn't even turn around.

Lamont stood. The face that had looked so stoked to get Gina's attention was contorted with rage. He picked Vinnie up by the armpit and waistband and tossed him down the row of booths. Like a bowling ball. He didn't quite hit the back wall.

"One honky down," someone said.

Gina screamed and covered her ears. She glared at Lamont. "What'd you do that for?"

He didn't answer her. Vinnie scrambled to his feet; he was coming back for more. Larry tried to block him, but it was useless. The mismatch in their sizes was extreme and pathetic. Vinnie threw a punch. Lamont swatted him away with one cuff to the jaw. Vinnie started bleeding from the right corner of his mouth. The other jocks rose to their feet, egging on Lamont.

"Stop it!" Gina shouted. "Stop it!"

I slipped out the front door. I ran back to school, clutching the McDonald's bags. The one with the soda and coffee fell to the sidewalk, brown liquid staining the white paper. I left them there and kept going. The door to the gym was locked, and I banged on it frantically. Finally, Immaculata opened it, sticking her head out into the cloudy late-afternoon light.

"You're late," she whispered hoarsely. She saw my face. "What's wrong?"

I rushed past her and out onto the stage where Mary Zaleski was waiting in a purple ruffled blouse, almost the same color as the one Ann-Margret wore in the movie, with her arms crossed, ticked off. I shielded my eyes from the footlights and saw Brian and Testagrose, down on the floor. They looked pissed.

"Nicky, we're waiting on you. Where have you been?" Brian said.

It took me a minute to catch my breath. "A fight broke out at McDonald's."

By the time Brian ran over to McDonald's, me and Maureen trotting behind him, a blue squad car was parked in front, red roof light ominously circling on top. There was a broken window near the booth where Lamont's crew was sitting. Vinnie and Lamont were handcuffed. Two officers took down their information.

I didn't see Larry. I didn't see Gina. I stared and stared at the chaos behind the windows.

"What happened?" Maureen asked.

"This punk from my English class started a fight with this black guy from Tilden. He called him a nigger."

Maureen looked in at the scene of arrested mayhem. "Asshole. Where is your coat?"

We stood back on the sidewalk, near the corner, out of reach of the garish yellow light of the McDonald's sign. I heard a siren wailing in the distance. "In my locker. I just want to see if my friends are okay."

Brian knocked on the restaurant's glass door and one of the cops—young and fit with a razor haircut—unlocked it. He went in and looked down on the floor, his expression aghast. Someone was hurt. The siren I'd heard before grew louder and a white-and-red ambulance from Brookdale Hospital pulled up behind the squad car. Two men in gray zip-up jackets and wool caps jumped out of the front seats and opened the back door, removing a gurney and wheeling it to the locked front door.

"It's Gina," I said, touching Maureen's shoulder. "Holy shit."

Inside the restaurant, I saw Larry standing next to Brian, his face drained. He pushed his glasses back on the bridge of his nose. I glanced down the dark street behind St. Mike's and saw members of the company come closer, their expressions bewildered as they took in the lights on the cop car and ambulance. Immaculata. Carole Esterhaus and the girls from the chorus. Some guys from the band.

I kicked an empty beer bottle across the street. "This is a disaster," I said. "A complete disaster."

The ambulance workers opened the door and wheeled the gurney out into the frigid air. Gina was strapped onto it, her bouffant caught in the raw yellow spotlight. Her face was a grimace of pain.

I gasped and ran forward, and one of the ambulance workers, the hospital logo stitched into the fabric of his jacket, near the pocket, told me to stay back. I called out her name, but she wouldn't look at me. Her face was turned away and her eyes were shut. The skirt of her suit was ripped on the side; her left leg was covered with a sheet. Immaculata came up behind me in her beaver coat as the gurney was loaded into the back of the ambulance. "Nicky, is that Gina? What the hell happened?"

I told her what I knew as the ambulance drove away, up Clarendon Road to Ralph Avenue. Larry came outside, looking right and left for a friendly face, and I waved him over. He told us Gina had gotten knocked down in the commotion. "She twisted her leg around one of the booth seats. I think it's broken."

Immaculata shook her head. I felt so dejected, I didn't know what to say. Wistfully, I remembered the Sunday afternoon Gina had sat with me in the kitchen while Maureen tried to make sense of the pattern pieces of my costume, yelling as she wrestled with the zipper. Gina had been so proud that she was going to wear her mother's Chanel suit. And now it was ruined.

You could have seen the rest of the scene on the eleven o'clock news. Two more squad cars pulled up. Cops jumped out, filing into McDonald's. Vinnie was slumped down in the booth where he had been sitting with Gina. His head was tilted back to balance an ice pack wrapped in silver Filet-O-Fish paper on his left eye. Lamont was sitting across from him, his back to us, hands behind his back.

"They're taking everyone in," I said.

"That's right," Immaculata said. "This is not for me. Let's go, Nicky."

She was wearing a burgundy wool cap and had pulled it so low over her head that her nose looked more Roman than ever. Now that I had cut my hair, my ears got cold really easily.

"Yeah," Maureen said. "We've seen enough."

"So, I guess there's no show tomorrow."

"Not without Gina," Larry said. "Who else can play her part?"

I felt tears coming on. Tears of rage. "The whole thing's over because of someone's stupid big mouth. I can't believe it."

Then Testagrose came trundling down the street in his black fedora and black overcoat. Flecks of saliva studded the corners of his mouth.

"As if there wasn't enough drama," Immaculata said.

"I told you schmucks to stay in the gym," Testagrose said to the kids lingering on the sidewalks in their absurd bobby-soxer outfits, like refugees from some time capsule. "You don't belong off school property." Then he banged on the door of the restaurant. The cops ignored him and he banged harder. Brian looked up and gave the okay to open up.

Larry said he was going to stay behind. I wondered if I should stick around, but Immaculata told me to stay out of it. Besides, Maureen and I would be expected to be home for dinner.

"So do we have a play or not?"

Larry shrugged. "I doubt it, sport."

"We're cooked," Immaculata said.

Larry tapped me on the shoulder and nodded. I looked down the block and saw a man wearing a tweed flat cap walking briskly in our direction, the collar of his peacoat turned up. Out of his black robes and black rosary beads, Brother Theodore looked like any other middle-aged Irishman, but the Babe Ruth nose was the dead giveaway. His expression was somber, as if somebody inside McDonald's were waiting for him to give Extreme Unction.

Testagrose must have gone to the top floor of the school and told one of the Brothers. That's why he was delayed in making his entrance. It was just our luck that the school principal was home.

"He's going to freak out," I said, my throat dry.

Larry agreed. "No shit, Sherlock."

No one had to tell me tomorrow's performance was canceled. I could see it on Brother Theodore's clenched pink face. Maureen pulled me aside and said, "Nicky, I'm cold. Let's call Daddy and ask him to come and get us."

"No," I said. "He'll have a fit." He was going to have a fit anyway when he found out the fight broke out the day I brought

Maureen to rehearsal; I'd just rather not have him have it in front of everybody.

Maureen said, "Well, we can't stay here."

We walked two blocks to the nearest gas station; the heavy smells of rubber and gasoline cast another pall over the day. Maureen and Immaculata stood under the sign, facing Ralph Avenue and the Midnight Pearl Lounge, a little hole-in-the-wall with two pink neon martini glasses flickering on the sign above the entrance. My shoulders tingled with the cold. Now that the excitement of watching the aftermath of the fight had worn off, the dampness of the outdoors was setting in and I wished I had my coat.

The pay phone was hiding in the corner behind the gas pumps. The phone booth smelled like a toilet. I picked up the receiver and held it away from my mouth. Fortunately, Mom answered.

"Can you ask Daddy to come get us?"

She sounded very serious. "What's wrong?"

"Something happened during rehearsal. There was a fight. We're okay, but we need to get out of here. And we have one friend with us who needs a ride home. We'll be in front of the school."

We went back into the gym to get our clothes. Immaculata had left her clothes backstage in a bag. She found them and said she would get changed at home. I handed Maureen the white bag from McDonald's. The pies were no longer warm. "We can eat while we wait," I said.

"Now you're talking," Immaculata said, rubbing her hands together. "I'm starving."

Maureen slid the pies out, breaking them in uneven pieces. One for each of us. And one left over. The filling was tartly sweet. While I cleaned out my locker, hanging my jeans and shirt on the hanger inside my garment bag, I remembered why I brought her with me today. I found the girls sitting on two folding chairs, facing the stage where the empty scenery, abandoned instruments, and interrupted melodies told today's story.

I dumped my parka on another empty chair and ran up on stage. I had a few minutes before Himself came to fetch us. I stood in front of the microphone, snapped my fingers and began to sing the opening of "A Lot of Livin' to Do."

Maureen wiped her mouth with a McDonald's napkin. "He made me listen to this in his room like fifteen times," she said.

Immaculata laughed. "Oh, let him do it. He's good."

I stopped singing. "Some say I stole my look from Liberace. Others say I stole it from James Brown. But my sister is the one who gave it to me and she didn't steal it from anybody. It makes me sad to think this may be the only time I'm going to sing in this costume, but hey, it was worth the trip to Orchard Street and the Sundays at the sewing machine because we did it together."

I picked up where I left off.

Sizzlin' steaks all ready for tastin'
And there's Cadillacs all shiny and new!
Gotta move, 'cause time is a-wastin',
There's such a lot of livin' to do!

SEVENTEEN

The show did go on, in a halfhearted way. With Vinnie Sorrentino suspended, Brother Theodore reversed his initial decision to cancel the performance and we were allowed to do the play once—on the weekend before Palm Sunday. Brian plucked Carole Esterhaus out of the chorus to learn Gina's part, but she kept flubbing her lines and her singing was nervous and jerky. I felt bad for her, but nobody's heart was really in it, including Brian's. Me, I focused on my family, out there in the audience. I would perform for them. They were all there, except for Himself.

He wasn't in the school lobby when I met my family after the show. "If it isn't my son, the star," Mom said, assembling me and my sisters for a photo with her Instamatic. I was still in my costume. "Where did you learn to move like that?"

The sound of the applause was still ringing in my ears. That was the big wow. "Rehearsal," I said, wiping my grimy forehead. "Lots of rehearsal."

Mom was decked out—she was actually wearing makeup—in a dark blue dress I'd never seen. Her lips were bright red and full; traces of iridescent green colored her eyelids. She really turned on the charm when she met Brian. "Tell me, you must have had your hands full, working with so many teenagers."

"Nah," Brian said. "Give kids some encouragement and some freedom to be creative and they really surprise you. And you have two talented children."

Brian left to meet other parents and Larry took his place. He asked me where my old man was.

"He has a new job," Mom said. "He's working weekends."

He had quit the Mermaid and was driving for a car service called Pronto.

"Missing the big moment," Larry said. I tried to shrug it off and Larry ushered me over to the other side of the lobby to meet his parents. As he led me through the crowd, all I could see were the fathers. Men in suits, ties, and overcoats. In another life, any one of them could have been my dad and they would have seen me on stage. I wondered if I was the only cast member whose father didn't turn up and I got distracted, slow to shake Larry's father's hand. Steve. Steve Cahill. That was his name. And he had the same black-frame glasses. It made me laugh, to see how alike he and Larry looked. I supposed I should have been glad Himself wasn't here because he would have made some facetious remark and embarrassed me, but his absence gnawed at me in a melancholy way.

And then it was back to school. Brian seemed like he was in a bad mood in class on Monday. We didn't put our chairs in a circle. When he looked at you, he looked right through you as if he wasn't there. At the end of the period, he was gone. So I thought of the one place I might find him: the stage in the school gym. I found him moving the ruins of Sweet Apple, Ohio, to the trash bins out by the track. He didn't see me at first. All that was left on stage was some living room furniture. I hung around and waited for him. He came back in and said, "Nicky, what's up? I wish I could talk, but I have to return a couch."

"Let me help you."

Reluctantly, he let me help him tie the faded sofa to the top of his car, a silver Plymouth Duster parked down the block from the Wyckoff House. I opened the passenger-side door when the couch was secured.

Brian frowned at me over the top of the upside-down olive-colored sofa. "What are you doing?"

A German shepherd watched us, open-jawed, from behind the fence at Collisionville. "You need someone to help you take it down, don't you?"

"I was going to handle that by myself." He seemed reluctant and glanced back at St. Mike's, like someone was watching him. "If we're gonna go, let's go."

He didn't want to drive past the school, though, backing up the car until he could head out on the street that ran along the side of the wrecking joint. We made a right turn on Ralph Avenue, past the Brooklyn Terminal Market.

"Where's this one going?"

"A friend of mine. Kevin Di Napoli. I took it from his parents' basement."

"Where does he live?"

"Nineteenth Avenue."

It took us half an hour to get there. The house was semi-attached brick on a block of semiattached homes, very clean and orderly. I didn't recognize the neighborhood, but the street name sounded familiar. We took the ropes off the couch and carried the sofa, which wasn't that heavy after all, down a long alleyway. The alley led to a yard with two garages; the basement door, the old slanted kind that opened out from the center, was on the left. A small woman with a salt-and-pepper beauty-parlor hairdo stood there in a white cardigan and navy slacks, smiling.

"Oh, it's so good to see you."

"Hey, Mrs. D.," Brian said. "This is my friend Nicky. He's one of my students."

She smiled at me and led the way down into the basement, holding on to the green wooden door, taking halting steps. Brian followed her, backing up to the top step and pausing to catch his breath before he went down.

"You okay, up there?"

"Yeah." I balanced one end of the couch on my pelvic bone so I could wipe my hands on my coat. Then we went down into the cellar. The first room seemed to be some kind of shed with tools hung on nails and planks of wood resting on a cutting board. Mrs. D. led the way. "Watch out for the toolbox over here," she said, and we shifted to the right. The next room was a finished basement, brightly lit with walnut-color paneling, a gray linoleum floor, and a bar over in the corner made out of bamboo and some kind of white countertop.

"Can we put it down over here?" Brian asked.

"Yes. That's good. I should really throw it out, but I have nothing to replace it with."

We set the couch down under a framed poster of Van Gogh's *Sunflowers*. I rubbed my hands together; my palms were red and stretched out. Brian thanked Mrs. D. profusely for loaning out the couch and began to walk toward the cellar door, which was still open.

Mrs. D. held a set of keys in one hand. "Would you like to say hello to Kevin before you go? I know he'd like to see you."

Brian looked at me. "Nicky, do you mind?"

I shook my head. A staircase on the left led to the first floor, but we didn't take it. Instead, we went into the yard again, so Mrs. D. could lock up. Then she took us through the front entrance, a wide stoop painted red with a nice-sized brick patio—a great place to spend a summer night if it wasn't too hot. While she was fiddling with the lock, Brian turned to me and whispered, "Kevin was injured in Vietnam."

"What?"

Brian touched my shoulder. "Just be cool."

I followed him inside the house, glancing up at the address over the front door: 6225. I had no time to think about what I was about to see; suddenly, we were in the living room and there was Kevin, a handsome young man with long, straight hair, medium-brown and parted in the middle, the way mine used to be, and toffee-colored eyes. He looked like he could have been on the cover of a folk-rock album, something by James Taylor or Crosby, Stills & Nash, except that his legs were gone, shot off or blown off by a bomb, and he was sitting in a wheelchair.

I stood stock-still and tried not to stare, but there was nowhere else to look. Kevin wore shorts, blue but not denim, and they were long enough to cover the stumps. Brian stepped in front of me—maybe he saw me standing there, horrified—and shook Kevin's hand, squeezing his shoulder. He introduced me again as one of his students but also one of his friends. I felt myself blushing. Even though the play was dead, we would still be friends. That's all I cared about.

"Nicky, how ya doin'?" Kevin said in this casual way, like he already knew me or knew about me. His eyes were kind and engaging, actively making contact with mine. I tried to smile and say something, but I just shook his hand instead. Mine felt very cold from carrying the couch. I thought I was going to burst into tears and I was breathing heavily through my nose. It was too sad, too much to look at, too much to take in. The floor beneath me swayed and I looked for a place to sit. I felt like I was seeing something obscene, forbidden. Yet it could have been me, if I'd been older and had a low draft number and had Kevin's bad luck. Himself sneered at guys like Brian who may have become teachers to escape the draft, but how could you blame them?

"Why don't you take off your coat and have a seat?" Mrs. D.

said merrily, showing me the couch, tweed with wooden arm-rests. I shook off my parka and balled it up next to me. "Would you boys like some coffee?"

She didn't wait for an answer and disappeared down a hallway with Brian's peacoat. I let Brian do the talking. Kevin told him about his rehab, his time at the V.A. hospital in Bay Ridge. The doctors were talking about prosthetics. Brian nodded and offered to drive him to appointments if his parents couldn't. All I could think was: *How old is he? Twenty-two, twenty-three? Younger? And this was it for the rest of his life?* I'd march on Washington too, if this had happened to someone I knew.

Mrs. D. brought the coffee in this beautiful white china cup patterned with tiny strawberries. The cup shook as I brought it to my mouth, some coffee spilling onto the saucer. The coffee was delicious and it seemed to settle me down. I leaned back against the sofa, settling my shoulder blades into the fabric.

Mrs. D. sat next to me in an armchair. She was smiling also, as if relieved to have company to break up a Monday afternoon. I wondered if she had other children who could help her take care of him; she seemed too frail to do it herself. A gold crucifix peeked out from under the collar of her white blouse. Her eyes were the same color as her son's. She told me that Brian and Kevin had been friends since high school.

"He was the first of Kevin's friends to visit him in the V.A., when he came home."

All of the questions I was going to ask Brian about where he stood with Brother Theodore had flown out of my head. No matter what they thought of him at St. Mike's, I couldn't imag-ine knowing a nicer guy.

Now I could look at the wheelchair, which was shiny and silver—the Di Napolis must have bought it brand-new—and the man in it, who was so laid-back, maybe medicated. Brian was sitting next to me on the couch, gratefully drinking coffee.

"We used to live closer to Brian's family, in Midwood," Mrs. D. said. "Then Kevin's father got a big job with the phone company, and he wanted to buy a house. So here we are. Almost ten years later."

It was the most innocent remark, but it suddenly hit me.

"My dad worked for the phone company." The wheels were turning. "Patrick Flynn. Maybe they know each other."

"Probably. Jim, that's my husband's name. Jim Di Napoli."

Brian was making plans to take Kevin out for a drive this weekend. "That would be great," Kevin said. "I get kind of cooped up in here with the TV on all day."

"Oh, I don't watch it all day," Mrs. D. said, fingers picking at her sweater. "Just my stories."

I imagined Kevin rolling himself from room to room to get away from those agonizing afternoon dramas. My mother had stopped watching them now that she was working.

I sort of wanted to get out of there. I knew this house—or maybe I should say Himself knew this house. This is where he took me that day after rehearsal and I had to remember this address for him. The time I asked one too many questions and he hit me. I couldn't ask Mrs. D. if her property or car had been vandalized. But I bet that's what happened. My father the punk. Vinnie Sorrentino had nothing on Patrick Flynn.

I finished the coffee, the cup steady in my hand, and put it on the end table. Somehow I'd gotten hold of myself. The shock of seeing Kevin had worn off. He and Brian were finishing up their conversation. Brian made everything steady and smooth, for Mrs. D. and Kevin and me. My father walked into a room and you held your breath. With Brian it was the opposite. I could see that he would forget the play too, and devote his time to taking care of his friend.

I was glad when Brian started saying his goodbyes: I wanted to go outside and have a look around. I stood up and put on my coat, shaking Kevin's hand one more time. While I walked down the stoop, I saw the public school Himself drove past on our first visit to this neighborhood. This was definitely the house. I should have stopped him. Gotten out of the car and taken whatever implement he was carrying out of his hand. I had to make it up to the Di Napolis somehow.

"You handled yourself well in there," Brian said, patting my knee in the car. "Once you got your bearings."

I thought of the night I helped Mom fix Himself up on the bathroom floor. I could handle an emergency. I smiled and leaned against the door. The sky was a sharp darkening blue. "You know, if you ever need help, with your friend, taking him around or stuff, I can help you."

We were driving on Sixtieth Street, toward Eighteenth Avenue. "That's very thoughtful, but you don't have to do it," he said.

"I can do something, Brian. You've done a lot for me. You're like the only guy who ever gave me any encouragement. And you got me out of the house and that was good. 'Cause now I'm not going back in."

EIGHTEEN

Two weeks had passed since the play shuttered and I was stuck in the house, actively moping. I dialed Larry's number from the pay phone in the gas station on Snyder Avenue. He was back at St. Thomas Aquinas, playing the organ. They paid him thirty dollars each time, plus the tips he got when he did a wedding. It sounded like a fortune to me.

I hated making calls from the gas station. I dreaded the moment when the line would be interrupted and my location would be exposed by that nasal recorded voice: *Please deposit five cents for the next five minutes.* I didn't want to have to tell the story of why I was using a pay phone. But it wasn't all about my pride. The booth smelled like cigarettes and piss. I had to keep the door open just to breathe.

The line rang several times before anyone picked up. It was Saturday morning, probably too early. Fortunately, Larry answered but he didn't have good news for me. "Sorry, sport. I have a wedding and two deads this weekend," he said.

"Deads" were his nickname for funerals. "One at ten. One at eleven. The wedding's at four. I'm just putting a little polish on my Thom McAns."

I was going to have to find another way to amuse myself. "Call me later and I'll see who's around," he said before hanging up.

Now what? I had no backup plan and when I got back in the house, Himself was up, watching *The Quiet Man* on TV. He watched that freaking movie every time it was on, but I was damned if I was going to watch John Wayne and Maureen O'Hara bicker for the umpteenth time and went up to my room. About half an hour later, there was a knock at my door and he leaned in.

"How about a drive?"

He'd never let me drive the Red Devil. I hadn't driven since Christmas, the night I safely brought everybody home. I asked if we could go out to the beach.

We switched places when we came off the Marine Parkway Bridge, right next to the old coast guard building, a brick and white shingle box across from Fort Tilden. If you drove west, you ended up in Breezy Point; if you drove east, you went to Uncle Tim's house. I adjusted the mirror and cruised down a windswept four-lane street, with the window cracked open. One day I wanted to drive the way Himself did, with my right hand on the wheel, left hanging down the front door. The epitome of nonchalance.

After a mile or two, we came upon the entrance to Breezy Point, a private community with a guardhouse, a small sturdy hut with a shingled roof. Nearly everyone who lived here was Irish, but the families didn't live here year-round; the homes, one story, modest, and crammed together, lined the "streets," cement paths named Gotham Walk, Jamaica Walk, and Kildare Walk. I drove up and down one of the few paved streets, looking at the homes with some vestiges of summer left behind—colored lanterns strung around an empty patio's slender iron fence—and one house that had Christmas lights in the bay window. At the end of each street boardwalks led way, way out to the beach. It was hard to believe we were still in New York City. I drove to the end of Rockaway Point Boulevard. The sky, a clear powder blue ringed with scalloped white clouds that never moved, was right on top of us. The sand was almost white, as if mixed with snow, and the ocean a flat, sleepy blue.

"So how do we get out of here?"

I needed a little help making a K-turn to go back down the avenue but after that I was fine. Himself asked to pull up in front of Kennedy's, on Jamaica Bay.

"Let's enjoy the view."

Kennedy's, as far as I knew, was mainly a bar. The older kids from St. Mike's told stories about hanging out there in the warm weather where they danced on the patio, made out with the girls from St. Brendan's, and drank until they threw up. But it also had a real restaurant. It couldn't have been open yet, so that meant we were going to the bar. Himself's time on the wagon was about to end. No way could he sit two, five, twenty feet away from a beer tap without asking a bartender to fill a glass and quench his thirst. The lifelong thirst.

I didn't want to go in. "What are we doing here?"

"We are going to look at the view," he said, door already open.

The bar was a vast improvement on the Dew Drop, and Versailles compared to the Mermaid. The walls were paneled in knotty pine with floor-to-ceiling windows on two sides and double doors that opened on a small patio facing the beach. Two miniature flags, green, white, and orange for Ireland, and the Stars and Stripes, listed from either side of a Budweiser clock on the wall behind the bar. We sat at a small table near the doors, Himself letting me have the bay view.

There didn't seem to be any waiters, just a bartender who was stacking glasses. He was a Paddy down to the shock of white hair, the runny blue eyes, and the brogue.

"What can I get you?" He was getting up to go to the bar, all smiles, back in his element.

What did I ever drink in a bar with him? "Ginger ale."

He came back with a soda and a pint of something amber in a frosted glass. He took the first sip before he even sat down, hooking his lip on the rim on the side of the glass with relief.

We had to sit back from the table so our legs didn't collide.

"They have cabanas here, don't they?" I said.

Himself nodded. "Your grandfather and grandmother used to rent one when I was a young lad."

Whenever I was near a beach, I thought of the summer. I knew this summer was going to be different. I'd be old enough to get my working papers and had stopped at the Baskin-Robbins going up on the corner of Church and Utica and filled out an application. The store was going to open in another month. If that didn't come through, I'd try to get a job out at the beach. I wasn't a good enough swimmer to be a lifeguard, but maybe I could be a cabana boy. What would I have to do—carry lots of canvas folding chairs and fetch old Irish ladies their cans of Bud?

"You think Uncle Tim would let me live in his house if I got a job at the beach this summer?"

Himself raised one eyebrow, but didn't answer. The scar on the bridge of his nose was healing nicely.

"You don't have to ask him," I said. "I will."

"Let's see if you get the job first."

I drank some of the ginger ale. It tasted flat; I bet very few people here ordered soft drinks, and it probably just sat around. "My friend Larry has a job." I told him about the organist gig at the church.

"Is he that guy I drove home that night? Big fellow."

I nodded.

"You know, just 'cause that play is over doesn't mean you can't see him or that other gal who was in the car."

I shrugged. "I see Larry in school every day, but Immaculata—"
I paused. "I mean, I can't call her. She can't call me."

He blushed. "Shame on me. Gotta get that phone turned
back on or your mother will kill me," he said with a chuckle. He
took another sip, one that left foam on his upper lip. He glanced
at the TV screen and wiped his mouth with the sleeve of his
jacket. There was an aftershave commercial on. He turned to me.
"You see the Martinucci girl? She got pretty banged up."

I'd knocked on Gina's door once. Maybe it was too soon because she wasn't really in the mood for company, but her mother
let me talk to her for a few minutes. Gina was reclining on a
gold plastic slipcovered couch in the living room, staring at the
television.

I felt like an idiot standing there. I asked her how she was
doing.

"Not great," Gina said, not really looking at me. Her hair,
short now like mine, was brushed back behind her ears and
bobby-pinned to the sides. Her left leg was in a full cast. It looked
like a plaster-of-paris monstrosity. Someone had done her the
kindness of painting her toenails a sunny peach color.

Her acoustic guitar was lying on the cushion next to her, as
if she tried playing it but lost interest after a few chords. "I'm
probably going to gain a hundred pounds sitting here for the next
eight weeks."

Himself had dropped me off at school the first Monday after
the fight, driving past the boarded-up window of McDonald's. He
was convinced there were going to be some repercussions. "The
school doesn't want those jigaboos from Tilden coming on school
property, looking for that guinea. What's his name? Sorrentino."

Vinnie wasn't coming back for a while, I'd told him.

More regulars were drifting into the bar for something to

tide them over till lunchtime. Himself had finished one beer and ordered another. I switched to Coke.

"Tell me again how your sister got mixed up in all this," he said, training the blue beams on me.

I sat up straight. He obviously wanted to have this discussion far from home, where Mom wouldn't tell him to give it a rest. "She was backstage with me during dress rehearsal. She wasn't there when the fight started. I told you. I was with Larry."

"So she was there on the sidelines after."

Our little driving lesson was turning into a cross-examination. I was fed up. "Nothing happened. We left. It was all over in fifteen minutes."

"You could have been followed."

I leaned in. "We can be followed anytime we walk down Church Avenue. People like us get mugged there all the time now. I told you: the restaurant was locked. The cops didn't let anyone out."

I stirred the ice cubes in my glass with a straw and waited for his comeback. A nasty smile crept across my father's face. "He's on his way out, you know."

"Who?"

"The director." He looked over at me. "The school's gonna pin it on him."

I was so naïve. "Brian had nothing to do with the fight. He wasn't even there."

"Doesn't matter. He and the other teacher, the Mafioso, they were supposed to know where everyone was. They're out."

"You don't know that."

"Let's see what happens at the end of the school year. I'll bet you fifty bucks."

I pushed the Coke away. "I don't want to talk about it anymore."

It was always going to be like this, until the day I left the house. Himself needling me or setting fires I had to put out. It was such a drag. I left him in the bar and strolled on the tiny beach. Across the bay, the sun shone down on the Coney Island boardwalk, the green circle of the Wonder Wheel, and the Parachute Jump. I sucked in the salt breeze and went back to the parking lot and the Red Devil, leaning on the hood. The headlight I'd kicked in had been fixed, without a word.

He came out of the bar smoking a cigarette, the collar of his jacket pulled up. He took the wheel for the drive home. I asked if we were going to pay a surprise visit to Uncle Tim over in Belle Harbor.

"Not today. I owe him money," he said, chuckling and leaning on the steering wheel as the Mercury entered the on ramp for the bridge.

It made me sad to be going back so soon. I could spend the entire day at the beach, even when it was chilly outside, but I didn't say anything as we passed the brown golf course and the deserted brick buildings and airplane hangars at Floyd Bennett Field. Eventually we stopped at a red light on Avenue U. Long lines of people were waiting to get on the buses pulling in front of Kings Plaza.

Then I decided to ask him a question that had been on the tip of my tongue for months. "Remember that book Uncle George gave you?"

He kept his eyes on the traffic. "Your uncle has given me lots of books. Son of a gun likes to read."

"The one he gave you the night he left for Germany."

Why was he playing dumb? He knew which book I was talking about. He sat back in the seat as we cruised past the Torregrossa funeral home and the Floridian diner with its dull chrome exterior. "What about it?"

My heart was beating wildly. "He gave you that book to help you. Did you ever open it?"

"That's between your uncle and me."

"What did you do when you went to the Di Napolis' house?"

"I never gave you that name."

"I got it from the operator," I lied. "I gave the address and they gave me the name. A James Di Napoli lives there. What did you do to him?"

We were driving on Brooklyn Avenue. The mailbox he'd knocked over with the Black Beauty on Christmas had been replaced. "Did you know his son was a Vietnam vet? He had his legs blown off. Did you know that?"

I expected to feel the crack of his hand across my face. But he kept driving. When he did say something, his voice was raspy and you could cut the sarcasm with a knife.

"Who told you that?"

"It doesn't matter. Just know that I know. And if you thought you were teaching that guy a lesson, believe me, whatever you broke or damaged can be replaced. But their son is in a wheelchair."

I turned away. He had to know how small he was in my eyes. My face was hot but inside I was chilled to the bone. I didn't care if I never had another driving lesson. And if he hit me again, I would tell Mom everything.

V.

THE PINK PANTHER

NINETEEN

My mother shook me awake. "C'mon, Nicky. Get up."
I struggled to open my eyes and when I did, the room was pitch-black. Her hand gripped my arm outside the blankets. She was wearing her car coat. What time was it? Where was she going? I couldn't see the digital radio behind her on my chest of drawers.

"What's the matter?"

Her voice trembled. "Your father's in Kings County."

I shot up in the bed. *He was in an accident*—that was the first thing that flew into my head. "What's wrong?"

"He was robbed." Then she burst into tears. "He was stabbed, Nicky. Oh my god."

My heart jumped and I felt my throat close up. I cradled Mom and stroked her back and she told me what happened. The cops had called Uncle Tim after the ambulance had brought my father to the emergency room because, of course, our phone wasn't working. She took a tissue out of her coat pocket and blew her nose. "Your uncle's downstairs. He's driving me to the hospital." She stood up and wobbled, as if she was going to faint. "Can you come downstairs?"

Queenie was at the bottom of the staircase, her tail wagging as if we were going to have an adventure, her small black

eyes alert. Uncle Tim was standing in the living room, in a short
jacket and jeans, ready to go. His face was ashen.

"Can I come?" I already knew the answer.

Mom touched my shoulder. "Stay here and watch your sisters."

This was nothing we could fix with a bottle of boric acid
and some cotton swabs. Uncle Tim put his arm around Mom's
shoulders and led her out the front door. I watched them walk to
Uncle Tim's car, parked across the street by the lamppost. The
sky was midnight blue with a stark waning moon. In the garden,
the first hyacinths, blue and white, were opening up. I felt myself
tearing up. It would be all right. At least he hadn't been shot.

I closed the door and stayed in the vestibule with the dog,
not knowing what to do next. It was Saturday morning; the
clock in the living room said four thirty. I was tempted to wake
one of my sisters to keep me company, but if I roused one, they'd
all be up. And freak out. As much as we wanted Himself to stop
it, or just go away, I never thought it was going to happen this
way. The car service job was supposed to get him out of the bars,
but it had only put him further in harm's way. He could not win.

The living room was conspicuously empty, the only sign of
Himself a half-filled handmade mosaic ashtray on the end table
next to his chair. I decided to wait in the rocking chair, but I
dragged it to the front porch, where it had been before the fire,
and wrapped myself in Mom's afghan. I gazed at the cars and the
stoops across the street till I drifted off.

Patty woke me sometime later, when the streets were fully
light. She was wearing a flannel nightgown with a yellow ribbon
around the collar.

She pushed her hair behind one ear. "Where's Ma?"

I sat up straight and told her. She turned away and burst into
tears. "I knew this would happen," she said. "I didn't know how,
but I knew."

I stood up and hugged her. She smelled like sleep. "Uncle Tim is with Mom at Kings County. We have to wait. I'm going to get dressed and walk the dog." I went up to my bedroom and put on a pair of pants.

It was one way to kill time, walking the dog up and down the length of Holy Cross, reading the names on the tombstones while Queenie did her business. It was a fine morning. The air made my eyes tear. Crocuses were blooming around some of the graves and many of the trees—soaring oaks and black maples—had budded. When I came back home, Maureen was at the stove, pouring pancake batter from a Tupperware mixing bowl into a frying pan. She looked up at me, teary-eyed but focused, her right hand gripping the spatula like a sword. Queenie jumped up on her, and she stroked the fur under her chin with her free hand. The batter was already bubbling up in the pan, and I reached over and turned down the gas. Suddenly, I was famished and sampled a discarded pancake on a plate on the dishwasher.

"Don't eat that. It's burnt," Maureen said.

I gobbled it down. "I don't care. I've been up for hours. Where's everybody?" The clock over the cabinets said 7:30 A.M.

"Getting dressed," she said, flipping over the pancake. It was the right shade of golden brown.

We were going to pretend it was a normal Saturday, as if Mom had already left for work and we were about to do our chores after breakfast.

"At least he wasn't shot," Maureen said, placing the cooked pancake on a stack of six that she was keeping warm under a pot cover.

I got out some plates and set the table. "So we have to look on the bright side?"

Breakfast was like a wake without a body. No one sat at the head of the table. Dee Dee and Mary Ellen looked truly bewil-

dered as Maureen set a plate of pancakes in front of them, like
they didn't know whether they should be eating because she had
cooked for them or crying because we hadn't heard anything yet.

Patty drowned her pancakes—three of them, more than the
rest of us—in syrup and dug in. "Maybe we should walk up to
the hospital. It's only three blocks away."

She was all of twelve years old. Very bold.

"Yeah, let's go," Dee Dee said.

"Mom told me to wait here, so we're waiting," I said. "Kings
County's a really nasty place."

"How do you know?" Maureen asked, a forkful of pancakes
held in midair. "Have you ever been there?"

"You read about the place all the time in the paper. They see
the worst of the worst."

"I don't want to go," Mary Ellen said.

"Neither do I." I was almost finished eating. I couldn't stop
anyone from going, but I was still going to try to talk them out of
it. Besides, Mom would have a fit if we showed up at the emergency room. "We could get there and they could already be on
their way home, while we are walking around looking for them."

"Yeah, but if they're there, we can sit with Mommy so she's
not by herself," Patty said.

"She's not by herself."

"You know what I mean."

"What about the dog?" I asked. "We can't just leave her here."

Maureen volunteered to stay with Queenie and Mary Ellen
while she did the laundry; three loads were waiting. "Patty really
wants to go, so take her," she told me.

I did the dishes and cleaned the stove in five minutes. Maureen went down into the basement to load the washing machine.
Patty, Dee Dee, and I put on our shoes and got our coats. We
all looked pretty scruffy. No one had combed their hair, and I

hadn't showered. Well, Kings County was no fashion show, so at least we wouldn't stick out.

The hospital was a ten-minute walk from our house. We crossed Linden Boulevard, Lenox Road, and then Clarkson Avenue, facing the fortress of hospital buildings, buildings named with a single letter, like *G* or *M*. Kings County's main building looked like it could hold off an army, a carnelian red-brick box with a sloping slate roof topped with a weather vane. Three cop cars were parked out front. A lone vendor sold hot coffee and pastries out of a portable silver cart. Across the street, a beaten-down diner and candy store looked defeated in the sunlight.

I turned to my sisters. "Are you really sure you want to do this?"

Patty's freckled face was resolute. "If we can't find her, we'll turn around and go home."

"Maybe I should go in first. In case it's really gross."

I'd never been in a hospital and braced myself for the worst. But when I went inside, I found a huge waiting room, already half-full, and all I saw was strung-out people, half-asleep in their coats, dressed in the shiny clothes they wore the night before. The room had a high ceiling and pale blue walls, and it was very warm with that old radiator heat that has a certain stale odor. I didn't see Mom or Uncle Tim, and I gave the nurse at the counter Dad's name. She directed me to admitting, which was down a corridor to the left. I went back outside for Patty and Dee Dee.

"He's been admitted."

This was good news, I told them, smiling, but they didn't look convinced. They wanted proof. So I took them down the corridor, skirting the edge of the ER waiting room and heading where I'd been directed. The smell of ammonia tickled my nostrils. We stepped aside for an orderly wheeling a gurney past us, accompanied by a pair of nurses.

A black kid with a bandaged head lay on it, under a snow-white sheet. I caught the horrified look on Dee Dee's face as she took it all in. We were distracted again by doctors, some in scrubs, others in white coats, striding in our direction and a young Indian nurse with a red dot painted on her forehead pushing an elderly woman in a wheelchair. A priest on crutches trailed after them. Patty and Dee Dee stuck close behind me as I searched feverishly for the admitting desk, hoping it would be around the next corner. And it was. The desk faced another lobby of seats. These had cushions, unlike the plastic bucket seats in the ER, and fewer people were waiting in them. I was feeling a little light-headed and thought if I were to sit down, I would conk out in two minutes.

The lady behind the desk was older than Mom, but maternal-looking, wearing a simple, striking navy suit. Her curly brown hair fell in her face as she looked up Dad's name.

"He's on the fourth floor," she said, smiling. She gave me the room number, and we went back to the elevator bank, this time without a crowd of hospital personnel.

"Stop rushing," Patty said, behind me. "Dee Dee can't keep up."

The elevator opened on the second floor for another patient on a gurney—this time, a fat, dark-skinned woman whose head lolled about on the sheet. She emitted a faint medicinal, stale odor. We backed against the elevator wall to make room for her team of nurses and orderlies and then squeezed past them when we got off. Room 423 was easy to find: the one with the cop outside the door. He was talking to Mom and Uncle Tim. Mom was holding her coat over her folded arms. Maybe they were getting ready to leave. I called her name and Dee Dee went running to her, hugging her from behind.

"Oh, Jesus," she said, jumping back, her shocked face taking a minute to register that this little girl at her waist was, in fact, her daughter.

She looked up at me. "Nicky, what are you doing here?"

I knew she wouldn't like it. Five minutes and we would go. "They made me." I sounded like an eight-year-old.

Patty stepped up, next to me. "Is Daddy okay?"

Uncle Tim came over, smiling, amused at our nerve. "Well, he's had a rough night, but they fixed him up and he'll be himself again in a few days." He squeezed the back of Patty's neck. Always the optimist. He yawned widely and said, "Excuse me."

A chunky nurse came out of the room and in a thick Jamaican accent said we could go in.

"I hear voices," Dad said from within. He sounded really groggy.

I smiled and poked Dee Dee in the ribs. "He hears voices."

The cop was watching us like we were suspects. Under his blue cap, he had very bushy black eyebrows and a dark, focused gaze. He towered over my uncle, but not me.

"These are my nieces and nephew," Uncle Tim explained. "Pat's kids."

The cop tried to smile, but it wasn't a natural reflex. He shook Uncle Tim's hand and sauntered down the hall, as if he were on a break from fighting crime that Saturday morning.

"Let me go in first," Mom said. Uncle Tim said he was going down the hall to use the pay phone. There were no lights on inside the room, and Dad appeared to have it to himself. Mom stood at the foot of the bed and said, "The kids are here. They wanted to make sure you were in one piece."

She waved us in. Dee Dee went first, holding Patty's hand. "Hi, Daddy," she said, standing next to Mom. I was the last to enter. He was a sight, prone in the bed with a huge bandage covering his chest. The bed was partially raised and his hair was sticking out all over the pillow, the way it did when he was stationed in front of the television on a Sunday afternoon watching football. Or baseball. An IV drip stood next to the bed, the bag three-quarters full, the tube tracing down to a spot above his wrist.

Patty went over and kissed him on the cheek. I shook the hand that wasn't hooked up to the drip. He could barely grip mine. "Hey, Dad," I said.

"No hugs today," he said. His eyes were half-open, the blazing blue dimmed. Maybe it was the room's semidarkness, maybe the pain medication dripping into his veins, but I half-expected him to pop out of the bed and start railing against the guy who pulled the knife and took his money. My memory of him striding across the Belt Parkway to pick up that kid who was thrown from his motorcycle seemed very, very far away. The patient in the Kings County Hospital bed was someone else: a man who'd had the life force knocked out of him. He would never be the same.

I got a good look at the bandage. It stretched from the left side of his body almost to his right armpit. My eyes started to film over. Who could have done this? I glanced at Mom, who was sitting in one of the room's two chairs and reaching for a cigarette in her pocketbook. She was still young, but the fatigue of worrying about Himself, getting him off the kitchen floor and up to bed, and now, keeping him alive, was beginning to show—in the bags under her eyes, in the bewildered expression she wore when she wasn't busy keeping the house running. She had it now. Staring at the bed and the man in it as if at an abyss.

I leaned against the window ledge, very dizzy now, and tried to steady myself. I cracked open the window for a little air. From this vantage point, I could see the homes on Winthrop Street and the main building of Wingate High School, white brick and circular; the track team was doing laps outdoors in sweatpants. I looked back at Dad, dozing, a hidden trail of stitches across his stomach and chest, and wondered what was next. Would the cops find the guy who did this—or would my father find him first? We all knew he wasn't going to let it rest.

Uncle Tim slipped into the room and said he was heading back to Rockaway, if anybody wanted a ride. I couldn't wait to get home and crawl into my bed for a while. I left with my sisters while Mom and Uncle Tim talked to Himself. I made it out to the hallway, but then the floor slipped out from underneath me. I reached out for the wall before I fainted.

TWENTY

H ello, the house!"
　　　The voice came booming from the bottom of the staircase.

It was still dark out, but I was already awake.

"Nicholas Flynn, get thine ass out of bed and bring your sisters with you."

I was still in bed when Maureen whispered from the hallway, "Didn't you hear him?"

This wasn't the usual morning shakedown, I knew. I got out of bed and found my slippers. Four tangled heads of hair bounced ahead of me down the staircase. Queenie was waiting for us at the bottom of the stairs, tail wagging, thinking it was time to play. Maureen patted the dog's head, but Queenie did not follow us into the kitchen. *Smart dog*, I thought.

Mom was at her usual station, leaning against the sink, smoking a cigarette, in her bathrobe and black wire rollers, cup of coffee on the counter. We filed into the kitchen, faces still pasty with sleep, lips glued together and blubbery. The yellow enamel of the kitchen cabinets was enough to make you queasy. The kitchen clock said 5:45.

Himself sat at the table, drinking a glass of grapefruit juice.

"Well," he said, a broad, sardonic smile breaking across his face, "good morning, everyone."

"Good morning, Daddy," Dee Dee said, trembling in her nightgown.

Nobody else said anything. I sat down across from him and tried to remember if me or one of my sisters had done something specifically wrong, but my mind was a blank.

Himself arched his eyebrows, his voice extra husky, spittle flecking the corners of his mouth. "And how is everybody this morning?"

"Fine," said Patty, more than a little ticked off.

"That's good," he said, dragging out the *os*. His eyelids were droopy. "Me, I'd have to say I'm a little tired."

He was without wheels these days. The Red Devil was stolen one night when he was shacked up at the Mermaid. Every time he came home now it took that much longer, by subway or bus. I looked over at Mom. She was biting her nails. "Pat, why don't you go up to bed?" she asked sharply.

"*Sios siogh*, for Pete's sake." It was the only Gaelic he knew. It meant: Sit down.

Then he brought out the gun.

He pulled the gun out of his shirt and rested it on the table, on the plastic flowered tablecloth. We froze in terror. He was going to shoot us. That's how this story was going to end. No one dared move.

"Jesus Christ," Mom said. "What the hell is that?"

"This here, Mrs. Flynn, is a .357 Magnum," he said, picking up the firearm. "It is for this family's protection. *My* family." He eyeballed us—always the challenge to see who could eyeball him back. If you cast your eyes down or looked somewhere else, he won because then he knew you were *hiding* something.

He caressed the trigger with his thumb. "The .357 Magnum,

this here is a powerful weapon." He held the gun in two hands and trained his eyes, no longer droopy, on us. "And by the way, it will most certainly kill you. Or anybody else who comes in this house and who doesn't belong in this house."

I stared at him, like he was a disturbed stranger in the middle of Church Avenue threatening passersby—not my father. I wanted to scream at him but knew I had to keep it together or God knows what else would happen. My sisters were not going to be able to take this and would start cracking. The last thing I could do was set him off.

"There are no bullets in this gun—yet," he said, as if he were threatening a group of hostages, not talking to his wife and children.

I didn't believe him, but then he flipped open the gun's chamber; mercifully, it was empty. Where were the bullets? In his pocket? Was he going to load them and pick us off, one by one? I thought my skull was going to split open with the pressure building inside.

He passed the gun across the table to me. I did what he wanted, picking up the weapon like it was a live snake. How heavy and smooth it was. My fingertip touched the trigger. The gunmetal gleamed in the overhead light. You could probably kill somebody just by cracking them over the head with it.

"Never point a gun at anybody unless you're prepared to use it," Himself said intimately, as if marksmanship was one of our after-school activities. "Do you feel how heavy it is?"

I swallowed and nodded.

"That's why it's important to have control of your weapon and not get sloppy. People who get sloppy—well, we know what happens to them." He nodded and sipped his juice. "Pass the gun to your sister."

"C'mon."

"C'mon, what? Pass it," he said.

I obeyed, handing the gun to Maureen, sitting on my left. I snuck a glance at Mom. Her bewildered face told me she didn't know where the gun had come from either. Maureen took the gun and put it down on the table, her hand shaking. She looked up with tears in her eyes.

Himself put the glass down. "What are we going for here, the Academy Award?" he said.

"I'm not touching it," she said, silent tears rolling down her cheeks.

"Pat, that's enough," Mom said, coming over to the table. "Goddammit, what's gotten into you? These kids have to get ready for school."

"Why are you always doing these things to us?" Maureen asked, sobbing now, her nose running, her face crabbed and red. "Why do you hate us so much?"

Himself paused, lips parted. I was afraid he was going to knock Maureen out of the chair.

"And where did you ever hear that?" he shouted, glaring at Mom, as if she'd been talking to us behind his back.

Maureen's voice was choked with sobs. "Then why did you bring that home?"

"Why did I bring it home?" he said, mocking her, his eyes huge and full of pain now, blood vessels stretched against his eyelids. He was talking to us like we were strangers, as if we hadn't seen him in the hospital, bandaged and on the IV. "Gee, I can't imagine why I brought it—" He suddenly shoved the table into my chest and lifted his shirt and undershirt to brandish the foot-long scar he had from his knife wound. It was ugly and red, with crude stitch marks in the hairy flesh. The scar ended just inches below his heart.

"Thirty stitches because of some dumb fucking nigger, and you want to know why I brought home a gun? Are you kidding me?"

The tears streamed down Maureen's face, then Dee Dee started bawling. I checked Patty and Mary Ellen. Patty was scowling at him, and Mary Ellen bit her lip, eyes welling.

"Stop it," I said.

"What did you say?"

"You have to stop it. You're upsetting everybody."

He slammed the table into my chest. "I'll clean your clock, young man," he said. Then he clutched his chest, knotted up with pain.

"Cut it out," Mom said, wiping Maureen's face with a tissue.

I'd never heard Mom talk back to him like that. He got up from the table. "Are you telling me how to talk to my children?"

She walked right up to him, nose-to-nose. "I said that's enough. They have to get ready for school."

He checked the clock. "Bullshit. It's only six thirty."

"I said *that's enough*." She was screaming. "Did you hear me?"

My head was splitting. I was sure Mrs. Garrett was in her kitchen catching every word of this. Maybe she would call the cops, the way she'd called the fire department.

He turned back to us kids. "Now understand this: if anybody does anything to hurt you or to hurt this family, you tell me and I'll take care of them. You just leave it alone and you come home and tell me. That's what this is for."

The cops hadn't found the guy who stabbed him, and he was going to try to finish the guy off himself. I saw it coming, the nights he sat in the wing chair after he came home from the hospital, glowering at the television and emptying one can after another of Budweiser—and then finally going out when that no longer did the trick.

I pushed the table off my chest and stood up. "You have really lost your mind now."

"Don't give me any back talk. If someone tries to hurt this family, they're going to try to do it here."

"And this is your solution?"

Mom told Mary Ellen and Dee Dee to go upstairs and get ready for school.

The rest of us were trapped, listening to him drone on. "You will not see the gun; you will not hear the gun discussed. The gun will be hidden, and if we're all lucky, you will not hear the gun, until such time as it is necessary to use it." He gave the gun to Mom. "Put this in the buffet drawer for now," he told her.

Mom flung him one final, violent look and took the Magnum out of the room. I heard her open the drawer in the buffet, where she kept assorted junk.

Himself turned to Maureen and said, "This was not done to upset you."

"Really? Well, it does." Maureen left the table and disappeared upstairs.

Mom came back into the kitchen with the ironing board, trying to get us back on course, ending the horror show before Himself rolled the final credits. She said quietly to Patty, "Do you want to start ironing your blouse?" She filled the iron with a cup of water. Patty went upstairs to get her blouse for the day.

Now I was left alone with Himself. I couldn't feign the excuse of having to get ready too: I wouldn't get near the bathroom for another twenty minutes. Well, I could try to eat breakfast. That would kill some time.

He watched me eating a bowl of Corn Flakes. "Who's using drugs in your school?" he said. I looked up at him, incredulous. Only Himself could top Himself. "Now, I am being very serious here. I want you to write down the names of the people in your school who are doing drugs. I have a friend who's a detective who will pull these varmints out of school and put them behind bars where they belong."

I didn't know what to say. He leaned in. I could smell the sour contents of his mouth. "I am not fucking with you, young man."

Twice in the last two weeks I'd patrolled the streets of Brooklyn, as my grandfather had done when Himself was a teenager, pulling him out of bars, even the worst dive of all: Shanahan's, where he disappeared for two days, and now he smelled like the back booth of that shithole.

I couldn't eat anymore. "I don't know."

"Anybody offers to sell you drugs, I don't care how easy it seems, I don't care how friendly they are, I want to know."

Patty came down with her blouse and gave me a fed-up look. Dee Dee came down in her bathrobe, carrying a terry-cloth towel, to wash her hair in the kitchen sink.

He finally left the kitchen, ducking under the cord of the iron after Patty had plugged it into the outlet.

"Ah, yes, the morning ablutions have begun. I'd better give my daughters the floor before they take over. Have a nice day," he said as he climbed the staircase with weary steps.

Patty and I waited to say anything until we heard the back bedroom door slam shut. Mom returned to the kitchen with the dog's leash in her hand.

"Ma, you better do something," Patty said. "He's a drunken lunatic and I am sick of being woken up at the crack of dawn."

The words shot out of her so articulately, like tiny spears, as if they had been on her lips for a long time.

"Sshhh," Mom said. "He's right upstairs."

Patty maneuvered the blouse from panel to panel on the ironing board as she continued to vent. "My teachers want to know why I look so tired. Maybe I'll tell them, 'Oh, Sister, my father woke us up early this morning because he wanted to show us how to use his new gun—'"

Mom slapped a dish towel at her side. She glared. "Did you hear what I said?"

Patty would not back down. "I don't care if he hears me. I'll tell him to his face. What the hell kind of house is this?"

"Ma, she's right. He's completely insane. Like where did he get the gun?"

Mom threw her arms up in the air. "How do I know? Do you think he tells me anything? Your father knows every gangster in Brooklyn."

Patty did not look up from the ironing board. "Yeah, well, what are you gonna say to the cops when he uses it on one of us one day? That you didn't know where he got it?"

Mom was livid. "That is enough. He is not going to use the gun, period. I will take care of the gun."

"Bathroom's free," Maureen called from upstairs.

"You have to get it out of the house," I said.

Mom gave us a desperate look. "Stop tormenting me. I told you I will take care of it." She looked up at the clock. "Jesus, will you look at the time? I have to get to work." She went into the dining room to get the clothes she had to iron. Patty stomped upstairs.

I watched Mom at the ironing board, getting on with the business of life. If she didn't work, we didn't eat. "Have you taken your shower yet?" she asked, without looking up. She began pressing her own blouse. "Well, I don't know what you're waiting for."

• • •

I was the first to escape. I was in school half an hour early and hid out in the library, combing the shelves for something to distract me, and came across *The Best American Plays*, an anthology with works I'd never heard of: *The Price, The Boys in the Band, Ceremonies in Dark Old Men*. The actors pictured were nobody I recognized from TV or the movies; their expressions were so serious, like they were all getting bad news and had to act fast, but I kept seeing that name in the text: Juilliard. The school Mary Zaleski wanted to go to. One minute I was reading the first act of *The Price*, the next someone was tapping me on the shoulder. The school librarian, Mrs. Reynolds. "The bell rang for first period. Didn't you hear it?"

I jumped out of my seat and stumbled out of the library. My first class was biology. It met down the hall; fortunately, I had my textbook with me. The teacher, Brother Crane, was about to shut the door and get started when I slipped in, ignoring my classmates as I sank into my seat, grateful to have something solid beneath me. I barely paid attention; it was a good thing we didn't have to dissect anything, and I prayed I would not get called on. And that's pretty much how the morning went, with me present in body only. All I could think about was the gun.

I met Larry on the cashier's line in the cafeteria. We hung out at school all the time, usually in the cafeteria, sometimes across the street in the playground; once or twice I was able to confide in him. One day in the playground across from St. Mike's, I told him how Himself was stabbed and ended up in the hospital. I watched his expression: he was shocked, concerned, but there was something else flickering behind his Clark Kent glasses, especially when I filled in the blanks with the story of the holdup. He looked at me warily, as if he didn't know what to do with the information.

So of course I didn't tell him about the gun and only half-listened as he told me about the weddings he played at this weekend. I was deciding to cut class, something I'd never done. The prospect filled me with anxiety. You were supposed to get a slip from the front office to leave the building. I knew Brian would cover for me.

"You're pretty quiet today," he said, as he polished off his French fries.

The lemonade I bought was a little watery. "I've felt weird all day. I think I'm coming down with something. If I don't show up, could you tell Brian I went home sick?"

"Sure. Is that all? You've been a veritable church mouse lately."

• • •

The television was on when I walked into the house. The door to the basement was open in the kitchen. Mom—or worse, Himself—was down there. I dumped my books on the dining room table and began looking for the gun. I first checked the buffet drawer, where he'd told her to put it. The drawer was full of meaningless envelopes, kerchiefs not worn in years, group photographs of Mom and Himself on a date with other couples at some weird club with palm trees. Everybody wore leis around their necks.

I heard footsteps coming up the basement steps—Mom, carrying a basket of wet laundry on one hip. She was home earlier than usual, but I wasn't going to ask why. She looked at me without smiling. It was too late to shut the drawer. I felt like I'd been caught with my hands in a safe. "You're home early," she said.

I closed the drawer and followed her into the kitchen. She lit a cigarette on the gas burner.

"My English teacher was sick. They didn't have a substitute." I paused. "Ma, what did you do with the gun?"

"Why do you care?"

"I want to know where it is. It's not here."

"Well, I wasn't going to leave it in the dining room where anybody could find it."

She carried the clothes out to the back porch, where she'd rigged up a clothesline with a long plastic rope. I squinted in the warm midafternoon sun. "So where did you put it?"

Mom hung a pair of Himself's gray work pants upside down. "I took care of it."

Her voice had an edge. I knew the tone: she was answering questions but the controlled tone and clipped phrasing implied that each question should be my last. I knew she wasn't going to tell me where the gun was, but I didn't trust her to get rid of it. She let Himself run roughshod all over us. I could check the vestibule coat closet later. Inside, there were deep shelves where Mom had once hidden a bottle of scotch we received as a Christmas present from somebody who didn't know how dangerous that kind of thing was around here. Maybe it was there.

Mom hung up some socks next—navy, black, and the yellow pair I'd given Himself for Christmas. Then she moved on to female underwear. She raised her eyes above the hanging wet laundry, looking for a second like a veiled woman from the Middle East. "I just woke your father up and I want to talk to him," she said. "I want to talk to him before your sisters come home, so if you wouldn't mind, I wonder if you could take the dog for a long walk somewhere, maybe around the cemetery. It's a nice day for that, right?" She turned to face me. "Do you think you could do that for me?"

Her expression said *I need you to do this*. I was still her soldier.

I went into the kitchen and got the dog's leash. Queenie heard it jangle and roused herself from the living room floor. I heard Himself turn on the shower upstairs. I wondered what they really said to each other in these private discussions, whether she laid down the law. She kept telling us she would take care of it, but I no longer believed her.

TWENTY-ONE

I had a dream that woke me up in the middle of the night the week after Himself brought home the gun. I was out riding my bike through the empty streets and I was being followed by a white convertible. I rode past the NBC studio on East Fourteenth Street and took a right on Elm Avenue, trying to get to Ocean Parkway. I rode against the traffic on the side streets to lose the car, but it always seemed to find me. The top was up, then the top came down, and when the car passed me at an intersection on Ocean Parkway, I couldn't see the driver's face, just his hands on the wheel. But I was sure who it was all the same.

The house was drawing round us, the walls coming together. During the week, my bedroom was my refuge and I stayed there, reading and doing my homework until it was time to walk the dog.

Come the weekend, I had to get out of the house. One of the last student dances of the year was happening at St. Mike's and I went. The cafeteria was an open cavern, its tables and chairs folded and stacked away in the corners. It didn't look like the place where I ate lunch every day. Purple and blue crepe paper hung from the ceiling. Posters of Jimi Hendrix and Jim Morrison and the Rolling Stones were taped to the walls. A platform set up in the middle of the room displayed a sparkly set of black drums, guitar stands, electric and acoustic guitars, and an electric keyboard, all waiting to be played.

Larry said he was coming to the dance before we left school on Friday. Now I couldn't wait for him to get here. Slowly, the room began to fill up. I nodded to one of two guys I knew, but I wasn't starting any conversations. I was just going to listen to the music. Rock hits mixed with oldies blared out of the giant black speakers in the back of the cafeteria. "Woodstock," "Instant Karma," "House of the Rising Sun," something insipid by Credence Clearwater Revival. One group of girls bobbed up and down with one another, impatient for the band to start playing. I was dressed down, just jeans and a denim shirt, but there were some squeaky-clean students in chinos and plaid shirts, and some of the Italian guys had gotten all dolled up in striped tight bell-bottoms and hip-huggers with white vinyl belts.

I told myself if I didn't like the dance, I didn't have to stay.

The guys in the band were coming out now, from behind a pair of silver doors that led to the kitchen—long-haired, lanky boys in jeans and faux-suede vests over button-down shirts. They called themselves Déjà Vu, after the hit album by Crosby, Stills, Nash & Young. They took their time getting started, tuning guitars, checking amps, and flashing smiles at their groupies, girls with long bushy hair whose loving gazes told me they would wait as long as it took to get their attention. It wasn't like when we were doing the play and the girls in the chorus moaned for me when Brian gave them the cue—their shiny-faced infatuation was real. I wondered if I would ever give off that kind of charisma again on stage.

The band kicked off its set with "Carry On," the one song I knew by heart from the *Déjà Vu* album. The girls up front jumped and quivered with short screams. The harmonies weren't anywhere near as good as the record, but the guitars, rigorous and rhythmic, made up for it. Moving in from the sidelines, I rocked back and forth on my feet with everyone else. This wasn't going to be so bad, as long as I didn't have to talk to anybody I didn't want to.

Somebody tapped me on the shoulder. Larry. Finally. I was so glad to see him.

He usually shook my hand, one of his old-man gestures, but instead I gave him a hug, nearly knocking his eyeglasses off his nose.

"Whoa. Hey there," he said, nodding at the stage. "Who are these hippies?"

"Crosby, Stills, Nash & Young, in their dreams."

Larry wasn't alone, but I couldn't believe whom he was with: the black girl who'd waited on us at McDonald's the day the fight broke out. Obviously, while I was dragging Himself out of bars, Larry had been sneaking across the street for more than his usual cheeseburger and fries.

I jabbed him in the ribs. "You've been holding out on me."

He touched the frame of his eyeglasses. "Nicky, you remember Rolonda."

She still had that smile that wowed us at the counter, the kind that would make you switch lines just so she could wait on you.

"Yes, I do. We'll never forget that day."

"No, we won't. Cops kept those doors locked for two hours."

Rolonda had to be the only black girl here, and I could see she was nervous. There were maybe three black guys total at St. Mike's, and I put my hand on her shoulder to convince her she would be all right.

I gestured to the room. "What do you think of our swanky accommodations?"

"Looks like my school." She had a slight accent, not quite Southern, and it was delightful to hear, especially when you thought about what most people in Brooklyn sounded like. Rolonda went to South Shore, in Canarsie, a neighborhood I didn't know at all.

"What do you think of the band?"

"It's like beach music, you know. Like when you go to Riis Park and all the girls have their radios. It's pretty good, I guess."

The first song ended and the band segued into "Get Back" and more people were dancing, guys and girls, and girls without dates, in clusters. I wasn't sure if Larry wanted me to get lost so he could take Rolonda out on the floor. I caught some of the girls near the front of the stage stealing glances at her, and I asked, "Aren't you guys going to get out there?"

Larry reached into his pants pocket and pulled out a ten-dollar bill. "Can I trust you to get us some drinks? And pick one up for yourself, sonny boy."

I snatched the bill out of his hand. "Only if I can have the next dance."

Rolonda waved goodbye as Larry led her deeper into the dancing couples. She wore tight jeans and a ribbed white turtleneck that accentuated her tiny waist. Most of the girls who hung around with the guys at St. Mike's dressed like boys, loose shirts and straight pants. Rolonda wasn't afraid to look sexy. I couldn't wait to dance with her, even if she was Larry's date.

The ten dollars covered three sodas. There was no alcohol served—even for the seniors, though they always tanked up before walking in the door. While I was waiting, somebody else found me.

"Nicky, I didn't see you come in."

It was Brian. He was standing two ahead of me in line, holding a yellow plastic cup. Smiling at me, but it was more a curious smile than a friendly one. The guy in front of me gave his order and stepped aside. I gave my order to the long-haired string bean behind the counter and looked down while he filled three red cups. Brian was off to the side, waiting for me. I couldn't sneak off if I'd tried. I grabbed the plastic soda cups—they were a little unwieldy—and hoped Larry would see me from the crowd to take his.

I had to walk past Brian. "What are you doing here?"

I must have sounded cocky because he was taken aback. "They recruited me. I'm what you call the faculty moderator."

"Like the chaperone?"

He laughed. "Gee, Nicky. That makes me feel like somebody's aunt." We moved away from the line, which snaked behind the refreshment table. He nodded at the dancers. "What a turnout."

I nodded, distracted, looking through the open blue doors of the cafeteria to the brightly lit school basement. The language lab, where I listened to French tapes, was directly across the hall. I hadn't spoken to him at school since the day I cut his class. He never asked me about it and I assumed there was no problem.

The band was playing something by the Stones. One of the girls from the play—I couldn't think of her name—approached. "Mr. Ventresca, would you dance with me?"

It was Carole Esterhaus, Gina's replacement as Rosie. Her tight-fitting yellow top just met the waistband of her jeans.

"I'm on duty, Carole, but I think I'm allowed one dance."

She pushed a strand of lank brown hair behind her ear and kissed me on the cheek. "Long time, no see."

"Hey, Nicky, make sure you find me before you go home," Brian said as he walked away with Carole. I looked for Larry and Rolonda in the crowd. They were way over by the windows. Larry's geeky flamboyance—arms and legs spazzing all over the place—made him easy to spot. That and his Revenge of the Bronx lavender shirt. Rolonda was going to need a real dancer on the next song—my cue to cut in.

I took a slug of flat ginger ale and raised the cups above my head as I moved through the throng. Larry reached for them and passed one to Rolonda.

"What dance were you doing just now? The telethon chicken?"

Rolonda laughed into the cup of soda and turned away. "Stop. It's going to come through my nose."

"Let's see you out there, Mr. James Brown," Larry said, wiping his forehead with the back of his hand.

"Give me the right song and I'll show you."

The lead guitarist, a wiry, handsome guy with a good tenor voice and an electric guitar strung casually across his chest as if to say "Me? I just play this," stopped the set to flash his great smile and say a few words to the crowd before the band took a break. The baby-faced drummer stroked the cymbals with his brush while he spoke. When the band disappeared, their groupies followed, curly heads bobbing through the silver doors, and the taped music resumed. This time, it was something I could dance to: "I Was Made to Love Her."

I handed Larry my soda cup and reached for Rolonda's hand. "This is more like it. Come on."

Rolonda passed her cup to Larry and followed me into the middle of the crowd. "Be back in a flash," she told him.

I was half the dancer that Rolonda was. Her shoulders and hips moved in a syncopated rhythm like she had the beat down. I tried to copy her moves instead of jumping around like an excited white boy. She knew what I was doing and winked at me. It was easier for me to dance with a girl who came with someone else than approach a stranger—even if that's what Rolonda really was. She complimented my dancing, which was all I needed to hear. I could leave when the song was over and the night would have been a success.

It was a Stevie Wonder double play. The song segued into

"Uptight," and then the entire floor was wall-to-wall bodies. I wondered if the guys in the band knew everybody was really rocking out to Motown when their imitation folk rock only brought half the crowd to its feet. The place was completely packed now. The back of Larry's loud shirt peeked through the mob, and I was glad he had found someone else to dance with.

"Wow, that was great," I said when the song ended. Rolonda was pulling out the collar of her turtleneck for some air. "If you see Larry, tell him I went to the ladies' room." She snaked through the crowd as "Sally Go 'Round the Roses" came through the speakers. In grammar school, when the classes were mixed, I got along better with the girls, or at least had more to talk about with them. How much could you actually say about the track team, which was all anybody at St. Mike's seemed to talk about? I was glad when the play came along, when I could hang out backstage between numbers and have something in common with most of the kids there. I wished Immaculata was here right then, even if she didn't strike me as the type who went to school dances.

"Sally Go 'Round the Roses" ended in the middle of the second verse and the band strolled back to the stage. I decided to take a walk. I drank about a gallon of water at the fountain outside the cafeteria and went down the hall to the bathroom. An Out of Order sign was taped to the door, so I went upstairs to the first-floor bathroom to splash some cold water on my face. A whiff of acrid-smelling smoke came in through an open window. I heard some voices outside and gruff, rumbling laughter. I took a leak and crept over to the window. Three guys were smoking a joint in the outdoor stairwell that led from the basement to the parking lot. One looked up and saw me. It was Vinnie Sorrentino.

"Well, if it isn't Conrad Birdie," he snickered. He had been back in school for a week, with a moustache, dark and bushy; he had the look of lurk all over his face. "You ever talk to Gina?" I didn't say anything. He held up the joint. "You want a hit? Or you gonna run and get the cops?"

I backed away from the window and heard them cackle. I almost asked what they were doing there. If Vinnie was hanging around, nothing good would come of it. My gut told me to go home.

I went back into the darkened room and looked for a bright lavender shirt, elbowing my way past the tangle of sweaty dancers as the band played a song I didn't recognize. I thought Larry might be in the back of the room, but I didn't see him. He was off in the corner, making out with Rolonda.

I stopped and looked away. Then I looked back at them. Her long arms, sheathed in the ribbed white fabric of the turtleneck, gripped the back of his purple shirt, and I felt washed out. And jealous. Damn him for having the balls to bring a black girl to the dance and kiss her like that.

I didn't know what to do next. The only other person I knew here from the play was Carole. Maybe she was dancing with people from the play or the girls from her high school. I went back into the jostling crowd of bodies and looked for a girl with a yellow shirt, but I didn't see her. I stopped by the bandstand and checked out the groupies. The same fan club clung to the sides of the stage. Were they all competing for the affections of the lead singer? Maybe that was the thing: learn to play the guitar, instead of faking it like I did in the play. I checked my watch. It was eleven thirty; these dances usually ended around midnight. If I left now, I'd have to wait awhile for the Church Avenue bus. I had never stood out on that corner, next to the gas station and the White Castle, at this time of night, but I imagined it would be completely desolate. I made up my mind to leave.

The cafeteria was starting to empty out and the dance debris was already in evidence: discarded plastic cups littered the floor, along with straws and gum wrappers. When I saw Brian out in the hallway, by the language lab, saying good night to a bunch of upperclassmen, I asked, "Do you have to stay and clean up this mess?"

He shook his head. "That chore belongs to the Student Activities Committee. I think they can handle it. So, I think I'm free to go. Can I give you a lift?"

The prospect of walking four long blocks in the dark to the bus stop did not thrill me. I said yes.

"Good. My car's right out front."

He led the way up the stairwell and past the rows of lockers and empty classrooms on the darkened first floor. Only the school lobby was illuminated and that's where we saw him: Vinnie Sorrentino, trailing in behind two upperclassmen I didn't know, guys with shag haircuts. Vinnie kept his head down but raised it long enough to shoot me an evil look. Brian intercepted him, putting a firm hand on his shoulder.

"Hey, Vinnie."

Vinnie looked up, blushing, glassy-eyed. The two older students stopped.

"How you doin'?"

Vinnie shrugged. He was in full Italian stallion gear: black bell-bottoms and a tight red muscle shirt. A thin gold chain peeked out from under a glossy bomber jacket. He looked over at his friends. Brian turned to them. "Fellas, why don't you go down and enjoy the dance."

They nodded and disappeared through the double doors to the hallway. Then Brian gave his full attention to Vinnie. "The dance is almost over. I know you want to go downstairs, but not tonight. You're on probation. You can't attend school activities. And I think you might be a little high."

I stepped back. I didn't want to see Vinnie's face as Brian escorted him out of the building. I didn't want to be here at all.

"C'mon, Mr. Ventresca. Five minutes, I swear. Ten. I just wanna say hi to my friends."

"You'll all see each other in class on Monday."

I moved to the exit and could see in the glass's reflection that Brian was steering Vinnie around, gently pointing him toward the door.

"I can't, Vin. Let's go."

Vinnie gave Brian this halfhearted shove, as if he knew he was no match for him. "So what, did your little boyfriend rat on me, tell you I was here?" Brian didn't say anything, but I turned around. "What are you lookin' at, faggot?" he said.

"I don't have to listen to this," I said.

I pushed through the double doors into the vestibule and then through another set of doors. Brian called my name, but I was going, going, gone, down the front steps and up the block. A strange kind of light shone down on the street, exposing things I wouldn't have normally been able to see: the chipped seesaws and interlocking boxes of the jungle gym in the playground across the street. I looked for the moon, but I couldn't find it. The sky was a spectacular indigo studded with shy, blinking stars. It was dead quiet. I was alone and I was free, free to slip back into that limbo between school and home, where nothing could touch me as long as I kept moving.

Then I heard Vinnie's voice, yelling, something garbled and obscene. God, he was such an ingrate. I wasn't getting involved. It would be like dealing with Himself, a junior version. If I was going to make it in this world I'd have to get better at eluding these steamroller guys with their anger, the problems they couldn't fix, and that constant urge to fight. I was no track star but if Vinnie was going to come after me, I'd run, all the way to

Church Avenue. I didn't care if he thought I was queer or weak or anything. I just wanted to get away from him.

I decided to get a head start, trotting across the intersection at Clarendon Road and down the next block. Soon I was walking next to the high brick wall that surrounded the Tilden football field. A car engine idled behind me. For one crazy second, I thought: the white convertible from my dream. I turned, expecting to see it. Instead, there was Brian waving at me through the windshield of his car.

He pulled over as I was crossing Tilden Avenue. "Come on, get in," he said through the rolled-down window. "I sent that clown home."

I bent down and looked at him. "What was that? It's not my fault he got thrown out of school."

"I know. It's okay."

I put my hands on the window frame. "What do you want from me?"

Brian looked through the windshield. "I just wanted to make sure you're okay."

"I'm not okay. Okay? I just wanted to get out of my crazy house and have a good time. Things are not right and maybe I wanted to have a good time. And if this is about last Tuesday, I'll tell you why I cut class. My father came home with a gun that morning and I had to go home and find it."

I turned away from the car and looked up the street. A light came on in the front room of one of the darkened houses. I waited to hear someone open the door to see who was making this racket.

Brian got out of the car and came around to my side. "Nicky, come on. Get in the car."

The interior of the car had an old, oily, metallic smell. I nestled into the groove between the door and the back of the seat.

Sweat ran down my neck. The door on the driver's side creaked as Brian got in and sat behind the wheel. "Where are we going? You haven't told me."

"Right. Sorry. You can take Tilden." I pointed out his window. "I live over in Flatbush. Or East Flatbush as they're calling it these days."

"East Flatbush," Brian mused. "I don't think I've ever been over there."

"You're not missing much."

The engine coughed as he pulled out.

"This car's seen better days," Brian said. We were driving east, past this tiny playground, the kind that still had aluminum baby swings. I directed him to Schenectady Avenue, where we came upon the mute granite expanse of Holy Cross Cemetery. Brian had never seen it.

"This is where my father taught me to drive," I said.

I remembered that first trembling day behind the wheel of the Black Beauty on that green spring afternoon—the last time Himself and I sat side by side without conflict—and now where were we, sitting across from each other at a kitchen table with a gun between us. And that's when the whole story came spilling out, the days and nights that led up to the morning he brought home the .357 Magnum.

"My father lost his job earlier this year. He's an alcoholic," I said. My face was hot with shame, and I was fighting back tears. I tried to collect myself but it was no use. "He disappears. He comes back. He gets into a fight. We fix him up in the bathroom with boric acid and cotton swabs. Then he gets stabbed. And then they sew him up at Kings County. It just never ends. He wakes everybody up at five in the morning to yell at us. He checks our arms for needle marks. Everybody's afraid of him," I said with a loud gasp. "Even my mother."

I covered my mouth, as if Himself was sitting in the back-seat. There would be no absolution for this confession, just penance. It was the kind of confidence that could get me killed.

"He probably thinks he's protecting you guys," Brian said. "But he sounds like he's gone over the edge."

"That's one way of putting it," I said.

"Is the gun still in the house?"

"I can't find it. I've looked everywhere. My mother said she would"— I made quotation marks in the air—"take care of it."

"Is there anyone you can tell? Someone who can get through to him?"

I thought of Uncle Tim. If I dragged him into it, Himself would really have a fit. I could call my grandfather in Florida. Then I would get crucified. Maybe it was a chance I would have to take. I wiped my wet fingers on my jeans. "I can't go home like this."

"I suppose people have talked to him about AA?"

I told him about Uncle George and the Big Book. "That was a waste of time."

I told Brian to turn left at the next light. After we passed Albany Avenue and the field of graves reappeared, he said, "This cemetery goes on forever, doesn't it?" I looked ahead at the midnight strip of Snyder Avenue, the distant traffic light turning yellow.

"I apologize for lying to you. It was a really bad day."

"You don't have to apologize. You've got a lot on your shoulders, Nicky. Everyone needs someone to talk to. He wasn't always like this, I bet."

"No."

"That day I saw you by Brooklyn College, he was teaching you how to drive. That was pretty nice of him."

"Yeah." I nodded to the cemetery outside Brian's window.

"I aced parallel parking on the first try." There were two sides of Himself: the fearless man who walked across the highway to rescue the guy who had the motorcycle accident, and the sneak who got even with his elected enemies. That was the father I was living with now.

"I can talk to somebody about this if you want me to."

"Like who?"

"The Department of Social Services. They deal with troubled families all the time."

That's where we got our food stamps. I shook my head. "You can, if you want to see me in the grave. I shouldn't even have told you."

We were almost home. I wished I didn't have to get out of the car. "This is my street," I said, rolling down the window. "You can pull over here."

Brian sounded incredulous. "C'mon, Nicky. I can drop you off at your house. I don't have to leave you on the corner like this."

He turned left and went slowly down the block. Before I got out of the car, he reached into the backseat and wrote his phone number on a piece of paper. I tucked it into my back pocket.

"Call me if you want to talk. Anytime."

I nodded. I already had the door open. Then he reached out and hugged me. It was so unexpected that at first I tensed up, as if it was some kind of threat. He smelled like aftershave, something with a lime scent.

He looked me directly in the eye and I was startled by the intensity of his gaze. "Be careful, Nicky."

TWENTY-TWO

Some guy named Morty Rifkin called my mother at the bank two days later. He wanted to see me about a job at Baskin-Robbins. It had been a while since I filled out the application, writing Mom's work number and extension in the box for our telephone number. I went over to the store, on Church and Utica. Morty was the manager. He interviewed me in the back room, behind the counter. I wasn't quite sixteen, didn't have my working papers, but he didn't seem to care.

"I think you can learn to make a malted," he said, shaking my hand. His voice was thick and deep; when he spoke, vowels died. He wore a black polyester shirt and hip-huggers, the kind they sold at Benhil, with a couple of gold chains draped around his neck for good measure. Except for his "I am the walrus" moustache, he looked like Neil Diamond, with wavy, almost kinky brown hair, parted on the side.

Himself didn't want me working there but I took the job anyway. Not to spite him, although he didn't see it that way. "I can't let you work in jigaboo country, Nicky," he said at breakfast one morning while perusing the sports pages of the *Daily News*. He did not raise his voice. "It would behoove you to ask your boss for a transfer."

I chewed the rest of the Total cereal in my mouth and swallowed. As long as he was kind of sober, I tried to reason with him. "I can't. I just started. It's okay up there. Nothing's going to happen."

Patty and Dee Dee were finishing up their bowls of Lucky Charms. Like everybody else in the family, they were all for it. Who wouldn't be? It was free ice cream. Dad put out his cigarette and closed the paper. "Don't try to fight me on this one. You will not win."

"It's not as bad as you think."

I rode the bus past Utica Avenue every day and knew that wasn't true. The slide was well under way. The Rugby Theatre, where I had last seen *Wait Until Dark* with Audrey Hepburn, was now showing porn, things like *Tower of Screaming Virgins*. A few remnants of the neighborhood from my grammar school days hung on: a kosher deli, Nettie Post's costume jewelry, and Roma Furniture, an emporium of crazy, massive cut-glass chandeliers and ceramic collies standing three feet high. But I didn't care if the place was going down the drain. I wanted the money. I wanted a reason to say I might not be home. Mom had her job. And now I had mine. My way out.

This was my schedule: Friday nights, one day on the weekend, and two days after school. I wasn't going to get rich—I made $1.60 an hour, minimum wage—but it would help me save enough money to get the phone turned back on. I was tired of being cut off from the world.

In my first week at the job, I learned the ice cream business. The store was shaped like a rectangle, with a long plate-glass window facing Utica Avenue and a vertical window facing Church. Inside, the space was divided by a chrome counter and a freezer to hold the trademark thirty-one flavors. The cardboard tubs holding the big sellers were always half-empty while the obscure, this-must-be-a-joke flavors, like Pink Bubblegum, which had chunks of Bazooka in it, sat untouched. A black guy named Delmar from Lenox Road taught me how to make milk shakes, malts, and sundaes. Those supplies were kept on another counter that ran along the back wall. Delmar was a senior at Tilden with a friendly manner and a big Afro that did not fit under the pink and white hat we were all supposed to wear while scooping. Morty made him prune it.

My sisters were forbidden to come to the store but that didn't stop Maureen, who showed up after school with her friend Kathy Fitzgerald, and these guys she knew from Linden Boulevard. Boppo drove them to the store in an old Buick, but he didn't look old enough to have a license. With his Coke-bottle glasses, he didn't look like he could see past the windshield.

Maureen gave my work uniform the once-over. "Do you go out in public like that?"

As costumes went, this one—a white apron and a white zip-up shirt with the company logo on the left breast—was several notches below the gold lamé jumpsuit she sewed for *Birdie*. "I change in the store. You think I walk down Church Avenue like this? I'd be dead." I leaned in. "Let's make this fast because you're not supposed to be here."

Larry came on a Friday after school. He'd slimmed down since he'd started going out with Rolonda, shedding about fifteen pounds, mostly from his gut, but today he wanted a double-scoop Dutch chocolate cone. He'd just passed his road test and he wanted to celebrate. As a reward, his old man was going to "give" him his old Plymouth to tool around with this summer.

"Jones Beach, my friend," he said. He put his mouth on the ice cream scoop so lovingly I could tell he'd been dreaming about it on the walk over from St. Mike's.

We walked up and down Utica Avenue on my break. Shopkeepers were pulling the store gates down—everyone was usually gone by six P.M. but some left an hour earlier—and people, mostly black, were heading home with paper bags of groceries and plastic bags from the local pharmacy. Larry wanted to check out the Rugby Theatre. "*Pamela, You Are Many Times a Woman*," he said, reading the marquee as we crossed the street. "Now in its eighteenth week." He looked over his shoulder and smiled at me. "What do you think? Must be good."

I smiled. "Let's see what the flesh peddlers have to offer," he said, striding past the beady-eyed ghoul at the box office to check out the posters in the windows, licking his cone, and motioned for me to join him. The movie poster showed a naked blonde with heavy black eyeliner and pendulous breasts. Her red nails covered her crotch and her mouth was partly open. Black stars covered her nipples.

"What a bod," he said.

"If I'd known you were going to drool, I would have given you extra napkins."

A rank smell of air-conditioning and unidentified filth wafted out of the lobby.

"Man, I bet it wouldn't be too hard to sneak in," Larry said.

The magic-markered sign in the box-office window said No One Under 18 Admitted. "Well, if you can convince that creep you're eighteen, I guess Pamela is all yours."

"You're just chicken," he said.

"Anytime you want to go to the Astor Theater, let me know." It wasn't a porn palace like this place but a real movie theater on Flatbush Avenue where they showed European "art" movies. One of the actresses was guaranteed to be naked, like Olivia Hussey in *Romeo and Juliet*. "Besides, I'm on a fifteen-minute break," I reminded him. "Besides, you have a girlfriend now. She's got a hot body."

Larry shot me a look. "Thanks for noticing." I blushed and

he dug his hands into his pockets. "Don't get me wrong. Rolonda is fun. But she is a good girl. I go to church to make money. She goes to church to go to church."

I laughed, sure he was exaggerating. Larry and Rolonda hadn't been going out that long. I didn't know what he should expect. I also hadn't known he was that horny. Larry didn't talk about getting laid all day long like some of the guys at school. I didn't have a comeback to his remark. I also didn't have a girl-friend. Larry asked me if there were any prospects at the ice cream emporium.

"All the people on my shifts are guys," I said. That was about to change.

We parted at the corner of Church and Utica. I wasn't ex-pecting any more visitors but as soon as it got dark, I looked up from the counter and saw the Pink Panther parked outside, behind the bus stop, like a sentinel. It was the latest car, a 1956 Ford Fairlane convertible. Himself called it "Puerto Rican pink," a dusky salmon with a cream-colored upper body and trunk. The hood was also pink, as were the fender skirts and the Continen-tal kit. Naturally, the car had a portable record player under the dashboard radio.

When I went outside to offer Himself a cone, the car was gone.

He came back later, parked this time on Church Avenue. The crowd had dispersed, and I told Delmar I was going outside for a few minutes. The evenings were warming up, with that fa-miliar trace of humidity that hinted of summer, complete with trash in the gutters, but you still had to wear a jacket. I knocked on the window of the car.

"Hey, Dad, can I get you anything?"

He was listening to the Mets game on the radio. Someone had hit a grand slam and Dad was slapping the dashboard. I waited until the commotion was over. "So, what brings you over this way?"

"Just making sure things are the way they're supposed to be."

I wondered how long he'd been patrolling the joint. "Everything's fine," I said, trying to smile. I was chilled in my skimpy company shirt. "You want to come in and I'll make you up something?"

He checked his watch. "You got anything like Vanilla Fudge in there?"

I brought out a double-scoop cup with chocolate sprinkles. "I figured a cone would be too messy with the steering wheel and all."

I didn't know where he was driving from or to; it seemed that he was just out. Maybe he was trying to stay out of the bars. Maybe that's what all this driving was about.

He stuck the cup on the dashboard. "Okay. I'm going to go. Maybe I'll stop back. Give you a ride home."

He didn't come back that night or for several nights after that, and I assumed the surveillance test was over, that he had proof I wouldn't get killed scooping ice cream.

One Friday night, I reported for duty and found Morty behind the counter with a girl. "I'm adding more staff," he said. "This is Valerie. I trained her this afternoon. She knows ice cream."

Valerie shook my hand and said, "Is this a great job or what?"

"Yeah, I'm having a blast," I said, looking down at my right hand. She had a good grip.

Valerie's last name was Conway. I always liked tall girls. She was five-eight and slim with bright, almond-shaped blue eyes and a thin mouth that conveyed impatience. She wore her long, light brown hair in a ponytail. As it turned out, she was all business when Morty was around, brisk and efficient, but the first to turn up the store radio when he was gone and a good song came on.

"Smokey Robinson, 'Tears of a Clown.' C'mon, Nicky, let's dance."

She took my hand and we did a few steps in the narrow aisle between the counters. Our dance lasted almost as long as the song, but someone came in for a milk shake. And then we were slammed all night. I didn't know if she had a boyfriend. All I knew was that when we weren't working the same shift and there were no customers, the time really dragged.

We became friends quickly, but not more than that until later that summer, after Himself left. For the first time in a long time I felt I could breathe. I knew we were going to end up going out, though, because I hung on her every word. One day, when Morty was out of earshot, she leaned over to me and said, "And how about this uniform? I can't believe I had to buy this."

The girls who worked at Baskin-Robbins had to wear a pink jumper that looked, Valerie said, like a Catholic schoolgirl's gym uniform. Only a girl who went to a Catholic high school would even think that. Valerie was a junior at Bishop McDonnell, and she lived on East Seventeenth Street, a mile away from me, in Holy Innocents' parish. In fact, she lived right across the street from the rectory.

"That sounds scary," I said. Priests made me nervous. I always used to see Father Byrne walking by himself on Church Avenue, looking a little stewed, his hand over his heart, where he held, no doubt, the Blessed Sacrament to bring to someone needing Extreme Unction.

"Tell me about it," she said. "We're always having priests over for dinner." I raised my eyebrows. Not even the Martinuccis did that. I asked Valerie if she knew Gina.

"Isn't she the one who plays guitar at those masses they make us go to? The nuns just love her."

I suppressed a smile. Gina would have that folk mass label attached to her for the rest of her life.

Even though she started working at the store after I did, Valerie was much better at dealing with the customers. I had been talking to them in polite, complete sentences until she took me aside and said, "They're lookin' at you like you're nuts. This is the jungle, not the perfume counter at Macy's."

She called the neighborhood "the jungle" the same way Himself did, but I didn't bristle when she said it. So when some black guy with a low-rise Afro came in and said, "Hey, man, let me get a Pralines 'n Cream," I said, "Cone or cup?"

"Not you," he said, sliding his hands deep into his pockets. "I want her to get it."

I had been through this before with Valerie. A lot of the black guys who came in only wanted her to fill their orders. They knew her by name. Some campaigned to come back at closing time and drive her home. One Friday night, a cluster of guys came in, standing on her side of the counter. It was about an hour before closing time, and we were waiting for Morty to swing by. As she filled their orders—Blueberry Cheesecake, Rocky Road—the two guys at the front of the line slowly ground their pelvises against the counter. I stared at them, amazed. Valerie bent her head over the tubs in the freezer, beet red, strands of hair falling out of her ponytail.

I stepped over. "Let me help the next person here."

There were about five guys in all, average height and above. The third in line said in an overly polite tone, "We're waiting for the white, I mean, the young lady to wait on us." He was wearing a bright yellow sweatshirt and jeans. His buddies snickered behind him.

Valerie handed cones to the first two customers. The guy in the sweatshirt wanted a milk shake, so Valerie filled up a silver malt cup with chocolate ice cream at the back counter. The next guy in line stepped up, and I leaned in. "What can I get you?" I asked.

"If I wanted you to wait on me, don't you think I'd be on your line?" He was short with a close-cropped haircut, and he wore a shiny black vinyl jacket with the word HAWKS printed in yellow on the back.

I assumed HAWKS was short for Tomahawks, the Brooklyn gang. The jacket was a couple of sizes too large for him, especially in the sleeves, which he kept pushing up, above his elbows. I had a bad feeling about these guys and wondered when Morty was coming back. "There are two of us, but only one line."

He ordered a cup of Jamoca Almond Fudge with sprinkles.

The whirring sound of the malted machine drowned out whatever remarks the guys were making. I dug the scooper into the brown swirled tub then tossed a few teaspoons of sprinkles on the ice cream at the toppings bar. The kid in the Tomahawks jacket threw some singles on the counter. While I made his change, Valerie served her customer his chocolate milk shake. She handed it to the kid too soon, because he couldn't pay for it. He made a big show of looking in his pockets, pulling them inside out to show they were empty.

"Must've left my wallet home," he said, winking and wrapping his lips around the straw sticking out of the cup.

Valerie crossed her arms. "Why did you order something if you had no money?"

The kid broke into a sneering grin. "I was kinda hoping you were gonna give it to me for free."

Valerie lay down her scooper and addressed the group. "Okay. Who's paying for this?" Her cheeks were flushed. "'Cause I'm not."

The guy in the Tomahawks jacket turned to one of his buddies. "What she say?" Valerie nodded to the last guy in line. He was huskier than the others, with wild, woolly hair and glasses.

"I'm not waiting on any of you until someone pays for that shake."

The kid with the Tomahawks jacket was licking his cone and talking to his friends when I put his change on the counter. The husky guy stood with his hands on his hips. He showed Valerie a five-dollar bill from his pocket. "I got money."

I asked, "Are you paying for the milk shake?"

"No. Why should I pay for him?"

"One of you has to. You're all together."

He turned to his friend. "Fool, why'd you come out the house without any money?"

The boy in the yellow sweatshirt shrugged.

"If I had known that, I would have made you get in line behind me. So I don't get no ice cream? That is fucked up."

Valerie looked him in the eye. "You guys have been jerking me around since you came in and now you're going to talk to me like that? Why don't you just take your ice cream and leave?"

I was in love. This girl had balls.

A swelling chorus of jeers and snickering rose up. The guy in the Tomahawks jacket came up to the counter and paid for the shake. He poked the husky guy in the soft flesh around his ribs. "Now get your cone, so we can get the fuck out of here."

I stepped up. "What can I get you?"

The guy shook his head. "Not you. I came here 'cause I want her to do it."

"I think she's had enough for one night."

Valerie stood beside me. "It's okay, Nicky." She stared the guy down. "Make it fast. What flavor?"

He glanced at the board on the wall behind us. "Let me see. The only flavor I think of when I look at you is Cherry Vanilla," he said, cracking himself up.

"You want that with hot fudge?" Valerie shot back.

"You can give it to me any way you want, mama, as long as you give it to me."

I heard the door swing open. I was hoping it was Morty—it was almost closing time—but instead Himself was standing there, in the center of the room. He had that watchdog face: he was looking for a fight. Now the shit was really going to hit the fan and I couldn't do a thing to stop it.

He sauntered over to the group. Valerie stood stock-still.

He started with the kid who ordered the milk shake. "Hey, pal, you have your ice cream?"

The boy nodded. "And did you pay for it?" Before the kid could say anything, Himself pointed to the door and said, "Then get in the wind."

He turned his blue glare on the rest of them. He must have seen the whole thing, but from a hiding place. "You would all be well advised to hit the road with your friend."

"For real?" The guy with the Tomahawks jacket laughed.

Dad's hand was resting on his pocket.

"For real." Then, it was out, out of the pocket and at his side.

The guy in the yellow sweatshirt was the first to speak. "Holy shit. Motherfucker got a gun." Then he was out the door.

So much for Mom getting rid of it. Valerie ducked behind the counter.

He raised the Magnum, pointed it at the ceiling, and fired one shot. I covered my ears and watched a small avalanche of plaster tumble to the floor. The blowback made him stagger backward. He wiped plaster dust from his face.

I slapped my hand on the counter, exasperated. "What the hell are you doing?" I almost called him Dad in front of everyone. "You can't bring that in here."

He was admiring the breadth of the gash in the ceiling. Valerie's fan club made for the front door. "Damn, trying to get a cone, not get shot," said the last one to leave.

Himself waved the gun. "Keep walking, scumbag."

I had to get him out of here. What if one of these kids came back with his own gun? Valerie looked up at me from behind the counter, bewildered.

Finally I said, "Dad, what the hell are you doing?"

"Doing what I do."

"You could have killed somebody. We had it under control. They were about to leave."

He lay the gun flat on the glass, barrel pointed outward, and flung me a look. He wasn't even drunk. "Mr. Flynn, you are full of soup."

"Someone's gonna call the cops."

He clapped his left hand behind his head and his right arm shot out straight in front of him. "Feed 'em cheese."

This gesture of defiance took me by surprise. His fuck-you to the world. I was dumbfounded.

"Nicky, I've been watching this place almost every Friday night since you started, and I've seen maybe four cop cars drive by."

I didn't believe him, but now was not the time to rile him. Valerie broke the tension. She stood up and poked me. "This is your *father*? Introduce me to my hero."

Hero? So that's what girls wanted: A man I would come to think of as Brooklyn's Clint Eastwood barging in with a .357 Magnum to pick people off. My voice stammered as I did the honors. Dad leaned on the counter heavily, a mischievous gleam in his eye.

"Young lady," he said, "does your mother know you are working in this godforsaken place?"

"Please," Valerie said, with a wave of her hand. "She gave up on me a long time ago."

"Some of us are still trying," Himself replied with a wink at me. He put the gun back in his pocket.

If he wasn't drunk, then what was up with him? I wondered.

"You know, there are assholes in every crowd," Valerie said. "I don't scare that easily."

Valerie's nonchalance was making it harder for me to stay mad at him. I was relieved he had chased those guys away, even if he was a madman. I didn't know what I would have done if they'd kept it up. But I had to get him out of here.

"Let me fix you up, before Morty gets back," Valerie said brightly. "After that I can only give you a cone and I have to pay for it. How about a banana split?"

"Actually, I thought I would bring home a little pint for the missus."

I stared at him. The missus? By now, the missus was probably sleeping on the couch; now that she was supporting the family, the missus worked six days a week and had to get up early tomorrow to go to work.

"Make it two pints," Valerie said. "I'll throw in the second one for free."

I couldn't figure out why she was so eager to please him. She had to see that I wanted him gone. He ordered one pint of Pistachio, another of Butter Pecan. Valerie put the pints in one of those pink-and-white Baskin-Robbins paper bags. I told Valerie to lock the door until Morty got here and walked Himself out of the store, the first time I'd been outside since my shift started. The night air, scented with something floral and the exhaust from a passing bus, was strangely refreshing; anything to get away from the smell of sugar. The Pink Panther was parked on Church Avenue, nearly a block away, between two newer cars, more of a throwback than ever, like someone spliced it from an old, deckle-edged photograph.

The street was smoky in a glow of headlights from the cars filling up both lanes. A B-35 bus roared past us to beat the light on Utica. I wanted to talk to him seriously but I couldn't do it through the open window on the driver's side. As he settled himself in the front seat, putting the ice cream on the dashboard and the gun on the seat next to him, I walked around the front of the car and waited for him to pull up the button on the passenger side. I got in.

"You want a ride back to the store?"

"No. I wanted to say something, but I don't want you to take it the wrong way."

He chuckled. "You been talking to your uncles? Try me."

He was under control now but my heart was racing. "I know you got attacked, and they never caught the guy, but you can't go around like this."

I looked down at the gun, silent on the seat between us. The portable record player was open; some of my old 45s lay, forgotten, on the turntable. The Magnum's likely hiding place. As long as I lived, I'd never be that clever or that sneaky.

He put his left hand on the top of the steering wheel, then turned on the engine. "The only place I'm going now is home. Let me get this ice cream home before it melts. You want me to pick you up in an hour?"

"I'll be all right." I didn't need him back here tonight, but I did need one more thing. "I'm a little worried about you driving around with this."

"Don't worry about me."

It was the saddest thing he ever said; that's all we ever did. "You know I'm not going to do that," I said. He could take off as soon as I left him, driving up and down Utica Avenue, Linden Boulevard, Lenox Road until he saw that kid in the Tomahawks jacket, the one who mocked him. I'd sat across from him in this seat enough times to know the kind of trouble he could get into.

"How about if you give me that?" I said.

"I cannot do that."

I pressed on. "Come on, Dad. You keep this around, you're just gonna hurt someone else or hurt yourself. Let me keep it in the store over the weekend. In case they come back."

He laughed out loud. "You've gotta be kidding me. Those mutts are not coming back, believe me."

"You don't know that." I picked up the gun. It didn't feel as heavy as it did the morning he passed it around the kitchen table, like a time bomb. Tonight, the bomb went off. If I had my way, it never would again.

"Don't pick that thing up when it's loaded."

He reached over and opened the chamber. He told me to remove the remaining bullets. I slid them out—five brass slugs that felt dirty in my palm. I couldn't imagine ever being able to pull the trigger.

"Let's get out of here," I said.

He flung me a look.

"You heard me," I said. "Pull out, but don't drive past the store. I'm taking you home."

He made a U-turn in the middle of Church Avenue, cutting off a westbound bus. I didn't know where to put the bullets and placed them on the dashboard, next to the bag of ice cream. Must be going soft now. I checked my watch. Ten thirty. Morty was most likely in the store by now. I would have to come up with a story as to why I had to leave early. My first job and I was already going to lie to my boss to protect Himself. It didn't get any better than this. I felt like I was picking up my own teenage son on the street and taking him home.

He made a left turn on Albany Avenue. An idea came to me as the gloomy granite headstones of Holy Cross came into view. I asked him to stop the car when we turned onto Snyder. I picked up the gun off the seat.

"Hey, where're you goin' with that?"

"You were supposed to get rid of this," I said over my shoulder. "Now I will."

I took the gun and ran across Snyder Avenue. I climbed up on the fence, placing my feet between the iron bars, and threw it as far as I could.

TWENTY-THREE

The warm weather was here and guys were just dragging themselves to classes. Even the cafeteria, usually a rollicking scene, was a snooze. I was eating lunch in the cafeteria with Larry the week after Himself made his appearance at the store when he leaned over and said, "I hear not all the first-year teachers are being asked back."

I only knew one first-year teacher. "How do you know?"

Larry made a face. "I played at a wedding on Saturday. One of the ushers is the son of Mrs. Caputo."

I finished my lemonade. "Who's that?"

Larry was having rice pudding for dessert. "She works in the front office at St. Mike's. She knows everything."

I seldom went into the front office so I wouldn't know Mrs. Caputo from a hole in the wall. I was getting impatient. "So what did she say?"

Some guys walking down the aisle between the rows of tables called out to Larry. There were three of them, carrying trays and heading our way. I thought I knew all of Larry's friends but I didn't know these guys. "Hey, fellas," he said, pointing to the empty chairs at our table. "Come join us."

"So what did she say?"

Larry took off his glasses and cleaned the lenses with a handkerchief. "That was all, but I think our friend Ventresca might be on his way out."

How did he know things even I didn't know? "You're kidding, right?"

"I hope I'm wrong, kiddo."

I did too. I told Larry I would see him later and went upstairs to the first floor and poked my head into the faculty lounge, a room as large as one of the classrooms, but carpeted in dark-orange pile. Desks lined the perimeter of the room. Brian was one of the lucky ones: his faced the window. He wasn't there; nobody was. I wasn't sure if I should go in, but I wanted to leave a quick note. A stack of tests, with students' names and their class written in blue ink on the covers, were weighed down with a gray rock on one corner.

A voice behind me asked, "Can I help you?"

I turned and saw Mr. Probst, who taught chemistry to the juniors. Like Brian, he was one of the ultra-tall teachers, about six-four, with a conservative, square-back haircut, almost military style. He dropped his textbook on the desk adjacent to Brian's with an authoritative thud.

"I was going to leave Brian a note," I stammered. Students weren't supposed to be in the faculty lounge, but I'd been in here often enough that most of the teachers knew me.

He glanced at the stack of tests. "I saw him headed to the parking lot," he said. "Maybe you can catch him."

The parking lot was on the other side of the gym and by the time I reached it, Brian's car was gone.

In my next class, I listened to Brother Methodious drone on about the Nazi occupation of Paris. He loved to talk about World War II and he would surely include questions about it on our world history final; I took a lot of notes. A warm breeze came through the open windows; soon enough, we would all be sprung from this beige building. Summer. Long bike rides to the beach. I wondered if Valerie had gone out to Rockaway on a bike. She had a ten-speed, a Peugeot she sometimes rode to work. That convinced me to do the same thing. And sometimes we rode home together, if our shifts ended at the same time. Morty was an easy-going boss but he really didn't like clutter and there wasn't much room in the back of the store for bikes. So we had to lean them against each other. The way I wanted to be with Valerie.

● ● ●

Morty switched Valerie's shifts after the night with the gun—a total bummer—and I didn't see her as much as when she first started at the store. She only worked weekend days and every other Friday night, when Morty could be there. Profits were down.

When she was there, though, there was always a crowd. And now her friends were visiting, a couple of girls from Bishop McDonnell and some guys too. They came in with car key rings dangling from their fingers. Guys with Jesus hair and an easy swagger, all older than I was. Valerie always introduced them as friends of her brother Chris, though he never made an appearance.

"Which one is your boyfriend?" I asked one day when we were loading new tubs of ice cream into the freezer.

"None of them. I'm not really in the market for a boyfriend," she said, not looking at me. "So don't get any ideas."

Mind reader. I blushed, and I had no comeback. So how did I think I was going to get anywhere with her? It was going to be a long campaign. I envied Larry his luck of walking into McDonald's one day and having Rolonda wait on him. They were both on the same level. Me and Valerie, it was different, like I was at the bottom of a seesaw.

Larry came by the store to check her out and thought she was out of my league. "Too grown-up for you, sport," he said, when we took our walk around the block on my break. The ceramic collies in the window at Roma Furniture were gone, along with the blinding chandeliers and the game-show bedroom sets. Roma had gone out of business, though the sign was still there. A large For Rent sign had been taped inside the window.

"You'll have to invite her to a group thing," Larry said, glancing over at the marquee at the Rugby. The feature attraction was *Naughty Nurses*. A silhouette of a naked woman adorned the marquee, next to the title. "Somebody will have a party. If she can hang with you and your friends, then she's good to go."

Until then, I rode with her down the tattered streets of my neighborhood and hoped she would invite me to hang out at her house.

"You don't have to ride home with me," she said the first time we rode together. She took the lead, her long legs pumping the pedals, silver spokes catching the lights from passing cars.

"I want to."

We rode straight down Church Avenue, slipping between the buses and parked cars, past Erasmus, the high school that looked like a castle, and the movie palaces on Flatbush Avenue, the Albermarle and the Loew's Kings. The bright marquees lit up the street and Valerie's brown ponytail. I kept my eyes on her shoulders and the small of her back, where her blouse rode up above the waist of her jeans. Thinking we were going to get cut off by a turning car or knocked off our bikes when someone decided to exit their car into the street, but we didn't. I don't think we even stopped at a red light. My thighs burned as I tried to keep up with her. After taking a right turn on Beverley Road, the light and the noise left us, as if we had crossed into a suburb. Valerie lived in a Victorian mansion with green shingles on the upper floors and white on the first floor. There was a wraparound porch but it took several rides before she invited me to hang out for a bit. She only asked to see my house once. Maybe once was enough? One night, we sailed through the intersection at Albany Avenue and she asked, "You live somewhere around here, don't you?"

"A few blocks."

"Show me."

I turned onto my block and braked my bike in the street. The Pink Panther was parked in the driveway. Himself was probably fast asleep in the wing chair with the television on.

"This is your old man's car?" she asked, riding onto the sidewalk for a good look. She laughed and shook her head in amazement. "My god, it's a tank. Is this what he drove when he showed up with his gun?"

She hadn't mentioned the gun once since the night of his visit. I paused and said, "He likes the old cars."

"Very old. Why does he have a gun? Is he a cop or something?"

Sergeant Flynn, Brooklyn's patrolman. I would have laughed if I wasn't so fed up with him. "No. He thought he was protecting us."

She nodded. "Sounds like you didn't agree with that."

I looked over my shoulder at the front porch. The center window was open but it didn't look like anyone was in the room, eavesdropping. "None of us do. Not me, not my sisters, not my mother. That night he came in the store and scared off those kids, maybe that impressed you. 'Cause he's outrageous and knows how to get attention. Try living with it."

She ran her hand over the chrome curve of the Continental

kit. "You shouldn't let him bother you so much. You're not going to be here forever."

Every day felt like forever with Himself. "I know that, but my mother will. And my younger sisters. What'll they do?"

"They'll leave when they can. That's what happens. I'm the last one left in my house."

A dog barked nearby. I looked at the front porch windows. Queenie was observing us, her forelegs up on the front porch radiator. She was waiting for me to come inside and hook the leash to her collar.

"I have to go in," I said, leaning on the car, folding my arms. I didn't want to talk about Himself anymore.

Valerie turned her bike around, got on the seat, and rode over to me. She kissed me on the cheek.

I smiled. "What was that for?"

"Don't worry so much."

Then she was off, riding toward Holy Cross. I put my bike in the garage. Larry was wrong, I decided. A girl who kissed you was not out of your league.

●　●　●

When it was finally time to go to English class, Brian was talking to a few students outside the classroom so I couldn't grab him, but he called me over after the period ended.

"You came by the lounge?"

I nodded.

"Everything all right?"

"Everything's never all right. I wanted to ask you a question."

The classroom was empty now, but students were milling about outside, waiting for the next teacher. Brian was through for the day and asked me to wait for him on the front steps while he packed up. I was finished too, but had some free time. I went upstairs to my locker, put back the books I didn't need, took some notebooks, and left the building.

Brian was on the sidewalk, pacing. He started walking toward Collisionville as I came down the steps. It was too warm to wear my windbreaker and I tied it around my waist. The mongrels behind the fence at the junkyard yapped as we approached.

"I'm headed to the V.A. hospital in Bay Ridge," Brian said. "Otherwise, I'd give you a ride. How's the job going? Seems like it suits you."

"Money suits me is more like it." Mom and I had scraped together the three hundred dollars it took to turn the phone back on. The first time it rang, after so many months of silence, it made everyone jump.

Brian's car was parked across the street by the playground. I looked at the faded body. Our midnight confessional seemed like a long time ago.

"Who's in the hospital?"

"My friend Kevin's getting his prosthetic legs fitted today," Brian said, smiling. He opened the front door and threw his satchel on the front seat. "I'm going out there to pick him up."

That was great news. "Larry heard something about some faculty leaving."

Brian put his hand on my shoulder. "Well, I don't know about anybody else, but I had a job interview. Keep that under your hat. I may not get it."

So it was true. I had only one word. "Why?"

Brian looked up, squinting into the sun. "Brother Theodore hasn't asked me back for next September."

"Oh." I lowered my head. They wanted him gone because of the *Birdie* fiasco, even though it was long over and Vinnie Sorrentino was back in school, his court date pending. "He still has a few weeks to ask me. But most of the other first-year teachers got the call already."

I didn't know what to say. He was being fired, like Himself, but not because he deserved it.

Brian tried to cheer me up. "Friend of mine teaches at Tech and told me there was an opening for an English teacher. So I'm talking to them."

Brooklyn Tech was one of the best public schools in the city. You had to take a special test to get in. I did and passed. But the school was in a terrible neighborhood—Fort Greene, where Himself had been stabbed.

"So even if you can stay at St. Mike's you might go anyway?"

"It's a public school. More money."

Combat pay, I thought.

"I can get my own place. Kevin and I will probably be room-mates. I've paid off my student loans, and it's just time." He gave a sly smile and got behind the wheel, closing the door. "It's a good change, Nicky. Don't freak out on me."

"I'm not." I looked at the sidewalk, dotted with old black chewing gum. I felt like a five-year-old. Brian was my teacher and my friend, but he was almost ten years older. He could make sweeping changes in his life if he wanted to. I had to stay put—trapped in Patrick Flynn's haunted house.

He started the engine. "You're looking daggers at me, Nicky. It's going to be all right. Who knows? Maybe I won't get the job and I'll have to go begging to Brother Theodore and they'll take mercy on me."

He said this very casually, as if it wouldn't happen in a mil-lion years and as if he didn't want it to. He backed the car into the street behind St. Mike's, then took off the back way. I stayed there on the corner, staring at the things I saw every day like I suddenly didn't recognize them, like I was in the wrong neighborhood. I had assumed Brian would be at St. Mike's until I graduated, persuading Brooklyn's least poetic students to recite Shakespeare and directing the annual play. He was my good-luck charm. As long as I could see him in class, I could face whatever happened at home.

TWENTY-FOUR

First, I heard the banging. Then his fist, brought squarely down on the kitchen table. Next came the royal summons; the volcano rumbled up the stairs and rattled the floorboards in our bedrooms.

"Maureen Flynn—"

I rolled over and heard the door to the front bedroom open.

"Can my eldest daughter be deaf? Maureen Flynn, get your ass downstairs. Noooowww."

I heard my sister going down the stairs and then Queenie's paws as she met her on the landing. The kitchen table turned into a boxing ring.

"Who's your boyfriend?"

"I don't have a boyfriend."

"Look me in the eye, young lady, I'll ask you again. Who is your boyfriend?"

"I don't know what you're talking about, Daddy."

The first slap, cracking across her face, made me jump out of bed.

"What were you doing last night on Church and Utica?"

Morty asked me to come in last night for someone who was sick. Maureen volunteered to pick me up when I was done, but

I told her not to come to the store after dark. And he must have seen her, with those eyes that could see around corners.

She didn't answer at first. Her voice came in petrified spurts.

"I was getting ice cream. We went to pick Nicky up."

"Oh yeah? And who's 'we'?"

I stood in the hallway, hand on the railing. I could just see that watchdog face snarling at her, leaning across the table. "It was me and my friend Kathy and some of her friends."

"What did you think you were doing on Church and Utica with every jigaboo in kingdom come on the streets?"

"I told you, we were getting ice cream."

"And who was driving the car?"

"Kathy's friend."

He had seen her in that guy's car. One of Kathy Fitzgerald's sketchy friends. That's what got him going. That's what he'd been obsessing about all night in his saloon of choice.

"I didn't get his name."

"Boppo."

"Boppo? Is that really someone's name?"

"Yes. He lives in her building on Linden Boulevard."

"And how old is this Boppo?"

"I don't know. How am I supposed to know how old he is?"

"Never answer a question with a question. Is he old enough to have a driver's license?"

I started walking down the staircase. I paused five steps down. Maureen's voice was trembling, the words getting stuck in her throat. I could see her, holding back the tears while Himself bore down upon her like some sick balloon, ready to burst.

"I ought to break your legs, young lady, for getting into a car with some guy you don't know. And what is Boppo's last name?"

"Gutierrez."

"You're going out with some motherfucking spic. Are you kidding me?"

Another slap. Finally, my mother intervened. "Knock it off, Pat."

I made it to the landing, next to the telephone bench. It was now or never. I came into the kitchen slowly, as if I knew what I would find there: Maureen sitting in the chair that faced the tiled wall, wiping her teary eyes with tissues, Himself in the inquisitor's chair, next to the dining room doorway, and Mom cowering over by the sink, puffing on a cigarette. When she saw me on the threshold, her eyes bugged out and her hand went to her head in disbelief.

"I was the one who invited her to come to the store," I said. "So if you have to scream at someone, you can scream at me and leave her alone."

He stood up. I was nearly as tall as he was now, in my bare feet. "Mister, you are talking out of your ass." He had stopped yelling; maybe he was giving his throat a rest. "Go back to your room. This discussion is between me and my daughter."

"Not when you're waking up the whole house and hitting her." I glanced at Maureen. She was looking away from all of us now, down at the tablecloth or her lap. And she was shaking.

"Come on," Mom said, helping her out of the chair. "Move," she said to Himself. She led Maureen upstairs.

He went to the stove, to pour more coffee into his cup. "You have to quit your job," he said. He turned around and sipped his coffee, leaning against the stove. The drink always made his eyes look huge, maybe the same way vodka made his ankles and fingers swell up. He pushed his fingers back through his hair. "It's got me crazy. You've got my daughter standing around with all those jungle bunnies so you can show off in front of her friends. I want you to quit today."

"I'm not doing it. I'm not quitting."

In one move, he was on me, clutching my T-shirt. The shirt ripped as I jumped back. "Are you circumventing my authority? When I tell you to do something, you will do it."

"Keep your hands off me."

"Ahh, little Nicky got his T-shirt ripped."

"You touch me again and I'll go straight to the police."

He laughed. "And what are they going to do? This is my house."

Mom came downstairs and told me to go get ready for school. I looked at the kitchen clock. Seven A.M. I turned to leave the room and his final words—he always had to have the last word—came like a kick in the small of my back.

"You and I are not finished, mister."

TWENTY-FIVE

Mom took us to Holy Cross to visit her mother's grave. Even though the prospect was melancholy, it almost felt like we were sneaking away for a secret outing. The only full day we had with her was Sundays.

The five of us bounded out of the house, leaving Himself at home with the Sunday *Daily News*, the television, and the dog.

We stopped at a florist on Brooklyn Avenue, across from the cemetery. Some flower arrangements, pink carnations attached to Styrofoam crosses, were displayed on a tiered stand outside. Mom went inside to look at the better stuff and came out with an azalea bush, a miniature version of the pink one in our backyard. She didn't really remember the exact spot of the grave, except that it was near Cortelyou Road, but I did. We walked under the double-gated entrance and set off for the chapel. I wondered if anyone had found the .357 Magnum I'd thrown over the fence.

I was wearing corduroys and a new white turtleneck. My skin had cleared up, and my hair was grown in again, finally. My sisters were wearing slacks and skirts. Mom wore a light sweater, a pair of slacks, and her car coat.

"Did Daddy really take you driving in here?" Mary Ellen said as we passed the chapel.

"Yep. All around the roads. Out to Schenectady Avenue and then back."

"Creepy." I didn't see any green maintenance trucks driving around and hoped that perv who'd followed me had the day off.

A lot of Irish immigrants were buried here. Their tombstones included the names of the counties, inscribed near the base, they'd come from in the old country. Our phantom grandmother was Irish too, real Irish, from County Mayo, not like the people who wore fisherman sweaters and blasted Clancy Brothers records at three in the morning on St. Patrick's Day, like Himself.

The path to the grave was halfway between the chapel and the Cloister. I could always find it by looking at the tops of tombstones; the last name, Jurgensen, Mom's maiden name, was engraved in a decorative panel. Catherine Jurgensen was buried along with a daughter who had died shortly after birth, two years before Mom was born. The inscription on the headstone read: To Our Darling Baby Daughter, Maureen, and My Beloved Wife, Catherine.

She was only thirty-nine when she died. Mom had always told us that she died of a heart attack. But that was so young to die that way. I thought about those five years, between the death of our phantom grandmother and my birth. Mom must have been so miserable that she needed an escape. For better or worse, it was into the arms of the first boy she fell in love with, Patrick Flynn. They'd met in high school.

Despite the "Permanent Care" marker in the lower left-hand corner of the stone, the ground around the stone looked nearly barren. Mom sadly told us that the soil was terrible and nothing would grow there.

"Your grandfather and I once tried to plant an azalea bush there, but it just died," Mom said, handing me the green plastic pot. Maureen helped me shake it loose. "But nothing says you can't try again." From the pocket of her car coat, she took out a garden trowel. She was tense and businesslike. "Do you want to start digging?"

I got down on my knees and scraped at the dirt.

"When was the last time you came?" Maureen asked.

Mom was smoking a cigarette. "Last year. I think it was around the time of her birthday. She was born June 11."

I looked up at the neighboring graves and didn't see any visitors. The absence of bouquets seemed a shame. This section of Holy Cross looked a little forlorn. Dee Dee and Mary Ellen sat on two low tombstones nearby. An empty green watering can— ours—lay on the ground. The soil was dry and orange; this azalea bush was going to need a lot of water to survive. I knew where there was a faucet. After I had patted down the dirt, I walked over to the main road. The pipe for water was directly across the road from the Cloister, and I filled the can. The dry earth soaked up the water and I filled the can again. Already the pink blossoms brightened the tombstone.

"They met at a school dance at St. Jerome's," Mom said when we were walking home. "She lied about her age because she was older than my father. Four years."

"You're kidding," Maureen said. "When did Grandpa figure it out?"

"That I'm not sure of," Mom said. "Maybe when they got their marriage licenses."

We all laughed and it felt good to do that. My sisters said they would remember that when they were old enough to have boyfriends.

When we walked down Medallion Street, we saw a car parked in the driveway, in front of the Pink Panther. Uncle Tim's car.

"Who's that?" Maureen asked.

"Your uncle," Mom said, stopping in front of the next-door neighbor's garden and staring at the car like it belonged to the coroner. She threw her cigarette on the sidewalk and stepped on it. "What the hell is he doing here?"

We hadn't seen Uncle Tim since that day Himself was in Kings County. Obviously, Mom didn't want him just showing up.

I was the first one in the back door. Uncle Tim was in the living room, leaning forward in the rocking chair and petting Queenie. He was talking very seriously with Dad. I heard the tail end of the conversation.

"C'mon, Pat," he said. "Why won't you let me help you? I don't see how you can keep on doing what you're doing."

Dad glanced at me and then back at the TV. The collie roused herself and came trotting over to greet us. Uncle Tim turned his head sharply, startled. He stood up and gave my mother a kiss. He was wearing chinos and a faded navy sweatshirt. His mop of gray hair was hidden under a Mets baseball cap.

Mom was trying to smile, but she just couldn't pull it off. And I couldn't hold it against her. I didn't trust this visit. Nobody in our family just showed up. Nobody decided to take a drive into our bad neighborhood, walk up the broken stoop, and knock on the peeling front door. It was an ambush.

Then I heard someone coming down the stairs. My grandfather, William Flynn himself, standing on the landing by the telephone bench, in all of his Floridian glory. He flashed a broad smile and gave my hand a good, hard shake. "Nicky, what's the good word? How ya doin'?"

I could barely find the words. "Fine, fine."

Grandpa had had no trouble adjusting to retirement, a tropical climate, or a different selection of men's clothing. Pale yellow pants—was he wearing flares?—fanned out over white patent leather slip-ons. He also sported a navy blue polo shirt and a white belt. He was trim, certainly in better shape than Himself, with a killer tan and freckles popping out on his wide, high forehead and over his black, bushy eyebrows. The lenses of his glasses were thicker, and the remaining fringe of hair that ringed his head just above the ears was snowier than I remembered. Even though his voice still boomed, he looked like an old man. It seemed like a long time had passed since we packed up the dining room furniture from Grandpa's house and took it home in the Black Beauty, but maybe I thought that because Dad had really gone downhill since that day.

"When did you get in?" I asked, still seeing yellow.

"Yesterday afternoon." Grandpa stepped into the living room and looked at the television for a minute. The volume had been turned down. Dad slumped deeper into the wing chair. "Pat, you've gotta get that bathroom in order. It's a disgrace."

I guess he'd noticed the missing tiles everywhere while he was using the facility. Hopefully, he wouldn't go into the kitchen, where Mom had retreated, and see the ceiling. I suspected Dad was letting the house fall apart the same way he was falling apart, as if to see how bad things could get before it just fell in on us. I'd tried to repair what I could of the bathroom after I was done with *Birdie*, scraping the ceiling, tearing off a lot of the old wallpaper. I had been ready to repaint the entire room. All I had to do was get the can of Benjamin Moore and a can of spackling compound. Then Himself said he would do it. But he didn't. And I knew it would never happen.

It was embarrassing watching my father get scolded by his old man, so I was glad when Patty broke the silence. "Where's Grandma?" she asked.

Grandpa cupped his ear. "What's that?"

Patty chuckled and shouted, "Where's Grandma?"

"Resting. She's at your uncle's house. Long car drive. Not me. I was up with your uncle. Drove to Breezy Point. Then checked out that ratty golf course on Flatbush Avenue. Florida has spoiled me, I'm afraid."

Maybe they drove past us as we were walking into the cemetery.

Grandpa was surprised that my sisters had all gotten so tall and grown-up. He stared at Maureen's chest and said, "Blouse a little tight?" She blushed and looked at the floor. I was waiting for Dad to come to her defense, but he didn't. Maureen wasn't speaking to him. Whenever he came into the room, she got up and left.

Dad was leaning back in the wing chair, one eye on the game on TV.

"Hadn't you better get yourself ready?" Grandpa asked.

Whatever discussion they were having would continue out of the house. Dad roused himself, slipped his feet into his beat-up slippers, and went upstairs to the bathroom. Grandpa took his place and raised the volume on the baseball game. The scorecard on the screen told me the Mets were losing. Maureen sat next to me and asked Uncle Tim how our little cousins were doing.

"Maybe I can come out and babysit for you sometime."

She was making the most of the time Himself was upstairs. Uncle Tim gave her a long look and tapped her knee. "That would be great." He had this broad, ready smile, and I didn't know how he was able to change his expression so quickly after scowling at Dad. "Then your aunt and I could go out and have a date."

When Dad came down, he had combed his hair, probably with just water because I couldn't smell any VO5, and he was wearing black oxfords. He grabbed his spring jacket off the back of the dining room chair, went into the kitchen, and mumbled something to Mom. And then he sauntered through the living room, without looking at us. I could see the humiliation in his stony face.

Grandpa and Uncle Tim said Dad would be back for dinner and then they said goodbye, following Himself out the door. I got up from the couch and shut off the television. The silence was eerie and bewildering.

The adults were cooking something up and I found out what it was a few days later when I woke up and Maureen was sitting on the edge of my bed.

"What?"

She was in her yellow cotton nightgown. "They're down in the kitchen. Daddy's going to Florida."

I knew it wasn't us going on a family vacation; the Pink Panther wouldn't make it to Delaware. He was going to live with my grandparents. That had to be it. I followed Maureen to the staircase. We sat on the top step and listened intently.

Mom went first. "So what are you going to do about this Florida thing?"

"Which Florida thing is that? Damn good meat," he said. Even with his mouth full, his voice carried beyond the kitchen. He must have been eating the leftover pot roast we'd had last night. "What'd they get you for this?"

Mom told him the King Kullen sale price. "This truck-driving school in Florida. It would be a good way for you to get back on your feet. Have you given any thought to going?"

Truck-driving school. What a strange idea. Maybe a brilliant one. There was no answer right away. Then he said, "Why, are you trying to get rid of me?"

Was she sitting across from him at the table? Or standing away from him, at the sink, taking drags on a cigarette—her usual position—while he shoveled the food in his face? Behind, I decided. She didn't give bad news face-to-face.

Mom sighed in exasperation. "Would you just stop it? This Florida thing sounds like a good idea. I mean, the way your brother explained it."

"I'm not so sure about that. What do you do if I go to Florida?"

She laughed, a mocking hoot. "What do you mean, what do I do? I do the same thing I do every day." The unspoken word "work" hung in the air like an anvil, waiting to be dropped.

"Oh yeah? You think you can handle it?"

"Handle what? I'm handling it every day, mister."

I wondered when they had come up with the plan to get him out of the house. Had she called Uncle Tim from the bank and then he called Grandpa in Florida? I couldn't even imagine him not ruling the roost, voice booming from the bottom of the staircase, fist coming down on the kitchen table. It would be like getting out of prison.

"So you are trying to get rid of me. . . ."

"Goddammit, nobody is trying to get rid of you. But if that's what you want, believe me, it can be arranged."

He mocked her with a whistle. "Now she speaks the truth. Well, you've been carrying me. I'll never deny that." He paused and asked, "We got any of that crumb cake left?"

The Entenmann's box was always on the kitchen table, under a package of melon-colored Marcal napkins. All he had to do was look for it. "Tim said the deadline for the application is in two weeks."

"Oh, he did now, did he?" There was always a knife inside the box. "Mother of God. Which one of your children is cutting the crumb cake around the edges?"

He probably meant that as a joke, but Mom didn't think it was funny anymore. "Jesus Christ, Pat, would you give it a rest? If one of them so much as blinks, you're all over them like a ton of bricks, waking everybody up at the crack of dawn to give them

the third degree. They're afraid to be in the same room as you."
Mom said, "You're drinking too much."

That was the understatement of the year but Himself, as always, had a comeback. "Don't blame it on the drink," he said emphatically. "I can't do anything right around here. Once the bad guy, always the bad guy."

It had to be time for some of us to be getting up for school, but Mom was on a roll. She was saying everything she'd held back, and I was proud of her.

"You're the one who made yourself the bad guy around here. Nobody but you." She hurled something into the kitchen sink. The plate and silverware he had been using. "I'm in that bank six days a week, and you sit on your ass in some frigging bar. Well, I am sick of it. Sick and tired—"

"Do not go down this road, Mrs. Flynn. I am warning you."
She turned on the faucet and we couldn't hear anything.

Maureen said, "You think she would catch a clue and leave him." She stood and went into the bathroom.

The water stopped. Mom's footsteps reached the dining room. I went back into my bedroom and pretended to sleep. Then she was on the staircase. "I have to start getting the girls up," she said. "Just make up your mind, Pat. Two weeks."

His voice was at the bottom of the staircase now and she was on the landing, to wake us up. "I thought you were trying to get rid of me—"

"Think whatever you want."

TWENTY-SIX

I cleared out the spring garden to make way for summer. I cut back the yellowed iris leaves and dug up the spent tulip and hyacinth bulbs, storing them in a paper bag in the garage. Mom had done the summer planting, when the seeds from the Burpee catalog arrived. Soon enough, we would have marigolds, gladioli, and dahlias. The roses were already out.

I had changed out of my school clothes into jeans. I filled up a garbage pail halfway and carried it into the backyard. When I was finished, I went into the house through the back porch and washed my hands in the kitchen sink.

Mom came up the basement stairs. She was still in her work outfit: a green-and-white shirtwaist dress. The day's application of lipstick for customer smiles had worn off. She was wearing slippers—sky blue with a banded front. Shoes and stockings came off the minute she walked in the door. The varicose veins on her left leg looked like busted champagne grapes.

We drank cups of tea at the kitchen table, and she told me that Himself was probably going to Florida. I had to act surprised.

She took a drag on her cigarette. "He wants to learn to drive a tractor-trailer. I don't know if it's going to change anything around here, but it's better than nothing, which is what he's got right now."

She sounded resigned but determined to see things through. These few months of working had made her steelier. She spoke in short, clipped sentences. "Your uncle told us about it."

Good old Uncle Tim. Determined to save his brother. The rest of us were exhausted.

"The program lasts a couple of months. Then he could stay on and work there for a while."

A house without Himself? It was hard to picture. In so many ways, he *was* the house. It was his voice booming from the kitchen saying he was sick and tired of being sick and tired. His cheering from the wing chair when the Mets scored a run. His creaking footsteps on the staircase when he was struggling to make it to the back bedroom. He bonded us together, even in numb dissatisfaction, rebellion, and misery. Without that, we might all just float away.

"You mean he'd live in Florida?"

She finished her tea and rose from the table, moving to the stove and pulling pots and pans out of the top drawer. She took a package of green beans out of the freezer and dipped the green square into one of the pots. "I don't know. Let's see if he can finish the program."

It had to cost something, but I didn't ask what. I was sure Uncle Tim was covering that too.

The front doorbell rang and Queenie trotted ahead of me into the vestibule. When I opened the door, she pushed her snout past my knee to see our visitor.

A petite woman with a pile of curly dark hair stood on the intact side of the stoop, two steps down, as if she expected the dog to lunge at her. Obviously, she had encountered people's pets this way before. Queenie thrust her shaggy head forward, giving one last bark. Then she merely looked at the stranger, sizing her up.

"That's a pretty dog," the woman said, giving a weak smile. She wore an open, mint-green raincoat over a print dress and carried a brown briefcase.

I glanced at the briefcase. *This is not the Avon lady.* "Can I help you?"

"Yes. Good afternoon. I'm looking for Mrs. Flynn. Does she live here?"

Something electric tingled up my spine, like I'd just touched a light socket, and I shooed the collie inside. Mom appeared behind me, dish towel thrown over her shoulder. She must have heard the strange voice.

"I'm Mrs. Flynn. What can I do for you?"

The woman climbed up one step. She spoke in a smooth, businesslike voice trained to convey the utmost consideration even as it lowered the boom. "Mrs. Flynn, good afternoon. My name 's Ruth Weingarten, and I'm with the Department of Social Services." *The same agency that gave us food stamps.* "Mrs. Flynn, if I could come in for a minute . . ."

Mom folded her arms. No way was Ruth Weingarten getting inside this house. "Please just tell me what this is about."

"We've had a report of a problem in the home concerning your eldest daughter, Maureen."

Holy shit. I shrank back into the vestibule.

"We tried calling you several times, but the phone seems to be out of service," she said. The phone had only been turned back on a few weeks. How long had Miss Weingarten been trying to get through?

Mom bent her head closer to the woman, and the towel fell to the tiled floor. "My daughter called you?" Her tone was incredulous, offended.

As I picked up the towel, I saw Mrs. Garrett watering her front garden next door, most likely listening to every word.

Miss Weingarten opened her briefcase and handed Mom a cream-colored business card printed with black lettering. Mom barely glanced at it. "I didn't speak to her directly, but as I've said, I've had a report."

Mom asked me to go inside. I sat on the rocking chair in the living room, holding the towel. The dog sat next to me on her hind legs, and I stroked her dark fur to calm myself. After my midnight confessional in Brian's car after the dance, he had asked me more than once if I could see myself calling a social worker. Someone had beaten me to it. But who? Not Brian. He would have said something. Mrs. Garrett? My mind raced with possibilities, but it didn't matter. Someone who knew what went on in this house had persuaded a New York City government agency to investigate.

Mom shut the front door and came into the living room. She glared at me. "Where is your sister?"

I shrugged. "Not home yet."

I knew where everybody else was. I had passed Dee Dee and Mary Ellen playing in front of the Spallinas' house when I walked down the block. Patty was upstairs changing out of her school uniform.

Mom stalked off to the kitchen and I looked out the window. Miss Weingarten was walking back toward Church Avenue. I watched the back of her green raincoat until it disappeared from view. She had traveled all the way from downtown Brooklyn to put us on notice. I was sure she would be back—or send someone more forceful. If I'd had more gumption, I would have opened the door and run down the street after her and told her everything—the morning shakedowns, the months of anxiety and terror. They all could have ended then and there.

I found Mom in the back porch, glowering past the window screens at the garden.

"Why did you send her away?"

"Oh, give me a goddamn break, would you?" Her hands were shaking and her eyes were glassy. "What did you expect me to do? I don't need any social worker ringing our doorbell." She shook her fist at me. "Did you call her?"

My voice went up several notes. "No."

"Then who did?" Clouds of paranoia floated across her face. She picked at a hole in the window screen. "This is all I need," she said bitterly. "If your father finds out about this, it's going to be World War Three around here."

"They're onto him, Ma," I said quietly. "It's not as if you can't hear him screaming all the time when he comes home drunk at five in the morning. Don't you think somebody might have heard him? He has to go and you know it. Before they send somebody else to the house."

She wasn't even listening. "Your sister did not do this alone, I'll tell you that much."

I didn't know what to say.

I heard footsteps in the kitchen, too light to belong to Himself. Then Patty walked onto the back porch. She wore jeans, a blue crop top, and flip-flops. "What's going on?"

Mom turned to her. Her eyes were dry and she wasn't looking so wounded now. "Do you know where your sister is?"

"Probably at Kathy Fitzgerald's house." Patty pulled her hair back and slipped a rubber band around the mane. "That's where she usually goes after school."

"Could you do me a favor and take a walk over there?"

Patty shrugged. She left by the back porch, flip-flops clapping on the wooden steps that led to the yard. I left Mom to hang up the wash, leaving the house by the front door. As Patty neared the corner, I caught up with her and told her what was going on.

She gave me an even look. "If Maureen didn't call, someone at her school did. She told me she'd been called into the guidance counselor's office a couple of weeks ago."

We turned the corner and walked toward Brooklyn Avenue. In my fantasies, Ruth Weingarten would still be at the bus stop, waiting in her green raincoat for the next B-35. She wasn't there, of course. By now, she was probably in the IRT subway station, waiting for the train to take her back downtown. I had missed my chance.

Kathy's building was between New York and Nostrand avenues, a five-minute walk from our house. The block was swallowed up by a fortress of apartment buildings; set back from the sidewalk, each in a different color brick, they had been designed with an effort at elegance, with wide, brick-walled gardens and arched entrances. Patty led me to the correct building, in the middle of the row. It was massive and made of a red brick so dark it looked brown. The slanting sun glinted off the fire escapes, giving the black paint a blistered patina. A group of black girls played double Dutch on the sidewalk outside, braids lifting as their feet bounced off the pavement. I envied them. They were so lighthearted, while I was filled with dread, trying to head off a disaster. Maureen was being made to feel she'd done something wrong, and I knew there was a lot wrong with that. We were expected to keep Himself's vices a secret, but it was too late.

To reach the entrance, we walked past an oval garden filled with weeds. The vestibule was rectangular and painted yellow, with a silver board of dozens of bells nailed to the wall next to the double glass doors. Patty found the name FITZGERALD, typed in white on a red plastic strip, and pressed the bell. And we waited, two long minutes. Maybe there was nobody home and Maureen was somewhere else. We were about to leave when a girl's voice crackled through the intercom. "Who is it?"

Patty identified herself. "Is my sister there?"

We were buzzed in. The lobby did not look promising, with catacomb lighting and a scuffed black-and-white tiled floor. We squeezed in on the elevator with a shopping cart full of folded laundry and a woman, pale and careworn, wearing white beaded moccasins and black slacks, leaning on the handle. We got off on the sixth floor and walked down a brightly lit hallway with a terrazzo floor and woodwork painted black. The door to the Fitzgerald apartment was painted black too. A faded Easter Seals sticker was placed next to the doorbell under the apartment number: 6G. While we waited for someone to answer the bell, I spotted an old mezuzah stuck to the doorframe.

I knew Maureen was going to feel ambushed, but I had to know if she called Ruth Weingarten's office before we went back home.

Maureen answered, with the most quizzical expression on her face. Her eyes traveled from Patty and then me, standing behind her. "What did Daddy do now?" she asked.

I wasn't expecting Patty to do the talking. "Somebody came to the house. Looking for you."

Maureen still looked clueless, so maybe she didn't know anything.

"It was this lady from the Department of Social Services," I said. "Did you call them? They had 'a report,' she said, whatever that means."

Maureen came out into the hall. She was wearing her uniform and no shoes, just a pair of white socks. Like Patty had said, the guidance counselor at St. Edmund's—not a nun, but a lay teacher—had called her in when her friends had found her crying in the schoolyard.

"I didn't tell her everything, but she got the picture," Maureen said. "But she didn't say she was going to call anyone. What about your teacher? Maybe it was him."

"I won't get to ask him until tomorrow."

We could guess all we wanted to. The elevator door creaked open and a man carrying a briefcase walked to the other end of the floor, unlocking the door to his place with a loud click. There was no point in standing here and I told Maureen we'd meet her downstairs. She asked us to wait while she put her shoes on and fetched her schoolbag. The three of us headed back in silence like we were on our way to our own funeral. The carefree girls jumping rope were gone now and the sidewalk was filling up with grown-ups dressed in work clothes, coming back from the subway station. When we crossed the light at New York Avenue, Maureen said, "What did Mommy say?"

I could see the worry in her eyes. "She was panicking, that's all. Just tell her you didn't call anyone," I said.

"What if she doesn't believe me?"

I had no answer. "Tell her the truth."

We went into the house through the back door. Dinner was cooking in the covered silver pots on the stove—I smelled the string beans—and Queenie was eating Alpo out of the yellow dish on the floor. Mom was sitting on the telephone bench in the dining room. In the dark. It was a very quiet conversation, maybe with her sister in Staten Island. She only called her when we were out of her hair and she was guaranteed some privacy. Maureen dropped her schoolbooks on the dining room table.

Mom hung up the phone. "Would you like to tell me what's going on?"

"I didn't call anybody."

"Then how did that woman know your name?"

Maureen didn't answer. I nudged her. "Tell her."

She told Mom about her meeting with the guidance counselor. Her voice was shaky but she didn't shed a tear.

"This is great. Just great," Mom said. Exasperated, she rose
from the telephone bench and went into the kitchen and continued making dinner. Maureen and I set the table. "And what am
I supposed to do if your father finds out? What do you think's
going to happen then?"

"I don't know," Maureen said. "But I can't take it anymore.
Tell him to get out. Why can't you do that? You know what he's
doing is wrong."

Mom flung her a look. "Of course I know what he's doing is
wrong."

Before Maureen could reply, the front door opened with a
familiar shove and Queenie took off, tail wagging, to greet her
master. Maureen rolled her eyes at me and left the room, stomping up the staircase. How I wished I'd been upstairs doing my
French homework. Now the shit was really going to hit the fan.

Himself strode into the kitchen, grinning, as if someone had
just told him a great joke. "Good evening, Mrs. Flynn. What's
all the commotion about? I think I overheard a loud discussion."

"You didn't hear anything," Mom said.

He flashed a cocky smile. "You sure about that?" He looked
from Mom to me, eyebrows raised. "No work today?"

"Day off."

He was mildly stewed but friendly. He must have run out
of money at the Dew Drop because he pulled a six-pack of Bud
from a brown paper bag and peeled one can off the plastic ring.

"You're just in time for dinner," Mom said, pulling a sizzling
meat loaf out of the oven. She wiped her forehead with the back
of her hand, as if relieved to be off the hot seat.

Patty picked up Queenie's leash off the closet door handle.
"Come on," she said, cocking her head.

"Tell Dee Dee and Mary Ellen it's time for supper," Mom said as the collie trotted after Patty out the back door.

Himself opened the refrigerator door to put the remaining cans inside. He offered me one and I shook my head.

"Ah, yes. My son is not a drinking man."

Mom drained the string beans in the sink, put them back in the pot, and covered them. "Go inside, Pat," she said. "I'll have your plate in a minute." She went upstairs, no doubt to have a word with Maureen.

"Yes, ma'am." He took his Bud and left the room.

Disaster averted. But I wondered how much he'd heard. It would be just like him not to say anything now, but wait a week or maybe two, then have us all downstairs for a lecture or a promise that he was the last one who would be leaving the house.

TWENTY-SEVEN

Maureen left us one week later, packed off to Rockaway for the summer to be "a mother's helper." Or, as she explained it while she was packing, "I'll clean up and take the kids to the beach while Aunt Julie sits on her ass and reads magazines."

Leave it to my sister to crack jokes about her exile, but I was sorry she had to go before Himself did. She was the first of us to move far away from home—all the way to Colorado, where the bitter winters were preferable to the contact sport of being the eldest girl in the family.

The last day of school rolled around, a short day, only morning classes. We would all be set free by one P.M. Everyone was going to the beach afterward. That was the tradition at St. Mike's. I'd never done that, but I decided if I was there I could visit Maureen. Now that Larry had wheels, getting there would be a breeze.

I cleaned out my locker, tossing Bic pens into the trash along with some notebooks and my trig textbook. As long as I lived, I never wanted to see another isosceles triangle. I pocketed my combination lock and walked over to McDonald's to meet Larry. I had never seen so many cars parked outside the school. Volkswagens, Valiants, Chevy Novas—every senior who had a license and enough money to buy a used car was ready to tear out of here.

Without the school crowd—Tilden had already finished for the year—McDonald's was pretty dead. Larry was at the counter, trying to cajole Rolonda into coming with us when I walked in. She was filling extra-large soda cups with Coke and Sprite for two sweaty guys in UPS uniforms. I looked at their long brown pants and thought they must be dying in this heat. One of the men took the sodas from Rolonda while his buddy paid for them.

"Wish these were a couple of cold beers," said the younger of the two, maybe in his early twenties, a few years out of high school, with thick, muscled arms and hands the size of dinner plates. He called Rolonda by a nickname when she handed him her change.

"One of your frequent customers?" Larry asked. He had already changed out of his school clothes into shorts and a Mets shirt. "I'm gonna have to get a job here to keep tabs on your fan club."

"Oh, that's Lonnie. He works at the warehouse up the street." Rolonda had pinned her hair back and her face, lovely with those bright brown eyes, looked out of place under that McDonald's cap. "I know him from the neighborhood. His sister is in my school. You boys want some drinks for the trip?"

Now that she and Larry had been going out awhile, she never charged us. We both ordered Cokes.

"It's too bad you can't come with us," I said, grabbing some straws at the condiments counter.

Rolonda leaned on the counter, looking out the front door at the long day ahead of her. "I really don't like the beach. I told Larry if he wants to take me to Jones Beach, where they at least have a pool, that's a different story."

Larry gave her a kiss goodbye and we were off.

"Pick me up at six," Rolonda said after us. "Don't forget."

When Larry told me his father was giving him the Plymouth, I thought it was going to be some dad car—sedate, pastel, pile the kids in the backseat and drive out to Ronkonkoma to visit Grandma. I didn't think it was going to be a Fury. I could see it at the end of the block, across the street from Collisionville, as we walked down East Fifty-Eighth Street.

"Wow, it's really gold. Did you give it a name?"

"Not yet." Larry stuck the straw through the hole in the plastic cup.

"You have to."

"Maybe I should ask your old man. You tell me: What would he call it?"

All I could think of was the Goldfinger, after the movie and that Shirley Bassey song: *He loves GOLD.* The car was a two-door in gold with a black hardtop, a panoramic windshield, and stacked headlights. Larry rested his drink on the hardtop while he searched his pants pockets for his keys. I looked inside. Some stitching was coming out of the seats and the vinyl was shiny in spots from all the backsides that sat there.

I got in on the passenger side and pressed the button to lower the window. A smile spread across my face. "This is great. I'm gonna have to wait another year for my license, but this will do."

"See? There are advantages to starting school late."

Larry was born at the end of December, and his mother kept him out of school for one year so he would have no problem getting into a Catholic grammar school, where kids were admitted in the order of their birth dates.

We went to the beach the back way, cutting through the Brooklyn Terminal Market to Remsen, where we picked up the Belt at Rockaway Parkway and headed west. Larry fiddled

with the radio until he found a station that came through. It was
Simon and Garfunkel, singing "Cecilia," a song I didn't really
like, but their good-natured harmonies seemed to fit with the
day. We were doing about fifty and soon the Marine Parkway
Bridge, battleship blue and shaped like a steel caterpillar with
two curved towers, came into view. The land was completely flat
and the sea air rushed at us.

"Too bad about Ventresca," Larry said. "I'm going to miss
having him around next year."

"Makes me want to transfer," I said.

Larry laughed. "You in Brooklyn Tech? It's a rough scene
down there."

"Maybe it's not so bad." Valerie had survived going to Bishop
McDonnell for the three years, taking the subway to Franklin
Avenue. You just had to be careful, mind your own business.

"So what do you think of the car?" Larry asked. "I know it's
no Pink Panther, but it rides pretty well."

"It's great. Do you freak out when you're driving on the
highway? I've never done that."

Larry stopped at the tollbooth and tossed some coins into
the box. "Piece of cake," he said. "I don't go when it's rush hour.
I'm not an idiot."

The road made a horrible buzz-saw sound once the Fury
hit the bridge span. The view of Jamaica Bay could not be beat.
You could see the orange brick bathhouse tower at Riis Park and
beyond that, the cold blue Atlantic, dotted with distant ocean
freighters that looked like toy ships.

I was wearing my bathing suit under my khakis and had
packed a ham-and-cheese sandwich with my towel. "It's probably going to be too cold to swim but I don't care," I said. "I'm
going in."

Larry took the first exit and made the first left, onto an as-

phalt strip that ended at Bay 14, the last bay at Riis and the
hangout for kids from the Catholic schools.

He parked near a small firehouse that serviced this end of
the Rockaway Peninsula. The strip divided Riis Park from Fort
Tilden. A half-dozen or so cars were already parked alongside
Larry's, with more on the way. Larry pulled a heavy metal cooler
out of the trunk and lugged it to the beach, towels and a blanket
stacked on top, finding a spot not too far from the water, on the
left side of a slightly sagging volleyball net. Sweat dripped from
my forehead, and I stripped down to my suit immediately. My
skin was nurse-white and I quickly applied some Coppertone
before the sun found me. A volleyball game was in full swing—
more guys than girls playing—and they all looked older. One of
them called Larry over to join in. The girls wore faded denim
cut-offs over their bathing suits and the guys wore tank tops and
denim shorts. An open cooler with cans and bottles of beer was
sunk into the sand next to one of the net's poles. Larry asked
me to play, but I wanted to get my feet wet. I hadn't been near a
beach since my last trip to my uncle's house.

The tide was out. The shore was covered in tangled, glossy
clumps of seaweed and crushed shells, all glistening in the sun.
Waves were rolling in slowly, as if the ocean was on a ten-minute
break. The cold brine slid up my calves and then my knees as I
made my way toward the few swimmers who had braved the
temperatures. One of them waved at me, a girl with thick, matted, wet dark hair.

"Rainone!" I called out.

I dove into the water and swam out to meet Immaculata.
Without her aunt Chickie's beaver coat and those squeaky orthopedic shoes, I barely recognized her.

"The dead arose and appeared to many," she said. That crazy
grin, which seemed to paralyze her face, was the same.

I hadn't expected to see anyone from the play, but the girl swimming with her was also from *Bye Bye Birdie*—Mary Zaleski. They both wore one-piece bathing suits—Mary's red and Immaculata's royal blue—that seemed to flatten their breasts. I hugged them both at the same time and felt their hard nipples against my ribs. I dove straight down after that, my balls tingling. When I surfaced, I knew Immaculata would have a million questions, and she did.

"What have you been up to? I tried calling you, but I couldn't get through. I thought I would have heard from you."

I must have seemed like a complete weirdo, but I wasn't going to tell her the story of my family's exile. I stuck to the good stuff, the good news: my job and the scene up on Church and Utica.

The waves were gathering strength. I forgot to bob and one smacked me right on the ear. I told Immaculata I was surprised to see her out here and that's when Mary said she'd twisted Immaculata's arm into going.

"I agreed to make a cameo appearance. How'd you get here?"

"Larry has a car. He passed his road test."

Immaculata turned and looked at the shore. "He's here too?" She gave me a meaningful look. "I didn't hear from him either, Nicky. After the play, nothing."

We had let her down. I was sure Larry had no clue. I didn't know what to say. So I said something stupid. "Larry's a busy guy. He's got this girlfriend now."

She nodded and looked down at the water. "Well, I guess it's old home week. You look good, Nicky. Your hair grew out."

"I would have called you, really, but our phone was disconnected. There was a lot of stuff going on at home."

She looked at me intently. "Your father. I could tell."

From one ride in the back of his car? She was smarter than most people I knew. "It's better now. I can call you."

My excuses sounded hollow to me, and they must have sounded worse to Immaculata. We weren't moving anymore and my legs were getting cold. We decided to swim over to the bathhouse. The girls were good swimmers, effortlessly rotating their bodies through the water. The tide had turned and the big waves were rolling in now, cresting right over my head. The cries of children carried over the water as we came closer to the bays where families set down their towels and beach equipment.

"This is about as far as we can go," I said. "Let's go in."

It was a short swim back, but the undertow pulled at my bathing suit like a pair of lonely hands. Clumps of hot sand stuck to the soles of my feet as we walked. I couldn't wait to get up to the boardwalk.

Immaculata was telling me about her summer job—she was an usher at the Alvin Theatre on Broadway—when a tall Puerto Rican guy in a pink jockstrap slinked past us and said, "Hello, gorgeous."

"Get a load of that one," Mary said, shielding her eyes with the palm of her hand. "He must be headed to Bay 1."

That was the nude beach. I looked over and saw the man walking away, the waistband of his jockstrap a stark contrast to his exposed, hairy rear end.

"He was checking you out," Mary said, lifting her wet hank of hair off her back and pulling the chain of her crucifix along with it. If she yanked it any faster, she would choke herself.

"He was?" I opened my mouth to say something back to him—not that he would have heard me. I wasn't going to call him a name. But I didn't want him thinking I was flattered. He had settled down on a giant white terry-cloth towel.

Immaculata touched my arm. "Don't, Nicky. It doesn't matter. You'll never see him again."

We stopped at the restrooms on the way back to Bay 14.

I looked at my face in the cheap, wavy mirror. A flush of pink was already there and on my shoulders. I had a T-shirt to cover myself with back at the blanket. Larry came in and rinsed off his glasses in the sink.

"Hey, where'd you go to, sport?"

"Ran into Mary and Immaculata in the water."

His Mets T-shirt was soaked to the skin. "Oh yeah? Where are they now?"

"Outside. You should cool off in the water. It's a little icy, but you get used to it."

The girls were standing next to the old cement drinking fountain, talking to some guy with dark hair and a bandanna tied around his head. He tapped a can of Bud to his lips, draining it. Then he crunched and dunked it, like an aluminum basketball, into a dented steel trash can.

I should have known from the peacock stance. Vinnie Sorrentino. I hadn't exchanged one word with him since the dance.

Larry and I walked over. He made an affectionate bow to Immaculata. She grinned and gave him a big kiss. "It's so good to see you. I was hoping you'd be here." She gave him the once-over. "You lost a lot of weight."

He blushed and lowered his head. "I've got someone counting my calories."

Vinnie was smiling. His black hair was knotted; sweaty tendrils stuck to his forehead. His eyes had a glassy, blurred cast. He was completely lit.

"You're not going to believe who's here," he said. "Gina. Down by the volleyball net. Good as new. Check it out." He started walking to the restroom. "I gotta take a piss."

I'd only seen Gina a few times since the accident, but usually in the backseat of her family's Dodge. The image of her being carried out of McDonald's on a gurney flashed before my eyes and suddenly I was worried. I looked out at the ocean as if I expected to find the funnel cloud of a freak tornado whirling in, but the water was clear and bright, in bands of deepening blue. A perfect day, for our reunion, but there was a hidden warning in the waves: something told me to be careful.

We were all thirsty, so we had to walk back to the cooler. A dozen or so bikes, ten-speeds and English racers, were chained to the fence that ran along the boardwalk; their spokes glittered in the sun. First thing I did was slip my undershirt, warm now and still smelling of Clorox, back over my head. Larry handed out Cokes, Tabs, and ginger ales. The volleyball game was over and the players were splashing around in the ocean. Mary padded down to the tide line and cajoled Larry into joining her. "I don't see Gina anywhere," he said, peeling off the wet Mets shirt. He handed me his black frame glasses and wriggled out of his khaki shorts. "If she shows, don't let her get away."

Immaculata and I sat on the blanket, and I rubbed some more suntan lotion on my legs—the backs of my knees smarted—and she told me about the people she had seen at the theater. The play at the Alvin was *Company*, and it was a hot ticket. This guy I'd never heard of named Stephen Sondheim wrote all the songs.

"How's the show?"

"Very good. It won all these awards. Remember the movie *That Darn Cat?* That guy from the movie, Dean Jones, is the star. Who knew he could sing?"

I smiled.

"You know who came in one night? You'll never guess."

"The Pope?"

"Close. Jackie Kennedy. I almost had a stroke. She was so striking. But she has a big face. Big, Nicky." She burst into a paroxysm of laughter. I remembered her backstage, cracking everyone up. *Well, if that's liquid gold, you can pour it all over me.*

"Beats making double-fudge sundaes for junior gang members on Church Avenue." Then I thought: *I can hand out playbills to Jackie Kennedy. And Ari Onassis, if he comes with.* "I can hold a flashlight. Any job openings over there?"

"I don't know. I can ask."

"My father hates me working on Church and Utica." I paused briefly. "I'm going to see a play next month. My first. I think it's off-Broadway. Brian invited me and Larry and a couple of other students to see *A Moon for the Misbegotten*."

"Eugene O'Neill," she said. "He writes a lot about alcoholics."

Brian had filled me in after our last class together. He'd said, "O'Neill was haunted by his past but he turned it into art." Knowing that I'd be seeing Brian so soon after he left school cheered me up. Come September, Larry was going to be my best friend—my only friend—at school.

I told Immaculata Brian was leaving St. Mike's for Brooklyn Tech.

She nodded thoughtfully. "Well, we knew he wasn't going to make it after that fight at McDonald's with that Tilden crowd. That was ridiculous."

Immaculata could take a word like "ridiculous" and stretch it out to seven syllables. I smiled, but I didn't say anything else; I figured she'd let it drop. She didn't.

"How's your sister, Nicky?"

"She's living out here for the summer, helping my aunt out with her kids. She's got a lot of little kids, and it gets Maureen out of Brooklyn for a while."

"Oh, brother. You said it. You still have that gold jumpsuit?"

I laughed. "Yeah."

Vinnie came over to the blanket with a dripping vanilla ice cream cone, soft serve, with sprinkles. "You guys seen Gina?"

I shook my head.

Then I heard her voice. "I'm right here."

She was standing right next to us, facing the water. Except for the curly hair, which had grown back to half its Judy Collins length, I wouldn't have recognized her. All that time in a cast had made Gina plump—she wasn't even wearing a bathing suit, just denim shorts and some kind of loose-fitting muslin shirt, white with thin aqua stripes, that was long enough to cover her rear end. Her calves were wet, bouillon-colored.

"I didn't ask you to get that," she said to Vinnie as he presented her with the cone. "Come on, I'm trying to lose weight here."

"Don't 'come on' me. It's a hot day."

Gina accepted the cone and licked the dripping vanilla ice cream off the sides. Vinnie watched her with a grinning satisfaction. For once, the smirk had left his face. He picked up a folding beach chair, the old-fashioned kind, with crisscrossing vinyl strips, and brought it over. This, I guessed, was Gina's convalescent throne.

"I can't sit all the way down on the ground," Gina explained, taking a seat. The chair's strips were orange, shot through with silver fibers. They brightened the stripes on her shirt. "This is my first trip anywhere by myself, except for going to school to take my finals."

Immaculata picked at the blanket. I didn't want to bring up the brawl at McDonald's. It didn't seem like Gina was going to either, but when Vinnie was out of earshot, she bent forward and said, "Excuse me, but he's like my fucking shadow."

"Oh, brother," Immaculata said, shaking her head gravely.

"He called me almost every day after they set my leg, and at first I wouldn't talk to him. And finally my mother said, 'Talk to him for five minutes. It's not going to kill you.' And now I can't get rid of him."

I had to ask. "So you forgave him?"

Gina nodded. "But I'm not going out with him, even if in his mind he thinks we might be seeing each other. I mean, he was arrested, for God's sake. Vinnie's father had to pay to fix everything—the broken windows, all of it. It cost a fortune."

It was depressing to think Vinnie had worn her down to the point where she was almost taking his side. Immaculata shook her head; she'd heard enough. "It's hot," she said, "I'm going back in. What do you say, Nicky?"

We didn't have to walk out to meet the tide. The surf was rough and after a couple of cold slaps from the waves, I swam out past a group of guys who were holding Mary by her feet and hands and then tossing her into the water. I waved to Larry to meet us. The three of us swam over to the fence separating Riis Park from Fort Tilden.

"Let's check this out," I said.

The water was warmer on the other side of the fence and the waves gentler; we let them push us across several bays. The beach wasn't entirely deserted. Scattered fishermen sat at the edge of the sand, squinting at the water, fishing lines stretching way out into the ocean. Jagged chunks of driftwood littered the shore along with pieces of Styrofoam and a few large-sized 7-Up bottles.

Immaculata was the first one out. Her hair was tangled with seaweed. I told her to stand still while I separated her thick matted clumps of brown hair from the slick, shiny mess.

We stood on the wet sand, just below the tide line. "What's over here?" Larry asked.

"Not much. There's an old army base. My old man told me about it. Want to look around?"

"My life is in your hands," Immaculata said.

The beach wasn't as wide as Riis, with a border of dunes broken up by narrow paths. I picked one, and we trudged over.

A discarded fish lay on the shore, gills still breathing. I picked up the slippery, silver thing and tossed it back in the ocean. Then I rinsed off my hand.

"You really do throw like a girl," Larry said.

"Bite me."

Without the bathhouse and the concession stands at Riis, the sky here seemed limitless. A plane trailing a Coppertone banner growled overhead, passing under thin cirrus clouds. Seagulls dipped below the waves, hovering until it was time to dive again. We walked three abreast, enveloped in the quiet, me in the middle. Farther back, naked sunbathers camped out against the dunes.

"You would never catch me doing that," I said. "I'd fry."

I was following Immaculata across the path that crossed the dunes when Larry tapped me on the shoulder. I stopped and followed his gaze. In one of the depressions in the sand, a dark-haired guy was reclining on a rose-colored blanket. Next to him lay a woman in red bikini bottoms. Her forearms rested on his thighs and her head was positioned over his crotch. Straight blond hair curtained off her face as her head went up and down on his dick.

"Fuck me," Larry said, squinting. "She's got balls."

"Man, she is really into it," I whispered. "This sure beats the Rugby Theatre."

"I'll say. Think I can get Rolonda to do that?"

"You can't even get her to go to the beach." I burst out laughing and left Larry there to leer. Immaculata was waiting for us down on a cement walkway dividing the beach from a wide thicket of scrub pines, wild rosebushes, and honeysuckle. Monarch butterflies flickered past, their wings like saintly apparitions.

"Where's Larry?" she asked. "I'm ready to go back."

"Taking a leak," I said. "Come on, let's go this way."

A dirt path in the thicket beckoned us onward, under canopied trees that provided some welcome shade. I soon heard Larry's footsteps behind us. Some of the ivy plants had red stems and leaves, which looked like trouble to me. "Don't step on that," I said to Immaculata.

She jumped, and I caught her shoulder. "What is it? A bug? I hate bugs."

"Where are you taking us?" Larry asked. "Not for nothing, pal, but I am barefoot."

We emerged from the cluster of trees onto a soft sandy path that wound to a series of steps. A loose rope threaded through a procession of wooden posts provided the only banister. At the top of the steps, there was an empty bench and another path that split off to the left. We were standing above the scrub pines and a complicated tangle of honeysuckle and rosebushes. This was all beautiful, but I couldn't shake the image of the woman going down on that guy. I was dying for a Coke or even a water fountain and thought we should turn back.

Then I saw the bunker.

"What the hell is that?" Larry said.

"It's a monstrosity," Immaculata said, punching up the syllables.

It must have been left over from Fort Tilden's salad days. The sandy path took us to the right and then sloped down, ending at the base of a concrete prison with ominous rusted gates that looked like the entrance to hell. A black gravel path bordered by tamped-down, yellowed grasses divided the bunker from the fenced-in forest we'd just visited.

"This is not for me," Immaculata said. She stood in the shade of a cottonwood tree and crossed her arms.

I knew we should go back, but there was a wooden staircase on the right side of the bunker and I wanted to climb it. I couldn't persuade Immaculata to come with us, so we agreed to come back down in five minutes. It was a tricky way up, an invitation to get splinters. The banister was loose and two steps were missing entirely, exposing the curved, blackened shell of the bunker. A few minutes later, we reached a landing and a small wooden platform with a sturdy railing on three sides. We could see everything: the bridge we'd crossed, the small collection of buildings at Fort Tilden, the sandy path to get here, and the beach dunes (but not the couple having sex). Something about the breadth of the ocean beyond made me choke up, like I was staring at my unknown future.

"Well, we came, we saw, we'd better leave," Larry said.

"Wait a minute," I said, stammering. "I want to tell you something."

Larry put his finger to his forehead, as if he was wearing his glasses and wanted to push them back. "What's up?"

"My father. I think he's leaving. For good." I shrugged.

"I'm sorry to hear that. It's going to be rough on your mother."

"It's already rough."

"Forget about it for now," Larry said, putting his arm around me. "Let's enjoy the rest of the day."

We started walking down the staircase and retraced our steps to the concrete walkway by the dunes and followed it past deserted buildings with missing windows and long shadows that fell across the glass-strewn floors inside. Our feet were hurting, so we tried to walk on the sand under the cottonwood trees, the white undersides of the leaves showing almost indecently as they fluttered in the sultry breeze. The scene was pretty trashed when we made it back. Another volleyball game was going, but this one was happening in slow motion, the players' reflexes blurred by all the beer they'd consumed. One girl missed the ball and went splat, facedown in the sand.

I was wondering if anyone else was ready to leave Beach Blanket Bingo and suggested we go see Maureen at my uncle's house. We could rinse off in the outdoor shower and maybe my aunt would give us something to eat. My sandwich must have turned to mush by now.

"That's enough incentive for me," Larry said. "I still have to pick up Princess Rolonda, so I can't stay long. Does anybody know what time it is?"

"You have time," I said, though I had no idea what time it was. I wanted a ride to Beach 138th Street. "It won't take long for us to pack up."

Larry elbowed Immaculata. "Rainone, you in?"

She laughed. "I love it when you call me by my last name. I feel like I'm in the in crowd again."

He put his arm around her. "You were never out, dollface."

She'd been waiting for that kind of encouragement all day and leaned into his armpit. I'll always have that image of my *Birdie* friends from the last day I saw them together, Larry letting his arm lie across Immaculata's narrow shoulders as they got ready to leave the beach.

I carried the blankets and towels while Larry and Immaculata carried the cooler. The asphalt strip was packed with cars on both sides. I reached Larry's car first, resting the stack of beach things on the hot trunk. I wanted to call ahead to Uncle Tim's to make sure Maureen would be there, and jogged down the strip to a phone booth next to the bus stop. When the line rang on the other end, I was hoping my sister would answer, but Aunt Julie picked up instead.

"I'm at Riis with my friends. We were gonna come over and see my sister. She there?"

The line crackled, but I could hear enough of my aunt's answer. "Went to the store," she said. "She should be back in five minutes."

I put my index finger in the return coin slot. My dime came back to me.

I started back down toward the Fury. Larry was walking my way, eyewear back on his face. He carried the cooler himself, awkwardly bouncing it off his thighs as he headed down the strip, talking to Immaculata on his left side. They too had put their clothes on over their bathing suits. They would have been hard to miss, right there in the middle of the sunbaked strip, but right then a bright green Volkswagen bug backed out of one of the parking spots closest to the boardwalk. It was packed with guys. One of them was standing up through the sunroof, arms waving, the upper half of his body gyrating as if rocking out to a song on the radio. The driver was going fast, and the car was weaving because the guy sticking out of the sunroof kept jumping around. He was an idiot. He had to be drunk.

I cupped my hands around my mouth. "Larry! Watch out."

Why didn't he hear me? Immaculata waved but must not have seen me pointing. And then the car swerved again to the right and Larry went flying, along with the cooler. I screamed and ran down the strip, an angry thud in my chest. The VW screeched to a halt; the guys inside jumped out, rushing over to Larry, facedown on the asphalt. I broke through the crowd and knelt next to him, calling his name, my voice breaking. He was unconscious.

I picked up his cracked glasses and held them, stunned and shaking while bright blood pooled under his head. I wanted to put something under his head, the blanket stacked on the trunk, but I knew I shouldn't move him. I got to my feet and turned around, staring at the guys. They were all muttering excuses and apologies. I recognized their faces from the hallways at St. Mike's, the cashier's line in the cafeteria, but I didn't *know* them know them.

"Don't just stand there. Go to the firehouse and get someone," I finally said.

Immaculata was kneeling. She was bleeding profusely from her nose and mouth, but she was alive. The asphalt was doused with carbonated spray from the burst soda cans. The car was aslant on the asphalt, doors flung open, by the Fort Tilden fence. One guy was leaning against the green car, covering his face. I recognized the bandanna tied around his head. Sorrentino. He was the guy standing up through the sunroof. I ran over and jumped on him. He didn't even push back.

"Didn't you see him? Tell me that you didn't see him. If you killed him, I am going to kill you."

"I'm sorry, I'm sorry." His eyes were glazed and tearful. He had a half a bag on; I knew that smell anywhere. Then he staggered away from me, over to the fence, and puked.

Two firemen were standing over Larry now and a third was helping Immaculata to her feet. She limped a little, dazed and trembling.

I went over to the fireman. "Where's the nearest hospital?"

"There's an ambulance coming."

"What should I do?"

"Wait here."

By the time the ambulance driver reached the firehouse, a crowd had gathered. The cops were there too. I had to give one officer Larry's name and address; Immaculata was able to give him her phone number to call her family. The other officer was questioning Vinnie and the driver of the VW, a tall guy with a Yankees T-shirt and cut-offs. He thumbed through his wallet for his license. I watched the medics strap Larry to a gurney and load it into the back of the ambulance. Then I helped Immaculata climb in. We sat on gray benches and rode to the hospital with the fireman.

He told us his name: Raymond. He wore a blue T-shirt and uniform pants. His hair was strawberry blond, his face covered with freckles.

"So what happened?"

"We were about to leave the beach. Then those clowns in the Volkswagen started veering all over the place."

Immaculata sat next to me, a terry-cloth towel pressed up against her face.

"He's dead, Nicky," she sobbed into the towel. "He's dead."

I put my arm around her shoulder; she was trembling. "Don't say that. Let's get him to the hospital."

The ambulance tore ass down Rockaway Beach Boulevard, siren blaring. I looked down at the gurney. Larry's T-shirt was soaked with blood. The blanket wrapped around him was soaked too.

"My head is killing me," said Immaculata.

There were doctors waiting outside the hospital for us and they took Larry away on the gurney. I walked with Immaculata and the fireman into the ER waiting room. I was in a daze, the world shifting around me, from the beach to this dire place. It was all happening too fast and I felt suspended, like I was in the scene and out of it at the same time.

I settled into an orange plastic bucket seat after the nurses took Immaculata to an examining room. I had to call about ten people, and I only had the dime that came back to me from the phone coin slot at the beach. I asked Raymond if he had any change. He dropped a handful of coins into my palm.

The pay phone was down the hall. I loaded the first quarter and dialed my uncle.

"Jesus," Uncle Tim said. "Are you all right?"

"Yes," I said. "But my friend's unconscious."

"I'll be there in ten minutes."

I hung up and wiped my eyes. I should call my mother; she would be home from the bank by now. I didn't know how I was going to tell her.

I went to the men's room to wash my face. My face was bright red, and my hair was matted against my skull. I couldn't wait to use the outdoor shower at my uncle's house—as soon as I knew Larry was in good hands. I leaned against the sink and said a fast Hail Mary. I tried to think good thoughts. We had the whole summer ahead of us. Maybe I would get a job as an usher like Immaculata and have my days free. We could take those car trips out to Jones Beach. I could practice driving on the highway with Larry.

A man in a striped bathing suit holding a surfboard was talking on the pay phone when I went to call home. He had a bandage slapped on his forehead. I wondered what bad news he was giving out. Uncle Tim and Maureen, in shorts and flip-flops, looking very carefree, came into the waiting room. Uncle Tim was twirling his car keys on his finger.

"I'm over here!"

They turned and smiled, relieved to see I was in one piece. Uncle Tim placed his hand on my shoulder. "Are you hurt? Do you need to see a doctor?"

I shook my head and started to tremble. A wave of dizziness hit me and I leaned on my uncle's other shoulder. My right leg was shaking.

"Whoa, steady there."

"I didn't call Mom yet. Is that guy with the surfboard still on the phone?"

Maureen looked over my shoulder. "Oh, Jesus. I'll get him off."

I handed her the leftover change the fireman gave to me. "And then I have to call Rolonda. Larry was supposed to pick her up."

"Who's Rolonda?"

Before I could tell her, a nurse came into the waiting room and asked, "Where's the boy?"

I gulped. Maureen took my hand.

"Your friend, he's gone," she said. Just like that. She probably didn't mean to be gruff. Partly it was her accent. She was from the West Indies. I couldn't understand her. But I still thought she was blunt.

I stared at her. She was chunky and short. She wore thick, aviator-style eyeglasses.

I heard myself yelling. "What do you mean, he's gone?"

"He had a severe blow to the head."

I knew that, but I wasn't hearing her. "You mean you couldn't do anything? You couldn't save him?"

How many times had Mom and I patched Himself together after one of his collisions, applying swabs dipped in boric acid to the cuts in his face while he twitched on the bathroom floor? And when he was in Kings County, it took so many stitches, the meticulous skills of the doctors, to save him. But they did.

This time, with a kid who never walked in calamity's shadow, nothing could be done.

"Nicky—" My uncle's voice behind me.

The nurse bowed her head. "The car was going too fast. I am sorry. Do you know if his parents are here yet?"

I didn't answer. They say if you get hit by a car going thirty miles an hour, you have an 80 percent chance of survival. With a car going forty, you have an 80 percent chance the other way.

I looked up, over the nurse's head, at the people waiting in the seats for good news or bad news. Took one last look at that guy with the surfboard, sitting now, his arms wrapped around the board between his legs like it was his last friend in the world. After that, everything was a blur. I covered my face.

"Nicky, I'm so sorry—" Maureen said.

"Get me out of here," I said through my tears. "Just get me out of here."

TWENTY-EIGHT

Come on, Nicky. Wake up."

Himself was sitting on the edge of my bed. I rolled over to face the wall.

"This is a terrible thing that happened." He shook my leg. "Are you awake yet?"

"Leave me alone. I'm sleeping."

"I want to talk to you."

I had to face him. In the dark, I could make out a short-sleeved shirt in a light color. His hair was hanging down in his eyes. He squeezed my calf under the blanket.

"I want names."

That day at the beach, I didn't know the names of Vinnie's friends, but now I did. But it didn't mean anything. Because they were still walking around.

"What for?" I asked.

"Just because."

Rain fell outside my window, stirring up night fragrances of dirt and pollen. I hadn't been out of the house since my uncle drove me home from the beach. I told my boss there was a death in the family and I didn't know when I would be back. Then the phone, silent these past months, never stopped ringing. And I told the story over and over to Brian and Valerie and even Mary Zaleski until I couldn't tell it anymore.

Mom let me lounge around in shorts and a T-shirt, without even taking a shower until the afternoon, for the whole weekend. I took Queenie for walks, around Holy Cross and past my old school, St. Maria Goretti, as if I was trying to recover lost time. When Mom was at work, I weeded the garden, clipped the rose hips off the rosebushes, and did my chores and my sisters', even the laundry. The tasks steadied me. I should have gone to see that stupid porno movie when Larry wanted to sneak into the Rugby on my break. I should have indulged him.

Himself yawned and scratched his head. I thought he was going to fall back on the mattress. But he had wisdom to share. "Life's a bitch, Nicky. And you're finding out the hard way. You've got many years ahead of you. Me, I figure I've got about fifteen. But you're a great kid, you know that. You're not going to fuck it up the way I did."

He had never said anything like that to me. I sat up with my back against the wall. He had my attention.

"I'm going away for a while. Your mother may have told you."

He eyeballed me to see if this was news to me. My face did not lie. "I'm going to figure some things out, learn some new things," he said. "I can't make it work anymore, Nicky. Things are gonna be rough for your mother."

"They already are."

"That's why your mother's gonna need a hand around here, with the house and with your sisters. So I need you to get out of bed and step up now."

A huge lump formed in my throat. He was beaten and he was finally admitting it. "Sure," I said. "Whatever you need." Then I started crying again.

"Come on, none of that."

He reached out, put his heavy hand on my neck, and I was able to calm myself. "When is the wake?"

"Tomorrow. McManus." The funeral parlor where all the Irish Catholics were laid out, in Marine Park.

"I want to drive you there."

"What?"

"Let me take you."

Himself in a funeral parlor with my friends? I snapped out of my funk. "I'm sure I can get a ride, Dad. Really."

He cocked one eyebrow. "Goddammit, Nicky. Let your old man take you."

It was a done deal. We drove to McManus on Monday night, the first night of the wake, and parked around the corner on Flatbush Avenue. Dad looked spiffy, with black slip-ons, slacks, a blue shirt, and a black sport jacket. The hair: perfect after ten minutes' preening in front of the mirror. He'd had one drink before leaving the house but any trace of alcohol was buried under the bouquet of VO5 and Old Spice. I was dressed up too, in navy trousers and a green checked shirt.

I had never been inside one of these places and didn't know what to expect. Dad seemed to know his way around. The walls were papered with something neutral: thin gold-and-white stripes. Viewing rooms peeled off a long hallway carpeted in dark plush green. An open coffin in an empty room caught my eye and I looked at the carpet. It wasn't Larry's though. I had never seen an embalmed body and I steeled myself.

Larry was laid out in a large room with a dozen rows of cushioned chairs. I wasn't the only kid from St. Mike's there with a parent. The room was packed with kids whose seersucker jackets clashed with their sunburned faces; their moms and dads stood nearby, smoking their brains out.

It was too weird, like we were starting the school year all

over again when it had just ended. I spotted three couches in the back of the room, done in green brocade.

"So how does this work?" I asked once Dad and I sat down.

The crowd blocked the coffin from view but I did see the line of people waiting for their turn to approach it and I heard the soft sorrow of a weeping woman. That lump came back in my throat again.

"You kneel down in front of the casket," he said. "You say a quick Hail Mary. Or Our Father, if you like that one better. Then you walk over and express your condolences to his mother and shake his father's hand. Make it short and sweet, because there's somebody behind you waiting to do the same thing."

I nodded and wiped my moist palms on my chinos.

"You'll feel much better once you get it over with."

I scanned the line, looking for a friendly face. Then Immaculata came into the room with an older woman—maybe one of her sisters.

"There's my friend from the play," I said, getting up.

We hadn't spoken since the accident. I tapped her on the shoulder and she turned very slowly toward me. I guess it still hurt, after getting knocked to the ground, or maybe it hurt more now that she was home and recovering. She smiled and touched my face. Hers was still pretty banged up—bruises, mainly, and two black eyes—but she could walk okay.

She introduced me to her sister, Antoinette. She looked like a bouncer: tall and chunky with a blunt cut. A skunk stripe of white parted the waves of thick brown hair. She said hello tersely and took the first seat she could find.

"This is going to be grim," Immaculata said as we moved up the line. "But we've seen the worst, Nicky. We were there."

The coffin came into view: a gleaming gunmetal color with a pale blue lining. A sweet fragrance lingered in the air, though

I did not see the stands of flowers, a profusion of them, white, yellow, and one blood-red arrangement of roses, until we were facing the bier. Two empty kneelers flanked the coffin. It was our turn to go up. Suddenly I felt like I couldn't find my feet and halted; I thought I would stumble onto the corpse. I reached out for Immaculata's hand and she guided me to the kneeler. I was praying—I chose the Hail Mary, it was shorter—and when I was done, I looked out of the corner of my eye. Immaculata's head was bowed, as if she couldn't look at the body again after that ride in the ambulance. But I raised my head and exhaled, gripping the kneeler, and I looked into the coffin. There was my friend, wearing enough pancake to mask the trauma his skull withstood when it collided with the asphalt. He was dressed in a plain black suit, white shirt, and white tie, understated in a way he never was in life. I smiled, expecting him to sit up and start singing "Kids! What's the matter with kids today?" in that Mermanesque tenor. I would never laugh that hard again as I did the first time he sang it, at his audition.

Immaculata tapped my elbow. I rose slowly, wiping my eyes, wishing I had a tissue. Now that I was standing in the front of the room, it seemed everyone was crying too. A man who was the spitting image of Larry, but older and jowly, took my hand and introduced himself. Steve Cahill, the father. Immaculata explained who we were, thank God; I had no words and wasn't going to remind him we'd met briefly that one time we did *Bye Bye Birdie*. And then we met more people. His mother, his older brother, Pete, his sister, Jane. A blur of sad faces meeting all the people who had gravitated toward the baby in their family. More people came up to express condolences: guys who were in the school band, some of the Brothers from St. Mike's. I backed away. Dad was standing over by a marble fireplace. Photos of Larry were displayed on a mantelpiece. He pointed to one Polaroid where

Larry, dressed in a navy suit, white carnation in his lapel, folded his hands in prayer and crossed his eyes. The caption said: First Communion.

"I can see why you liked him," he said.

There were family vacation shots on a lake. Birthday parties. And the baby pictures, a big kid with startled, comic-strip eyes, his mouth open, ready to give somebody some lip.

Immaculata came up and told us she was going to sit down with her sister.

Himself watched her walk away. "She got hit too?"

"She was the lucky one."

He nodded slowly, but I could practically see the smoke coming out of his ears. If Vinnie Sorrentino walked in the door, he would be dead meat. But that wouldn't happen. That would be the height of bad taste, right? We were heading back to our seats when someone tugged my shirtsleeve. It was Rolonda, standing next to an equally stunning, slender woman of medium height. Had to be her mother. Rolonda threw her arms around me, sobbing into my shirt. I held her close, imagining Himself's stunned expression. I introduced her as Larry's girlfriend and she hugged him too. "Whoa," he said, while she clung to him.

"Hello, I am Hetty," said Rolonda's mother, smiling. "My daughter's told me all about you. Sorry to be meeting on such a sad occasion."

"I am too."

With all the commotion, I forgot to ask Rolonda how she found out, who'd told her. I certainly meant to. I just dropped the ball. So much for having the phone turned back on.

The funeral was Wednesday morning, the burial at Holy Cross. The irony was rich. Who would have thought with all the family ghosts in that cemetery that I would actually know someone my own age buried there? I'd never cut through the fence at Cortelyou Road and walk among the dead again.

The room was packed. We let Rolonda and her mother get in line. The couches in the back were taken; we found empty seats behind a group of guys from school telling stories about a school trip they all took together to Washington, D.C., the year before I had started at the school. It made me feel empty to know there would be no more stories. Larry had told me he wanted to drive a GTO across the country. He had wanted to go to a dude ranch. Crazy things I would never think of.

We had been at the funeral home an hour and Himself asked me if I wanted to leave. I didn't see Gina and I didn't see Brian, but I didn't feel like waiting. Besides, my head was stuffed up from all the crying. I felt like I had a sinus infection.

The night air, sultry and thick, felt better than the smoky air inside McManus. Insects buzzed around the streetlamp bulb that shone down on the Pink Panther. We pulled out and stopped at a red light on Kings Highway. Standing at the bus stop were Rolonda and her mother. I didn't know how long one could expect to wait for a bus at this hour, but I thought they deserved door-to-door service.

"Hey, let's give them a ride home."

Himself looked out the window. "You know where they live? I'm not driving to any—"

"Don't worry. She works near my school so it can't be that far from there."

We pulled over to the bus stop. I rolled down the window. "Where to, ladies?"

Rolonda stepped off the curb. "C'mon, Hetty. We'll be here all night."

They sat in back and the Pink Panther traced the graceful

arc of Kings Highway, heading east. Hetty gave an address in Canarsie, south of the Brooklyn Terminal Market. I leaned over the backseat and asked Rolonda her summer plans. I doubted that she was going to stay at the place where she met Larry and I was right.

"Friday's my last day," she said. "I'm going to spend the summer down at my granny's. She lives in Charleston. You ever been to South Carolina? They've got all these tiny islands. That's where she lives. James Island."

We dropped them off in front of a two-family brick house on Remsen Avenue. "I'll ride by before you go," I said as they got out.

"Sure. Come by for your last free Big Mac."

"Thanks for doing that," I said when we were on the road again. "And thanks for keeping me company tonight."

"My pleasure." He paused. "Let me ask you something: Your friend's family didn't say anything about him going out with a black girl?"

"They grumbled, but once they met her, what could they say? I was always jealous that Larry thought to ask her out first."

"Jesus, Nicky, give me a break. I'm driving here."

I smiled and sank into the seat, feeling my spine relax. We drove back on Ralph Avenue and took a left on Church. I asked him if he was taking the Pink Panther to Florida. He laughed. "What are you, kidding me?" he said. "Your uncle and I are going to drive down and meet your grandfather in Virginia. Then I'll go the rest of the way with him."

A system was in place to make sure he got there. The rest was up to him. "I'll leave the Ford in your hands, if you don't mind. You'll have to move it now and then, drive it around the block, check the oil, but you know how to do that."

"Really?" I said, grinning. "I wasn't expecting that."

"That's all right. You earned it."

A tangle of police cars blocked the traffic at the intersection of Church and Utica. There was a commotion on the sidewalk in front of Baskin-Robbins. One of the plate-glass windows was boarded up with a huge piece of plywood. We stopped at a red light. "Holy shit," I said.

"Somebody got ambushed," Dad said.

All I could think was that those kids had come back, from the night of the gun. "Can you pull over?"

"You don't need to be involved in any of that."

The light turned green and we crept through the intersection. That's when I saw two cop cars in the middle of Utica Avenue. "I'm getting out."

He warned me to stay inside the car, but I already had the door open. He stopped to let me go and I ran onto the sidewalk, peering inside the empty ice cream parlor. The odors of sugar and chocolate were as familiar as my middle name. There was nobody behind the counter and the place had a strange silence, as if the night had passed without anybody ordering so much as a vanilla cone.

"Anybody here?"

Morty came out of the back office and stood next to the freezer. Wire-rimmed glasses were tipped halfway down his nose; he must have been doing the books. Gold chains dangled from his open nylon shirt. "We're unofficially closed," he said before he realized who I was. "I thought you were at a funeral."

"We were just driving back from the wake. What happened?"

"They tried to rob me. I pulled a gun on them. Shot one of them in the leg."

"Are you kidding?"

He was weirding me out. Who knew he was packing? Where did he keep it? Morty was the real vigilante around here.

He smiled. "Your father's not the only one with a gun, Nicky. I should thank him for giving me the idea to get one." I hoped Dad was still waiting in the car. "I had the cops here and an ambulance."

I supposed he didn't know the cops were still here. "Who was behind the counter?" Hoping it wasn't Valerie. But it was. Valerie and Delmar. "He talked to the cops and went home, but she's outside somewhere. He'll probably quit on me after this. Say, can you work this weekend? One shift. I could use a hand."

His face showed a sweaty desperation. "Can I get back to you?"

He nodded. "Deal."

He locked the door behind me and I went looking for Valerie. She was standing in her uniform, minus the hat, in front of the drugstore, taking in the scene and chewing her fingernails. I pushed through the throng of gawkers, like a swimmer moving toward a life raft, and tapped her on the shoulder. She seemed astonished to see me, as if I'd been gone for months, when only a week had passed since we last worked together. When we hugged, people around us whistled.

"What are you doing here? I thought you were at a funeral."

"No, that's Wednesday." I explained why we were passing by. "It's good to see you. So who held up the store? Was it the same guys as that night with my father?"

"They were older," she said, nodding at the cop car where one guy with dark curly hair sat in the backseat. "The other one was taken away in an ambulance."

I put my arm around her shoulder. Her hair smelled like sugar. "You must have been scared out of your mind."

"Never a dull moment," she said, laughing. "I'm good at ducking behind a counter now. Can you believe this?" She looked back at the boarded-up window. "Is Morty even going to open up tomorrow?"

"He asked me to come in this weekend, but I don't know. This might be it for me."

She laughed. "Chicken."

I was. "Let's get out of here," I said, leading her away. When we turned the corner, my father was walking toward us. "Look who I found," I said, releasing my arm.

We piled into the Pink Panther, parked a block away. I sat in the middle and we waited for a bus to pass before pulling out. Valerie gave her address and we drove her home. To end this night of tears sitting next to her comforted me. We didn't even say that much to each other. She put her head on my shoulder just before I was about to put my head on hers.

The night strip of stores sheathed with riot gates was as long as the summer before me. I looked out at the corner boys milling about outside bodegas, drinking out of paper bags. I was damned if I was going to spend my summer walking up and down this street.

"I'm going to get a new job." I let the announcement hang in the air. "Broadway theater usher. Something with a little more pizzazz to it. And better uniforms."

"Amen to that," Dad said.

TWENTY-NINE

Mom packed his bags two days before he left, two dark blue suitcases that had been stored in the basement for so long first I had to wipe the dust off them with a sponge. The luggage was manufactured by a company called Amelia Earhart, the name embossed on a brass plate above the brass buckles. The suitcases were waiting upstairs in the back bedroom.

Mom had phoned Aunt Julie, giving her fair warning. "I know Tim wants to get on the road, but Pat's not here yet."

As usual, all we had to do was to get Himself to show up for his own appointment.

When he did, it was after two days and some time out in the field—the Mermaid, the Dew Drop, Harkins. Any of them and maybe all of them. He came crashing home about six P.M. on a Saturday, forgetting to shut the front door behind him. He paced the first floor of the house like a grizzly, his hair in wild tufts, as if he'd been trying to pull it out, his white shirt a sweat-yellowed rag. His face was livid. His body teetered when he stood in one place like a loose chunk of masonry atop a building.

It was time to go. He didn't want to.

Mom asked us to stick around, like she was going to need us

to intervene. Patty and I were in the house. Dee Dee and Mary Ellen stayed outside, in front, by the garden. They were learning the value of making themselves scarce.

The voice boomed throughout the house. Patty, hiding upstairs with Queenie, could hear him. Mrs. Garrett across the alley could hear him. The Provenzanos next door could hear him through the walls. This evening, we were all his enemies.

"I am sick and tired of being sick and tired—"

It was a hot evening, heavy with the threat of thunderstorms. A gray shadow had fallen over the day. Tonight I was going to see *A Moon for the Misbegotten*.

Then again, maybe I wasn't going anywhere.

"You don't like me hanging out on Nostrand Avenue. Well, who asked you?"

He was talking to me but looking out the front porch windows. In any case, he didn't wait for me to answer but went into the kitchen. An old argument started all over again.

"You carried me, babe. You really carried me. None better by far—"

Mom kept her voice level. "Pat, we've all been waiting for you to show up. And where are you? Everywhere else except where you're supposed to be."

I stood in the dining room doorway, at the ready.

"Well, I'm here right now. Does that meet with your approval?"

"Pat, I don't have time for this. God, I am disgusted with you. Absolutely disgusted—"

"That's all right, Mrs. Flynn, because I am absolutely disgusting—"

He picked up the drainboard from the sink, half-full of glasses, plates, pot covers, and flatware, and flung it across the room. The glasses crashed to the floor with a woeful tinkling and the plates—they were Melmac—rolled and spun on the floor, settling facedown on the linoleum with a hollow clap.

Mom slapped at his swinging arms.

"You stop right there, mister—"

Patty came halfway downstairs with the dog and peeked into the kitchen from the staircase. I stood in the dining room while Mom swept up the broken glass and picked up the scattered pot covers and plates. My heart hammered in my chest. Patty took the dog back upstairs with her. I hoped Mary Ellen and Dee Dee would stay outside.

"I want to know what's going on here," he said.

"You're leaving, that's what's going on here."

The telephone rang. I jumped. Upstairs, Patty answered it on the first ring.

"Yeah, well, how come I'm the one who's goin'?"

Mom shut the gas off under the pot of boiling potatoes and moved it to a back burner.

"I don't have to tell you why you're the one who's going," she said. "I didn't tell you to spend the past two days holed up in some frigging bar. You know you're supposed to leave. Your brother's on his way."

No reply. I stood in the dining room, ready to pounce. And then I heard a loud tearing sound. One of the seat cushions from the kitchen chairs flew across the room, hitting the rim of the sink. He was ripping them off their metal bases and throwing them around the room like Frisbees. Then he flung one chair over his head at my mother. It crashed into the closet door and down on the dog's bowl, turning it upside down. A puddle of water spread under the half-stripped chair. I heard a terrible thud and Mom's furious cry.

"You stop right there, mister. What the hell is wrong with you?"

"Leave it there," he thundered.

"Go to hell!"

"I said, leave it there."

This was not going to be the night he killed one of us. I hoped Patty was calling the cops right now. I went into the battlefield. I said, "Knock it off! Leave her alone."

He swung around and gaped at me. "Well, look who's here. If it isn't the Anointed One."

The kitchen table was capsized, the toaster smashed up against the tiled wall. "You lay a hand on her, I'll call the cops."

"You pick up the phone, I'll break your arm."

My blood ran cold. He was that guy you could never trust, the one who could keep me company at the McManus funeral home one night and who could turn on a dime into this other creature: Himself. I had spent the past two years anticipating the arrival of the latter while longing for the former. After tonight, it would never be the same.

He took a swing at me, and I ducked.

"You're out of line, mister," he said. "I can still clean your clock if I have to."

"I'm not out of line and you know it. I dragged your ass out of every bar in Brooklyn. I saved your ass when you almost shot those black kids at Baskin-Robbins. I never told anybody when you vandalized the property at the Di Napoli house. Remember? So don't talk that way to me."

He clocked me. Huge smack across the face. I staggered back against the basement door, and he was on me, pinning me against the wood. My right ear stung. "Stop it," I said, trying to shove him off, but he was a silo of flesh. He landed a punch and blood rushed into my mouth. Mom was trying to get hold of one of his arms. I pushed my hands against his leathery face, contorted with fury, so he couldn't see what he was doing.

Then I heard someone calling his name. Uncle Tim had finally shown up. "Pat, Pat, goddammit, what are you doing?"

Although he was several inches shorter than my father, Uncle Tim was able to seize him with both arms and get him off me. I broke free and ran. My fingers were covered with blood. I tripped on one of the dog's toys in the living room and fell on the couch. My mother came after me with a wet washcloth filled with ice.

"Jesus Christ. Put this on your mouth."

The cold wet cloth felt good, but the bleeding didn't stop. "Get me some tissues," I said, and she came back with a handful. I divided the wad in half and pressed it against my nose, still stunned.

Patty crept down the stairs without the dog. "That was your friend Brian on the phone. He said he's on his way."

He was driving everyone to the show. Great. I was going to have to get in the car with a swollen lip and a bloody nose.

The racket in the kitchen got even louder as the Flynn brothers raised the rafters. I had to change for the play but couldn't get off the couch. Queenie came in and sat at my feet, and I hugged her with my free hand. I wiped my eyes and waited for the trembling in my shoulders to subside. I wouldn't say a word to him before I left. Gone was any sense of duty. Gone was pity or forgiveness. I had opened my heart and was met with a fist. I was done. Done with Himself.

THIRTY

I opened the medicine cabinet. Razor, shaving cream, tube of VO5, even the trusty bottle of Old Spice: all gone. Already it was weird not having him here. We got what we wanted and now what?

I closed the medicine cabinet, checked my lip in the mirror. It looked like a beesting. From a queen bee. I went downstairs. The kitchen was back to normal. Mom must have put the chairs back together herself.

The keys to the Pink Panther lay on the kitchen table. I was amazed he remembered to do it, with the state he was in, but he was true to his word. I picked them up, examining them in my palm. There were two keys, white gold with a fan shape cut into the round part of the key and the letters FORD imprinted onto the metal. Horizontal lines rose on either side of the fan shape, a fancy key for a car that had been, in its day, the snazziest thing on the street.

I put them in the pocket of my jeans and went through the back porch into the yard. A fresh load of wet laundry hung on the clothesline, detergent smell wafting toward me through the window screen. There was a fresh breeze: thunderstorms had rampaged in the night and cleared out the fetid, stale air. Mom was sitting with the door open, on the back step, drinking coffee and reading the comics.

She was wearing her yellow duster. "You're up early."

I went down the steps and stood in the yard. It was so cool in the morning shade on the cement. The dog lay there, with her paws crossed and her head shaking. For a minute, I thought she winked at me.

"So he got off okay?" I asked.

I was waiting for Mrs. Garrett to make one of her cameo appearances. "It took a while, but yes, he's on his way," she said, rubbing the purple bruise on the back of her leg where the kitchen chair had hit her.

She looked up at me. "Say, I was walking Queenie, and I ran into Flo Martinucci walking Muffin. She and her daughter Carmella were all dressed up for church. Is Gina still doing that folk mass?"

"I think so. She should be back on the altar by now."

She had a dreamy, distant expression as she skimmed through the news section of the paper. "If your sisters get up soon, maybe you can go and take them with you. You can stop at the bakery on the way back, get some jelly donuts and crullers. I'll make a big breakfast. How would you like blueberry pancakes?"

So we were going to celebrate.

"Do we have blueberries?"

She nodded. "I got them on sale at King Kullen. And after breakfast, we'll take a ride out to the beach and get your sister."

The beach. I covered my mouth and looked at the peach tree in the garden for a minute. I hadn't been to Rockaway since the accident and supposed I wouldn't return for a long while. But if Mom wanted to go, I'd do it. We'd take the bus and I'd take an aisle seat, so I wouldn't see Riis Park if I didn't want to—or the asphalt strip where Larry died.

I broke into a smile. That was the second best bit of news this morning. "You mean we'll just go get her?"

She flicked her cigarette butt across the yard. "I'm about to call your aunt."

I waited another instant and asked, "Is Dad gone for good?"

There were no guarantees. "Who knows? Maybe he'll straighten himself out down there."

I wanted her to tell me he couldn't live here anymore. But that statement was not going to come today. I knew how hard it must have been for her to pack his bags. But true to her promise, she had taken care of the situation her way.

● ● ●

Gina Martinucci tightened the strings on her Wilson acoustic guitar, turning away from the parishioners at St. Maria Goretti to hear if the instrument was in tune. Then she strapped a capo across the top fret and gave the cue to her fellow troubadours, including her younger sisters Connie and Carmella. They had the same allure as Gina: good girls in summer skirts and dresses with long, flowing hair, the hope of Vatican II.

The first chords had a tinny sound—maybe somebody needed to check their tuning again—but the congregation didn't seem to notice. They didn't need to check the words to the songs, printed on the back of the church bulletin. They knew the words by heart. As did I.

Sons of God
Hear His Holy Word

Gather round the table of the Lord
Eat His body, drink His blood
And we'll sing a song of love.
Allelu, allelu, allelu, allelu-u-ia!

I hadn't been to mass in a long time, but I knew Gina's greatest hits. There was the offertory song "Take Our Bread," the post-Communion filler "They'll Know We Are Christians by Our Love," and the walk-down-the-aisle song "Allelu!" when the ceremony was over.

Gina smiled at me and my sisters from the altar. I had to admire her. If anybody thought she was corny or square because she headed up the folk mass, she couldn't give a shit. She was a believer and didn't care how much anybody laughed behind her back.

I smiled as the priest told everyone to give the sign of peace. Most people in the pews shook hands, but I kissed my sisters lightly on their foreheads. We smiled with a strange sense of relief, as if we couldn't believe Himself was really gone. Had our lives really changed overnight?

While Gina and her band played "They'll Know We Are Christians," my attention drifted to the stained-glass windows on the aisles. There was one for each of the apostles, St. Simon with his saw, St. Jude with his lance, St. Peter with his keys, and, overhead, the clerestory windows with angels clad in emerald robes with red and coral halos, their wings flat against checkerboard panes of sage, periwinkle, and maize. The laws of the church unfurled in gilt scrolls across their chests: Confess at Least Once a Year, Do Not Marry Kin or at Forbidden Times. All my life, I had regarded these figures as decorative, spooky bystanders to the unproven creeds of my religion. Pray and the Lord will take care of you. I was taught to revere them in school, even when the message about faith and redemption seemed to exclude what went on in our house. But now I thought maybe one of the angels up there had finally come through for us.

It seemed like a long walk back home. I was starving and I could smell breakfast cooking in the apartment houses we passed on Church Avenue. On the way, we stopped at Sylvia's Bakery and I ordered a baker's dozen, crullers and donuts. I split a jelly donut with Dee Dee.

She tapped me on my elbow and asked, "Is Daddy gone for good?"

It was the question of the day and perhaps the rest of the year. Her blue eyes, so like my father's in their shape and the intensity of their color, were rimmed with red. Another one of us who hadn't slept through the night.

I patted her head, her dirty-blond curls. "I don't know. He's gone for a while, I know that much." I didn't know anything but didn't want my little sister to think that. "Mom says we'll have to see what happens."

People ask me why I never went to the cops or why my mother didn't leave him and all I can say is we did everything we could not to make things worse. We fixed the little problems and covered the big problems, surviving one thing, then the next, like needles. The endurance made us numb. My youngest sisters would forget half the scenes we had witnessed. Me and Patty and Maureen, we'd never forget. Even when we were in college or nursing school or on the New York stage, where I eventually found my calling, we'd still talk about the night raids, the burning of the Blue Max. We'd never forget the story of a man, still young, who lost his place in the world and never found it again. Even though everyone offered to help, it was never the right kind of help. Because it didn't come from Himself.

● ● ●

As custodian of the Pink Panther, I decided to drive everyone to Rockaway. The bus would be packed with people going to Riis Park, and I couldn't see my mother standing in the aisle with a bunch of strangers and their beach gear. But I couldn't drive the car in its present state. After breakfast, I went into the basement, filled up a yellow bucket with Tide and hot water, and carried it up the cellar steps. I faced the hood of the Ford. As I squeezed a hunk of soap onto the pink expanse, I wondered how many coats of paint it took to achieve this color. It wasn't bright or soft like a flower or medicinal like Pepto-Bismol or industrial like the Pink Pearl erasers we used in school. The layers had built up over time to a deep, earthy, claylike color—nothing feminine about it. When I washed the front of the car, I tossed the sponge into the pail of suds at my feet to take in its gleaming authority. I had to admire Himself for picking it out among all the jalopies being auctioned at the Sixty-Ninth Precinct the day he brought this home. Even without a .357 Magnum, he always knew how to get noticed.

I tried the best I could to clean the sides of the car, with one foot in the garden while bending to wash the chrome strips, well nicked with raisin-sized spots of rust. Over my shoulder, I saw the new marigolds and gladioli getting ready to bloom, green heads turning orange, yellow, and peach. There were some dead leaves around the rosebushes, some dead cane on the bushes themselves—but they would have to wait for another day.

"Well, hey there."

I turned around and saw Mrs. Garrett standing in the alley. She had just come from church—Southern Baptist, on Lenox Road—and wore a blue suit with white buttons and a demure white hat pinned to her straight gray hair.

The suds dripped off the fender onto my sneakers. I wondered if she was going to complain about the car being in the driveway. I would park it on the street when we got back from the beach. "Hi. Doing a little spring cleaning. I'm going to start with my father's car."

She wore silver-frame eyeglasses that reflected my unshaven face. "What happened to your lip?"

The swelling was down but still noticeable. I looked at her. She lowered her voice to a whisper. "Your daddy did that, didn't he?"

I nodded.

"I heard him, you know. Last night. Giving somebody the business." She paused. "He's gone now, isn't he?"

I flushed. The bucket handle felt clammy in my right hand. I nodded, but I felt foolish somehow.

She now reached out and touched my hand. Her skin was dry as paper. "You're going to be all right. I can tell."

● ● ●

I eased the Ford, still wet, out of the driveway, parking in front of the house, and went up the front stoop, stepping over the suds in the gutter, and shouted through the window screen, "Ladies, your beach transport has arrived. All aboard."

The stoop was a mess. I didn't know how to fix it, but Uncle Tim had to know someone who could teach me. And I'd paint the front door too. I'd do all the things around the house Himself forgot to do. The summer was mine and I had the energy and focus to make it different.

I adjusted the rearview mirror while everyone got themselves situated and made room for Queenie on their laps. For once, Mom did not sit in the back, and the girls spread out, with their wicker beach bags next to them, on the backseat. Mom was nervous because I didn't have my license yet, but I promised her I wouldn't go over 40 miles per hour and I wouldn't take any main streets until we reached the Flatbush Avenue extension. I knew all the back roads.

"You're going to have to buy an air freshener or something," Mom said, rolling the window down as I pulled out. She was smoking a cigarette.

"The sea air will fumigate the car for us, hopefully," I said.

She laughed. "Oh, sure. Did you put the hose away?"

"Yes, Mother."

"Just remember, I'm not looking to spend the whole day out there."

Really? I had my bathing suit on under my jeans.

"I need a break from your father's family for a while."

"I know, but I don't think we can honk the horn, get Maureen, and go."

Why was she in such a huff? Exhaustion, probably. I never did ask what time the Florida expedition finally got on the road. I drove around the corner and took a left on Brooklyn Avenue and another on Cortelyou Road, riding along the back end of Holy Cross. There were seldom any cars on this stretch because the road was so old and narrow.

"We're getting her out of there at the right time," said Patty, sitting behind Mom. "Maureen told me she's had it up to here with Aunt Julie's bratty kids."

"Come on, they can't be that bad," I said. "They were nice at Christmas."

"Everyone's nice at Christmas. They're getting presents," Patty said.

It was already heating up and I was hoping the cooler beach air would change Mom's mind about spending the day in Belle Harbor. The needle on the gas gauge was poised just above the middle. Was that enough to get us there and back? I hoped so.

I was driving on Clarendon Road, passing Utica Avenue and looking for East Fifty-Third Street, a wide residential street in a quiet neighborhood I could take almost all the way. There'd be a lot of cars on Avenue U when we got to Kings Plaza, but I wasn't going to attract that much attention, even with a pink car. After all, I was tall enough to pass for an adult now. I just had to shield my face with a baseball cap.

"Maureen thinks Rockaway is boring," Patty said. "I think she misses the action on Church Avenue."

"Who would miss Church Avenue?" Mom said, flicking an ash out the window. "That's what I'd like to know."

I thought of Maureen riding in Boppo's Buick to see me at Baskin-Robbins. Trouble would always find her, whether Himself was in the house or not.

Mom asked me about the play. I told her it was great but telling her about the plot could not describe it. After all, no one in my house needed to see a play about a man who made Himself look like an amateur at life's cocktail party. So I told them about the scene I'd never forget, when Josie cradled Jamie Tyrone on the edge of the stage, bestowing a forgiveness upon him he'd never give himself after he went with a prostitute following his mother's death. I could barely breathe. I knew then that the stage would be my destiny. To command an audience like that, why would you want to do anything else? I just had to figure out how to do it.

"Did your teacher say anything about your lip?"

"Why wouldn't he?" I sat in the backseat of Brian's car with the washcloth and melting ice cubes pressed against my lips, but didn't want to get into it when he asked me what was going on because we weren't alone. His friend Kevin was in the front seat. He had his new legs. All I said was "I'll tell you later," but then I never did. I was too caught up in watching the play. My mouth may have been numb, but the rest of me was on fire.

The blocks clicked past like flash cards. Glenwood Road, Avenue H, Avenue J. The alphabet of my childhood. I swung over on Avenue M to East Fifty-Sixth Street, by Mary Queen of Heaven. I wondered if the portable record player was working. At the next red light, I looked for the switch under the dashboard and flipped it on. A record with a purple label dropped onto the turntable. Gordy Records. The needle hit the worn grooves of the 45 and soon the mellow harmonies of the Temptations floated on the summer air. They were singing "The Way You Do the Things You Do," and my sisters, surprisingly, knew most of the words. Without Himself at the wheel, I could blast it.

"Your father called—collect—while you were at church. He's left Virginia with your grandfather and your uncle's on his way home," Mom said.

"Glad I'm not sitting in the backseat of that car."

We hit a line of cars at Avenue U and just sat there. The song finished and I felt around inside the record player for another single to play. I pulled out singles by Martha and the Vandellas, the Four Seasons, and the Supremes. As I removed the last record, my fingers touched something else. I pulled it out. It was one of the bullets from the .357 Magnum. I placed it on the dashboard. Then I popped the Supremes on the record player. "You Keep Me Hangin' On."

"What's that?" Mom said, nodding at the lone bullet.

"Something Dad left behind," I said.

Diana Ross and her backup singers were all fired up, tearing through the song with brassy gusto. *Get out, get out of my life and let me sleep at night. . . .* I made the wide left turn onto the Flatbush extension. I pressed a button below the dashboard and the hood lifted, retracted, and folded back, letting summer warm our necks.

"Ladies, we are living the convertible lifestyle," I said.

The towers of the Marine Park Bridge came into view, blue-gray in the full sun. I had come down this road several times in the last year and each trip had the whiff of danger about it. One left a trail of tears. Today felt different. I tossed fifty cents into the basket at the tollbooth and drove up onto the noisy bridge, the streets of Brooklyn behind me and the Atlantic, wide and blue, up ahead.

EPILOGUE

I had to wait until I made it to Broadway for Himself to see me on stage—and even then he had an ulterior motive. I was playing Edmund Tyrone in *Long Day's Journey into Night* at the Booth Theatre and George C. Scott was playing my father. The show was going well, with the critics saying Julie Harris was a shoo-in for the Tony as Mary Tyrone. But the critics I most cared about were sitting in row G. It was weird doing my monologues knowing they were out there.

After the curtain calls, I waited backstage for my family and they were moved yet humbled, as if I was finally doing the real thing after one TV lawyer show in LA. Mary Ellen gave me a bouquet of tulips from our garden. Himself shook my hand. He had a handlebar moustache now that gave Yosemite Sam a run for his money. "You held your own up there with General Patton," he said, just a little too loud. "Very impressive."

He had a moderate buzz. I assumed he'd had some other refreshments before they left the house.

"Let's go to my dressing room. We can sit down," I offered.

Dad leaned over and said, chuckling, "Is General Patton reviewing the troops, or is he closeted in his quarters?"

Mom made eyes at me over his shoulder. "Do you think it

would be too much trouble for your father to meet George C. Scott?"

"Nah. We can meet him or anybody else you want to. I'll go knock on his door."

I led the troupe down the corridor and up two flights of stairs, through peeling hallways and industrial gray carpeting, to the dressing rooms. My door was open.

"Gee, it's not very fancy back here," Mom said. "I thought you were all big stars."

"Welcome to Broadway," I said. "We won't be long. Anybody else for George C. Scott?"

Patty and Dee Dee shook their heads, and Dad and I went back down the hall.

I knocked on the door. "George, do you have a minute? I have someone who wants to meet you."

I heard some rustling inside and then the great man opened the door, his brows raised with the kind of curiosity that made people pull themselves up short when they met him. He wore a terry-cloth robe over his undershirt and black nylon socks on his feet. I glanced at a glass of scotch on the table inside.

"Meet my father, Patrick Flynn."

Himself seemed so awed that I knew he wouldn't dare call him General.

"Very nice to meet you, Mr. Flynn," Scott said in warm appreciation. "Your son here's one of the finest young actors I've worked with." Gilding the lily, but who was I to argue?

"So I see," Dad said, chuckling nervously. I realized he didn't know how to talk to him. "Yeah, he's done all right for himself."

Scott pointed to the liquor glass on the table. "I was just having a postperformance drink. Would you gentlemen care to join me?"

"Don't mind if I do," Dad said, taste buds break-dancing.

He stepped forward into Scott's dressing room. I followed. He watched Scott pour the Johnnie Walker into a tumbler like a priest pouring Communion wine into a chalice.

Scott raised his glass and I thought Himself was going to salute. "Nick?"

"I should get back to my mother and sisters. They're waiting in my dressing room." I whispered to Scott, "*One* drink."

Himself was shooing me out the door. "Tell your mother I'll meet her out front in ten minutes."

I cleaned up, changed into fancier pants than the jeans I usually wore to work because I knew we were going out somewhere, and met everyone outside the theater.

Pointing up at the marquee, Mom said, "Everybody get together for a picture." We gathered for a minute and grinned while Mom snapped one with her Instamatic.

Suddenly Dad pulled up in his cab. The only car he drove these days was a yellow taxi. The Florida thing didn't exactly work out. He was gone about a year and a half, working for various trucking companies, driving the eighteen-wheelers, but then something went wrong and he came back, just in time for my graduation from St. Mike's. I had my license, my diploma, and a scholarship to Carnegie-Mellon. Maureen was the next to go—off to Maine, then Colorado. By the time I moved back to New York, there were three sisters left. And Queenie. And my mother. She never left him.

He got out and ushered the girls into the backseat. "Door-to-door service," he said with his bartender's smile. "It'll be a little cozy up front."

"So?" Mom said, smiling. "How was the general?"

"Very impressive. I wanted to salute him, but I couldn't find the right moment."

"Oh, Jesus," said Patty. Much of the crowd had dispersed

into town cars and taxis and now only the sketchy characters of Times Square remained. "Do you think we could get out of here before these bums start hitting us up for money?"

"Oh, by the by, wherever you want to go, it's on me," Dad said.

I shook my head. "Dad, don't be ridiculous." I knew he had given up a night of work to get the cab. I had an idea. "Hey, why don't you let me drive?"

Dad looked at me, surprised. "That would be against the law, I'm afraid," he said with solemnity. "You see, it's my face on the hack license."

"I know, but it's my big night, so I want you to let me drive. I've never driven—"

He glowered at me. "Are you trying to insult me?"

This flare-up was all too familiar. But I was a grown-up now; I could humor him. "I'll just drive downtown."

Mom leaned over in the front seat, calling out the window. "Let's go, you two."

He was giving me the hairy eyeball, and I gave it back. "I am not trying to insult you. I just thought I'd do it for the hell of it."

He threw me the keys, and they landed on the sidewalk. I scooped them up, smiling. *The old man surrenders in battle.* I slid in behind the wheel and looked back at my sisters. It wasn't one of those taxis with a divider between the front and backseat.

"And where would you lovely ladies like to go this evening?"

"Oh, let's go someplace fancy," Mary Ellen said.

"Yeah, let's be elegant," said Dee Dee.

I looked at her in the rearview mirror. "You're the one who said 'Yo, Nicky' at the curtain call, right?"

Dee Dee blushed. "Yep, I confess."

I adjusted the rearview mirror and pulled out. Himself sat in the passenger seat; Mom was in between us. "If you take a left at the corner and go down to Ninth Avenue, you can make all the lights," Dad said.

"I'd rather take Broadway. It's much prettier."

"You'll get stuck in traffic." A singsong warning.

I followed his instructions, driving to Ninth Avenue and making a left. A sea of cars. "Get into the passing lane, lose this dame from Jersey," Dad said. "Come on, Maryann," he said to the woman driving in front of us.

I was sweating, getting just a little nervous having Himself play backseat driver. I made every effort to look serene. Once we passed Thirty-Fourth Street, I took the first left and made my way to Broadway. The Flatiron Building came into view near Twenty-Third Street.

"If you put your foot on the accelerator, you can make this light," Dad said.

"That's okay. Is anybody here in a hurry?"

No one said a word.

"Well, if you're gonna drive a goddamn cab, drive it."

I swallowed. Would-be passengers stuck their arms out on lower Broadway, looking for a ride. They lowered their arms in disappointment and stepped back toward the sidewalk when they saw my cab was full. Yes, Himself was being a pain in the ass, but I still thought this was pretty cool, until we came to the intersection of Broadway and Houston, and we were set upon by a plague of zombies wearing baseball caps and dirty T-shirts. They were coming up to the car and pawing the windshield as if they wanted to reach through and grab our throats. Then they squirted the glass with sudsy Windex bottles.

"What is going on here?"

"Put on the wipers," Dad commanded. "Don't let these var-mints touch my cab."

"Where are the wipers?" I panicked, seeing one guy with a bumpy, dark face and a rag tied around his head approaching with a blue sponge.

Dad reached across Mom's lap and flipped the wipers on. At the intersection, the light turned red. The wipers swished back and forth while the guy made a wiping motion of his own with a rag. I shook my head, waved him away, and the guy gave me the finger.

"Ooh, he's so rude," Mom said.

I burst out laughing. "Who are these guys?"

"They call them the squeegee men. They're from the men's shelter," Patty said in the backseat.

You'd never see anything like that in LA. I really was back home. Dad muttered something under his breath and opened his door. "Daddy, don't get involved," Patty said. "The light's about to change."

It was already too late. In two strides, he was standing in front of the cab, yelling at the squeegee guy. The guy was yelling back, with wild gestures. Dad stepped back, as if the guy had grazed him.

I could make a living in the theater, but he was the real actor in the family. Never needed a script to put on a show.

"Nicky, go get your father," Mom said.

I shook my head. He was on his own. "I'm not getting out of this car." I honked the horn to get Himself's attention. A cacophony of horns honked behind me, and another taxi pulled ahead of us. The light had turned green. I stuck my head out the window. "Come on. You're holding everyone up."

He ignored me so I drove across the intersection, pulling over next to a car near the corner of Houston Street. In the rearview mirror, I watched Himself walking toward me.

He opened the door on the driver's side. "Slide over," he said, winded.

It was his cab and I did as I was told.

● ● ●

We ended up back at the house. It was the shank of the evening, but after a three-hour play, Mom was beat, and I said we would go out another night, when I didn't have a show. My family was the only white family still living on Medallion Street, and Himself was the only Flynn left in New York. Even Uncle Tim had taken off, packing up his brood for a fancy job in the Midwest. Uncle George had moved back from Germany but didn't return here. I wondered what size bomb I would have to light under Himself to get him to put the house up for sale.

Mom immediately got out of her dress-up clothes and into her nightgown when we arrived home. Dad opened up a Bud and tilted back in his recliner. Queenie, thirteen years old now and slowing down, the gray hairs fully grown in around her muzzle, lay at his feet.

"So what would you say the play is about?"

When I was on the TV show, sometimes he would call me to talk about the latest episode, slightly in his cups, late at night, working up the courage. He talked to me about my scenes, the other actors I was working with, whether there was enough dramatic punch. It was his way of telling me he wanted to stay in touch, despite everything, and I had to give in. He was proud of me, I knew. And now that I was making money, well, that was all this cabdriver from Brooklyn needed to know.

I sat on the couch, looking at him. "Oh, a lot of things— regret, hatred, love, whether people can still love each other after all the crap they put each other through, something like that. I don't know."

Now wasn't that articulate? I thought. Only people in Eugene O'Neill's plays discussed these things at one in the morning.

He gave me a serious look. "No, I mean it. In your estimation, what do you think this play is about, what makes these characters tick?"

Mom wouldn't have asked me a question like that. Sometimes he really surprised me. While I thought of an answer, I watched Himself drift off. Mom came into the living room with a cup of tea, the tag on the Lipton's tea bag hanging outside.

"Out already?" she said, glancing at him. "That was fast. He had a long day, though, worked a double shift last night. Thank God I don't have to go to work tomorrow."

"Yeah, but I do," I said, rising to use the phone to call a car service.

"Wake him up. He'll take you home."

"But he's fast asleep. Besides, he's had too much to drink."

"I'm telling you, he'll be offended."

Dad grumbled in the chair, but it was a false alarm. The snoring immediately began, the deep, satisfied rumble of a middle-aged man. He was under. I knew it. I called Arecibo car service. The driver was there in five minutes. I ran upstairs and said good night to my sisters and kissed my mother good night at the door.

She stood in the vestibule as I went down the stoop, the way she had the night we junked the Blue Max, cigarette in one hand, the dog at her side. I looked into the garden. The roses were in full bloom and there were new clusters of marigolds and salvia. "Hey, what about these weeds?"

"I know. I'll get to them."

The driver was waiting.

"Thanks for coming," I said. "It really meant a lot to me."

"We had a great time. We're very proud of you. But do me a favor."

"What?"

"Next time, do you think you could do a comedy?"

The streetlamps cast their fuzzy glow on Dad's cab, parked in the driveway. The driver from Arecibo was pulled up alongside it. I got into the backseat and looked out at the house. It looked good, even tasteful with the Wedgwood blue aluminum siding. Everything looked a whole lot better than it used to.

"Where to?" asked the driver, a man about Himself's age with dark hair combed in a swirl over the center of his forehead.

"Remsen Street."

"Mind if I take the Prospect? I don't like driving in this neighborhood."

"Who asked you?" With that snotty comeback, I felt like a New Yorker again and settled in the backseat. "Go whatever way you want to."

We made a left at the corner of Church Avenue and rode out in the star-blind darkness past Cliff's Pink Pussycat. It was the neighborhood's newest bar, on the corner of Brooklyn Avenue. Cliff had a clientele who rolled up every Friday night to the shocking pink aluminum siding façade in a parade of pastel Bonnevilles and Coupe de Villes, according to my mother.

It was funny how Himself had never gotten around to owning a Cadillac. Me, I drove back to New York in a Thunderbird. I didn't get it at a police department auction either. I made a commercial for acne medication, even after I was pimple free, when I was in college and saved the residuals for a car. It was a 1966 model, with a retractable hood and Cruise-o-Matic automatic transmission. The taillights were hidden behind a wide band of red plastic and the car's symbol, an art deco bird with a thin, wide wingspan that formed a V on its breast, was planted on the egg-crate grille. Best of all were the colors: diamond blue with a Wimbledon white hardtop.

I knew Himself would approve. He hasn't seen the car yet, but when he is feeling all right, I might let him take it out for a spin. We'll see.

ACKNOWLEDGMENTS

My editor Sara Nelson and my agent Liza Fleissig made everything come together quickly and seamlessly. I would like to thank these teachers for their guidance and encouragement: David Haynes, Dominic Smith, Victor La Valle, Ron Carlson, and Shelby Hearon. Thanks also to the staunch friends who read portions of this story: Lee Prusik, Rebecca Foust, Liz Gray, Bethanne Patrick, Anita Gates, Rolf Yngve, and Reine Arcache Melvin. Thanks to James Iacobelli at HarperCollins for the extremely cool license-plate font on the cover, Trent Duffy, Mary Gaule, Bryan R. Monte of the *Amsterdam Review*, Lindsay Ahl, John Timpane, and my family.

ABOUT THE AUTHOR

ROBERT RORKE was born and raised and lives in Brooklyn. He is a TV columnist at the *New York Post* who has also previously written for *Publishers Weekly*, *TV Guide*, *Los Angeles Times*, and *Seventeen*. He received his MFA from Warren Wilson College and his MA in English from Stanford University.